D1826400

THE PLOUGH, THE GUN AND THE GLORY

ISBN 978-1-84799-426-4

ANGUS HYSLOP

PUBLISHED BY LULU

ISBN 978-1-84799-426-4

AS WITH MY PREVIOUS BOOKS THIS BOOK
IS DEDICATED TO MY FAMILY

JACKET COVER BY AUTHOR

PUPLISHED BY LULU

PREFACE

An exciting powerful story unfolds between the pages of this novel... a book that will leave the reader spellbound, as they read through the pages of an earlier chapter of Australia's short, but nevertheless diverse and exciting history. Although the book is based on historical records it is predominantly a work of fiction and many of the characters, and their names are fictional, with the exception of famous persons and names recorded in military records.

BRIEF HISTORY

During the late 1890s, the seven Australian colonies (pre-federation) were gripped by the worst economic depression since the 1840s. The gold-rush boom-years of the early 1890s had ended and widespread droughts had weakened the rural industry plunging farmers into bankruptcy. Wheat and wool prices had fallen almost fifty percent, resulting in farmers being unable to recover their costs and pay their bills. Livestock, mainly cattle and sheep, perished from dehydration or were destroyed because farmers were unable to feed them.

Emerging trade unions only made matters worse by organising widespread strikes amongst Wool Shearer's and the maritime industry, crippling the fragile economy even further. Investments dried up and many banks collapsed, as speculators were unable to repay their borrowings. Inevitably, the price of land crashed and valuable property became worthless almost overnight. Thousands of men took to the outback becoming swagmen in search of work prompting the poet Banjo Paterson to write 'Waltzing Matilda.'

It was around the same period that Britain went to war in South Africa against the Boers (farmers). Consequently, the Australian colonies became enthralled in a display of patriotism and loyalty towards the crown. Thousands of volunteer's enlisted for service with the army; young men eager to join the fight for the glory of the empire, in what became known as the Boer War.

The Boers however, had proved to be a formidable foe with their unique style of guerrilla warfare and Britain's conventional armies suffered humiliating defeats in earlier battles, among the more significant Stormberg, Magersfontein and Colenso.

Originally, the Dutch were the first Europeans to colonise Southern Africa at the Cape of Good Hope in 1652. However, the British acquired the Cape during the Napoleonic wars in 1806. Dissatisfied with living under British rule the

Boers trekked northeast to Natal, which became the first South African Republic. Later, the British annexed Natal. The Boers however, had also trekked inland and settled in two main areas between the Orange River and the Vaal River, which later became known as the Orange Free State. Another area, north of the Vaal River was named the Transvaal. At the time they were separate republics, but these eventually became united as the SAR (South African Republics).

The discovery of gold and diamonds in the Transvaal led to the invasion of thousands of foreigners seeking their fortunes, among them Cecil John Rhodes, who the Boers called Uitlanders (Outlanders). This further fuelled the fire for imperial expansion in that part of Africa. Britain then annexed the Transvaal along with the Orange Free State. This in-turn led to the uprising by the Afrikaners and consequently the birth of the second Boer War.

In the colonies of Australia, certain politicians viewed the war in South Africa as somewhat of a blessing in disguise. It was seen as the ideal opportunity to kill two birds with one stone; to rally public enthusiasm and support for the British cause and offer to send Her Imperial Majesty Australian troops, volunteers, to assist the motherland in her time of need. The Australian colonies would be seen most favourably by Britain for their support, loyalty and patriotism. At the same time many unemployed men would no longer be on the streets.

Another more pressing reason was that both Canada and New Zealand had already agreed to send troops to South Africa. And so, during the four-year war, Australia dispatched around sixteen thousand men and thousands of horses. Many of those brave and gallant young men never returned to their homeland and not a single horse ever came back to Australia. To this day, their remains lie buried out on the veldt where they died in a bloody conflict, giving their lives so willingly for the glory of the empire. The dawn of the new century led to rapid growth in South Africa resulting in the expansion of sprawling cities, urbanisation and industry. Unfortunately, many graves were unmarked and sadly the last resting places of those young men have been lost forever.

The latter part of the war in South Africa became marred by what was commonly known as Kitchener's concentration camps. It left a bitter taste in the mouths of politicians and also many soldiers, and consequently when it was over everyone wanted to forget about the atrocities that had taken place. The two World Wars which followed and a rapidly changing world quickly overshadowed Australia's young heroes, in what was Australia's first war as a nation. The Boer War was a conflict, which Australia should never have become involved in and a war that should never have taken place. The year 2002 brought about the centenary of the Boer War and during the hundred years that have since passed the world has changed so dramatically, and so rapidly that it is almost impossible for us today to imagine what life was like back then.

Although a number of memorials were erected around Australia commemorating the soldiers who gave their lives during the Boer War, no memorial was ever dedicated to the thousands of horses sent to South Africa to die on the battlefields; horses that suffered the long and arduous journey by sea to face even harsher conditions on the African high-veldt. They too, died for the glory of the empire, only to be forgotten and to fade into obscurity along with men like James Mitchell.

AUSTRALIA 1899

1 On a sheep farm outside the town of Wickepin (200 kilometres south west of Perth) three young men are busy repairing a damaged fence to one of the paddocks. The youngest, James Mitchell, aged twenty-one, is the eldest son of four children born to Charles and Lily Mitchell. James is strikingly handsome with blonde hair and deep blue eyes. He's strong with a good physique and is six foot-three in height. Next in the family is the eldest daughter Alanna. She's nineteen and extremely attractive with long blonde hair and blue eyes. Both Alanna and James had taken their good looks from their mother's side. The other son, William, is seventeen. He's more like his father with brown hair and hazel colour eyes. The second oldest daughter is Elizabeth. She's fourteen and also had brown hair and hazel coloured eyes. The youngest in the family also a daughter is named Bridget. She's eight years of age and is the spitting image of her older sister Alanna.

James' grandparents, immigrants from Britain, who'd both since passed on, had originally started the farm Rambling Meadows. The farm had then been left to his father and a younger brother who had tragically died some years earlier, after falling from a horse. James, like his sisters and brother was born on the farm. His mother and father were of strong Christian faith and like most of the farmers in the area Sundays were family days when the whole family attended the local village church. After the service everyone would congregate outside in small groups chatting and catching up with the latest news and gossip.

James had been educated at the small village school in Wickepin until reaching the age of fourteen. After that he worked on the farm. Later, once he had a few years experience behind him, his father made him the supervisor, due to his own failing health. Rambling Meadows, like many farms at the time had suffered the terrible effects of the seven-year drought and crippling recession of the 1890s. Many of the hired hands had been laid off and the sheep flocks drastically reduced. The farms one blessing had always been a good supply of clean underground water, pumped deep from within the bowels of the earth by a windmill. This was now running out as the underground water tables dropped almost below the extent of the borehole. Along the one boundary of the farm was also a river, but this too had become a dry sandy bed excepting for several isolated pools.

THE SEVEN STATES OF AUSTRALIA
PRE FEDERATION

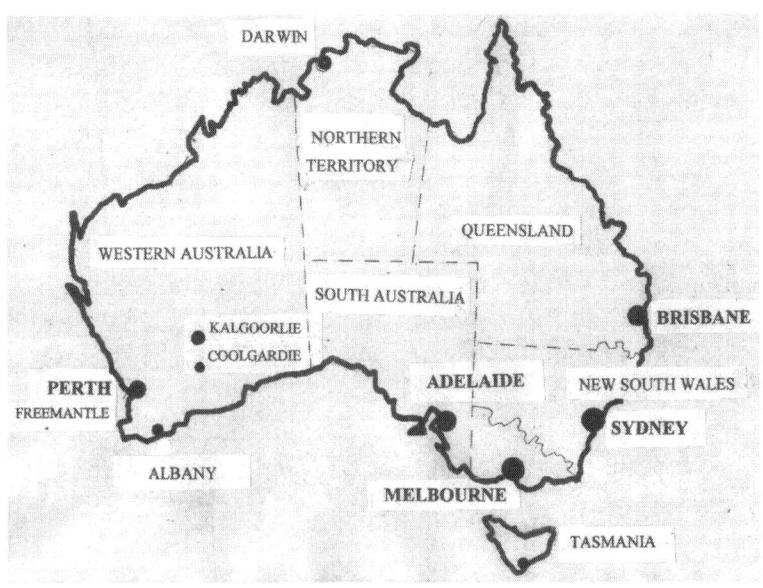

NEW SOUTH WALES – QUEENSLAND – NORTHERN TERRITORY -- WESTERN AUSTRALIA – SOUTH AUSTRALIA – VICTORIA -- TASMANIA

2   The morning was already uncomfortably warm although it was only 8.30a.m. James' short sleeve cotton shirt was damp with sweat. He stopped digging for a moment, firstly to wave a fly away from his face, and secondly to take a drink of water from the canvas water bag, he had previously left in a shady spot. The water tasted a little tainted, but at least it was cool and he had a long drink. He wiped his mouth with the back of his hand then replaced the cork firmly into the neck of the container. He waved another fly from his face as one of the dogs began to bark. James glanced in the direction the dog was barking, towards the large rambling house in the near distance. He could see his eldest sister making her way towards him. She was waving her hand frantically while calling out to him. 'James! ...James!'

He waited until she was a little closer before he shouted out, 'What is it?'

Moments later, she arrived at his side and was a little out of breath. 'Father wants... you to return... to the house,' she puffed out.

James couldn't believe it. 'What for?'

'He wants to... talk to you ...that's all I know.'

'Well, did he say what it was about?'

'Nooo!' She replied a little irritably, mainly due to being out in the hot sun and also having to deal with flies that were pestering her. 'But I think it has something to do with a letter... that he received from Perth.' She was still breathing heavily.

James frowned. 'How would you know that?'

...'He was holding a letter in his hand when he spoke to me.'

James waved another fly from his face. 'I wonder what could possibly be so urgent that I need to return to the house now?' he asked, 'I still have a lot to do here before I finish.'

Alanna looked at the canteen he was holding in his hand. 'May I have a drink of that?'

James handed her the canvas bag. Alanna had a mouthful and then she pulled a face and spat it out. 'Siss! That tasted awful James! God! How long have you had this water in here?'

'I don't know... a couple of days I suppose.'

She handed it back to him. 'You'll give yourself the dysentery if you aren't careful... Come on let's get going, you know father doesn't like to be kept waiting these days.'

'Just a moment!' He told her. He looked over in the direction of the two other men who were working a little way off from them. 'Hey Billy!' he called out loudly.

The big dark-skinned man stopped working and looked over in his direction. 'Yeah?'

'I have to return to the house. You and George carry on until I get back!'

'Right!' ...The young man then glanced towards Alanna and raised his hat. 'Gday Miss Alanna!'

'Morning Billy!' she shouted back.

James turned his attention to his sister. 'I'll race you back to the house,' he said smiling.

'Only if you give me a start first.'

'Go on then.'

Alanna picked up her long skirt and raced off over the rough ground with the dog barking as it chased after her. James pulled his braces up over his shoulders, which had been hanging loosely by his trouser legs. He waited for her to get about halfway to the house before going after her. They both arrived at the verandah almost together and out of breath, puffing and panting for air.

'Beat... you!' Alanna boasted, flicking her long blonde hair over her shoulders, while sucking more air into her lungs, her firm young breasts heaving under her thin cotton blouse.

'So... you... did,' he puffed out. For a moment James starred at her bulging breasts and for the first time he realised that his sister had grown into a beautiful young woman.

Alanna had noticed him starring at her breasts. 'James!' she said loudly with a look of disgust on her face.

'What?' he replied with a guilty expression on his face.

'You were blatantly starring at my bosom!'

'No I wasn't!' he replied defensibly as well as being slightly embarrassed.

'You were so!'

Without further discussion they climbed the wooden steps up to the verandah and were glad to be out of the hot sun. Alanna flopped down into one of the porch chairs while James dusted himself down with his wide-brimmed hat before entering the hallway through the fly screen door. His eyes took a moment to adjust to the dim light after the bright sunshine. His mother was standing there holding a small tray in both hands. There were two glasses of Rose's limejuice she had pored for Alanna and James.

'Hello mother,' he greeted her with a big grin as he took one of the glasses in his hand.

'You had better wash your hands and face first before you go into your fathers study.'

James drank the whole glass down in one gulp. 'Ahhh, that was really nice,' he said wiping his mouth with the back of his hand. 'That sure tasted a lot better than the water I have been drinking out there.' He gave his mother a kiss on the cheek. 'What would I do without you?' He placed the empty glass on the tray and then left for the kitchen.

In one corner there was a table with an enamel basin standing on it. It was half filled with clean hot water, which his mother had previously placed there for him. James cupped his hands and filled them with water then splashed his face. He repeated the action several times. There was a small cake of soap in a floral dish. James rubbed it onto a face cloth, then washed his face, hands and arms. Once he had finished he dried his hands and face on a towel. He then brushed his hair while looking into an ornate brass hand-mirror. He left the kitchen and walked down the dimly lit passage. James stopped outside the door to his father's study. He waited a moment before knocking three times.

'Come in!' his father's muffled voice called out from the other side of the door.

James entered the dimly lit room. The air was heavy with cigar smoke. The smell wasn't unpleasant to him though, he was used to it. 'I understand that you wanted to see me, father?'

He was pleased that James had come so promptly. 'Indeed I do James... take a seat my boy.' He pointed to one of the two vacant chairs opposite his oak desk.

Charles Mitchell was a tall, portly sort of man with a good head of hair for his age, and wore a large brown moustache. He was typical of many men of the Victorian period, being a strict disciplinarian with strong ties to his family's past. He wore a suit most days and carried a pocket watch, which he had inherited from his late father.

James sat in one of the heavily upholstered leather armchairs as requested. His father's desk was cluttered with an assortment of paperwork. He noticed there were a few opened letters lying on the opposite side of the desk. His father stared at him for a moment and then he walked over to a window, surrounded with heavy drapes. He gazed outwards through the lace curtain, seemingly deep in thought, and then he turned to face James. He puffed on his cigar sending more clouds of grey smoke spiralling towards the high ceiling. For some reason, James felt himself becoming a little uneasy.

'I called you here James, as I have decided that we need to further reduce the flocks of sheep. Tomorrow morning I would like you to organise the shearing. Bail the wool and place it into storage as usual. After that shoot the sheep and burn the carcasses.'

James gave a sigh. 'We are running out of space father! Soon, there will be no room left for any more wool bales and then what will we do?'

'We will cross that bridge when the time comes, my boy. Once the wool prices improve again we will be able to sell the stockpile for a good price... Hopefully we will even make a small profit.' He puffed on his cigar. 'There is something else... I know this news will disappoint you, but I am afraid that I am going to have to let George and Billy go shortly.'

'Ah no father! Please! ...Surely you can find someway of keeping them on?' he pleaded. 'They are both practically part of this family!'

His father nodded with a grim expression on his face. 'I know, son... I am terribly sorry... You must try and understand this has been a very difficult decision for me to make. I simply cannot afford their wages any longer. They can remain on until the tasks I have given you are completed.'

'If I ask them, I know they will stay on for food and keep only.'

...'I have no right to expect that of them James.'

'Why not father? ...They won't be able to find work elsewhere. They'll become swagmen. The country is full of desperate men looking for work. We have them passing through here in droves willing to work just for food and a dry place to sleep. I'll speak to them and see what they say.'

'Very well, son, as you wish.' He puffed a few times on his cigar. 'There is another matter of pressing importance which I need to discuss with you. As you know Great Britain has gone to war with the Boers in South Africa.'

James nodded. The probability of this happening had been reported in the newspapers and everyone was talking about it. Plus, a few weeks earlier, over two thousand people had attended a meeting at the Town Hall in Perth, to discuss the idea of volunteer troops going to South Africa. Another reason had also been to gather public opinion as to whether or not Western Australia should consider joining the federation of the Australian colonies, something that had met with a lot of opposition in the wheat-belt towns.

His father continued, 'His Excellency, the Governor of Western Australia, Sir Gerard Smith, has now sanctioned the formation of one company of infantry for service with Her Majesty's Imperial Forces in South Africa. Therefore, the army reserve is now calling for volunteers, as are the other Australian Colonies. I'm sure that you will understand, that it would be a proud moment for Western Australia if we were able to put forward a good sized contingent.' He puffed on his cigar again. 'I have decided James, that you should be amongst some of the first men to offer your services... to show our loyalty and support to the motherland, so-to-speak. This would also offer you a great opportunity to serve Her Majesty and also to be a part of the greatest army the world has ever known.'

James could feel his heart racing in his chest. He glanced around the room with its heavy, ornate styled furniture, all previously shipped over from England when his grandparents came out to Australia, forty years earlier. The portrait of a stern looking Queen Victoria hung on the wall behind the desk, seemingly imposing her rule here in the small room. James looked back at his father. 'I don't mean to upset you father or go against your wishes either, for that matter, but I hardly believe that the war in South Africa is any of our concern.'

'Hardly our concern?' his father interrupted. He had raised his voice a little and puffed more vigorously on his cigar. 'I am sure that I misheard you, James?'

THE PLOUGH, THE GUN AND THE GLORY

'No father, I'm sorry, but I just can't see why we should become involved in this war. This is a matter between Britain and the Afrikaners... it really has nothing to do with us.'

'Listen to me James!' He sat down in his chair, took several deep breaths of air and then puffed on his cigar. Grey smoke spiralled upwards. 'Western Australia is a British colony and therefore it is a matter of showing our loyalty... supporting the motherland in her time of need. It's our duty son. I don't have to remind you of where your grandparents came from... I can assure you that if I was thirty years younger I would have no hesitation in enlisting myself.' He puffed vigorously on the cigar sending more clouds of smoke billowing to the ceiling. He continued, 'Furthermore, I am of the opinion that the whole thing won't last long anyway... possibly a few months at the very most. The Boers stand no chance against such a mighty force as Britain.'

James was about to say something when his father continued, 'Besides, I have been thinking of late, that you have attained the age when you should to go out into the world. Spread your wings so-to-speak.' Charles Mitchell got up from the chair and went over to the window and gazed outwards rocking slowly back and forth on his heels. After a few moments he turned to face James. 'You have lived a sheltered life here on the farm, son. The war in South Africa is an ideal opportunity for you to broaden your horizons whilst also gaining some military experience. In turn, you will become worldlier and gain quite a different perspective on life... I trust that I have made myself absolutely clear, James?'

The young man swallowed the lump in his throat. This was an argument he could never win, no matter what. Sometimes it was far easier when dealing with his father, to let the current take him downstream, rather than trying to swim against it. He gave a sigh. 'If that's what you wish, father.'

'Excellent!' A broad smile beamed from his face. 'I knew you would come to the right conclusion. Now, will you care to join me in a brandy?'

James was taken aback for a moment. Was he hearing things? His father was actually offering him a brandy. This had never happened before, not even when he turned twenty-one. 'I'm still working over at the paddock father, repairing the broken fence. Besides, it's still early morning.'

'Never mind, this is cause for a celebration. Besides, you can delegate that task to George or Billy.' His father decanted them both a brandy from a crystal-glass container. He gave one glass to James, and then lifted the other glass in a toast. 'To Her Majesty and may the Empire be victorious in South Africa.'

James did the same and they drank them down. The neat alcohol made him cough. This was the first time he had ever drunk brandy. He usually only drank Swan Ale and even that was very seldom. He placed the glass down on the desk. 'May I go now, father?'

His father puffed on his cigar again. 'Just a moment James, I have not quite finished yet. I have also received in the post the volunteer registration forms from army headquarters.' He coughed a little before continuing. 'Therefore, tomorrow morning we should meet here and go over them as there are certain formalities that have to be completed, references to be obtained from our clergy, the local constabulary, and also the family doctor, etcetera.'

James nodded his head. 'As you like, father... What time would you like me to be here?'

'Let's say at eight o'clock sharp.'

James nodded. 'May I go now?'

'Very well.'

James left the study and closed the door behind him. He stood for a moment in the hallway. He felt flushed and the walls seemed to be closing in on him. He started to walk down the passage when his mother appeared from the parlour. She could tell he was upset and she was about to say something when he blurted out, 'I'm going over to the paddock to give Billy and George further instructions, mother.'

'James,' she called softly.

'I might also go for a ride afterwards,' he continued, 'maybe down to the river.'

She gave a sigh. She could tell he wasn't going to listen. He gave her a kiss on the cheek and then walked on through the hallway and out through the fly-screen door onto the verandah. At first he had to squint his eyes against the brilliant sunlight. He put his bush hat on and went down the wooden steps into the hot sunshine. The dog was still waiting in the shade for him. 'Come on Blaze!' he called out to it.

The dog immediately ran in front of him leading the way. After instructing the two station hands what to do, James walked over to the stables where he saddled his horse. When he was ready he mounted up. 'Let's go, Thunder,' he said giving the horse a few friendly pats on the side of the neck. They left the stables behind with James cantering the big, white stallion along the dusty, dirt road with the dog following closely behind.

3 James rode at a steady pace through the bush, between the tall Jarrah trees with patches of sunlight streaming downwards through the green canopy overhead and dancing on the dirt road. The wind in his face felt cool and refreshing and also dried the sweat on his forehead. Several kangaroos skipped across the path in front of the horse and then quickly vanished into the thick, dry bush. The dog took off after them.

A few kilometres later James came to the riverbank and he slowed the horse to a walking pace. Once he had dismounted he removed the saddle, then the blanket and dumped them on the ground. After that he removed the bridle and draped it over the saddle. A kookaburra laughed loudly from high up in the trees somewhere. James tried to spot him without success. Another suddenly swooped down and caught a small mullet from the river. James watched it for a moment as it flew off in the direction of several gum trees.

James sat down on the grass and pulled off his boots and then his socks. After stripping naked he plunged into the clear, cool water, and swam down to the bottom. When he resurfaced he hollered out at the top of his lungs, 'Woohoo!' The water was refreshing and he swam around for a few minutes enjoying it immensely.

A short time later, when James was making his way back to the riverbank, he noticed another horse arriving. He stood in the shallows with the water up to his waist and waited. He was surprised when he saw it was a young woman from a nearby orchard farm. Her name was Veronica. He knew her slightly from the small church that they both attended on Sunday mornings. James had thought her stunningly attractive from the first time he had seen her, with her sparkling blue-green eyes and long auburn hair, which she wore down to her waist.

'Hello James!' she called out to him in a friendly manner.

He felt somewhat embarrassed being naked and wasn't quite sure what to do about his unexpected predicament. Using both his hands he quickly covered his groin area under the water. His heart was beating loudly in his ears as he replied, 'G'day... I must apologise for swimming like this. I never realised that any-one-else visited this part of the river any longer.'

She didn't appear to be overly concerned about his nakedness. 'Oh that's all right there's no need to apologise. Actually, I come down here quite often, much the same as you.'

'Oh?' he was surprised to hear that. 'Well, I have never seen you down here before.' Not that he doubted her word in any way.

Veronica dismounted and walked towards the waters edge. She wore a wide brimmed hat, long skirt and a white lacy blouse. 'I'm afraid that's because I have been rather deceitful. If anything, it is I who should be apologising to you.'

James frowned and was now somewhat confused.

Veronica continued, 'Actually, I'm afraid that I have a confession to make.'

'A confession?' He was more puzzled than ever now.

'Yes... I hope that you're not going be too angry with me after disclosing that I have actually been... well... spying on you I suppose... from behind the bushes?'

'Spying?' James was somewhat surprised if not a little shocked.

She sighed. 'It happened one afternoon, quite by accident naturally. I had been down here alone swimming and was in the process of changing into my garments, behind those bushes,' she pointed, 'when I heard a horse approaching. Looking up I saw it was you. I wasn't quite sure what to do as I was only dressed in my underwear. I thought that perhaps you might ride off shortly, but instead, you striped naked and went swimming. I waited and watched you until you were finished. Later, I quietly led my horse away for some distance before mounting-up and riding home.'

'I see.' James scratched the back of his head. 'Well, as you say it was purely by accident, therefore, I see no need for you to apologise.'

'Another time,' she continued enthusiastically, 'when I came down here I noticed that your horse was here. I dismounted and crept quietly towards those bushes.' She pointed again. 'I waited there while you swam. When you got out I watched you drying yourself off before dressing. From then onwards I would come down here regularly and wait over in the bushes hoping that you would come swimming. Sometimes you didn't show up and I would return home disappointed.'

James scratched under his chin while he thought about what she had told him. 'How long have you been coming down here?'

...'A few months.'

James wiped a little water from his face. His heart was still racing wildly and he could hear it thumping in his ears.

'I'll quite understand if you're angry with me,' she added while pouting her lips.

...'Quite honestly I don't know what to say... surprised, shocked I suppose, more than anything.'

Veronica bent down. She placed her hand into the water to see how cold it was. James could see part of her breasts protruding above her camisole. They appeared firm and shapely. She gave a smile as she said, 'The water seems rather pleasant today.'

'It's a bit cold actually.'

She got to her feet. 'Would you object if I was to join you for a swim?'

James' heart thumped even harder in his chest.

Veronica continued, 'Of course if you would rather I not, I can always come back some other time.'

He shook his head. 'No. I'm sorry... you must think me rude? The river belongs to everyone. You are quite entitled to swim here wherever and at whatever time you wish. Please feel free to join me.'

'You will have to turn around and face away while I remove my garments. Unlike yourself, I will not be swimming naked.'

'Naturally.' James felt somewhat relieved to hear that. A few moments later he heard her enter the water.

'You can turn around now,' she said as she swam out a little deeper.

James watched her as she went towards the centre of the river, her long auburn hair flowing out behind. Veronica had moved to the region with her parents earlier that year, after her father had bought an adjoining orchard, together with a small vineyard from a deceased estate. They seemed nice enough people, but remained somewhat private, seldom mixing with the other farmers in the area.

'So, what made you pick this particular spot,' he asked once she had returned.

'I like the pools here.' She brushed a little hair from her face. 'Most of the river over our way is only dry sand now, excepting for one small pool.'

James nodded. 'When the river's running during the rainy season, there are several rapids over by those rocks and even a small waterfall.' He was pointing to the area as he spoke.

'Really? ...That must be rather beautiful.'

'Yeah... I also like the old boathouse and also the jetty... It used to be a good spot to fish from.'

She nodded... 'Do you do much fishing any-more?'

'No. ...I used to, when the river was still flowing. But now there are no fish really worth catching. Anyway, the kookaburras have taken most of them. You would probably be lucky if you caught a mud-crab. These days I only come down here to swim and cool off. It's also a good place for doing some thinking.'

'What do you mostly think about? ...Don't tell me you are a poet or something?'

'No,' he laughed, 'I am certainly not that. I don't know... a lot of things... mostly about life I suppose.'

'Is that why you came here today... to ponder about life?'

'Maybe.'

Veronica swam to a shallow part and stood up. Her white cotton undergarments were almost transparent now that they were wet. James could see her nipples protruding through her camisole, and there was also a dark patch where her vagina was. He could feel some movement in his loins despite the coldness of the water. He decided to take a swim to the other side of the river to get his mind off her. It didn't work, and anyhow he had to swim back. When he returned he said, 'You do realise that I will have to remain in the water until you have left before I can get out and dress?'

'Well, what on earth are we going to do then?' she replied teasingly. 'It will take quite sometime for me to dry off enough before I can redress?'

James scratched his head. He was beginning to shiver and his teeth were starting to chatter.

'I'll tell you what?' she said with enthusiasm in her voice.

'What?' he asked eagerly.

'I will face away from you, towards the bank on the other side. You can then get out and dress yourself. Then, I will join you on the jetty where we can both dry off in the warm sunshine.'

'That sounds fine to me.' Once she had turned around, James waded towards the bank and then made his way over to his clothes. He hurriedly dried himself with his shirt before dressing. When he was finished he let Veronica know and then they both made their way over to the old wooden structure.

4   Veronica climbed onto the jetty. 'I really would have thought James, seeing as that you have grown up with sisters, who I'm sure you must have seen naked at some time or other, that you wouldn't have been quite so bashful in the presence of a woman? Don't tell me you and your sisters have never been down here swimming naked together?'

'Well that's different! ...And besides we were much younger then... and you are virtually a stranger.'

She gave a little laugh. 'Oh James! I wish you could have seen the expression on your face when you saw me arriving. It was one of total panic... even horror, I would say.'

This time he also laughed. 'Well to be honest I never expected anyone else to come down here. Not to this part of the river anyway, and certainly not a woman on her own. To tell you the truth I had absolutely no idea what I was going to do.'

They both laughed together. At that moment a pair of pink and grey galahs swooped down and landed on the handrail of the jetty. They seemed quite oblivious of the two humans not far from them. James and Veronica watched them for a short while, until they suddenly flew off into the tall gum trees lining the riverbank.

'Have you noticed that all the gum trees are shedding their bark at present?' Veronica suddenly asked.

'Yeah... they always do at this time of year.' He looked over at nearby tree. A small squirrel was running along one of the branches. Once it had disappeared inside a hole James turned his attention to Veronica. Her beauty was striking and he couldn't help noticing her nipples protruding through her cotton camisole. 'What if someone was to find us together like this?' he asked with a nervous tone of voice.

She smiled seemingly unperturbed by the idea. 'Then I am afraid, that I would become the talk of the village. You can well imagine what all those gossiping old woman from the church would have to say. I would most probably be branded the whore of Wickepin and run out of town,' she laughed heartily. 'Does it worry you if we were seen together like this?'

He shook his head. 'No... I was thinking more of you... perhaps your father might come here.'

'My father?' she repeated with a surprised expression. 'No.' She shook her head. 'My father would never come down here. And, apart from you James, I have never seen anyone else here... have you?'

'No... well not for a long time... When I was younger the whole family would come down here. My father and grandfather built this boathouse together... My grandfather would take us out in the rowing boat... Sometimes we would go fishing together and catch a good-sized cobbler, a jackfish or a mullet. Other times we would net for yabbies... After both my grandparents passed away we stopped coming down here as a family.'

'I think that is so sad.'

'What?'

'That you don't come down here as a family any more.'

'Oh.'

There was and awkward moment and they both glanced around at the scenery without saying anything until Veronica quite boldly and unexpectedly asked, 'So, who's the special lady in your life James?'

He shook his head. 'No one... well, not any longer anyway,' he replied with a serious expression.

'What was her name?' she asked, even though she really knew the answer.

...'Christina.'

'Were you in love with her?'

James looked thoughtful for a moment. 'Yeah.'

'What happened to her? ... I mean, where is she now?'

...'She lives over in Melbourne. Her father was transferred on a promotion there with the bank.'

'Oh.' Veronica already knew that. Someone at church had told her. 'Do you correspond with her?'

...'No! The last news I heard of Christina was that she had become engaged to be married to someone from the bank.'

'Oh... I am sorry to hear that.' She wasn't being truthful.

He smiled. 'That's alright... and anyway, I am well over her now.'

'You came down here a lot together, didn't you?'

'Yeah.' He frowned. 'How did you know that?'

'I've seen the heart with the arrow that you carved into one of the gum trees. It's right over there.' She pointed in the general direction. 'It has the initials J. M. loves C. C. I guessed they must mean James Mitchell loves Christina Cartwright?'

He frowned again. 'How did you know her surname was Cartwright?'

Veronica smiled. 'A little bird told me.'

His brow wrinkled again. 'Oh, I can guess… one of my sisters, I suppose?'

'If it were, would you be annoyed?'

He shrugged his shoulders. 'I suppose not. Anyway, it doesn't really matter anymore.'

'Well anyway, it wasn't one of your sisters. Did the two of you ever swim naked together?'

James was surprised by her blunt directness, but at the same time amused by her obvious curiosity and interest in him. He thought he would tease her and pretend he was a little annoyed. 'That was a very personal question and I am not sure that I want to answer it.'

She realised perhaps she had gone a little too far this time. 'I'm sorry I shouldn't have said that. I didn't mean to offend you James, I apologise.'

The expression on his face didn't change.

After a few moments she became a little anxious. 'I did say I was sorry.'

He decided not to tease her any further. 'Alright,' he smiled, 'yes, we did swim naked together. Satisfied now?' He thought perhaps that would be the end of her questions.

She gave a sigh of relief and then moments later began with more questions. 'How did the two of you meet?'

James decided he might just as well tell her everything and get it over with. Besides, he was accustomed to his sisters always asking him questions, especially when he and Christina were courting. 'At school.'

'In Wickepin?'

'Yeah… she sat near my desk. I liked her when I first saw her and we became friendly.'

'So, you were childhood sweethearts?'

'I guess so.' James thought it was about time he asked a few questions. 'What about you? Is there a man in your life?'

She sighed. 'Only in my heart James, and I am afraid that I can't disclose his name. It's a secret... even he doesn't know.'

'He doesn't know his own name?' he asked teasingly.

'Nooo! ...I mean he doesn't know that I'm in love with him. That's why I can't tell you who he is. How would it look if was to hear about it from someone, and then he thought that it was me going around town spreading gossip?'

James nodded. 'I suppose that would be very embarrassing for the both of you?' He got to his feet and stretched his legs. James then felt the backside of his trousers to check if they were dry yet. They were still damp and there was a wet patch left on the wooden deck. 'You will probably need to move to another spot,' he advised Veronica, 'otherwise you will never dry off.' He then helped her to her feet.

'Thank you.' She then looked at the large damp patch on the timber. Veronica felt her garments. 'Not quite done yet,' she said with a smile.

They moved over to another dry spot and sat down again. The timber was warm from the sun. At that moment a kookaburra laughed loudly from somewhere in the trees which drew both their attention towards it.

'I can imitate a kookaburra you know?' James advised her with an almost boy-like enthusiasm.

She liked that. He was still young and fresh at heart. 'Can you?' she asked enthusiastically.

'Yeah.'

'Well come on! Let's hear you then!' She said encouraging him.

James made a noise, which sounded exactly like that of the kookaburra up in the tree.

'That was excellent James,' Veronica said, once he had finished. 'Please do it again for me.'

He repeated the sound again. 'I can also imitate a didgeridoo,' he said, a little more boastfully this time.

'Come on then, let's hear you,' she said excitedly.

James gave his best imitation of the primitive bamboo instrument.

'Once again Veronica was impressed. 'However did you ever learn to do that?'

'Billy taught me.'

She nodded. 'Who's Billy, may I ask?'

'He's a jackeroo on our station.'

'Oh.'

'He's part Irish part Aborigine. Well, more Irish, I reckon. He's a good bloke, one of the best. I would trust him with my life if I had to. He's been working for my father since he was a young boy... he's practically one of the family. I taught myself how to do the kookaburra sound years ago when I was still at school.'

'I wish I could do things like that.'

'There must be something you can do surely? Everyone has got some form of talent, you know.'

'Well, I can play the piano. I also do a little singing, but I think imitating noises by simply using your mouth, is so clever.'

'Well, I can't play a musical instrument. My mother plays the piano though. She's very good.'

They continued talking for over an hour until Veronica eventually said, 'I have to go now. My father will be wondering where I've got to... Will you come back again soon? Tomorrow perhaps?'

...'Tomorrow? If you like?'

'How about you is that what you would like?' she asked.

'Yeah, I would like that very much.'

Veronica got to her feet. 'Well, I seem to be dry enough now. It will only take a moment for me to dress and then I must hurry.' She made her way towards her garments hanging over a branch and then quickly dressed. Afterwards she said, 'I'll see you tomorrow then.'

James nodded. 'What time?'

'Around the same as today.'

'I'll be here.' He assisted Veronica as she climbed onto her horse and then she rode off.

5   James re-saddled his mount and then set off for home with the sun dropping on the horizon. When he arrived he unsaddled the horse and gave it some fresh hay. Then he walked over to the large, rambling brick-house with its wood and iron verandah. His mother was playing the piano, a usual early evening event prior to dinner. It was a ballad by Banjo Paterson. James liked his music especially Waltzing Matilda. He stood and listened for a moment before entering the hallway.

His mother stopped playing when she noticed him enter through the door. 'You were gone for a long time, James. Did you enjoy your ride?'

'Yes thank you mother,' he smiled while hanging up his hat on the rack in the hallway.

She got up from the piano. 'Did you go down to the river again?'

'Yeah.'

'How was it?'

'Pleasant, but as you know, there's not much water these days, not like how you remember it. Once the drought has broken, we should all go down there together again and have a picnic.'

'That would be very nice... Can we talk for a moment about something important James?'

'Sure.'

'I mean somewhere in private... come, let's go into the garden.'

His mother led the way with James wondering what she wanted to talk about. Once they had reached the centre of the garden they sat down on a wooden bench-seat. His mother looked over the garden before saying, 'It is all going to die I am afraid. Father says we can no longer spare the water. Soon, we will hardly have enough for ourselves. Each night I pray that God will bring us rain.' She gave a sigh... 'After you went riding this afternoon your father and I discussed the matter of you going off to the war in South Africa.'

He nodded... 'I was going to tell you myself tonight after supper.'

'I am not ashamed that my heart is heavy with sadness over this whole matter James, and I have told your father of my feelings. I shall truly miss you and I will not rest or be happy until I see you return safely home again. Furthermore, as you know my mother was originally from Holland and that I have a sister living in the Orange Free State. Your aunt Ruth and her husband Jacobaas, farm in the western part of the state. Jacobaas is Afrikaans and I am deeply worried for their safety and also that of the three children.'

'I understand how you must feel mother. I'm sure they will be all right. I can't exactly see the British storming homesteads. Besides, they may be nowhere near the war. However, father's right, we must support Her Majesty during this conflict. It would be cowardly and wrong of us not too. Anyway, with things the way they are, with the drought and recession, what choice do we really have?' Another thing, having now thought things over, I am quite looking forward to the experience. I think the whole thing is exciting,' he said enthusiastically.

'Oh James,' she said shaking her head, 'you are still so young and full of boyish ideas. War is a terrible thing son. It destroys everyone, even the victors. And it robs mothers of their sons and wives of their husbands and children of their fathers. If anything should happen to you it would kill me.'

'Nothing is going to happen to me mother. Besides, what would you have me do? Stay here and be looked upon as a coward by everyone in the village for the rest of my life? Perhaps even by my own father?'

She shook her head. 'No, James… I could never ask or expect that of you. Nor do I want you to go against your father's wishes. However, at the same time I am deeply concerned for your safety.'

James placed his arm over her shoulder. 'I have already told you mother; nothing is going to happen to me. I am sure that God will take good care of me.'

'I pray that the Lord does, my son. I really pray that the Lord does.'

6 The following days were taken up shearing, baling the wool and slaughtering the sheep. Afterwards, the carcasses were burnt to prevent any disease breaking out. James hated killing them but it was far better than watching them die a slow and agonising death through starvation and thirst. Towards the end of the day James would ride down to the river where he would usually find Veronica waiting for him. One afternoon he thought he should tell Veronica that he would be leaving soon to go to the war in South Africa.

She took the news rather badly. 'Why haven't you mentioned this to me sooner?' she said wiping her eyes and blowing her nose.

'I'm sorry. I suppose I didn't expect you to react this way. I honestly thought that you would be proud of me.'

'Proud? ...Why would you possibly think that? ...Why are you are so eager to go off to war?'

'At first it was my father's wish... then, after thinking about it, I decided he was right. After all we are a British colony. It's our duty to help the empire in her time of need. George and Billy have also volunteered.'

Veronica sighed.

'Britain needs our help to fight the Boers,' James added.

'You mean chase farmers from their land so they can take over? We should have nothing to with it.'

'Don't be silly we're not going to chase farmers off their land. We're going to fight a war. Listen, at first I wasn't keen on the idea myself.'

'Then please don't go James... Stay here,' she pleaded.

'I have to go.'

'Why?'

'I would shame my father if I wasn't to go now. Besides, everyone in the village and at church would think of me as a coward... and I'm certainly not that.'

'Oh God, James. You could not have given me any worse news.' Veronica wiped more tears away and gave a little sniff. She looked into his striking blue-eyes and at his handsome boyish looks. 'So when will you be leaving?'

'I'm not sure... soon though. It could only be only a matter of days now. Perhaps a week.'

Veronica wiped her eyes as she looked towards the old boathouse. She turned to look at James. 'Can you meet me here tomorrow?' she asked with a pleading tone to her voice.

'Yeah.'

'Come early... at say around three o'clock?'

'Okay.'

'I have to go now.' She made her way over to her horse. After mounting up she waved to James and rode off.

7

The following afternoon James returned to the river as agreed. Veronica was already waiting for him down by the jetty. He dismounted and walked over to her. 'G'day.'

'Hello James.' She was sitting on the grass next to a folded blanket.

'Have you been waiting long?'

'No, not long. I was just enjoying being here listening to all the birds. I love this place it's so beautiful and peaceful.' She got to her feet and then went down to the waters edge. Veronica took something out of the water and held it up for him to see. 'Red wine,' she said showing it to him, 'from our cellar.' She made her way back, picked up the blanket and handed it to him. Then she took him by the hand. 'Come, follow me.' She led James along the pathway towards the old clinker built wood-fabricated boatshed. They crossed over the jetty and entered the building. Once inside Veronica stopped and then glanced around the place for a moment before saying, 'I think this will do us very nicely.'

James frowned. 'What for?'

'Making love.'

'Pardon?' he swallowed hard.

'We are going to make love right here in the boathouse like you and Christina used to do.'

...'But... we haven't even known one another for very long.'

Without replying Veronica pulled the cork out of the bottle and took a long drink from it. Then she handed it to James. 'Here, have some.'

James had a good drink and then another before returning the bottle. Veronica had another few mouthfuls. She placed the bottle down on the floor and then came up close to

James. Her heart was racing as she took hold of him and kissed his moist mouth with passionate desire. When she was finished she said, 'You simply can't go off to war without having made love to me. What if you should be killed or something terrible?'

'Killed?' he hadn't contemplated that idea. 'I'm sure that won't happen.'

'You are going off to war James! Men get killed in wars! ...It's not a game!'

James swallowed another lump in his throat. Surely he wasn't going to die so young. And anyway, God was going to take care of him. He decided to take another long drink from the wine bottle.

Veronica hurriedly started undoing the buttons on his shirt. 'Help me to take off your clothes.'

James undid the remaining buttons and then he started to strip down. Veronica had seen him naked before, but only from the distance of the bushes. This was the first time really up close. 'You're not Jewish are you,' she asked.

'Jewish? No... why?'

'You've been circumcised.'

'Oh... My mother said it was for hygiene purposes.'

Veronica stripped off her clothing and stood naked in front of him. Her figure was firm and slim and her breasts round. Her nipples stood erect with goose bumps surrounding them. She took the blanket and placed it over a canvas tarpaulin, which was stacked on the timber floor. After that she asked, 'Would you like more wine?'

James cleared the lump in his throat. 'Yeah, thanks,' he replied as he took the bottle from her and drank another long drink down. He returned the bottle.

'Lay down next me,' she said softly, holding out her hand to him.

He knelt on the blanket with his heart racing. He was trembling as he asked, 'What if your father finds out?'

'Who's going to tell him?'

...'What happens if you fall pregnant?'

'You worry too much James. Leave everything to me.'

Veronica put her arms out and he lay down next to her. James placed his hand on her one breast. It was firm and her skin was soft and smooth. Her nipple was hard and he felt the goose bumps surrounding it. They were plentiful, far more than before.

Veronica stared into his eyes for a brief moment and then placed her lips onto his. His mouth was warm and his breath fresh. She kissed him lustfully and James did the same while caressing her breast. She could feel his penis pressing against her thigh, and she wanted him more now than ever.

Moments later James penetrated her with Veronica giving a slight moan. James began thrusting with vigour. Veronica closed her eyes and moved her hips in rhythm with his. James continued thrusting with Veronica wrapped her legs around his waist and clinging to him. 'Tell me... that you... love me James?' she said breathlessly.

'I love... you.'

James pushed harder. Veronica could feel him deeper inside her. The sensation was sheer ecstasy. There was no stopping now, not for anything. 'Tell... me... again,' she begged.

'I love... you... Veronica.' He continued thrusting harder and deeper.

'Tell me... again.'

He repeated the words in between catching his breath.

She opened and closed her eyes with pure, sensual pleasure. 'Oh James... I love you so much... Oh God! Veronica began to pump with her hips more vigorously. She was breathing harder and her heart was racing faster than it had done in a long time. They were both sweating as she continued to pump her buttocks, expelling her breath. 'Oh God! Uh! Uh! Uhhh! Oh God!' Veronica pumped harder. Her breathing was short and sharp now and moments later she orgasmed. James followed seconds after also making sounds of sexual pleasure and satisfaction. They lay next to each other with James' arm around her, both still breathing hard trying to get the air back into their lungs. Once Veronica had recovered she sat up. 'Would you like a little more wine?'

'Yeah, thanks.' He took the bottle, had a long drink and then handed it back.

Veronica swallowed down a mouthful. 'Did you enjoy that... making love to me?'

'Yeah.'

'I'm going to wash myself in the river now.' Veronica got to her feet and walked towards the open doorway.

James followed her. Veronica took the path down the side of the jetty and walked into the water. James decided to dive off the end of the timber structure. The water was cool and refreshing. After swimming around for a few moments they left the water and returned to the boathouse.

'I'm going to leave for home shortly James.'

'Why so soon?'

'I have to take care of a few things back at the house.'

'Oh,' he nodded. 'But you're still dripping wet.'

'The wind will dry me off on the way home.' She started to dress. At that moment they heard the sound of a horse galloping off. They looked at one-another with startled expressions.

'Darn!' Veronica said while pulling on her underwear. 'I think my horse may have bolted.'

'I'll go and take a look.' James hurriedly pulled up his trousers and then fastened the buttons. Then he scampered off. A few moments later he returned to the boathouse.

'Was I right?' Veronica asked while doing up the buttons on her dress.

'No, it was none of ours... Perhaps we were hearing things?'

Veronica shook her head. 'No, we both heard it. That was definitely a horse leaving in a rather big hurry.'

'I'll have another look around for signs of hoof prints.'

'They'll be there.'

James finished dressing and then he searched the ground while Veronica replaced the blanket and empty wine bottle into her saddlebag. A few moments later James came across a third set of hoof prints, plus several footprints. He looked at the hoof prints first. They were large and broad and they had left deep marks in the sand. He looked up at Veronica. 'These were made by a fairly large horse... a stallion or a gelding maybe.' He then glanced at the footprints. James wasn't sure if they were men's or not. 'Whoever it was, may have seen us in the boathouse?' he said looking at Veronica.

'Maybe... Anyway, I must get going.' She gave him a kiss on the cheek and then he helped her into the saddle.

'I won't be able to come down here for the next few days,' she said looking down at him.

'Why not?'

'I will explain to you another time... I'll meet you here Friday afternoon... say three o'clock.'

'I may have already left for the war by then,' he protested.

'Let's hope not.'

'Okay,' he replied a little disappointed.

'Bye James.'

He gave her a wave as Veronica galloped off in a hurry.

8   Veronica spurred the horse on at a good pace, up the gently sloping hill, between the wandoo and the sandalwoods, the huge gum trees, black-boys (grass trees), the hibiscus and honeysuckle and the Christmas bush (fire tree). She was an accomplished rider having been taught by her father, who had ridden in a number of equestrian events at annual shows, while they were still living further south in Manjimup.

It was a six-kilometre ride from the river to the orchards and vineyards known as Two Valleys. Veronica slowed the horse almost to a trot once the house came into sight. When she arrived at the stables, an aging, bearded Aborigine with curly grey-hair took the horse from her. 'G'day, Miss Veronica,' he said with a coarse, gruff voice.

She greeted him courteously. Veronica dismounted and was just about to walk off towards the house when she turned and faced the indigenous man. 'Tom!' she called out.

He stopped walking the horse and looked over in her direction. 'Yea, Miss.'

'Have any of the other horses been out this afternoon?'

'Only Master Karl's, Miss... it was all steaming hot and foaming at the mouth when he got back. I reck'n he rode the horse real hard, Miss.'

'I see. ...Thank you Tom.'

Veronica proceeded to the house with her heart pumping faster. When she entered the hallway she placed her riding gloves down on the table. Then she brushed her hair back with her hand, while looking into the ornate wall mirror. Veronica was about to proceed down the hallway to her room, when the door to the parlour opened. Her father stepped out. 'Ah, I see that you're finally back at long last.'

'Have you been looking for me, father?'

'No, but someone else has... Where have you been all this time anyway?'

'Out riding.'

A small boy came running up the passage. 'Mother! Mother! I've been looking for you the whole afternoon,' he called out. He threw his arms around her legs and held on tight.

'Hello, my darling.' She rubbed his head gently.

'Where have you been all this time mother?'

'I was out riding.'

'Why didn't you take me with?' he complained, 'you always take me when you go riding.'

'I'll take you tomorrow... Come let's go to your room.'

They left, with her father still standing at the door, and walked hand-in-hand to Samuel's bedroom.

9 James unsaddled his horse, removed the bridal and then walked over to the other horses. He felt each one in turn. They were all cold except Alanna's and Billy's. One at a time, he lifted a leg on each horse and checked the hooves. By the time James arrived at the house everyone had bathed and were ready for supper.

James washed his face and hands in the basin. Once everyone was seated around the table Mr Mitchell said grace, and then he began slicing the roast mutton into thin strips. Mrs Mitchell dished up and then everyone started to eat. James was starving and was swallowing his food down in large gulps.

'Siss! James! You're eating like a pig!' Elizabeth commented with disgust. Everyone then had something to say and a family argument broke out until Mr Mitchell rapped the table with his spoon. 'Now, that's quite enough from all of you!' he said sternly. He lowered his voice a little. 'You all know that I will not tolerate this kind of behaviour at the meal table. Is that understood?' He looked sternly at each one in turn and then he continued with his meal without anyone saying another word.

After supper everyone helped to clear away the dishes and wash up. There were pots, plates and cutlery, which had to be cleaned with lemon juice to remove the grease. Clean water had to be carried in from the outside tank. Water had to be boiled on the wood-stove and the dirty water taken out to the vegetable garden.

Once all the chores were completed James sat outside on the verandah with his sisters and brother. His mother was playing the Piano Concerto in A-Minor by Grieg. His father was sitting in his favourite heavy leather-armchair smoking a cigar and listening attentively to Lily, which he thoroughly enjoyed doing after supper.

'So, Alanna, where did you go to today?' James asked once a favourable opportunity arose.

'Nowhere... why?'

James frowned. 'I happened to notice that your horse had been ridden this afternoon.'

Alanna looked thoughtful for a moment. She then looked towards Elizabeth. 'Did you ride my horse this afternoon?'

Elizabeth's face turned pale. 'I only took it for a short ride, I promise.'

'I would appreciate it if you were to ask me first in future, Elizabeth.'

'Yes all right! I'm sorry! It won't happen again! ...I'm tired now. I'm going to bed. Goodnight.' She got to her feet and left before any other questions could be asked.

James swallowed the lump in his throat. Was it Elizabeth that had seen him and Veronica together, he thought, as he watched her leave? Or was it Billy's horse that had been down at the river? ...Or, had it been another horse from somewhere else?

'Elizabeth!' her mother called out as she entered the hallway.

'Yes mother.'

'I hope that you haven't forgotten it's your turn to empty the bath-water?'

'No mother.'

'And please don't forget to place a bucket of water on the stove so that James may bath later.'

James got to his feet. 'That's alright mother,' he called out, 'I'll do it! ...You go on up to bed Elizabeth!'

'You spoil her James,' Alanna protested. 'She gets away with murder with you.'

'She has school in the morning... Besides, she's only fourteen, remember?'

Alanna gave a sigh... 'I had to do it at that age.'

'Me too.' He gave her a friendly pat on the head.

She looked up at him. 'Well don't forget this time, that the bathwater goes into the drum for the vegetable garden.'

'I won't,' he replied with a smile.

10   Some days later George rode to the nearby village of Wickepin and by late afternoon he arrived home with the mail. Charles Mitchell had received a letter from army headquarters in Perth, telling him that James and the two other volunteers, were now to report to the infantry battalion barracks at Karrakatta, within five days for assessments and medicals.

James had only seen Veronica once since the time they had made love, although he had been going down to the river daily in the hope that she would show up. Neither had she or her family been to church the previous Sunday, which was also rather unusual.

After waiting down at the boathouse one afternoon James decided, out of frustration, to ride to her father's property to see her. James galloped the white stallion along the dirt road towards the orchards and vineyard. The Jarrah trees had thinned out and there were now open patches of land with gum trees and rolling brown hills, and he could see the house over in the distance. As he neared the property he slowed his horse to a trot, then brought it to a stop. He was feeling a little nervous about showing up unexpectedly and was worried that he may cause a problem for Veronica. Then he thought, 'To heck with everyone, I'm going there.' He spurred the horse on and made the final gallop.

When he arrived at the house there were two men standing on the verandah talking. One of them approached James as he dismounted. James recognised him from church as Veronica's father. They greeted one another first; then James said, 'I would like to talk with Veronica if I may, sir.'

The man removed his hat and mopped his brow with a handkerchief. 'I'm afraid that will not be possible, young man.'

'Can I ask why not?'

The man replaced his hat. 'You can leave a message with me if you wish?'

'I mean you no disrespect sir, but I would prefer to talk with Veronica if I may?'

'What has my daughter to do with you, young man?'

'We are good friends.'

'Friends? From where may I ask?'

James was stumped for a moment. He couldn't reveal that they had been meeting secretly down at the river. What could he possibly say without exposing their relationship? 'Well, as you know, Mr Van der Valk, I have seen her many times at church. I was also hoping to ask your permission to take her riding sometime... in the company of others naturally... having first asked Veronica of course.'

The man shook his head while replying, 'I'm sorry, but that will not be possible. I must ask you to leave now.'

James was disappointed and frustrated. 'Will you please tell her I called by then?'

'Please don't come back here again.'

James turned his horse and rode off down the dirt road. He was angry, confused and puzzled. Why wouldn't Veronica's father allow him see her? What kind of man was he? James trotted the horse for half a mile when he heard a horse galloping up from behind. He stopped and looked around. It was Karl who James also recognised from the church.

Karl brought his mount to a halt kicking up the sand and dust around James. 'I saw you back at the house,' he said, 'were you looking for Veronica?'

'Yeah, how did you know?'

'Just guessing.'

'It was without success I'm afraid.'

'If you continue a little further on down this road you will come across a turn off on the left. Take it. It will lead you down to the river. There is a small pond where you will find her.' He tipped his hat and then rode of at a gallop without James having thanked him.

James cantered his horse in the direction Karl had given him. The road down to the river was well worn from the wheels of a carriage. In the distance amongst the huge gum trees, he saw what looked like a gazebo, then a horse and buggy. James soon brought his horse to a halt and dismounted. After tying the reins to a branch he walked down towards the river. His heart gave a flutter when he saw Veronica a short distance away. He was about to call out to her when a small boy came running out from behind a tree. He was calling out, 'Mother! ... Mother! ...Look, there's a strange man!'

For a moment James was stunned. Who was this child? Why was he calling her mother?

Veronica got to her feet and turned around. Her heart started to race when she saw it was James. She started to walk towards him. 'What on earth are you doing here?' she asked, as they got closer.

'I was worried when you didn't show up at the boathouse for so long. I thought there might be something wrong... that you were ill perhaps?'

'Oh James, I am so sorry.'

The small boy arrived and clung to Veronica's skirt. She placed her hand on his head and gently brushed the hair from his face. 'This is my son, Samuel.'

James' mind was still spinning. 'I think you owe me some kind of explanation.'

Veronica nodded. She first told Samuel to see if he could catch a fish with his rod, which had been cut from a small branch. They both watched the small blonde-headed boy as he skipped off down to the waters edge. Veronica then turned to face James. 'We can talk over by the gazebo.'

They walked over to the timber structure in silence, which was positioned under the shade of several towering gum trees. There was a gentle breeze drifting through the open-air building making it cool and pleasant. 'Would you like a little lemonade?' Veronica asked opening up a cane picnic basket.

'No thank you,' he replied softly.

'I made it myself.'

'Well, perhaps just a little then.' James removed his hat and sat down on a bench seat. 'So, what should I make of all of this then?' he asked impatiently.

Veronica sensed the aggravation in his voice as she poured two glasses and gave one to James. She sipped a little of her cool drink first before saying, 'I often bring Samuel here. It's so nice and peaceful.' She gave a sigh. 'I am afraid that I owe you another apology James. I regret that I have not been very truthful with you.'

'It would certainly appear that way.'

'I am sure by now that you will have reached the conclusion that I am a married woman?'

'Either that or you have a bastard for a son.'

Veronica resented the remark but she knew James was angry, and that he possibly had every right to be. 'My married name is Veronica Pearson. My husband's name is Timothy.'

James' heart was racing as he swallowed the lump in his throat.

'But, if it is of any consequence, I am no longer living with him. I left him when we moved here from Manjimup, when my father bought this property.'

James shook his head. 'I just can't believe any of this.' He brushed his hands through his damp hair. His head was swimming as his mind tried to take in what he was hearing. 'So whereabouts' is this husband of yours then?'

Veronica shook her head. 'I presume he's still living in Manjimup.'

'Why did you leave him?'

Veronica sighed again. 'It's a long story James... He was a violent man. He would often get drunk and beat Samuel and me. One night when he came home drunk he beat me so severely that I was unconscious for over an hour. My father happened to call around unexpectedly that night. When he saw what Timothy had done to me he threatened to shoot him there and then. He took Samuel and me home with him. I knew then that the best thing for me to do was to leave Timothy permanently. My father was so determined about the whole matter that he sold up his property in Manjimup and we moved here. As far as I know Timothy has no idea of my whereabouts.'

THE PLOUGH, THE GUN AND THE GLORY

James got to his feet and then paced the small structure shaking his head. 'How did you meet this man, this husband of yours?'

'It was many years ago at an agriculture show. I was fifteen then, still very young. My father rode in the gymkhana events. He always took me along with him. That's where I first met Timothy. I thought he was the most handsome man in the world. He was ten years older than me and swept me off my feet. He told me that I was the most beautiful girl in the world. Anyway, he started courting me. Six months later I fell pregnant with Samuel and so we got married.'

James sighed. 'Why have you never told me any of this before?'

'Believe me I wanted nothing more, but I didn't know how, James. I was frightened that you would want nothing to do with me after that. I didn't want to lose you. I am so sorry that you had to learn the truth like this.'

James' mind was spinning even more now and his throat was dry. He took a gulp of the lemonade and then looked out of the gazebo at the small boy. Then he turned back to Veronica with his heart still racing in his chest. He shook his head again. 'I still can't believe any of this. I can't believe that you would deliberately deceive me the way you have... Lie to me... Leading me on pretending to be in love with me... and a married woman at that!'

'Is that what you think? ...That I was pretending to be in love with you?'

'I honestly don't know what to think anymore.'

'I love you more than my heart can bear... but I can't change the past... what has happened has happened and will always, I suppose haunt me... Anyway, you will be leaving for South Africa soon, so I suppose that it was just as well that you have found out the truth.'

James said nothing. His heart was sore and he was still angry and confused.

Veronica smiled. 'Do you remember the time down at the old boathouse when you asked me if there was a man in my life? And I replied only in my heart... and then I said that I couldn't tell you who he was... do you remember that?'

James nodded.

'That was you I was talking about... You! James Mitchell!'

At that moment Samuel came running up to the gazebo calling out to his mother. 'Mother look I have caught a fish.' He was proudly holding up a little tiddler for her to see.

James turned back to Veronica. 'I think perhaps I should leave now.'

She nodded reluctantly. 'May God take good care of you in South Africa, James. ...Please look after yourself and be careful.' The tears were streaming down her face.

'Thank you... and you take care to.' James turned and walked down the gazebo steps and over to his horse. He undid the reins from the branch and with a heavy heart he climbed into the saddle. Without looking back in Veronica's direction he rode off at a gallop.

11

Early morning two days later, James was standing on the verandah next to his mother, together with his brother and sisters. There was a fresh breeze blowing kicking up the dust. It made James shiver for some reason. It was a sad occasion for the family and his mother was tearful as she said, 'I have prayed to God to take good care of you James.' She wiped the tears from her eyes with a lace handkerchief.

'Thank you, and please stop worrying, mother.'

They embraced for a moment and then James kissed her on the cheek. She held onto him. 'I have given your father a letter together with a photograph of the family to post from Perth. It's for your Aunt Ruth explaining to her that you will be in South Africa shortly with the Western Australian army.'

'Mother, I haven't even been selected yet. I may not even get to go over there.'

'You will. Regrettably they always choose the best boys. They need fine young men like you. ...Now, I also have an envelope for you. It contains a photograph of your Aunt Ruth and your Uncle Jacobaas together with the children. They will be somewhat older now as the picture was taken a few years ago. I have written their address on the outside for you, in case you should find yourself near their farm.'

James took it from her and placed the envelope in the inside pocket of his jacket. He turned to Alanna and gave her a big hug saying, 'Take care of mother for me.'

'I will.'

'And look after yourself as well.'

Alanna nodded.

James then turned to William. 'Don't forget you have to chop the firewood every morning for the stove, and also for the boiler or you will have mother after you.' He smiled and then gave him a manly hug. 'Don't forget you also have to help with the bath water when it's your turn, the same as the girls do.'

The young boy nodded. 'And they have to help me water the veggie garden and to feed the chickens, the dogs, and also the pigs.'

'Yeah, all of those things to.'

'And what about the sheep?'

'Father will look after those as well as the bullocks.'

'Why are we keeping the bulls if we aren't carting the wool to Narrogin any longer?'

'Well, father may try and sell them if things don't pick up soon... And don't forget to do your homework. When I return from South Africa I want to see that you have obtained good marks from school.'

'Who's going to help me with my homework while you are away?'

'You have Alanna, mother and father, so no excuses.'

After that it was Elizabeth's turn and then finally Bridget's. James then said goodbye to the three dogs. His favourite, Blaze, had to be tied up so that he didn't follow after James.

Several Aborigines had gathered around from nearby farms. They said they belonged to the Nunga Clan, which apparently was the same as Billy's mother. They had come to conduct a sort of ritual. One of them approached the three young men who were about to depart. He was old with long straggly grey hair and a beard. He wore the skins of a kangaroo and his body was decorated with yellow ochre and red paint. He dipped his finger into a pot and then painted several markings on the three men's foreheads.

'What's he doing Billy?' James asked with curiosity.

'He's protecting us from evil spirits because we are going to a strange, faraway land. ...A land where we have no ancestral spirits to keep watch and take care over us.'

After the ceremonial dancing, chanting and wailing had taken place, the Aborigine clan left in silence and disappeared into the dry brown bush, as mysteriously as they had first appeared.

'Did you know any of them Billy?' James asked.

'No, none of them... But that makes no difference.'

'How did they know we were leaving here and going to South Africa then? Who told them?'

'No one James, they saw it in the dreamtime. The elder told me that he had seen us travelling over water and across hills and sand. He saw us in a hostile land, fighting many fierce and raging battles, and crossing rivers flowing with blood.'

'Yeah? ... Do you really believe in all that stuff then?'

'Yeah... don't you?'

'I don't know. No, not really. I think it's just a lot of primitive superstition.'

Billy smiled. 'Well, you believe in God, don't you?'

'Of course, you know I do. Anyway, what has that to do with it?'

'How do you know that your religion isn't just a lot of primitive superstition?'

'Is that what you think it is?'

'You didn't answer my question James.'

'Of course not.'

Charles Mitchell was eager to get going. 'Come on you blokes it's time for us to get moving now, we have a long journey ahead of us.'

Billy and George said goodbye to the Mitchell family and after James had mounted up he waved to everyone as he bid them goodbye. Then his father, Billy O'Reilly, George Gleniste and himself, set off in the direction of the capital city of Western Australia.

Lulu.

Lulu Enterprises UK Ltd
263 Putney Bridge Road
London SW15 2PU
United Kingdom

Business ID: 3714212

Order Date: 20/11/2009

PREFERED DELIVERY METHOD: Royal Mail 1st Class Mail

DELIVERY NOTE

Tink Bough
208 Dower Rd

Sutton Coldfield

T: 0121 3083140
B75 6SZ
UNITED KINGDOM

* 2 4 9 3 4 3 *

Type	Book ID	URC	DN	Title	Qty
Soft	736397	240077-1	249343	THE PLOUGH, THE GUN AND THE GLOR	1

Total: 1

Thanks for shopping at lulu.com!
Contact us at http://www.lulu.com/help/email_support.php
if you have any questions about your order

FSC

Mixed Sources

Product group from well-managed
forests and other controlled sources

Cert no. SGS-COC-2953
www.fsc.org
© 1996 Forest Stewardship Council

Tink Bough
208 Dower Rd

Sutton Coldfield

T: 0121 3083140
B75 6SZ
UNITED KINGDOM

Royal Mail 1st
Class Mail

In Case of Non Delivery, Please Return to:
48-50 Birch Close, Eastbourne, East Sussex, BN23 6PE

* 2 4 9 3 4 3 *

12   It was a good two-day ride through bush to the smallish settlement built on the north bank of the Swan River. Towards the end of the second day they arrived on the outskirts of Victoria Park, a new suburb built on the south bank, which they entered from the Albany Road.

At first, there was only the odd house spread out with miles of bush in between. Later, they came across hundreds of small single-storey rusty corrugated-iron shanties built closely together. Every now and then a few houses were built from clinker board with iron roofs and tiny verandah's. Periodically, there was a brick house. Most of the houses had galvanised-iron water tanks that stood at the sides of the houses or in the back yards. There were also dunnies at the bottom of the yards. Sometimes, in between the houses there would be trading stores, such as blacksmiths, hardware merchants and livery stables.

Several houses had small neat gardens at the front, while others had dry, lifeless sea sand. Several young children were playing games in the dusty dirt-streets with old bicycle rims and a ball. They wore no shoes and their clothes were shabby and torn. At the backs of many houses washing was strung out along lines and fences. James thought how lucky he and his brother and sisters were having grown up on a farm.

As it was near the end of the day crowds of people were walking home from town carrying things in baskets or pushing small carts. Others, more fortunate, rode on bicycles, mules or horses, and some rode in buggies. There were other larger carts pulled by a team of four horses, delivering water in wooden casks to many of the houses. James noticed a young woman walking with a small blonde headed boy. His clothes were shabby and he was crying, and for some reason they made him think of Veronica and Samuel, although they were far more fortunate than these two.

Scruffy, mongrel dogs barked at the horses, as they rode on their way towards Perth Bridge (now the Causeway) with the sun setting on the horizon. After crossing the long, iron and wood structure with the horse's hoofs clopping on the timber, they entered the suburb of East Perth. There was a sign 'Anglican Orphanage.' A few scrawny-looking children were playing in the dusty, tree barren grounds.

The three men continued along the sand and limestone road, deeply rutted from the wheels of carriages. The stench of horse urine and manure droppings was heavy in the air, and the horse's hooves kicked up the white dust. A street sign said 'Adelaide Terrace.'

Once they reached Plain Street the scenery changed somewhat. Adelaide Terrace was now lined on both sides with Cape Lilac trees (Jacarandas) in full bloom. Their purple bell shaped flowers filled the air with their perfume, against the backdrop of palatial brick homes two stories in height. Gone were the shanty houses, the clinker-wood houses, the rusty corrugated-iron roofs and water tanks. Instead, there were now slate and shingles, good quality masonry work wrought-iron fences and gates and splendid rose gardens.

'Hey George!' James called out, 'what about getting yourself a place like that when you get back from South Africa?' He pointed to a magnificent Victorian styled home.

George sniggered to himself. 'Are yah kiddin? What would I do with a bleedin joint like that? I only got this 'orse. Nah thanks mate. Anyways, it would take me a month of darn Sundays to bleedin clean it.'

James laughed. 'If you owned a place like that you wouldn't be cleaning it mate, believe me.'

The further they proceeded into town, the houses became more palatial, grander and more spectacular than the ones before. They crossed over Bennet and Hill Streets and arrived at Victoria Avenue. James looked to his right. Up on a small hill he saw a magnificent Gothic style building, which impressed him immensely. He called out to his father who was a little way ahead of him. 'Father! What's that place over there?' He pointed.

Charles Mitchell brought his horse to a temporary halt as he half turned in the saddle and looked in the direction James was pointing. 'That's Saint Mary's Cathedral. I can see that you are impressed and who wouldn't be?'

James nodded. 'I could never have ever imagined anything like it,' he replied thinking of the small corrugated-iron church he was used to, back at their home village of Wickepin.

They spurred the horses on. A new sign said Saint Georges Terrace. There was another fine building on their left. A signboard told them it was the Perth Roman Catholic Boys

School. From there, they came across magnificent grounds surrounded by a low brick wall with wrought-iron gates. A soldier stood proudly to attention. Behind the wall was the most spectacular gardens that James and the others had ever seen. The West Australian flag (Royal blue with the Union Jack in the top left-hand corner and a yellow circle with a black swan) flew proudly from a high pole. There was also a grand building of huge proportions set further back.

'This is Government House,' Charles Mitchell told them, 'another very fine building in the town,
I must say'.

Over to their right there were other magnificent homes and commercial buildings, which Charles Mitchell pointed out. 'That's the Brockman's mansion,' he told them, 'they call it Great Boulder. Mr W G Brockman is one of Perth's wealthiest entrepreneur's. He made his money in real estate and has built many fine buildings and mansions in the city.'

There were many others too, such as the Deanery of Reverend George Pownall and Saint Georges Cathedral and also the Post Office. Charles Mitchell brought his horse to a halt. 'I have to post your mothers letter from here, James.' He removed from a leather pouch hanging from the saddle.

'I'll do it for you, father,' James eagerly offered.

'Thank you, son.'

James dismounted and then went over to his father who handed him down the letter. As James crossed over the busy road he had to dodge horses and carriages that were travelling in both directions. James and the other two farmhands had never been to a town of this size. There were no others in Western Australia, excepting for Fremantle down the Swan River on the coast. Once inside the large building he came across a number of people queuing up in front of a long counter. James joined one of them. Finally, it was his turn. There was an attractive young lady behind the counter who asked if she could be of assistance. James greeted her in a friendly manner as he handed the letter over to her. She looked at the address first before she placed it onto a set of delicate brass scales. Then she added a few small round weights to one side of the scales. 'That will be sixpence, thank you,' she said politely.

James paid her the money. 'How long will that take to reach its destination?' he asked politely.

'Between eight and ten days from Fremantle to Durban.'

He thanked her and then he rejoined the others outside. 'It seems strange to be posting a letter to South Africa when I am about to go there myself shortly,' he said to his father as he placed his left foot in the stirrup and hauled himself back into the saddle.

'The letter will reach there a lot sooner than you will James,' his father replied. 'Besides, you are going off to war. You most certainly will not have time to worry about posting a letter when you arrive in South Africa.'

They reached Barrack Street next where Charles Mitchell stopped to let his horse drink from a trough outside Bowra O'Dea's (coach builders for the Boer War). James and the other two men did the same. Down the hill at the bottom of the street, in the far distance, they could see the river. There was also a magnificent pavilion that stood out over the water at the end of a pier. Several paddle steamers were making their way along Perth Water. Neither James, Billy or George had ever seen a ship before, excepting in sketches and paintings, and they were becoming more excited with each passing moment.

At the other end of the street the Town Hall towered above most other buildings. Men dressed in suits wore straw-bashers or bowler hats, and the women, long dresses with hats and fancy umbrellas.

'So, this is what Perth is like, father?'

'What do you think of it, son?'

'It's much larger and far busier than I had ever imagined... very much busier and noisier.'

'Actually, Perth stopped growing when they discovered gold in Kalgoorlie and also Coolgardie, mainly because many people left here to seek their fortunes there,' his father advised. 'The recession has not helped its cause either, for otherwise I think it would have been much larger today... perhaps the size of Brisbane or Adelaide?'

It was difficult for James and the other two men to imagine what that could be like. They continuously had to wave flies away from their faces, which anyway they were used to doing on the farm. At that moment a coach came racing down Adelaide Terrace with dust flying up from the horses hooves and wheels. It raced on past the four men standing nearby their horses. Royal Mail with a gold crown was painted on the sides of the doors.

Once the horses had finished drinking the men remounted and then they proceeded along Saint Georges Terrace. James was still fascinated by it all almost finding it overwhelming. Further on they came across several women with young children. They were dressed in rags unwashed and filthy dirty.

'Spare us a penny mate,' one of the women called out, 'to feed me starving kids.'

James had heard stories about the beggars in the towns who were mainly victims of the drought, which had crippled the economy. And others, who had sold up everything and joined the gold rush and who had returned poorer than before. There had also been the Trade Union strikes, which had damaged production and stopped investments. Workers had lost their jobs and land prices had crashed to an all-time low. James put his hand in his pocket and took out three pennies. He threw them to a woman carrying a small child. The woman grovelled on the ground collecting them up. 'God bless yah son,' she shouted back to him. 'God bless yah.'

An elderly man was busking with a banjo outside a hotel. Another was playing a violin a little further on down the street. There were well-dressed women standing on street corners as though waiting for someone. James had also heard of them. One of them winked at him and he felt a little embarrassed. Further down the road there was the Western Australian Club and then the Palace Hotel on the corner of William Street. Charles Mitchell stopped his horse for a moment while the four men watched a handsome cab, drawn by a team of four white stallions, drew up to the main entrance. A smartly dressed commissioner stepped forward and opened the door. He then assisted a wealthy looking gentleman and lady out of the carriage, who were then escorted into the hotel.

Charles Mitchell half turned in the saddle in order to see James. 'That's the grandest hotel in all of Perth. A wealthy American built it only three years ago. Someday, when the price of wool and mutton has improved again, I shall book all of us rooms there for one night. Would you all like that?'

They all thought that it was a great idea and made various comments and jokes about dress, table manners and meals, etc.

13   They crossed over William Street and continued along Saint Georges Terrace passing Shenton House (later Newspaper House), and then on past the Royal Insurance Buildings, Perth Technical School and Perth Boys School. On the opposite side of the road there was Harry Armstrong Sanitary Engineer and Plumber, and the National Bank of Australia and National Mutual Life Insurance Company.

Once they had reached the 'Cloisters' Charles Mitchell pulled up his horse. 'I won't be long,' he said dismounting. 'I need to purchase a box of cigars here,' he advised passing over the reins to James.

The other three men waited for him, still fascinated by the hustle and bustle of city life, as carriages horse-drawn buses and a menagerie of people proceeded in both directions on either side of the road. After that, it was on again past more splendid mansions. The road had now become steeper as they neared Mount Eliza (Kings Park) and the horses laboured along. Pensioners Barracks stood over to one side, a huge complex with a magnificent archway at the centre. After awhile there were only the single storey brick or clinker-board houses, corrugated-iron shanties and trading stores. Finally, only the odd house stood here and there and then there was only bush. The city of Perth had been left behind and the quietness of the evening was familiar and more comforting to James.

'So what did you think of it all, James?' his father eventually asked as they continued to walk the horses at a steady pace.

James had been thinking of Veronica and also the farm, of his mother, brother and sisters that had been left behind. His father's voice jarred him back to the present. 'Pardon?'

'Of Perth, son! ...What did you think?'

'Oh... I'm sorry... my mind was elsewhere. I found it truly amazing, but I didn't like seeing women and children begging for money... I found that disturbing to be honest.'

'I understand son. It had the same effect on me the first time. We can thank the Lord that we have been blessed. However, if it is any comfort to you, you do get used to it with time.'

'I don't think I could ever get used to that, father.'

'We will bed down under the stars again tonight and make our way to the barracks early tomorrow,' his father advised them all.

A little later they came across a small billabong and Charles Mitchell brought his horse to a halt. 'This looks as good a spot as any,' he said as he dismounted. 'And to be honest, I have had just about enough for the day.'

The other three men felt the same and climbed off their mounts as Billy commented, 'I sure could do with some tucker, me belly button's touching me spine.'

James collected a bundle of firewood and then he found two forked-sticks, which he knocked into the ground using a small rock. Once the fire was lit, George de-cantered a little water into a billycan. He then placed a stick through the handle and suspended it between the forked sticks. Later, George made a damper to eat with their bully beef.

They ate their supper and sipped their tea chatting around the fire about all the things they had seen in Perth. A train-whistle in the near distance came to their ears as a steam-train past on its way to Fremantle, about twenty-odd kilometres away on the coast. After that, they only heard the sounds of the night, crickets, an owl, and the crackling of the wood-fire.

James watched the flames as they leapt and danced about on the wood, sending tiny sparks shooting in all directions as the timber exploded. He thought of Veronica and the time they made love in the old boathouse and how much he already missed her. He would write to her at the first opportunity he could get, and apologise for the way he reacted. Maybe he would even tell her how he truly felt about her.

14   The bright early-morning sun shone brightly into James' eyes as he slowly opened them to find that it was already the beginning of a new day. He shivered a little from the cold before pulling up the blanket higher. All around, he could hear a variety of parrots and other wild birds chirping in the trees. They were familiar and comforting sounds to James... sounds that he had heard many times over ever since he could remember. His father was already up and about. George had also boiled the billycan and was making coffee, which they would have with homemade biscuits that James' mother had made for them all.

'G'day, father.'

Charles Mitchell turned around to see James throwing the blanket off himself. 'Morning James,' he replied with a smile, 'sleep well?'

'Like a log, and you?'

'I had an excellent night apart from the odd mosquito, thank you.'

James got to his feet stretching and yawning before greeting the other two. The first thing he had to do was to urinate. He walked a little way from the others, removed his penis and emptied his bladder onto the dusty ground. After breakfast they made the final leg of the journey towards Karrakatta. On arrival they came across a large crowd of men and women gathered outside the gates to the barracks. Many of them were carrying placards with anti-Boer slogans and were yelling abuse at pro-Boer supporters. The constabulary were trying to keep order as several scuffles and fistfights erupted amongst a group of men.

A few men suddenly rushed towards James trying to pull him from his horse. Thunder reared up whinnying at the same time almost pitching James to the ground. One of the men took hold of James' leg and was pulling on it with all his strength, while James tried to keep the horse under control. Finally, James managed to free himself and he spurred the horse on through the crowd. His father and the other two following close behind.

Once inside the barrack grounds they saw at least a thousand men of all shapes and sizes, waiting to be enlisted.

THE PLOUGH, THE GUN AND THE GLORY

They were standing in two long queues behind notice boards. One said 'Army Reservists,' the other 'Civilian Volunteers.'

Charles Mitchell brought his horse to a halt. 'Well, this is a far as I go son.'

James' heart gave a little flutter. 'There are a lot of men here father. I hope that we're not turned away because they have too many.'

'Don't worry, I'm sure that most of them won't be accepted,' his father told them with confidence as they dismounted. 'You are all strong and healthy young men. I am sure that you'll have no trouble being selected.'

James and the others nervously got their papers out of their saddlebags. James went to the front of his horse. He rubbed him gently on the snout saying, 'Well, this is probably goodbye for awhile Thunder... Don't worry, I'll be back soon and we'll go down to the river again.'

The horse gave a little whinny and shook its head as though it understood him.

James approached his father. 'Well father, I guess the time has come to say goodbye?' He put his hand out.

They shook hands firmly as his father said, 'Take care of yourself son... Write home whenever you can and let us know how you are doing.'

For the first time in many years there was a lump in Charles Mitchell's throat.

They embraced one another.

'I will, I promise,' James replied with a little moisture in his eyes. He quickly wiped them away using the back of his hand.

'I'll wait over in the shade of those trees until sundown,' Charles Mitchell said as he pointed in the general direction. 'Should any of you have the misfortune of being rejected you will find me there.' George and Billy shook his hand. He wished both of them good luck, telling them to write whenever they could. They left him holding all four horse's stirrups and went off to join the end of a very long queue. There was an army sergeant with a highly waxed moustache going along the queue checking papers. 'Right, you lot of rabble!' he barked. 'Straighten up this line and at least try and look like soldiers, if nothing else.'

The men shuffled their feet kicking up the dust. Somehow, the line wasn't any better though. Slowly, James got closer to where several officers were seated. They were checking papers and asking various questions. At last, it was his turn. 'Family name?' the officer called out impatiently.

'Mitchell,' James replied promptly.

The officer went through several papers in alphabetical order. 'Christian name?'

'James.'

The officer placed a tick next to his name with a pencil. 'Papers!'

James handed them over.

The officer looked through them then glanced up at James. 'Why are you enlisting to go to South Africa?'

James was surprised by the question. 'To fight the Boers.'

'Do you think you will be up to it?'

'Yeah, too darn true,' James replied cockily.

'Have you had previous musketry experience? You know, done any shooting before?' he asked a little sarcastically.

'Yeah, many times.'

'What type of weapons have you fired?'

'A rifle... and.'

'A rifle?' he interrupted.

'Yeah... and.'

'Anything else?'

James was now becoming a little frustrated. 'A revolver!' he replied aggressively.

The officer wrote it down. 'What did you shoot at, targets?'

'No! Ducks and rabbits and also sheep and roos (kangaroos).'

The officer looked up at him. 'Well, you won't be shooting those where you are going. You will be shooting Boers and they shoot back. From what I hear they do a good job. Do you think that you will be able to kill a man... many men in-fact?'

James swallowed hard. 'Yeah, sir.'

'Well, you will soon know well enough when the time comes I suppose... you may proceed.'

James moved onto the next officer who also asked him his name, which he politely gave again. After filling in a form he was told to proceed to the hospital tent. He followed a few other blokes and joined onto the back of the queue. When his turn came he entered the large, white canvass marquee, which had a red cross painted on the side. He was told to strip down to his underpants. A doctor dressed in a white coat was sitting at a desk. 'Have you ever had any of the following diseases?' he asked and then rattled off a string of names that James had never even heard, including gonorrhoea and syphilis.

'No, definitely not,' he replied indignantly.

James was then told to open his mouth and his teeth were checked. Next, a flat piece of wood was shoved inside and pressed down onto his tongue. He was told to say 'Ahhh.' The doctor then checked his ears and eyes. After that, his hair was examined for lice. Then, the doctor listened to his heart and from there he went into a cubicle where he was told to remove his underpants. Another doctor examined his penis and then he was asked to cough, while the doctor held his testicles. Once that was over he had to lift his feet up, one at a time, to see if they were flat.

The doctor wrote something down on his paperwork before saying, 'Take this card and join that queue.' He indicated by pointing with his pencil.

Fifteen minutes later, James arrived opposite another officer seated behind a desk. Once again, he was required to give his name, which he did while handing over the card. The officer wrote something down then stamped the papers. He looked up at James. 'You are classified as a Private. Your serial number is 127. Henceforth, you will be required to call out your rank, name and serial number in that order. Is that quite clear private?'

'Yes sergeant,' James replied a little nervously.

'Firstly, I am not a sergeant. I'm an officer... As you can plainly see I am wearing a crown on my epaulets. That means that I'm a major not a sergeant. While you are enlisted with the army you will address all officers as sir.'

'Yes sir.'

'You will also salute an officer at all times. Proceed to the next desk.' He waved him on with his hand.

The next officer looked him up and down before requesting harshly, 'Rank, name and number!'

James called it out as he had previously been instructed.

'Whilst holding the rank of private you will be paid four shillings and sixpence per day, of which two shillings and three pence will be deferred until your return to Australia. Should you be promoted in the field your pay will be increased accordingly. Should you become a deserter however, or you are court martialled the deferred money will be forfeited to the crown. Is that understood private?'

'Yes sir.'

'Sign here.'

James took the pencil and signed on the line that the officer had placed his finger next to. He put the pencil down as the officer said, 'You have been enlisted with the 1st Contingent West Australian Infantry. You will serve with Her Majesty's Imperial Army in South African for a period of not less than twelve months. Should the war be brought to a conclusion sooner, you will be returned to Australia as soon as possible there after. Any questions?'

'No sir.'

James was then instructed to form-up outside with the other men. There was a tall, thin sergeant who was yelling at the top of his voice, 'Come on, come on! Move your backsides you lot! We haven't got all day here, you know!'

James hurriedly joined onto the end of the line.

'That includes you too, soldier!' the sergeant said pointing at James.

James couldn't figure-out what he had possibly done wrong.

'From here,' the sergeant continued, 'you will be required to march to the quartermaster stores where you will then be issued with your kit. When I give you the command and not before then, you will come smartly to attention and look straight ahead. You will not look at me! ...I will then give the order for you to turn to the right. You will do that as smartly as possible!' He looked the men over for a moment and then bellowed the order. The men came to attention at various times. He bellowed some abuse at them. They were then given the order to turn to the right, which they did, but not in unison. They received more verbal abuse. They marched off out of step with the sergeant bellowing more foul language at the top of his voice.

15   The quartermaster's store was another large tent and there was a long wooden counter with several men standing behind. The recruits were instructed to approached the counter one at a time. After calling out their name, rank and number, they were then ordered to hold out their arms. Various pieces of kit were fetched from shelving behind and dumped into their arms. Each recruit would then move along the counter to the next man. More kit was dumped onto his arms. Each time, the particular item would be shouted out to the quartermaster who wrote it down.

The list was seemingly endless and the items got heavier by the minute, starting with two khaki drill jackets, three pairs of drill trousers, three flannel shirts, one blue-colour guernsey (jersey) blue putties and so on. Smaller items such as, socks, braces, razor with case, were thrown into a canvas kit-bag, including boot-blacking, brushes, spoon, knife and fork, soap, sponge and towel.

From there the men were told to form-up outside. Eventually, they were all marched off towards neat rows of small white-tents that were to become home until their departure. The men were then formed into sections of four men and allocated a tent. James, Billy and George, plus a bloke by the name of Joseph Allingham, who James had known from school, made sure they were in the same section. As soon as he was able, James raced off to where his father said he would be waiting until sundown.

'We have all been enlisted, father,' he said excitedly as he arrived.

His father had been resting by the trunk of the tree. He got to his feet dusting the back of his pants with his hands. 'Marvellous. I was confident you all would... Did they give Billy a difficult time?'

'No. No one even asked him if he was part Aborigine.'

'Good, that's how it should be, son.' Charles Mitchell put his hand out.

They shook hands firmly.

'You take care now, James, and don't forget to write home whenever you can.'

They embraced once again.

'Give my love to mother and the others,' James said as he stood back. He turned and walked off wiping his eyes with his hand.

The remainder of the day was spent organising kit and familiarising themselves with military life, and naturally the men were excitedly discussing the war which they would soon become part of. Later that afternoon the men were told to form-up outside their tents and from there they were marched to a large open field where several officers were waiting for them.

Once the recruits had been brought to a halt Lieutenant-Colonel Campbell, the Chief Staff Officer at Karrakatta, addressed them. After welcoming everyone he gave a short briefing about the training programme that was to be conducted. He then introduced the senior officer of the Western Australian Contingent, Major Moor and also Lieutenants Parker and Darling, and then the medical officer Major McWilliams and finally Company Sergeant-Major Edwards.

16   The following few days were hectic with reveille at 4am. After kit and tent inspection there was thirty minutes for breakfast and then it was drill-parade and marching. After lunch there were lectures on military procedure and the enemy. Later, there were practical battlefield procedures and at 4.30 pm, it was shower time. At 6 pm, it was supper. Some of the men were delegated picket duties during the night, while others prepared kit for the following day. By 8 pm, all lanterns were distinguished and the camp fell silent.

On the third day the men drew their rifles and bayonets from the armoury for the first time. Everyone was excited including James. 'Woohoo!' he yelled loudly to Billy and the two others in his section. 'Now I feel as though we really are in the army!'

A corporal approached James. 'Private Mitchell!' he called out.

James looked over at him. 'Yeah corporal.'

'Was that you shouting loudly like that?'

'I guess so,' he replied with a surprised look.

'You guess so, what?'

'Yeah, I suppose it was me.'

'Are you trying to be clever in front of the other men or something Mitchell?'

'No.'

'No, what?' He pointed to the stripe on his arm.

'No corporal!'

'We have a way of dealing with smart arses in the army! Place your rifle at the high port! That means above your head Mitchell!'

James lifted the weapon and held over his head as ordered.

'You will now run around the campgrounds twenty times! Move! Move!' he yelled.

James departed from the others. Half an hour later he rejoined the group, as they were about to march off to the shooting range. When they arrived there were a couple of NCOs (non commissioned officers) from Karrakatta Camp who were impatiently waiting, together with two armourers. Once the men had been brought to a halt they were addressed by one of the sergeants. 'Pay attention everyone. ...The weapon, which you are presently carrying in your grubby little hands, is known as the Martini-Henry. It fires a single .450 bullet. You will have observed that there is no magazine and therefore the bullet is breach loaded each time, before you can fire the weapon. The Martini-Henry is sighted to 1,400 yards.'

Mumbling was heard coming from amongst several of the men. The sergeant stopped talking and singled someone out. 'Obviously you have something that you wish to contribute to the lecture private? Why don't you speak-up and share your wealth of knowledge with all of us?'

The man looked a little puzzled before replying, 'I believe that someone made the comment that the Boers are equipped with rifles that have a ten round magazine.'

'I am well aware of that private!'

'Yes sergeant.'

'Perhaps if you weren't so busy talking instead of paying attention; I would have had the chance to explain to you that these rifles are for training purposes only while here at Karrakatta.'

'Yes sergeant.'

The sergeant then asked one of the men to hand over his rifle to him. He then held it up high so everyone could see what he was about to demonstrate. 'Firstly, this small leaver here is the safety catch.' He indicated by pointing his finger. 'Always check and make sure that it is in the safety position. The only time it should not be in the safety position is on the battlefield.' He glanced around at the men and then continued, 'The weapon is loaded by pushing this lever in a downward motion.' He showed them the lever located under the butt. 'When you do that the breach is opened ready to insert the bullet.' He demonstrated. 'After placing the bullet into the open chamber you pull the lever up under the butt.' He showed them. 'Now, I want all of you to try that... Carry-on at will.'

The men practised what they had been shown. After awhile the sergeant called out, 'Alright, I want you all to stop doing that now and pay attention!' He waited a few moments for the men to settle down. 'After removing a bullet from your bandolier you then place the bullet into the breach, like this.' He pushed a blank into position. 'Next, you close the breach as previously demonstrated. The weapon is now loaded and ready to be fired. Once you have fired the weapon you open the breach, as previously shown, and the spent cartridge is automatically ejected.'

The men were issued with one blank each and told to practice loading and unloading. After that they were taught the names of the parts of the rifle. Then they learned how to strip the rifle down, clean and assemble it and to also set the sights. Once that was over the blanks were collected up and then each man was issued with ten live rounds (bullets) that were fed into the bullet pouches on their bandoliers. Each man was then allocated a target and then two sections at a time commenced practicing their shooting. As each man finished his ten rounds he would leave the breach of the rifle open. The rifle was then placed down on the sandbag in front of him. After that he would raise his right hand in the air, so that the instructors could see he was finished. The instructors would then go down the line and check each rifle to make sure they were clear.

Once that was done the sergeant shouted, 'On your feet!'

The men did as instructed.

'Move forward!'

The men proceeded to their targets. Several targets had only one or two bullet holes in them. Others had four or five and a number of them had none. James and George's targets each had seven. Billy's had nine and Joseph's five.

After patching up the holes, using paper mixed with flower water for glue, each man received another ten rounds. The armourers also came around to each man adjusting the sights on the rifle as necessary. This time James got nine hits. George and Billy both got eight and Joseph seven.

Each man collected up his empty brass casings and once the armourers were satisfied that every man had twenty; they were thrown into a kitbag. James and Billy were given the job of carrying the heavy kitbags back to the armoury. After that it was rifle cleaning and inspection.

The NCOs spent the following day with the men observing demonstrations of bayonet drills. When it was the recruit's turn they were given the command, 'Fix bayonets!' They drew the long steel knives from their scabbards and attached them to the end of the barrel.

Lieutenant Parker then yelled, 'Charge!'

He took off with the men following, running and screaming at the top of their lungs… at the same time viciously thrusting their bayonets into fabricated dummies representing the enemy.

17   The morning of the 4th of November 1899 was a windy with clear-blue skies and the Fremantle doctor (sea-breeze) was churning up white horses on Perth Water. Paddle steamers, yachts and other nautical craft of all sizes and descriptions plied the river in all directions, in the hopes of getting a good view of the memorable occasion.

The pier leading out to the pavilion was crowded to capacity with spectators, as was the pavilion itself. On the grounds of the Supreme Court Gardens the public swarmed in the thousands to catch a last glimpse of their loved-ones and heroes, before they departed for the railway station.

The Governor of Western Australia, Sir Gerard Smith and his wife, the Mayor Alexander Forrest and his wife, town Councillors, Military and Navy representatives and guests of honour were all seated to one side of the large open grounds. West Australian flags flew alongside Union Jacks from tall wooden poles, flogging and lashing about wildly in the strong sea breeze.

One hundred and twenty-five men plus five officers were lined up, together with seventeen horses, two wagons, a spring cart and two maxim guns. The Military Band was playing 'The Girl I Left Behind Me.'

When they were finished the Governor addressed the troops with a lengthy speech, which for most of the time could hardly be heard, due to the strength of the blustering wind. Then, it was the Mayor's turn. The guests and onlookers clapped and cheered each time they finished. The band struck up with 'Soldiers of the Queen' and then 'Rule Britannia.' The crowds waved and cheered again and pistol shots were fired into the air.

The troops marched from the Supreme Court Gardens with the band playing another British marching tune with a detachment of Navy from HMS Rambler leading with the 1st Contingent troops behind them. After turning right into

Barrack Street they marched up the steep sloping street, passing Parmelia Barracks and Stirling Gardens to Adelaide and Saint Georges Terrace. James and the other troops felt proud of themselves, dressed in their khaki uniforms with their distinctive blue putties and their broad-brimmed bush-hats. The brim on the left folded up to enable their rifles to be carried across their left shoulder. The band was now playing 'When Johnny comes marching home again.'

The dusty limestone-streets were crowded with men, women and children who stood shoulder to shoulder without a space or an opening between them, pushing and shoving to get a better view of the heroes. They were excitedly waving Union Jacks. Someone shouted, 'Good on yah, cobbers!' And another; 'Go get 'em Boers mates!'

Decorations and banners alongside Union Jacks flapping in the breeze, were strung out along the fascias of buildings with goodwill messages, such as 'God bless our boys' and 'For Queen and Empire' and another 'Soldiers of the Queen.'

People in the hundreds hung from the balconies of two-story buildings lining both sides of the narrow street. Others poured out of windows or were standing on the flimsy canopies overhanging the pavements. James saw a man slip and then go tumbling out of sight. He wondered if he had been injured.

The Town Hall was past with the McNess Arcade buildings opposite. Then it was on past Hunter's-City Boot-Palace. The troops crossed over Howick Street (now Hay) and then past J M Ferguson Ltd., Timber and Hardware Merchants, the Bon Marche Arcade and the Commercial Hotel (Railway Hotel). Patrons were leaning out as far as possible over the wrought iron balconies throwing confetti and streamers into the air, the sea breeze gusting up the dusty road taking hold of it, swirling it over the troops and the crowds lining both sides of the street.

Young children ran excitedly alongside the soldiers trying to keep in step. Some had pieces of wood; others broom handles pretending they were guns. They were happy and laughing and were shouting good luck to the men in uniform, enjoying the atmosphere of the whole occasion. Accompanying them were an assortment of stray dogs that constantly barked as they weaved their way between the crowds.

Having crossed over Murray Street the parade turned left into Wellington for the final short distance to the railway station. The men were brought to a halt outside Boan's Bros store (Myers). Crowds of on-lookers lined the pavements cheering and waving. Others hung dangerously out of windows at the Globe Hotel and the Wellington Building.

The deafening noise of the crowds and band made it difficult for the soldiers to hear the commands of the officers. Finally, the parade came to an end and the men were dismissed. From there the troops started to make their way into the station, with the horses', wagons and maxim guns, all yet to be loaded into the waiting boxcars.

18

The platform was crowded with members of the public and the troops had to politely push their way through to make their way over to the train. James and the three others tried to keep together, but it became impossible and they were soon separated. James pushed ahead weaving his way between fathers, mothers, brothers, sisters and girlfriends all farewelling loved ones.

Suddenly and unexpectedly James saw Veronica. His heart gave a skip and for a brief moment he just stood there staring at her hardly believing his eyes. Then he made his way towards her. She had seen him earlier and was heading in his direction. As they made their way towards one another they were bumped and shoved about.

'What are you doing here?' he asked once he reached her.

She had tears in her eyes. 'Oh James, I had to come here and say farewell to you. I hope you don't mind?'

'Mind? No. I'm very happy. Thank you for coming all the way here. It's a very long journey from Two Valleys.'

'I don't care. I had to see you for the last time, especially after what happened. I couldn't let you go off to South Africa thinking that I had deceived you, and that I didn't love you.'

'I was going to write to you, but I haven't had the chance we have been so busy.'

THE PLOUGH, THE GUN AND THE GLORY

'I am so glad that I found you before you left.'

'So am I.' He took hold of her and they kissed one another passionately. 'Will you wait for me to return?' he asked. 'I will only be gone for a year at the very outside. Probably less if the war goes well.'

'Yes,' she replied excitedly. 'I was praying that you would ask me that.'

They kissed sensually once again. Someone in the background was calling out loudly, trying to be heard above all the noise on the platform, Veronica! ...Veronica!'

They stopped kissing. James turned around to see a man dressed in military uniform heading towards them. Veronica's heart started thumping in her chest. 'Oh God it's Timothy!' She quickly stood back from James, not wishing to implicate him in any way. 'You had better leave James! Quickly! Go! Go! ... I love you and God bless you!'

James' heart was racing in his chest. He reluctantly left her side and pushed his way through the crowd in the direction of the train. Veronica waited nervously for the uniformed man to reach her. 'What are you doing here?' she asked once he arrived.

'Never mind that! The question is what are you doing here! And who was that trooper you were with?' he asked in an abrupt manner.

She was trembling. 'Just someone I was saying goodbye to.'

'I'll have you remember that you are still a married woman!' He took hold of her roughly by the arm. 'Where have you been hiding, hey? I've been searching everywhere for you for damn months!'

Veronica pulled her arm away from him. 'Don't you dare put your hands on me! You keep your distance from me, you hear, or I will call a constable and have you arrested!'

'A constable?' he sniggered. 'And what do you think he will do? I am still your husband remember!' At that moment there was a loud blast from the steam locomotives' whistle. 'You are darn lucky that I am presently on my way to South Africa, otherwise I would settle this matter here and now and have you arrested, you slut!'

The shrieking ear-piercing sound of the engine's whistle blasted into the air once again. The conductor then blew on his whistle to add to the myriad of noises. Then he shouted at the top of his voice, 'ALL ABOARD!'

Moments later he waved a green flag and blasted loudly on his whistle again. The carriages jerked and clanged together as they began to slowly move along the platform. Steam hissed and blew out from between the large steel wheels of the engine, as they went spinning on the shiny metal rails. Clouds of grey-black smoke belched out from the smokestack over everything and everyone.

Veronica's estranged husband let go of her arm. 'I'll deal with you when I return.' He turned and walked briskly towards the moving carriages and then jumped onto the steps. One of the men gave him a helping hand and pulled him onboard.

James lent out of the carriage window as far as he could, in the hope of catching a last glimpse of Veronica. He saw her crying into a hanky and then she was gone as the crowd swallowed her up. The carriage passed the military band that was now playing 'Auld Lang Syne'.

There was a tap on his shoulder and he turned around to see Billy and Joseph standing there.

'We have been looking everywhere for you,' Billy said a little exasperated. 'Where the heck did you get to?'

'After we got separated on the platform I saw someone that I know from Wickepin.'

'Who was that?'

'Just someone... You don't know her.'

'Her?' Joseph said with a large grin. 'Come on James, who was she?'

'Just someone I know.'

'Ahhh, come on James don't keep us in suspense,' Billy added. 'Who was she? Come on tell us.'

'Alright, but you must promise to never tell anyone... Do you promise?'

'Yeah, we promise,' they both said in unison.

'Her name's Veronica Pearson... I met her one-day down by the river on the farm. Her father owns the vineyard called Two Valleys.'

Billy stared at him for a moment before asking, 'When was this then? And why are you keeping it such a big secret?'

James looked at each one in turn. 'Because she's a married woman.'

'Married?' they both said with a look of surprise on their faces.

James told them the story and finished by saying, 'And what's more her husband is also on the train. He's going with us to South Africa.'

Billy and Joseph were speechless for a moment. 'Come on,' Billy eventually said, 'let's go to our compartment. George will be wondering where the heck we have all got too.'

The three of them pushed their way through the crowds of soldiers blocking the narrow corridor, and made their way towards their carriage. Finally they arrived and got themselves inside the four-man compartment. George was pleased to see that they had James with them. 'I was beginning to give up on you. I thought you must have missed the train or something?'

James went on and explained to him what had happened. After they had all made their comments about the matter, James took up a seat next to the window. It was hot in the carriage so he slid the wooden window down to let the air in. The train was now making its way through the poor and derelict section of East Perth. Shanty houses, built one next to the other, their back yards facing onto the railway line, slowly past by the window. After awhile there was only dry bush. James didn't mind that. In-fact he found it comforting. The others in the carriage were talking, making jokes and laughing loudly, which he found a little annoying. He wished he could just jump onto Thunder and ride off down to the tranquillity of the river.

19   The remainder of the journey to Albany was fairly uneventful except when the train stopped at the small siding of Narrogin, to replenish coal and water supplies. Most of the men onboard hopped off to stretch their legs and have a break from their compartments. George spotted a hotel in the nearby and suggested to James and the others that they have a quick beer.

'Now that is a darn good idea George,' James replied, with the other two enthusiastically agreeing.

They sneaked off in the hope that none of the sergeants or corporals would notice them. As they approached the hotel they could hear that it was very rowdy in there. Billy was first to push his way through the swing doors with the others following close behind. To their amazement the place was half full with other troops from the train. The wooden floorboards creaked and groaned under their weight, as they proceeded to go further inside. There were several civilians seated at wooden, circular tables who lifted their mugs in salute to the four new arrivals in uniform.

They acknowledged them and made their way over to the counter where a stout barman, with a walrus type moustache, was in attendance. George pushed his way between two other soldiers. 'Excuse us mates,' he said looking at them both. 'Four pints of Fred Sherwood's Swan Ale, please.' he then called out loudly to the barman.

The ales were banged onto the wooden counter with the froth running over the sides of the mugs. 'That's a shilling,' the big man advised abruptly.

George paid him and then passed the beers over to the others. They said cheers and drank them down in a hurry. 'Ahhh, that was good,' James advised licking his lips. 'But it didn't touch the sides. I'll get us another round. He ordered another four and they drank those a little slower this time.

When those were almost finished Billy said he would get another round for the road. By this time the bar had become more rowdy with every-one talking loudly in an effort to be heard. He pushed himself between a few other blokes to place his order. 'Four Swan Ales please, mate' he asked the barman politely.

THE PLOUGH, THE GUN AND THE GLORY

The barman looked him over. 'You should know darn well you can't come in here! It's against the law for me to serve you alcohol! What if the coppers were to come in here, hey? You could get me a hefty fine from the magistrate. Now bugger off out of here!'

Not wanting to cause a scene Billy left the counter and returned to the group. 'I'm going back to the train, I'll see yah all later.'

'Hey, what happened to the beers mate?' George called out.

Billy didn't reply and was about to leave. James could tell he was upset and grabbed hold of his arm. 'Hey, what's up Billy?'

'Nothin.'

'Come on, I know you better than that mate.'

'The barman won't serve me them beers.'

'Why not?'

'You should know... It's against the law, remember?'

James immediately became angry. 'Come with me!' He approached the barman. 'My friend here wants to order!' James told him.

The barman reached under the counter and took a baton out. He placed it on the counter while saying, 'I already told him to leave the premises.'

'Why?' James asked out of frustration.

'Do you have to ask? Everyone knows it's against the law to serve blacks alcohol.'

'Can't you see that he's also half white?'

'It doesn't matter! The law's the law!'

James could see he was getting nowhere. Besides, the train would be leaving soon and he and the others wanted another beer. 'Alright then, give me the four ales instead.'

'I can't do that.'

'Why not?' he asked angrily.

'Look here soldier I'm busy! I haven't got time to stand here arguing with you! Now I want the four of you to leave this establishment before I call the coppers!'

At that moment Joseph, who had been the quietest one of them all, suddenly took a flying leap over the counter. Drinks flew in all directions and he landed on top of the barman. They both went crashing into the shelving and mirrors against the back wall. They scrambled back onto their feet. The barman tried to use his baton, but Joseph quickly swung with his right hand. He connected him squarely on the jaw and the big man dropped to the floor like a sack of potatoes.

At that moment there was a loud blast from the train whistle in the background. Complete panic and pandemonium broke out as the other troops bolted for the swing doors. They struggled as they forced their way through the double opening doors four or five at a time, and then headed for the train.

Meanwhile James had gone behind the counter and grabbed hold of Joseph. 'Come on, hurry, or we will miss the train!' he said with urgency.

The four men then bolted from the hotel and started to make a run for it. To their shock they heard the whistle blast again. Clouds of steam hissed and blew out from the locomotive as black smoke poured from the stack. The wheels of the engine spun wildly on the tracks as they tried to find traction, and then the train started moving off.

'Wait for us, damn it!' James called out puffing wildly for air. 'Wait! Wait!'

To their horror the train quickly gathered speed and started to pull away from them. They ran behind it along the tracks for a short distance then gave up the chase. They stood around speechless trying to get their breath back.

After a few moments James said, 'Now... what the heck do... we do?' He was still gasping for air and looking in the direction of the rapidly vanishing train.

'I think... we are... in big... trouble,' George puffed out. 'Big trouble.'

They were still staring down the tracks in despair when they heard the sound of horse's hooves behind them. They looked around and saw a pair of horses pulling a small cart at high speed. The driver was waving and yelling at the same time. The four men quickly jumped out of the way as the horses pulled up next to them and were brought to a rapid halt in clouds of dust, the driver shouting, 'Whoa! Whoa! Easy there! Easy!' He then shouted to the men on the ground, 'Come on you blokes! Hurry or you'll miss the Boer War!'

The four of them jumped onto the back of the open cart and the driver cracked his whip across the horses' backs. They immediately took off over the rough terrain with the four soldiers holding onto their bush hats, while bouncing and clinging desperately with one hand, to the wooden sides.

Moments later, James precariously clambered his way forward and joined the driver on the seat up front.

'You boys were lucky I was comin' along at the time!' the driver shouted above the noise from the horses' hooves and the cart.

'We sure were, and we appreciate you doing this for us!'

'That's okay mate! If you can't help a couple of blokes when they are in need, what good are yah?'

'Too true mate! Too true!'

Shortly, they joined the main road and the driver flicked the reins again, encouraging the horses to pull even harder with the cart bouncing and swaying over the rough road. Ten minutes later they saw the train ahead weaving its way between brown rolling, sun-drenched hills.

The driver shouted to James, 'I know a good spot where you can jump aboard! It's not too far from here!'

'Okay!'

The horses were driven on with a lash of the whip. Their hooves were kicking up dust and stones, with their ears almost lying flat, and the wheels of the cart sending debris flying in all directions. Shortly, the road drew parallel with the railway line. 'This is it mate! This is where you hop off!' the driver advised.

James told the others in the back. They prepared themselves to leap from the cart onto the train. They were approaching a low rise and the train began to slow down a little. The horses now started to overhaul the guards van and they soon drew alongside the end carriage.

James turned to the men at the back. 'Okay who's going first?' he yelled.

George was ready and he took a flying leap landing with his feet on the steps. At the same time he grabbed hold of the handrails on either side of the doorway. A couple of blokes who had been watching helped him onboard. George turned towards the men in the cart and yelled, 'Yah-hoo!' Obviously pleased with himself.

'Who's going next?' James asked.

Joseph made the transfer without any mishaps and then it was Billy's turn. He steadied himself for the jump, but just as he was about to leap from the cart, the wheel hit a hole in the road and the cart bucked into the air. It pitched Billy violently off, but as he came down again he made a desperate grab for the handrails with both hands. His feet dragged along the ground as George and Billy pulled him up and into the carriage.

He was out of breath as he gasped out, "Bugger me... that was... a close one!'

James thanked the driver and climbed into the back of the bouncing cart. He got ready to jump. The train was already starting to negotiate a bend between two hills. The cart was moving away from the carriage and James could see up ahead that the road was about to change direction from the rails. He made a desperate leap and grabbed hold of the handrails. He too was left dangling precariously until he was hauled up and into the carriage.

James was out of breath as he turned around to wave goodbye to the driver, but all he saw was a cloud of brown dust as the cart headed off in another direction. 'We didn't even know that blokes name,' he said to the others. 'I forgot to ask him his name.'

They were all grateful and very relieved at having been reunited with the train. Joseph patted James on the back of the shoulder saying, 'We are still going to the Boer War James.'

He nodded. 'We sure are.' He smiled. 'We sure as hell didn't want to miss that, did we fellows?'

20   During the journey, James took a walk through the carriages in the hope of spotting Veronica's husband but he never saw him. The following day they crossed over the King River and then the small picturesque whaling town of Albany came into sight, with the train rolling and lurching along the twisting, turning track. Eventually it ground to a jerky shuddering halt with steam hissing from several sources and black smoke belching from the stack.

Crowds of onlookers lined the small timber platform spilling out on both sides of the tiny station. A band from the Albany Military Garrison was bashing out Soldiers of the Queen as the crowds cheered and waved Union Jacks.

The troops onboard the train waved back, happy to see the crowds and also to be disembarking from the confinement of their compartments that were covered with a fine layer of coal dust. James and the others jumped from the carriage onto the platform except Joseph, who stayed behind so he could throw their kit down to them from the open window of the compartment. Several military personnel were yelling orders to the men as they swarmed from the timber fabricated carriages.

Corporal Vernon approached James. 'Once you lot have got your kit together form-up outside the railway station.'

'Right,' replied James.

Once they had their gear sorted out they made their way through the excited noisy crowds. An attractive girl of about seventeen approached James and kissed him on the cheek. 'Good luck,' she said above all the noise.

He tried to thank her but was pushed and shoved from behind and had to continue on making his way through the throng of men and women. The enthusiastic crowds were patting the troops on their shoulders and backs while wishing them the best of luck. Finally, James broke through the crowd to see the officers standing around impatiently waiting for everyone to arrive. Eventually the men formed into three ranks. Sometime later, the seventeen horses, two maxim guns, spring cart and the two wagons arrived. Once everyone had settled down, a corporal walked along the front row counting the men. When he was finished he approached the sergeant major. 'One hundred and twenty-six, sergeant major!' he shouted out.

The NCO frowned. 'We only have one hundred and twenty-five men listed corporal!' he replied with a sarcastic tone.

'Yes sergeant major.'

'Well then, you will have to recount them, won't you?'

'Yes, sergeant major.'

'I suggest you get on with it then!' he said impatiently.

The corporal proceeded along the front row once again. He was tired from the long train journey and the noise of the crowd plus the band in the background made it almost impossible for him to concentrate. This time he counted one hundred and twenty-seven. He scratched his head as he looked around at the sergeant major with a look of exasperation on his face. He could see quite plainly that the sergeant major was becoming irritated, so the corporal quickly began another recount.

One of the officer's was running out of patience and he told the sergeant major to go and count for himself. When he reached the end he had counted one hundred and twenty-four. He was also feeling tired and all the noise going on also made it difficult for him to think. He quietly cursed to himself under his breath. He briefly glanced at the corporal before turning around to face the officers. 'One hundred and twenty-five, sir!' he called out confidently.

'Well, thank goodness for that!' the officer replied somewhat relieved.

The sergeant major then brought the men to attention. After that the CO (Commanding Officer) addressed the men. He paced the front rank for a moment then stopped and looked the men over. 'We will shortly be marching down to the harbour where we will make our way along the pier to the transporter 'Medic' which is alongside the wharf in King George Sound. On-board there are four hundred and fifty-five men and officers from the colonies of Victoria, South Australia and Tasmania. I am sure that I don't have to remind you to look after your kit. If your things should go missing or are stolen you will be held responsible. Naturally you will be required to purchase any replacements at your own expense.'

THE PLOUGH, THE GUN AND THE GLORY

The major continued to pace the front row as though deep in thought. 'Fighting amongst yourselves,' he continued, 'or with troops from the other colonies is strictly prohibited. If any of you are caught during the course of the voyage you will be placed into the brig (ships prison) where you will remain until we reach Cape Town. Certain parts of the ship will be out of bounds to all troops. You will see notices posted to that effect on-board. During the voyage you will maintain army standards of dress and discipline. You will be clean-shaven and dressed by 6am daily. You will shower daily and be required to keep your uniforms clean and presentable. Laundry facilities will be available to each colony on a roster basis.' He stopped pacing the dusty road and faced the men. 'Other than that, I wish you all a pleasant voyage.' He handed the men over to the sergeant major.

As the men marched towards the wharf the crowds continued to follow them, still cheering, waving their flags, and wishing them all the best of luck. And, as the troops climbed the gangplank they waved a last farewell to them and went onboard.

21 A fresh gusty wind was blowing on the morning of the 6th November 1899, as the ageing White Star Liner 'Medic' rolled and pitched in the heavy swell, gradually leaving Albany behind, making her way through King George Sound. Several large sailing ships were lying at anchor and she had to weave her way between them. From there it was around the point of land known as Bald Head. Soon, the coastline of Australia disappeared in a deep purple-blue haze, as the ship headed west. As she pitched and plunged her way into the oncoming waves most of the men were seasick over the side, including James.

After a very uncomfortable night at sea the men were brought to attention on deck early the following morning, with the clanging of the ships bell and loud booming-voice of the sergeant major.

'Right you lot of layabouts! I am extremely pleased to advise you that your holiday has ended!' He looked the men over. 'As of this morning you will be required to earn your keep once again!' He stroked his large moustache several times. 'You will be expected to remain fit and alert by engaging in regular exercise! ...You will be required to practice parade drills, shoot at targets, and also attend lectures. You will also have regular weapon and kit inspections!' His eyes ran up and down the ranks. 'Are there any complaints so-far?'

He waited to see if any one was willing to challenge his authority. No one did. 'I thought not! ...To start the day off we are all going for a little run around the ship to clear our heads and get rid of the cobwebs! ...Follow me!'

He took off with a sprint catching the men by surprise. Seconds later they gave chase.

22   A couple of nights later around 10 pm, James felt someone shaking him by the shoulder. He opened his eyes to see a stranger standing next to his hammock.

'Who's the toughest fella in yah lot?' the man whispered.

James was still half asleep. 'Hey?'

'Are you bleedin deaf or something? ...Who's the best fighter amongst yah lot?'

'I don't know, why?' he replied rubbing his eyes.

'I'll challenge him to a fight. Four shillings says I can beat him.'

It was hot in the cabin and the sweat trickled down James' face. 'Four-shillings? That's a whole days pay.'

'That's right. So, who 'ave yah got then, hey?'

'I don't know.'

'How about yah then?'

'I'm no boxer.'

'Are yah sayin yah are yella, then?'

'I said I'm no boxer. I never said I was yellow.'

'Then it's on. Yah and me tomorrow night below decks in the 'orses' stables.'

The sound of voices nearby had woken Billy. 'What the heck is going on, James?' he asked blurry-eyed.

'This bloke wants to challenge somebody to a fistfight. He chose me.'

'What for?'

'For money... four shillings to be exact.'

Billy scratched his head. 'Four shillings?'

'Yeah,' replied James, 'tomorrow night below decks.'

Billy slowly got to his feet. 'Oh yeah. Well I'll fight him for you for nothin.'

The stranger glared back at him. 'Is that so? Well yah can have yah turn after I've done with him... same wager four shillings. Both of you be there at 9pm, sharp.'

He turned and walked off disappearing into the dark.

'I've seen that bloke before on deck,' Billy said scratching under his chin. 'He's with the Tasmanians. I don't like the looks of him. I don't think we can trust him he looks the type who would carry a knife?'

James climbed out of his bunk bed. 'Well, in that case we had better keep a sharp eye on him then.'

23

The following morning while they were dressing, James told George and Joseph the story of the proposed fight for later that night.

'We are both coming with,' George said as he did his bootlaces up and then his putties.

'Too right we are,' Joseph added. 'You and Billy are not going without us.'

James and Billy eventually agreed. They discussed the fight in some depth during breakfast, with George and Joseph offering tips on how James and Billy best take on their opponent.

It was another full day army-style commencing with physical exercise after breakfast and then running around the ship ten times. After that there was drill instruction and later shooting at targets which were apple boxes thrown out to sea. During a lull between activities James spotted the man who he was going to fight. 'That's the bloke George,' he pointed. 'The bald-headed one with all the tattoos.'

George took a good look at him. 'Bugger me James, he's as big as damn gorilla!'

James glanced in the man's direction again. 'You're not wrong mate. It's funny though, somehow last night he didn't look all that big. Maybe it was because I was half asleep and it was dark?'

'I reken you have a slight advantage over him.'

'How so?'

'He's not as tall as you, and look at his arms they're a bit shorter than yours. He hasn't got the reach.'

'Maybe, but what he lacks in reach he probably makes up for with experience. I reckon that bloke has been in a lot of fights. He's probably a pro (professional). Look at his nose it has been broken many times over and his ears look like darn cauliflowers.'

'Maybe you should just give him the four shillings and tell him you were just joking?' he said sniggering a little.

James smiled. 'Somehow I don't think he would accept that George. I reckon he enjoys fighting. I think it relieves the boredom for him. Don't forget that these blokes have been onboard ship for almost two weeks. Somehow I get the feeling that he just enjoys beating another man's face into a pulp.'

'You've got me worried now James. Let's find something more pleasant to look at.'

The day ended with them cleaning their rifles and handing them back to the armoury. Later, James and Billy had a light supper so as not to be bloated for the fight. After lights-out at 8pm, George and Joseph began wrapping bandages, which they had bribed from the ships hospital, firmly around both James and Billy's hands. Once he had finished George asked James, 'How does that feel?'

'Good... they feel good.'

Tension was beginning to build up, and the humidity of the cabin made the men perspire, which trickled down their faces and bodies. George picked up a towel and wiped James down, with Joseph doing the same for Billy.

'How much time have we got left?' Billy asked anxiously.

Joseph looked at his pocket-watch. In the dim light of the oil lantern it was quite difficult for him to see the hands. After squinting his eyes for a moment he said, 'Slightly over ten minutes.'

'Well then, we had better be going,' said James after having made a few practice jabs at Billy. 'Have you got the money?' he asked George.

'Right here.' He slapped his trouser pocket.

They followed Joseph, leading the way with the lantern, and headed along the narrow steel corridors. Now and then they had to stop and make sure that the night watch wasn't doing his rounds. After lights out no one was allowed outside of their cabins. If you were caught it meant a few days in the brig at the very least, and probably a fine.

The four men were barefooted so they made very little noise as they made their way down the steel companionway to the decks below. Finally, they arrived at the stables. The stench of manure and urine was strong in the confined deck space. The men could see a few lanterns ahead of them and proceeded in their direction. They were almost there when someone approached them from out of the shadows. 'Yah's are late!' the man croaked in a scratchy, gruff voice.

'No we aren't,' Joseph replied with a little indignantly, 'according to my pocket watch we are spot on time.'

'What kept yah so long?'

'We had to make sure the coast was clear,' Billy answered.

'We thought yah weren't comin.'

'No chance of that,' replied James.

They arrived alongside several other men who were standing around in an open circle. The lights of the lanterns flickered on their faces producing an eerie, ghostly look about them. At that moment another lot of men arrived, which made James and the others a little edgy. 'What are all these blokes doing here?' James asked the bald-headed man who had challenged him to the fight.

'They're here to bet on the fight. Where's yah money?' he asked impatiently.'

'I've got it,' George replied.

'Show me.'

George took the money out of the bag and showed it to him.

'Give it to that fella,' the Tasmanian ordered pointing, 'he's the purser. He'll take care of it until the fight's over.'

George reluctantly handed over the bag containing the cash while asking, 'So, what are the rules then?'

'Rules?' the Tasmanian sniggered... 'Yah fight until one of yah can't get up. No hitting below the belt. No biting. No eye gouging and no wrestling. Them's the rules. Now come on we're wasting time!'

The Tasmanian and James entered the circle and faced one another with clenched fists. Then, the purser called out, 'Okay, fight!'

The two men momentarily sized one other up, and then the challenger suddenly threw the first punch. James moved out of reach and quickly threw a punch of his own. He collected the challenger square on the jaw. George, Billy and Joseph cheered him on. The Tasmanian shook his head and than came straight back at James. They both continued throwing punch after punch, some finding their target, others missing. The challenger threw a right hook and then a quick left, then another right to James' head. The vicious blows stunning him, splitting his lip and cutting his tongue. James spat the blood out of his mouth. His head was ringing and his eyes were blurry and partly swollen.

'Come on James!' Billy shouted as loud as he could, offering encouragement.

The two men continued slugging it out, trading blow after blow, punch after punch, when James suddenly swung with an uppercut. He collected the man under the chin, which sent him reeling backwards into a group of men. A horse nearby, behind them whinnied while trying to rear up but was restrained by ropes. The Tasmanian's supporters yelled for him to get back into the fight. The bald-headed man returned to the centre of the circle for more. He swung at James with another right hook but this time James avoided the blow. James threw another quick punch to the man's head and then another left hook. Blood was now streaming from the Tasmanians nose. James instinctively knew that he must continue punching the man in the face. He struck him with another vicious blow to the head with his left fist, followed by another right-hand punch square on the nose. James felt the man's nose break under the impact as more of his blood sprayed out. James quickly went in with another right and then a left hook. The Tasmanians knees buckled and then he fell to the straw-covered floor.

His supporters shouted encouragement for him to get back onto his feet, with George, Billy and Joseph cheering loudly for James. The bald-headed man slowly got to his hands and knees. James was waiting for him to get up. Suddenly, the man lunged at his legs bringing James down onto the hard, steel deck. They rolled over, with the other men quickly jumping out of their way. The two men continued fighting it out on the floor. Eventually though, they became entangled amongst the legs of a horse. The animal panicked and started kicking wildly with its hind legs and several fencing posts were sent crashing down.

Saddles, harnesses, lanterns and other stable hardware went tumbling to the floor. One of the lanterns shattered spilling burning oil over the straw covered floor. The dry grass quickly caught fire and several men had to grab pails of water and extinguished the flames. The two men were still fighting it out. They rolled out from under the horses and ended up amongst buckets, straw bails and other saddlery items.

George suddenly noticed the challenger had produced a knife from somewhere. He yelled, 'Look out James!' as he grabbed hold of a pitchfork and shoved it close to the man's face. 'Don't even think of it mate! Drop it!' he yelled at him. 'Drop it!'

The man on the ground finally let go of the knife and it fell to the deck with a clatter. Joseph quickly gave James a hand and pulled him onto his feet. George looked around at the other men, then back at the man holding the prize money. 'Alright! I'm sure that you will agree that we won the fight fair and square! Your man broke his own rules! He cheated! So, hand over the money!'

James and the challenger were breathless trying to suck the smoke filled air into their lungs. The other men were arguing over who had actually won. Finally, the purser succumbed to defeat and reluctantly passed the purse over to George. Two men suddenly stepped out of the darkness surprising everyone. They wore scarves over their faces and both were armed with pistols, which they pointed threateningly towards the startled men.

'We'll take that now thank you very much,' one of them said looking over at George. 'Hand over the bag!' He then gestured with the gun for the money to be brought over to him.

Even in the dull flickering-light of the lanterns James thought there was something familiar about the one man. He had heard his voice somewhere before, but at that very moment he couldn't think where it had been.

George was still holding onto the money while glancing over at the masked men. He suspected that they were in cohorts with the others, as a back up, in case the Tasmanian lost the fight. 'Listen you blokes,' he said, glancing around at the other men, 'I don't know quite what's going on here but you lost the fight fair and square, so get your two men to back off!'

'Shut up you idiot!' one of the masked men told George. 'Get the money Albert,' he demanded.

This time, James was more positive about the man's voice. He now remembered where he had first heard it. It was on the railway platform in Perth. The man had been calling out to Veronica. She had then told James that it was her estranged husband Timothy Pearson. James decided to keep that to himself for the time being. Albert approached George cautiously and then he snatched the bag from him. He then rejoined the other man before they slowly backed away into the shadows and then vanished from sight.

The Tasmanian was furious. 'I'll kill them sons of bitches if it's the last thing I do! Nobody steals my money and gets away with it! Nobody!' Saliva flew from his mouth.

'Don't worry Fredrick, we will get the money back!' the bloke standing near to him advised.

Someone-else then added, 'Even if we have to tear this bloody rust-bucket apart!'

The Tasmanian's eyes surveyed the men standing around, while wiping the blood from his nose. 'Did any of yah recognise either of those blokes?'

The men shook their heads.

'Someone here must know who they are!' the challenger bellowed.

'They weren't from our lot,' someone advised.

'What about you, hey?' the challenger asked looking across at James. 'Do you know them? ...Are they with your lot?'

James shook his head. 'They both wore masks in case you hadn't noticed,' he replied sarcastically. 'And besides, why the heck would we want to steal our own money, it doesn't make any sense?'

'I don't know and I don't care! ...But, this had better not have been a set-up, I am warning you all,' the challenger threatened. 'I know where to find you. I swear to God that I will disembowel you if I find out this was a rip-off!'

The Tasmanian was about to leave when someone shouted from the shadows, 'Stand where you are! Don't move or I will shoot!'

Several armed sailors suddenly appeared from out of the darkness. An armed officer accompanied them. 'Place your hands on your heads!' he demanded.

The group of men were stunned but they did as ordered.

'So, what do we have here?' the officer asked, looking at each man in turn. He stopped at the bald headed Tasmanian observing the blood trickling from his nose. 'I suppose you will tell me that you walked into a door?'

The big man wiped the blood from his nose but didn't reply.

The officer's eyes then turned to James. 'Another one who walked into a door, I presume?'

James didn't reply either.

'Arrest these two,' the officer ordered pointing at James and the Tasmanian.

The two men were handcuffed and then taken down several flights of steel steps to the brig where they were then thrown into separate cells. The air was foul down there. It was also stinking hot and humid. James went and lay down on the hard steel-bunk with the perspiration running from him. He was thinking about his unexpected predicament when Lieutenant Parker came towards his cell.

'Quite frankly, Mitchell, I am extremely disappointed in you,' he said, speaking between the steel bars. 'I would never have taken you for the prize-fighting type.'

James got to his feet and then approached the officer. 'I'm not normally, sir.'

'Then explain to me how you got yourself locked up in here.'

James thought for a moment before replying, 'I'm afraid it was a matter of honour, sir.'

'Honour?'

'Yes sir.'

'Well, I can assure you that Major Moor is most unhappy about the whole matter. Insomuch, that one of our contingent should have become involved in a bout of fisticuffs. What's more, in the middle of the night with a trooper from another colony.'

...'Yes sir! Would the lieutenant kindly offer the major my sincere apologies.'

'I shall pass that onto the major. However, if this was a matter of honour as you claim Mitchell, then I presume that you were not fighting for a wager, that in-fact no money exchanged hands? Do I presume correctly Mitchell?'

James swallowed the lump in his throat. He wasn't in the habit of lying and he didn't really want to start now. 'I'm afraid there was a wager, sir.'

'Well then, I need not tell you that this is most serious Mitchell. Where is this... wager now? Who is in possession of this money?'

THE PLOUGH, THE GUN AND THE GLORY

James realised that he would probably have to lie to the lieutenant. He hadn't done that since he was a young boy when he blamed Alanna for something he had done and she was punished. Even though he had confessed later it was too late. He now believed however, that it was too dangerous to reveal the name of the man who he suspected. What if the masked man wasn't Timothy Person? He would be accusing an innocent man. There was also another slight problem. The Tasmanian was in the cell next to him. He was bound to be listening to everything that was being said. Furthermore, James had previously told him that he didn't know who had stolen the money. If he told Lieutenant Parker who he thought the suspect was, the Tasmanian would think the whole thing had been a set-up from the beginning. It wouldn't take long for a witch-hunt to get started. Someone was going to end up with their throat cut and James didn't want an innocent man's blood on his hands. In this situation telling a lie was a lot safer for everyone. 'I have no idea sir. It was very dark down there and the wager was stolen shortly before we were arrested.'

The lieutenant shook his head in disbelief. 'Do you honestly expect me to believe a concoction of a story like that Mitchell? …I must say I do regret having misread your character. I have always taken you for a person of upright morals and standing. You have disappointed me to say the very least.'

'I am extremely sorry, sir.'

'Very well, I will make my report to Major Moor. Quite frankly Mitchell, in my opinion you are nothing but a disgrace to the entire West Australian contingent. If I had my way you would spend the rest of the voyage in this stinking cell.'

James was left standing next to the steel bars with sweat running down his body. He returned to his bunk and lay down. He then rolled his tongue around the inside of his mouth feeling the cuts on his tongue and cheeks. Afterwards, he got to his feet, went over to a wooden pail in the corner of the cell and spat a mouthful of blood into it.

24   On the 26th November the coastline of South Africa was seen in the distance through a misty-blue sea haze. It was a welcome sight for all. After first rounding Cape Agulhas and then later Cape of Good Hope, the steamship changed course in a more northerly direction. They had now left the Indian Ocean and entered the South Atlantic. Now and then, spray from the bow-waves would be thrown up onto the deck as the 'Medic' ploughed her way into the large Cape Rollers.

The steel vessel pushed on past Slangkop Point and then Hout Bay and finally rounded Sea Point. James had been released from the brig the previous day. George, Billy and Joseph were standing together with him near the bow of the ship. They, like the other men onboard were eager to get their first glimpse of Cape Town. Everyone was eager to step onto dry land once again and maybe even get to see the enemy for the first time.

Table Mountain grew more majestic with each passing minute, towering 6000 feet above the town and harbour. The tall masts of sailing ships cluttered with ropes and furled sails were rolling, pitching and endlessly tugging at their anchors. Steam ships carrying troops from Queensland, New South Wales, Canada, New Zealand and Britain, were lying at anchor outside Victoria Basin Docks, anxiously waiting to be guided in by the steam tugs. The unexpected harsh rattling noise of the anchor chain as it went clattering over the iron rollers, made James and the others jump with fright. The anchor broke the surface of the ocean with a huge splash and then made its way down through the deep, cold water to the seabed below.

'Hey James!' Joseph called out, once the noise had quietened down.

'Yeah.'

'They call that Lion's Head,' he said pointing up at the mountainside. 'The one on the left is called Devils Peak... The long flat one in the centre is obviously Table Mountain.'

'How come you know all this stuff?' George asked him out of curiosity.

'When I first found out that I was coming to South Africa I read up on it.'

THE PLOUGH, THE GUN AND THE GLORY

'Yeah?' George was impressed.

'It sure is a beautiful sight,' James commented with the others agreeing.

Their attention was momentarily drawn to several seagulls circling above. They suddenly came swooping down low over the men's heads before landing on various parts of the ships superstructure. The men's attention however, was soon drawn back to the spectacular scenery that lay before them.

After supper James and the others returned to the deck. They gazed in awe and silence at the lights of Cape Town, and the myriad of other ships at anchor, as they glowed and sparkled in the dark almost like the stars in the heavens. Everyone onboard was in good spirits that night. Many of the men stayed up late talking excitedly, smoking their pipes while staring apprehensively towards the landmass, now hidden from them by the blackness of the night. Many of them were wondering what the future held for them. What lay ahead on this strange, mystical land far away from their homes in Australia?

25   At daybreak the ship was slowly guided into Victoria Basin by steam-tugs. Slowly, but steadily, the heavy vessel was manoeuvred and nudged into a berth while members of the ships crew ran around the decks carrying out various tasks. To add to the noise and confusion army officers and junior NCOs were yelling orders to their men, who eagerly disembarked down the timber gangways onto South African soil.

After several hours, the horses, guns and equipment were eventually unloaded, and from there the men were marched to the Maitland Cavalry and Artillery Depot. On arrival, one company of New South Wales Lancers, who had previously arrived via England on the 2nd November, greeted them with a rowdy reception.

The following day the six colonies were individually formed-up on a large open field for a kit and weapons inspection, where they were also given a briefing by their various commanding officers. Company Sergeant-Major Edwards brought the West Australians to the stand-easy position. After that, Major Moor began his briefing.

'Yesterday evening I attended a council-of-war meeting with the Garrison Commander of Cape Colony, together with other senior Australian officers, and senior officers of Her Majesties Imperial Army.' He stopped talking for a moment while he cleared his throat. 'Some weeks ago the Boer Armies besieged the towns of Mafeking, Kimberley and also Ladysmith. We were briefed as follows; Her Majesty's Imperial Forces are now deployed in four main areas... In Natal we have General Sir Redvers Buller, the commander-in-chief of the South African War, who at present is marching on the town of Colenso near Ladysmith. General John French is moving towards Stormberg where a large force of Boers has congregated. Then, we have General Sir William Gatacre who is advancing on Boer positions near the town of Colesberg. And lastly, at De Aar we have Lieutenant General Lord Methuen who is about to advance his army towards Kimberley.'

Major Moor cleared his throat once again before continuing. 'I am sure that it goes without saying that we have the finest British Generals and professional soldiers in the field. Therefore, it is anticipated that the war against the Boers will not be a long campaign. In-fact several Imperial Offices have indicted that they expect it will all be over by Christmas.'

Cheering broke out amongst the men. Major Moor then began to pace the front rank. 'During the meeting I learned that General Sir Redvers Buller has issued orders for the Australian colonies to be united as one regiment.' He cleared his throat again. 'We will therefore, shortly be know as 'The Australian Regiment.' Sadly, we will not have the privilege of serving under the colours of Western Australia. Instead, we will be integrated into Her Majesties Imperial Army to fight under the colours of the Union Jack.'

Mumbling broke out from amongst the ranks, which were then quickly silenced by Sergeant Major Edwards.

Major Moor then continued, 'Gentlemen, please believe me when I tell you that I can understand your heartfelt disappointment by this unexpected news. I cannot deny that I sympathise wholeheartedly with you. However, you should look upon this as a privilege and indeed an honour. It should be appreciated, that by being attached to Her Majesties Imperial Army will afford us the opportunity to gain at first-hand the experience and the enormous benefits of fighting alongside professional soldiers, in the greatest army the world has ever known.'

The major continued to pace the front rank while addressing the men. 'Even though we will no longer be fighting under our own colours, I know full-well that when the time comes you will all give of your very best. Two-days from now, we will take part in the initiation ceremony to be held on these grounds. That will be the last time that we will march under the West Australian colours. I know that you will march with pride in your hearts.' He cleared his throat once again. 'Tomorrow, there will be a rehearsal. Details will be posted later today.'

Further mumbling broke out amongst the men who were silenced once again by the sergeant major.

Major Moor looked the men over. 'Some good news however, is that later this afternoon you will be exchanging your Martini-Henry's for the latest Lee-Metford's.'

A round of applause broke out from the men.

'For your information, the Lee-Metford fires a .303 bullet. You will also no doubt be more than glad to learn that it has a ten round magazine. I understand that the Lee-Metford's are sighted to 1,600 yards with good accuracy.'

Another round of applause broke out from the men.

'There's one other thing,' the major continued. 'When you fall-out at the end of this parade, you are to hand-in your blue guernseys and also your putties to the quartermaster as they will no longer form part of our uniform. This includes all badges of rank, insignia's and colour facings.'

More rumblings broke out from amongst the ranks.

'This is not so much to do with being formed into a Federal Regiment, but is more for safety precautions. I have been advised that the Boers are crack marksmen and will single out officers and NCOs.'

26   Cape Town had laid-on a beautiful cloudless morning with a deep powder-blue sky and brilliant sunshine, with the exception of a single layer of thin white cloud that covered the top of Table Mountain, known locally as the tablecloth. The drum major of Her Imperial Majesty's Army, held the mace high as he led the parade onto the grounds to a brassy British marching tune. Nine officers and twenty-nine mounted lancers from the New South Wales 1st Contingent rode behind, their colours flapping wildly in the stiff sea breeze. Following them were one hundred and thirty-four remaining lancers who at the time were without horses.

They in-turn were followed by the 1st Infantry Contingent from Victoria with twelve officers and two hundred and forty men, plus several horses and wagons. Tasmania was next with four officers and seventy-two infantrymen, plus horses and wagons. After them was the South Australian Mounted Rifles 1st Contingent with six officers and one hundred and twenty-one men. Finally, the Western Australia 1st Contingent marched on, with five officers and one hundred and twenty-five infantrymen, plus several horses and wagons.

The colours of the Australian Colonies were carried high and proud for the last time and they fluttered wildly about in the strong wind. The troops of each colony were brought to a halt on the grass-covered ground. There, they turned to face towards a large white marquee containing over one hundred seated guests. The command was then given for them to open order and then to stand at ease.

A senior officer from Her Majesties Imperial Army garrisoned in Cape Town made the opening speech. He carried a sword hung from a belt and wore a white ceremonial uniform with a white-feathered pith helmet. The wind shook the plumage wildly as he clung to several pieces of paper in his hand. After grappling with them for a moment to prevent them from flying away he began his speech. 'On behalf of Her Imperial Majesty Her Royal Highness Queen Victoria, Lord Milner the British High Commissioner, the Commander-in-Chief of the Imperial Army for Africa, General Sir Redvers Buller, the Mayor and Mayoress of Cape Town and distinguished guests, ladies and gentlemen and soldiers of the colonies of Australia, it is my great privilege and honour to welcome you all here today on this historic occasion.'

He stopped speaking for a moment while a large gust of wind blew forcefully through the marquee. Once it had died down he continued, 'Regrettably, the Prime Minister of Cape colony the honourable Cecil John Rhodes, is not able to be here today to witness this historic event. Mr Rhodes is unfortunately taking shelter in the besieged diamond-mining town of Kimberley. It is hoped that he will soon be relived by Her Majesties Imperial Forces.'

Applause was heard amongst the crowd. Once they had quietened down the officer continued. 'We have gathered here today to witness the formation of a new regiment. This new regiment is to be known as The Australian Regiment, thereby uniting the six Australian colonies as one military body.'

During another strong gust of wind a pair of Union Jacks on either side of the dais flogged themselves against their staffs, virtually drowning out his voice for a few moments. The officer continued as soon as he was able. 'Colonel Hoad has been given command of this new regiment.'

Loud applause broke out from the general public. Once everyone had quietened down the officer continued. 'Major Eddy will be second in command.'

More clapping came from the public. The officer then went on to read out the remaining names. Then he called upon the Mayor to address the public and troops. He produced a long drawn-out-speech about the importance of the British Empire controlling the whole of Southern Africa. Finally, it was time to lower the individual flags of the colonies. They were rolled up and handed over to each of the colony's senior officers. After exchanging them for Union flags (Australian Colonies 1801-1901) they were hoisted to the anthem God Save the Queen. Everyone stood to attention with army officers at the salute. The military band then played Soldiers of the Queen and other British marching tunes, while Lord Milner accompanied by Colonel Hoad, plus two imperial officers inspected the troops. Finally, it was all over and the troops of the newly formed Australian Regiment departed from the parade grounds to the tune of Rule Britannia.

27   It was another beautiful cloudless day as the troops marched down Adderley Street towards the railway station. The band was thumping out imperial marching tunes as hundreds of onlookers, young and old, lined the streets waving and cheering. Others merely stood in silence, staring forlornly at the foreigners who had come to the aid of the British Imperialists. Despite them though, the parade somehow reminded James when they had marched through Perth. Only this time, they were on South African soil and much closer to the Boer War. Rambling Meadows suddenly seemed a very long way off.

The train pulled out of Cape Town station with the two steam locomotives, puffing and hissing and belching coal-dust smoke into the air. James and the others hung out of the open windows waving to crowds lining the platform. After passing the Cape Town Castle they slowly made their way around the base of Devils Peak towering 990 metres above them.

Other troops onboard the train were twenty-nine New South Wales Lancers, on their way to join Lord Methuen's forces. Another forty-three NSW Lancers were to be attached to General French's cavalry. The remaining troops were all infantry units.

THE PLOUGH, THE GUN AND THE GLORY

'Well James, at long last we are on the final leg to the Boer War,' Joseph said excitedly, with the wind from the moving train blowing his hair about wildly.

They were all in high spirits and they laughed and joked about what they would do when they eventually came across the first Boers.

'We'll show 'em what Aussies are made of, hey mates?' George added.

'Too bloody true mates!' Billy replied enthusiastically, 'and, we'll show the limey's how to fight.'

'Darn right we will,' James added, while making a fist and waving it above his head.

The carriages gently rocked from side to side, the wheels clicking noisily over the expansion joints in the rails, as the train wound its way snakelike through the steep twisting, winding hills. Sometimes, the men were able see the whole of the train ahead of them as it negotiated the sharp bends. And often, coal-dust would fly through the open windows of the carriages covering everything with a fine black-soot. The men didn't mind though, they were too excited as they talked loudly about what the war would be like. Then, slowly one by one the men fell silent as they gazed at the magnificent scenery gliding past the open windows of the carriages.

Hours later, having first gone through Paarl and later the twisting turning mountains at Du Toits Kloof, the train ground to a jerky halt at the town of Worcester, where the steam engines took on water and coal. After that the train huffed and puffed its way into the Hex River Mountains towering some 1800 metres above sea level.

The passengers starred in awe at the semi-barren, windswept hills and the myriad of vivid-green valleys hundreds of metres below the track. They saw vineyards and orchard farms with whitewashed Cape Dutch style homesteads. Others, had cattle, horses and sheep grazing on the slopes of the treeless hills. James thought of home and wondered how his parents were, and his sisters and brother. Then, his mind turned to thoughts of the old boathouse and Veronica. The gentle, continuous swaying and rocking motion of the carriage made him feel tired. Finally, he succumbed. His eyelids closed and he fell asleep.

The mountains slowly gave way to flat, barren, desolate landscape. Later, the hot, glowing, orange ball on the western horizon gave way to night, as the troop-train entered the Great Karoo Desert. The temperature soon dropped and throughout the cold night the train pushed on stopping only to take on water and coal, and also to change the weary drivers for fresh ones.

South Africa

Theatre of the 2nd Boer War 1899 - 1992

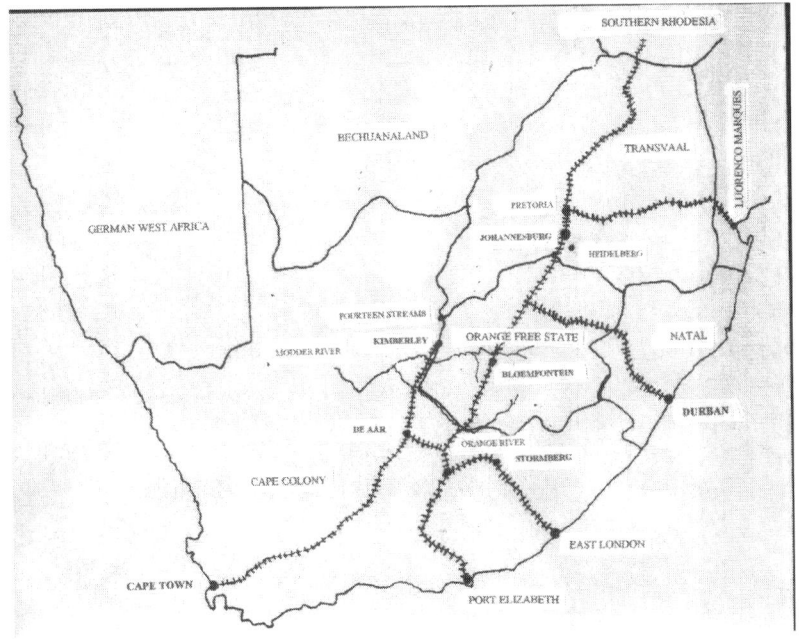

28   The early morning sun streamed through the window of the railway carriage into James' face, and he had to shield his eyes with his hand. He sat up, being careful not to bump his head on the bunk above him. He pushed his greatcoat over to one side of the bunk and then climbed out. The carriage was gently rocking from side to side and he could hear the sound of the steam engines up ahead.

Outside the window was an endless sea of colourful wild flowers, spreading as far as the eye could see to the distant kopjes in the background. James watched for a few moments before looking around the compartment at the three other bunks. George, Billy and Joseph were still asleep. James needed to go to the toilet as his bladder was bursting. He opened the door of the compartment and looked out both-ways along the passageway. It was actually empty for a change, which was pleasing. At least he wouldn't have to push his way through dozens of other men to get to the toilet.

James made his way along the narrow passage and then entered the cramped toilet compartment at the end of the carriage. Once inside he only just managed to close the narrow door behind him. With some difficulty he undid the buttons on his trousers and removed his penis. He gave an instant sigh of relief as his bladder emptied itself into the metal pan. When he was finished he placed the toe of his boot onto a small peddle at the base of the pan. The perforated plate inside the toilet, at the bottom of the pan, opened, and at the same time water gushed into the pan flushing the contents to the ground below. To James' amazement he could actually see lumps of red-hot coals, plus the railway sleepers as they went racing past. He removed his boot from the footplate and the lid closed with a bang.

After doing up the buttons on his trousers he started to make his way back to his compartment. As he moved along the carriage he glanced out of the windows at the passing scenery. There were men with guns hiding in the bushes and also behind rocks. The window near him suddenly exploded and shattered fragments of wood and glass went flying through the passage. James' heart skipped a beat as he realised the train was under attack. 'He yelled at the top of his voice, 'BOERS! BOERS! AMBUSH! AMBUSH!' Then he dropped to his hands and knees and continued making his way along the passageway towards his compartment.

The doors of compartments flew open and rifles were shoved through. The sound of gunfire and the smell of cordite was suddenly everywhere. Moments later, James reached his compartment. Billy and George were busy firing their rifles out of the open window. Joseph was lying on the floor. His chest and face were covered with blood. James knelt down next to him and called out above the noise of gunfire, 'Joseph! ...Joseph!'

Suddenly and unexpectedly, they were flung violently against one wall of the carriage when the train ground to a screeching, skidding halt. Another barrage of bullets blasted into the compartment, perforating the sides of the carriage, showering the men with bits of wood and metal. Billy and George scrambled to their knees once they were able, and continued firing their rifles, while James attended to Joseph. He knew that his old school friend was badly wounded and he quickly found a cushion to support his head.

Joseph grabbed hold of James by the shirt and pulled him closer towards him. 'James,' he said softly into his ear, hardly able to talk, 'can you please give me a drink of water?'

James searched through the debris in the carriage and quickly found one of the canteens. He removed the cork and placed the neck of the water bottle to Joseph's lips. Then he poured a little into his mouth. The wounded man gave a slight cough and then he tried to smile. 'It wasn't supposed to be like this mate, was it?'

James shook his head. 'I'm going to patch you up and then find the doctor for you,' he replied with the deafening sound of gunfire all around.

Joseph hung onto him. 'There's need James... I am done for.'

'That's not true. Don't talk like that.'

Joseph wouldn't let go of him. 'Will you write to my family?' He coughed again which made him wince with pain. 'Tell them that I loved them dearly.'

'You can write to them yourself once you have recovered.'

'Pray for me James.' His eyes had lost their colour and had become almost transparent. Blood was now drooling from his mouth.

James swallowed the lump in his throat then began to recite the 23rd Psalm. 'The Lord is my shepherd, I shall not want; he makes me lie down in green pastures. He leads me besides the still waters;' James felt Joseph go limp. 'Joseph... Joseph!' he shouted above the noise of gunfire.

Joseph didn't respond. He lay there limp and bloody. James knew that he was gone. He continued to pray until he had completed the whole of the prayer. Then he looked up at the others who were still engaged in battle with the enemy. 'He's dead... Joseph's dead!' he yelled.

They both stopped shooting. They turned and looked down at Joseph's blood soaked body lying on the floor. George and Billy quickly joined James on the floor. They were shocked that Joseph had been killed.

'It's not fair,' Billy commented in disbelief, 'he didn't even get to fire a single shot.'

Another hail of bullets entered the compartment sending feathers, leather and wood flying from the upholstery. Billy and George returned to the window and fired back at the enemy. James was still in shock as he grabbed his rifle and ammunition belt, and then made his way towards one of the vacant windows in the corridor.

A number of wounded and dead men were lying in the passageway. James crawled his way between them over to a window. He then got to his knees and peeped above the windowsill. Several Boers were amongst the rocks and bushes. James pushed the safety catch off and shoved the barrel of the rifle out of the window. Taking quick aim at a young Boer he pulled the trigger. The gun gave a solid kick against his shoulder and he saw blood explode from the young man's face.

James reloaded the Lee-Enfield by first lifting the breach-bolt upwards to unlock it and then pulling the bolt backwards to eject the spent cartridge. When shoving it forwards again a live round was pushed upwards and forwards from the magazine into the breach of the barrel. Another Boer was over to his right. He looked even younger than the first one. James quickly placed his sights on him and pulled the trigger. The young man's shoulder exploded sending blood and bone into the air. He fell to the ground screaming in agony.

THE PLOUGH, THE GUN AND THE GLORY

The carriage suddenly lurched violently as the stationary train took a direct hit from one of the Boers 75mm Krupp field guns. Billy and George were catapulted from the bunks they had been kneeling on. When they had both recovered they returned to their previous positions, by the window, and continued firing in the direction of the enemy. James noticed a Boer running between several rocks. He took quick aim and fired. The bullet missed and the man quickly vanished behind the bushes. James fired off another round in his direction in the hopes of hitting him.

29   Jacobaas Vorster lay still for a few moments, his heart pounding loudly in his ears, while trying to recapture his breath. He was feeling extremely relieved having made it to safety. He had accidentally fallen into a ditch shielding him from enemy fire. He first thanked God and regained his breath before crawling his way over to several rocks where he had a good view of the train below. He reloaded the Mauser in readiness while also surveying the scene in front of him. Perspiration trickled down his face and a few flies were pestering him. He tried to get rid of them with his hand waving them away from his face. The train had been ambushed while travelling through a port (cutting through a small hill). On each side of the port were steep embankments covered with rocks and bushes. It was an ideal location to ambush a train. The reason the train had come to a sudden grinding halt was due to two lengths of missing railway track. Luckily, two guards who had been riding on the front of the engine spotted the missing rails and shouted a warning to the driver. He had then managed to slam on the brakes just in the nick of time preventing a derailment. Clouds of black smoke and steam were gushing from the stationary locomotive as bullets and cannon shells rained down on the trapped train.

The driver had been slightly wounded in one shoulder, which had knocked him down for several moments. He had since recovered and got to his feet. He released the brake and then activated the controls for reverse. With the wheels of the engine spinning wildly on the shiny, smooth rails the train started moving backwards.

Jacobaas could see both the driver and fireman working frantically to get the train moving out of the ambush area. He took aim at the driver and as he came into view Jacobaas pulled the trigger. He saw sparks fly off the side of the engine as the bullet ricocheted off the coal layered black metal. He cursed loudly as he quickly reloaded the rifle and looked back at the train. His attention now turned to the troops who were shooting out of the carriage windows. He then noticed two civilians. One of them came into view for a few moments. Jacobaas took quick aim and fired at him. The bullet hit the bottom of the windowsill splitting the timber frame, sending jagged splinters of wood in all directions. The civilian was struck in the forehead and he immediately dropped to the floor to take cover. He felt inside his jacket and removed a handkerchief and began to dab the blood from his forehead.

James looked over at him. Blood was now streaming down his face. 'Are you alright mate?' he asked the youngish man, out of concern for his wellbeing.

'Yes, thank you. Fortunately I was only struck by fragments of wood.'

The train had now gathered momentum and was pulling away from the ambush area. Mounted Boers gave chase firing their rifles at the departing train. The troops fired back at them. A short time later the sound of gunfire ceased. James got to his feet and peered out the window. No Boers were in sight and the train was now travelling across open ground. 'I think they have given up,' he said turning to the stranger a few moments later. He approached the man sitting on the floor. 'Let's take a look,' he said kneeling down next to him. Several large splinters were protruding from the man's head. It took James a few moments to pull them out using his fingers. He showed them to the stranger. 'You were lucky. A little lower and you would probably have lost your eyesight.'

The man got to his feet and stuck out his hand. 'Winston,' he said shaking James by the hand, 'I'm a war correspondent with the Morning Post in London.'

James had been wondering what civilians were doing on a troop train. 'James,' he said, still shaking Winston's hand.

A second civilian approached them. 'I say, Churchill, old boy. We were certainly in a spot of bother back there for a moment, what?' The man spoke with a well-to-do English accent that made James smile.

'We certainly were.'

'By jove, Winston! The darn blighters have damn well wounded you!'

'It's nothing Rudyard, only a scratch caused by wooden splinters... Let me introduce you to James.'

The two men shook hands. 'James Mitchell.'

'Rudyard Kipling.'

Seconds later George popped his head out of the compartment door. 'James, are you okay mate?'

James looked his way. 'Yeah, I'm fine thanks. And you two?'

'We're okay.'

The train was slowing once again and moments later came to a screeching, shuddering halt. James returned to his compartment. For a few moments he gazed down at Joseph's body. It pained him to see his old school pal lying dead on the floor in a pool of blood.

Corporals and sergeants were now quickly making their way through the narrow corridors shouting orders to the troops. One of the corporals looked into the compartment. 'Keep to your sections! Take up defensive positions outside of the train! On that side!' he pointed. 'Move it! Move it!'

Billy placed his hand on James' shoulder. 'We'll take care of Joseph shortly. We had better get going now.'

James nodded and the three men made their way through the corridor and jumped from the train. It was a long drop to the hard ground below. The men landed heavily onto small stones, cutting their elbows and knees. They rolled over a few times in the dust before scrambling to their feet. From there, they ran a short distance from the train and then went to ground.

30   General De la Rey had given orders for his men to attend to the wounded and to bury the dead. He was bitterly disappointed that the train hadn't derailed at the chosen location. He was also angry because the train had managed to escape altogether from the ambush area. He rode his horse along the side of the port surveying the situation. He had lost five good men, plus several wounded despite having had good cover, plus the element of surprise, and also having been on higher ground. He would make certain in future that this didn't happen again. He then thought to himself, 'Those vervloetes (cursed) colonials were lucky this time, but it wouldn't happen again.'

Jacobaas Vorster dug a shallow grave, in the hard stony ground, with the help of another man. Then, they buried the body of the sixteen-year-old boy. After that they gathered loose rocks and packed them on top of the mound of dry earth, to prevent wild animals from digging up the corpse. Once they had finished they stood at the side of the youngster's last resting place. Jacobaas was about to say a short prayer. He looked skywards at the dark rain-clouds building up. He could tell there was going to be a storm before the day was out.

'Dear Heavenly Father,' he began in Afrikaans, 'again we humbly stand before you in order to bury one of our young boys... a young boy who has this day given his life in the struggle to free our country from the rooineks (British). We ask you Lord to take his soul that he may join the others in Heaven who have gone before him... Give his mother and father strength in their grieving and bring peace to their minds and hearts. Amen.'

'Amen.'

Jacobaas picked up his rifle and slung it over his shoulder. Then, he also picked up the buried boy's rifle and bandolier. The other man collected the shovel and then they made their way towards a cart. The man threw the shovel onto it. The rifle and bandolier were then handed into the armourer's wagon. A little later, orders were given to move out. Jacobaas mounted his horse and then the Boers rode off. A bolt of lightning lit up the sky followed by a loud clap of thunder overhead, which startled the horses and riders.

31   The Australians lay on the hot ground staring towards the flower-covered veldt that lay before them. James waived a fly away from his face that was annoying him. He was still upset over Joseph's death and was thinking to himself, 'It all happened so fast without any warning. One minute Joseph was alive. Next, he lay on the floor of the carriage dying.' He remembered Joseph's last words and wiped the moisture from his eyes with the backs of his hands. He then looked at them and realised that he was still trembling.

A loud clap of thunder gave him a fright and made him look upwards. He could smell the rain in the air and knew there was going to be a storm soon. He turned his head and looked back at the motionless train. The medics were still attending to the wounded, while others removed bodies from the carriages. Officers and NCOs were running around frantically, assessing the damage and giving out orders. Moments later Lieutenant Darling approached a group of the men.

'Corporal Brown!' he called out.

'Sir!' The man jumped to his feet and braced-up smartly.

'I want you to take a section of men over to the train. There are a couple of dead horses that need to be removed from one of the boxcars.'

'Yes sir.' The corporal turned to his men. 'Right, you lot,' he said while pointing towards James and the others. 'We've got some work for you to do.'

The men got to their feet, dusted themselves down and then made their way over to the train. A couple of them helped to heave the others up onto the boxcar. The corporal was first up with the others following. A sickening sight greeted them. Two horses were dead and one was badly wounded. Blood was everywhere. It was difficult for the men not to lose their footing as they proceed further in. James knelt down next to the wounded horse. It neighed constantly in pain as it stared back at him. He could tell by its face that it was in terrible agony. James gently stroked its head and then along the snout while talking softly trying to comfort the animal. It reminded him of the horses on the farm and he felt sorry for it. He stood up and looked at the other men standing around. 'I've never shot a horse before, have any of you?'

The men shook their heads.

'Only once,' George replied. 'It's something that you never forget.'

The corporal became impatient. 'Come on you lot let's get on with it!' he said, seemingly without compassion for the animal. 'We haven't got all day here, you know.'

His apparent lack of feelings angered James. 'You shoot it then!'

This annoyed the corporal. 'Let's get one thing straight here Mitchell. I am in charge here, not you! I'm not asking you, private! I am giving you an order to shoot the horse! Now get on with it!'

James glared at the man for a moment. There was a burning rage in his heart, now pumping rapidly in his chest. He pushed the safety catch off and then placed the barrel against the horse's head. The horse stared back at him. James swallowed the lump in his throat and then closed his eyes. He pulled the trigger. The rifle kicked hard in his arms. There was a deafening noise inside the confinement of the boxcar. Blood, brains, hair and bone exploded everywhere, some of which sprayed over James.

Without looking at anyone, he turned around and walked briskly towards the large open doors. He then jumped down from the boxcar and walked away from the train as fast as he could. The corporal followed him as far as the doors yelling, 'Mitchell! ...Mitchell! Where the hell do you think you are going! ...Get back here now, this instant! ...That's an order Mitchell!'

James ignored him. He continued walking with lightning flashing from the clouds. Thunder boomed as it rolled across the dark blue-black sky. Moments later James felt large drops of rain falling. He kept on walking until he was well away from the train before stopping. He placed the rifle against a large rock and then removed his bush-hat. A heavy gust of wind blasted across the veldt kicking up the dust, sending it skywards. The smell of rain was strong in his nostrils and he took several deep breaths of the air into his lungs.

The corporal shouted once again, 'I'll lay charges against you Mitchell! God is my witness!' He then turned his attention back to the other men. 'Well, what the hell are you lot waiting for?' he shouted.

Billy and George, plus two other men, took hold of the legs of the recently slain horse and started dragging the body towards the open doors. It was extremely heavy and under the prevailing conditions very difficult to move. The blood-soaked timber floor also made the job more difficult. Half of the head was missing, and as they dragged the body a trail of blood and brains poured out from the wound making the floor more slippery than ever.

At last though they finally got the dead animal over to the doors puffing and panting for air. Some of the men had slipped and fallen and their hands and uniforms were covered with congealing crimson liquid.

'Right!' the corporal's loud voice echoed in the boxcar as the men gathered their breath. 'Let's get this darn thing over the side.'

The men gathered around the animal and began to heave and push with all their strength, but they were unable to get it over the side. After awhile the corporal bellowed, 'Wait! Wait! You will never do it like that in a month-of-Sundays!' He looked at Billy and George. 'You two, go and get a couple shovels.'

They returned moments later and handed up the shovels. Billy and George were then given a hand onto the boxcar. The corporal took hold of one of the shovels and placed it under the carcase. 'I want you to use them like this... like leavers.' He demonstrated to them.

Two men took the shovels and put all their strength behind them. They heaved in unison as the corporal called out, 'One! Two! Three! Heave!'

The carcase moved 300mm. Finally, after several more attempts it flopped over the side of the boxcar. It crashed heavily to the ground sending up a cloud of brown dust, which was swept away by a gust of swirling wind.

It was now the turn of the two remaining horses. They were also eventually shoved over the side, landing one on top of the other with a solid thump. They lay there like a pile of discarded sacks of potatoes. Billy stood on the edge of the boxcar looking down at them. He felt a sadness and pain in his heart as he thought. 'This is an undignified end for such majestic creatures. Horses should never be treated in this manner. No creature of the earth or the sea or the sky should be treated this way. The earth spirit will be displeased with what has happened here today. The spirits will be angry and will punish the men who have done this.'

Several men were given the task of cleaning the blood out of the boxcar. Others handed up wooden pails of water drawn from the bowser. They were thrown against the walls and over the floors. Other men brushed the bloodstained timbers with brooms, sending red-stained coloured water gushing between the openings in the floorboards to the ground, together with bits of bone, hair and flesh.

Outside, the men tied ropes to the dead animals legs and then they were dragged away in an undignified manner, using other horses that had survived the massacre. A streak of jagged white light lit up the ink-black sky, immediately followed by a sharp crack of thunder. Heavy rain began falling and several men bolted for cover under the carriages.

James was now heading towards the train to rejoin his section when he noticed Billy and George were approaching him. He waited for them to arrive with the rain stinging his face and shivering from the cold wind sweeping across the open veldt. Billy and George soon arrived and then the three men made their way to their previous defensive positions.

Half an hour later the storm ended with warm sunshine bursting out from behind the clouds. It was a welcome relief and the men tried to dry themselves off a little. Meanwhile, a temporary command post had been organised. Colonel Hoad requested that a telegraph message be sent onto the next station, which was De Aar, approximately five miles north. After discovering that the telegraph lines had obviously been cut somewhere he decided to send a dispatch rider with a coded message. A volunteer was requested from the New South Wales Lancers, as they were equipped with horses onboard the train.

The man was soon mounted up and on his way. Major Moor was then given instructions to arrange four sections of men to accompany him and Lieutenant Parker, together with a senior officer from the NSW Lancers, to go forward along the line and inspect the damage to the rails. Winston Churchill, the war correspondent, requested to accompany the party, in order for him to write something for his column. It took half an hour to reach the ambush area on foot. Two sections climbed one side of the loop with the other two climbing the opposite side. It was tough going up the sides of the rugged kopjes (hills). James and the others puffed and panted as they scrambled their way upwards between rocks and thorn scrub. They soon came across dozens of empty bullet casings and freshly dug graves with small rocks piled on top.

'There's another one over here corporal!' Billy called out.

The corporal made his way over to him. 'That's three so-far,' he remarked, 'and we don't know how many more we will find, or how many there are over on the other side.' He glanced across the cutting towards the opposite side of the kopje as he spoke.

Down below three army officers together with Winston Churchill walked along the wooden railway sleepers. They soon came across the area where the rails had been removed. They observed that the rails had been left lying on either side of the track. After examining them they found that they were still in reasonably good condition.

'I think we were very lucky gentlemen,' Winston said excitedly, looking up at the two army-officers. 'If they had used dynamite to remove them, it would have taken days to obtain new rails and repair the damage, possibly even a week.'

'Thank God they didn't,' Major Moor replied. 'Perhaps they thought it would alert the garrison at De Aar, which as you know, is only about five or six miles from here.'

'I think we have been darn lucky all round,' Lieutenant Parked added. 'If the guards at the front of the train hadn't seen the missing rails in time, we would have most certainly been derailed and never made good our escape.'

'The blighters could very well have wiped us out to the last man,' Winston added.

'Indeed,' Major Moor replied, 'however, quick thinking by the engine driver certainly helped save many lives.'

'Absolutely,' Winston agreed, brushing a fly from his face. 'So, what's the plan now, major?'

'We will return to the train. I will make my report to Colonel Hoad. After that we will organise a work party. There are tools in the guards van that we can use.' He looked skywards. Vultures were circling overhead. 'We also need to bury our dead. After that we will return here together with the train and then repair the rails. Then, we will proceed onto De Aar with all haste.'

'What about the dispatch rider, major?' Lieutenant Parker asked.

'We will more than likely come across him enroute on his way back to us.'

The lieutenant nodded in agreement.

The major waved a fly from his face. 'Two sections will remain on here and keep watch in case the Boers return,' he advised the lieutenant. 'The other two sections will accompany us back to the train. I also want a report on anything that they may have been observed up there.' He was pointing to both sides of the kopjes.

Once the sections rejoined the officers Sergeant Lessey approached the major. 'We found five shallow graves in total, sir. Three over that side,' he pointed, 'and two on this side.'

'Those were most probably the two Boers that fellow shot,' Winston advised, 'what's-his-name?' He then pointed towards James. 'That young fellow over there.'

The sergeant glanced in the direction that Winston was indicting. 'That's Private Mitchell, sir.'

'That's him, James Mitchell,' Winston replied, 'I remember now.'

James was asked to come forward by the sergeant. He then saluted the officers.

'He is a terrific shot major,' Winston continued, 'I saw him kill at least two Boers. I was by the window next to him. Later, he kindly removed several wooden splinters from my forehead.'

'Well private, you appear to have won-over Mr Churchill's admiration. Well done.'

'Thank you, sir.'

'You may rejoin your section now,' the major ordered.

'Yes sir.' James saluted, turned and walked away.

32 Later, a gravesite was selected not far from the railway line, and eight shallow graves were dug. It was hard work despite the fact that the rain earlier had softened the ground slightly. Wooden crosses were also fabricated from a length of timber taken from a damaged carriage. They were then bound together by thin strips of leather, cut from the reins of a dead horse.

It was now time to bury Joseph and the other men. Colonel Hoad took the service reading a passage from the bible. 'Blessed be the Lord, my rock, who trains my hands for war, and my fingers for battle; my rock and my fortress, my stronghold and my deliverer, my shield and in whom I take refuge, who subdues the people under him.'

After he had read the entire psalm there was a twenty-one-gun salute, followed by a bugler who played the last post. George and Billy assisted James to place Joseph's body into the shallow grave and cover it up. They then gathered small rocks and placed them on the grave. When they were finished James took a wooden cross and knocked it into the ground using the butt of his rifle. He had previously carved Joseph's name and date of death and stood back in order to observe it. He was pleased; at least Joseph's grave was marked. James said a short prayer with Billy chanting in the traditional Aborigine custom with George looking on.

The horse's carcases, now swarming with flies and ants were left out on the open veldt for the hyenas and vultures to feast off. Once everyone had climbed onboard the train, it was then moved closer to the repair work to be carried out to the track. The men had now sampled their first taste of war. The war they had come to fight on behalf of the Empire. It had come to them suddenly and unexpectedly and had caught them completely unaware. In future they would be ready. Next time the Boers wouldn't find them such an easy target. Several of the men glanced around the carriages. They were bullet ridden with bloodstained walls and shattered glass, which had previously been windows. Smashed woodwork, splintered panelling, ripped upholstery and broken lamps lay strew around. Other men gazed outwards at the arid brown-land covered with thorn scrub. This was the country they had readily volunteered to help claim for the Empire...

the land, which a few of them had already paid the ultimate price.

Several men spoke excitedly, a few nervously, while others sat quietly saying nothing. The three jackaroos from Rambling Meadows were amongst the latter. James was deep in thought. As soon as possible he would write to Joseph's family as promised, even though the army would officially notify them of his death. He would also write home to his family and also to Veronica.

33 War correspondent, Winston Churchill, paced the confined area of the compartment. He was busy going over the previous events in his mind and then hurriedly recording them into a small notebook. His constant pacing aggravated Rudyard a little. 'I say, Churchill old boy, is that absolutely necessary?'

Winston stopped for a moment. He looked down at the man seated on one of the bunks. 'I always do this. It helps me to concentrate.'

'Yes, but we are in such a confined space in here.'

'May I suggest that you go for a walk along the corridor or something?'

Rudyard sighed and then gazed out of the window. Moments later he turned his eyes to Winston. 'I am rather worried about Rhodes,' he said, changing the subject. 'I can't imagine him being happy held a prisoner in Kimberley.'

Winston stopped writing. 'I am sure that he has made himself quite comfortable knowing him?'

'Mm, perhaps... That foolish stunt of Jameson and Rhodes' brother, Frank, trying to relieve Mafeking has brought nothing but pressure on Cecil... Furthermore, he has lost much of his credibility with the loyal Afrikaners of Cape colony.'

'Yes, that was a most unfortunate blunder altogether. I cannot for a moment fathom out what was going on in their minds.' Winston continued to write in his notebook.

'Neither can I... And, I am afraid that this whole business will pull Rhodes down if it goes on for too long... He is also not a well man.'

THE PLOUGH, THE GUN AND THE GLORY

Winston stopped writing and looked at Rudyard. 'Quite frankly I wouldn't worry if I was you, old chap. I think this war will be all over in a matter of some weeks. Everything is falling into place very nicely at the moment. Once we have relieved Ladysmith and then Mafeking, and also taken possession of Bloemfontein and Pretoria from the Boers, the whole thing will simply fizzle out. It will be the end and probably forgotten in a matter of months.'

'I wish I were as confident as you... It must be very comforting?'

Winston sat down on the bunk opposite him. 'Listen, in the next few days Gatacre will move into the Free State. Methuen will relieve Mafeking and Buller Ladysmith. That's why I'm so eager to get to Natal, so I can be there when Buller rides into Ladysmith. Can you imagine what a story that will make for the Morning Post, and your paper naturally? Perhaps we will even be able to return to England in time for Christmas as there will be no war left worth writing about?'

'Well I hope so. I truly hope so, or I fear that my old friend Rhodes will become gravely ill otherwise.'
Winston patted him on the knee. 'You worry far too much about him. He's a tough old horse, I'm sure he will survive this little uprising.'

Rudyard lent against the padded backrest of the seat and tried to relax. He glanced out of the window for a moment before looking back at Winston. 'What are you going to do when you return to England, write another novel? ... Another Savrola, perhaps?'

Churchill scratched his head looking thoughtful. 'No,' he gave a little chuckle. 'I think that book is best forgotten ...I think I might rather pursue a career in politics the same as my father.'

34 Lieutenant Parker was seated opposite Major Moor. The two officers were discussing something when one of the corporals approached their compartment. He knocked on the open door. 'Permission to speak with you, sir,' he asked bracing-up while looking at the lieutenant.

'What is it corporal?' the junior of the officers asked.

'I wish to lay a charge against one of the men, sir.'

...'I see... And what is the nature of the charge?'

'Failing to obey a lawful command, sir.'

...'Did this incident take place while under enemy fire, corporal?'

'No sir.'

The lieutenant stroked his moustache while looking thoughtful. 'Explain what happened.'

The corporal then began to tell him the story.

'Private Mitchell you say?' Major Moor asked, interrupting the conversation.

'Yes sir,' the corporal replied, 'a most disagreeable young man, if I may say, sir.'

'Not according to Mr Churchill, corporal... In fact, he spoke very highly of Private Mitchell.'

'I am afraid that I am not acquainted with Mr Churchill, sir. Is he with the military?'

'No. He's a war correspondent with the Morning Post... a London newspaper.'

'I'm afraid that I have not had the pleasure of meeting the gentlemen, sir.'

'Quite frankly corporal, after Mr Churchill's high praise of Private Mitchell, I believe it would be unwise to charge the man over the incident.'

'May I remind the major that Private Mitchell was also involved in an incident on-board the Medic, sir. If you recall he was placed in the brig for fighting, sir.'

'I recall the incident quite clearly corporal. However, I'm sure that a verbal warning would be quite sufficient on this occasion.'

'If I might just add, sir, Private Mitchell was one of the men who was involved in a bar brawl during the train journey from Perth to Albany. Furthermore, should Private Mitchell be allowed to go unpunished he may well undermine my authority with the other men, sir. Soon, everyone will think they can disobey orders and get away with it.'

'I understand your concern corporal. Nevertheless, I have given the matter some consideration and I still believe that a verbal warning would be quite adequate.'

'As you wish sir. Thank you.' He saluted the officers and left.

The major looked over at Lieutenant Parker. 'I think we should earmark Mitchell for future promotion once we are in the field, Francis. I believe he has the qualities of becoming a good soldier. Make a note of it.'

35   With the steam-train steadily making its way towards De Aar a lone rider was seen approaching alongside the track. The guards sitting on the front of the engine shouted to the driver to slow the locomotive down. Once the rider was nearer they could see it was the NSW Lancer who had previously been sent to De Aar. The driver then brought the train to a grinding halt.

Major Moor was the first to jump down from the carriage together with a lieutenant from the NSW Lancers. They both waited by the side of the track for the rider to arrive. The horse was pulled up alongside of them, frothing at the mouth and kicking up small stones and dust. The rider dismounted and saluted the officers before handing over an envelope to Major Moor. He then handed it up to Colonel Hoad who was standing in the carriage doorway.

The colonel hurriedly opened the sealed letter addressed to him and read the coded message. 'Sir, news of the attack on the train thereby delaying your arrival at De Aar is most disappointing to say the very least. However, whilst I can sympathise with your regrettable predicament, I must however advise that I am unable to assist you, as I can no longer delay my departure for Stormberg, as this would leave the garrison undermanned for a short period. Therefore, I urge that you make every effort to proceed by road with as much haste as possible; Lieutenant-General Sir William Gatacre De Aar Garrison.'

The colonel then handed the message over to Major Moor saying, 'Get the man and his horse loaded-up as quickly as possible and let's get moving again.'

36   The battered troop train from the Cape Colony finally crawled its way into De Aar station grinding to a jerky halt alongside the crowded platforms. This was a main railway junction for trains heading north, south and east. The station was extremely busy with the arrival of troops from Britain, Canada and New Zealand plus South African volunteers.

Horses, cannons, wagons, crates of ammunition and a myriad of other necessary military equipment were being unloaded. To add to the noise and confusion imperial officers from the De Aar garrison, were yelling orders at seemingly everyone. The troops from the newly arrived train were led outside the station where they were formed into their ranks. Troops, carriages and field guns were being carted in both directions along the dusty dirt road, with bullocks hauling the heavily laden, slow moving wagons.

Some hours later the Australian Regiment was then divided up, much to everyone's disappointment, and the contingents were then placed under various Imperial Commanders. The twenty-nine NSW Lancers and the infantry companies proceeded onto Enslin, along the western railway, to join the 1st Battalion Gordon Highlanders, plus a section of the Royal Horse Artillery under Lord Methuen's command.

The remaining NSW Lancers were despatched by rail eastwards to join General French's Cavalry-Brigade in the Colesberg area. The two war correspondents, Winston and Rudyard, took the train to Naauwpoort and from there went onto Stormberg.

37   Once the train had reached Orange River Station it was unable to continue further, due to the Boers having cut the line two miles further up. Orders where waiting for the Australians to proceed to Lord Methuen's laager a couple of miles to the west.

Having first crossed the bridge over the Orange River on foot, the Australians headed for the British position. The echo of the booming cannons was clearly heard amongst the semi-barren kopjes as the troops made their way across the veldt. The once blue-sky was now littered with large yellow cottonwool-clouds, as Lyddite shells rained down on British troops from Boer positions. The air hung heavy, filling the men's nostrils with the stench of death and the smell of exploded cordite.

During the march they came across the ruins of several burnt-out farms. Freshly dug graves made James think of his aunt and uncle, and he wondered how they and the children were surviving the war. The mutilated carcases of cattle and sheep lay strewn around. Wagons were smashed to pieces, still attached to dead bullocks and horses. Flies and ants were swarming over the bloated, decomposing bodies, and vultures circling above were anxiously waiting to feast on the blood-soaked carcases.

Half a mile further on they saw thousands of white tents strung out in neat straight rows as far as the eye could see. Wagons, men, horses and bullocks were rushing in all directions. There was a large marquee to one side, with a red cross painted on the sides. Horse-drawn ambulances and stretcher-bearers were bringing men in from the battlefield. Some were crying out in agony, while others lay silent staring aimlessly at seemingly nothing. James swallowed the lump in his throat. He hadn't thought the war was going to be anything like this.

Once they arrived at Methuen's headquarters the men were brought to a halt and allowed to take a brief rest, while the senior offices from the various colonies went forward to announce their arrival. Amongst the first officers to approach the marquee, where a single Union Jack fluttered in the gentle breeze, was Major Eddy of the Victorian infantry.

Accompanying him was Captain Cameron of the Tasmanian infantry and Major Moor of the Western Australian infantry

Upon arrival, the senior officer Major Eddy reported to a guard outside. After a short wait the officers were escorted inside. They saluted Major General Lord Methuen, seated behind a large table, together with other senior imperial officers.

'Major Eddy of the Australian Regiment reporting for duty, sir,' he advised proudly.

Methuen slowly got to his feet. He looked tired. 'I am rather pleased to see that you have finally arrived major. I received word yesterday by telegraph from Colonel Hoad at De Aar Garrison that you were on your way. Welcome to the Boer war.' He extended his hand.

Major Eddy shook it firmly. 'Thank you, sir.'

The major then introduced the other Australian officers accompanying him. After that, Lord Methuen introduced the imperial officers. The officers shook each other's hands. Once the formalities were over the Lieutenant General turned to a map laid out on the table.

'Quite frankly gentlemen, we are not making the progress that I had hoped for. Although the Boers are fewer in numbers they have however, held the upper hand. Firstly, in my opinion they are equipped with better rifles. The German Mauser can accurately kill a man at over two thousand yards. Our rifles are only accurate up to fifteen hundred yards.'

The General gave a cough, cleared his throat, then continued, 'Furthermore, to worsen matters, their artillery is also far superior. The Boers have light displacement mountain-guns, which are easily and quickly hauled up and down the kopjes. They use these to great effect whenever they can. They have also converted fortress artillery for use in the field... ninety-four-pounder Creusot's, commonly known as Long Toms, which can clearly outdistance ours. In addition, they have a field gun known as a pom-pom, a German Maxim repeating one-pounder. These guns fire explosive Lyddite shells up to three thousand yards and are most effective against our machine-gun positions. Another thing, the Boers infantry are fully mounted on horseback. Generally speaking, they do not stand and fight unless they have no option. Instead, they attack at will and then retreat when it suits them. They make use of trenches and kopjes to ambush us whilst we are on the move. Their knowledge of the surrounding terrain is clearly to their advantage. Their tactics have been most effective in delaying our advance towards Kimberley. For over two days now we have taken a severe pounding... Both my men and horses are exhausted.'

'Lessons the Boer's no doubt learnt from studying the American Civil War, sir,' one of the Australian officers remarked.

With his brow wrinkled Lord Methuen looked thoughtful for a moment. Then he took a long drink of water from a glass before saying, 'Explain yourself, sir.'

'Yes, sir... I'm sure that the General will recall that the Confederacy used trenches to great effect against the Union during the defence of Atlanta.'

Lord Methuen became a little agitated. He was annoyed at the thought of a junior colonial officer having the audacity to give him a military history lesson. 'Are you insinuating sir, that I am lacking in knowledge concerning the art of military warfare?'

'No sir, not at all,' he replied defensively.

'What are you saying then, sir?' he asked angrily.

'I was merely making an observation sir... I humbly apologise if I have offended the General, sir. That was most certainly not my intention.'

'Well major, let me enlighten you. As you have been afforded the privilege of serving under my command I would prefer that you keep your observations to yourself in future.'

'Yes sir.'

General Methuen then pointed to the map. 'We estimate that there are two thousand Boers occupying well-concealed positions in the surrounding kopjes. Here and over here.' He pointed to the map. 'They command good views of our positions in the field... Over here.' He pointed to another spot on the map. 'There are three mountain-guns which have caused considerable havoc. Two attempts have been made to capture them, regrettably without success.' Lord Methuen drank more water. 'Today however, we will endeavour to drive the Boers out into open ground and finish the fight. We will mount a frontal attack with British regulars, the Guards, Northumberland Fusiliers, Royal Marines and Naval Brigade.' He glanced at Major Eddy. 'The Australians will be held as reserves and only used if the need arise.' He looked at

Major Moor. 'Your men will be held in reserve on the left flank under the command of an Imperial officer, Captain Ferguson.'

'Yes sir.'

'Should we require your services, which I very much doubt, you will be signalled. You will then be required to advance on the larger of these two kopjes. This one.' He placed his finger on the map.

'Yes sir.'

'Major Eddy.'

'Sir.'

'You will fall under the command of an Imperial officer, Captain Brown. If required, your troops will attack this position here.' He pointed to the map. 'There are approximately five to six hundred Boers there.'

'Yes sir.'

'Captain Cameron's troops will come under the command of Lieutenant Pondsworth, who will take up positions on the right flank. If needed, you will attack the two mountain-guns positioned over here on this kopje.' Again, he pointed to the place on the map.

'Very well, sir.'

Further questions and discussions took place until finally everyone was in agreement about what had to be done. The Australian officers were about to leave when a man came running towards the tent. He pushed his way through the guards. 'Lieutenant General! Lieutenant General, sir! Urgent message from De Aar Garrison, sir!' he blurted out, struggling to catch his breath.

The message was handed over. The Lieutenant General opened it and read it to himself. Then, he placed his hand to his forehead as he said quietly, 'My God.' He sat down in his folding canvas and wooden chair.

The officers saw the distress written on his face, wondering what had caused him to appear this shocked. Lord Methuen looked grimly at each one in turn before saying, 'I have extremely bad news gentlemen. Gatacre's third division was ambushed near Stormberg. They have suffered a terrible defeat. Five-hundred and seventy of his troops have either been killed, wounded or captured.'

The imperial officers were shocked by the news.

THE PLOUGH, THE GUN AND THE GLORY

'But, sir,' a junior rank amongst them burst out unable to contain his emotions. 'They were professional soldiers, the Royal Irish Rifles and Northumberland Fusiliers, sir. How could the Boers have possibly defeated them? Surely there must be some mistake, sir?'

The Lieutenant General looked up at the young man. 'Mistake?' he repeated quietly. 'Yes, you are right, there has been a terrible mistake... General Gatacre's.' He looked at the heliograph message again. 'It is more important now than ever gentlemen, that we secure the area here immediately and then press forwards to Belmont with all haste. I want all available troops to be ready and in position within the hour.' He gave a wave with his hand saying, 'Dismissed.'

The officers saluted, turned and left the Lieutenant General reading the heliographed message once more. They returned to their troops who were then formed-up behind the Royal Horse Artillery and the Guards Brigade, the Northumberland Fusiliers, Royal Marines and Naval Brigade. In-all 9,500 British and Australian troops were spread out across the open veldt in preparation to do battle with the Boers.

James swept his eyes over the myriad of colourful wild flowers blossoming in abundance due to the onset of the rainy season. Butterflies floated lazily in the air. Grasshoppers sprung from place to place. He was thinking, 'If God has intended me to die here today, then he has chosen a burial ground not without some beauty.'

Lord Methuen rode his large white-charger amongst the troops. 'I want all of you here today to remember!' he shouted loudly in order to be heard above the sound of cannon fire, 'that you are fighting for your Queen! ...Her Imperial Majesty, Queen Victoria, will expect every one of you to give of your very best on the battlefield! ... Some of you will die here today! ...You will not have died here in vain! ...YOU WILL HAVE DIED FOR THE GLORY OF THE EMPIRE!' he yelled at the top of his voice.

James' heart was pounding wildly in his chest as the adrenalin surged through his veins. He whispered a short prayer for everyone. The Lieutenant General then rode at a gallop towards the centre of his troops. Moments later, he drew his sword from the scabbard and held it vertically in the air. He quickly brought it down giving the order for the artillery to move forward. Signal flags were thrust into the air. Following that, four batteries of Royal Horse Artillery with fifteen-pounder field guns were hauled across the battle-strewn veldt to positions previously given to them.

38   Across the veldt to the north on a low kopje, General Piet Cronje sat astride his horse. He was surveying the British forces through field glasses. 'I have a feeling that the rooineks (rednecks) are going to try everything to break through us today,' he said in Afrikaans to the Captain on horseback next to him.

'Yah, it looks that way General?' He was also peering towards the enemy's lines through binoculars.

'Look at them Van! Only a blind man could miss them. Men being sent to the slaughter dressed-up like peacocks. They belong on a parade square in England not out here in the veldt.'

'All to our advantage sir.'

'Of course... However, I can't help feeling sorry for them. After today many British wives will be without husbands and many children without fathers.'

'I'm sure the British don't feel sorry for our wives and children sir.'

The General took the field glasses from his face and let them hang by the neck-strap. He stroked his beard a couple of times while gazing thoughtfully over the veldt. Then, he removed a stick of biltong (seasoned game-meat) from a small bag and cut off a slice with his knife. He chewed on it while placing the glasses to his eyes. 'I see that additional reinforcements have arrived today. The Australian colonies are joining in the fight now. Probably the troops that Koos De la Rey ambushed on the train outside of De Aar?'

'It's quite possible sir. However, I'm not sure.'

'We should keep an eye on them Captain. These Australians are much like ourselves, you know?'

The captain frowned. 'In what way general?'

'Like us, they too are volunteers. They have come from a country not unlike ours. I have a feeling they will be

THE PLOUGH, THE GUN AND THE GLORY

keen to prove themselves on the battlefield alongside the British soldier.' Cronje then swept the glasses across the veldt to the kopje on his left and surveyed the positions of his men. His eyes then focused on the two mountain-guns. After that, he checked the kopje on the right. Three mountain-guns waited patiently for the order to open fire. He then looked at the man next to him. 'What's our present strength, Van?'

The Captain removed a notebook from his top pocket, turned to the last entry he had made and said, 'Two thousand one hundred and twenty-three, sir. That was yesterdays count.'

'And the rooinecks?'

'Our last calculation was approximately nine thousand, sir'

'Does that include the Australians?'

'No, sir.'

'Nine thousand,' he repeated thoughtfully. 'How many on horseback?'

'About eight hundred and fifty, sir, plus twenty-nine Australians who arrived today.'

'Mmm... Okay, Van. We will hold our position here as long as we are able, then I want to withdraw.'

The young captain was somewhat disappointed. 'But sir, we have a great opportunity to defeat the British heavily here! Our artillery out distance theirs. Our rifles are more accurate over a greater range'. Why does the general wish to withdraw from the engagement?'

'In your enthusiasm to defeat the British captain, you have overlooked a very important statistic. We are considerably out-numbered. How long do you think it would take before they over-run us with sheer numbers? We can't afford our artillery to fall into the hands of the enemy. We have done well here, Van. Let us not tempt fate. We will withdraw when I say! And not a moment before!'

'As you wish general.'

39   Four batteries of Royal Horse Artillery sent their shells hurling towards the Boers. This time, they were closer to the enemy and were far more effective. Their shells exploded against the hard granite rocks sending stone shrapnel flying in all directions. Chunks of black earth, grass and rocks were hurled into the air before raining down on the veldt below.

The Boers however, had previously placed white painted stones out on the veldt, giving them the range to set their sights, and they returned an accurate barrage of shells on the British. In addition, Pom-Pom guns sent exploding shells bursting onto the veldt. Boer machine guns also opened fire and the air soon became a dirty mixture of yellow and black gun smoke.

Signal flags went up from Methuen's side. The bugler sounded the charge and the cavalry, the 2nd Dragoons (Royal Scots Greys), together with the 5th Mounted Infantry galloped away towards the enemy. The bagpipes of the Gordon Highlanders sent their eerie squeal into the already noise-filled air as the regiment pressed forwards into the throng of battle.

The Boers fired their rifles and artillery on the advancing British troops. The air became thicker with the stench of gun-smoke, choking both men and horses,' and the sky became darker. The veldt was churned-up and trampled. Wildflowers became spattered with the blood spilled from both horse and man.

From their concealed positions the Boers found the British shoulder-to-shoulder targets easy prey out in the open, their bullets ripping into the flesh of the enemy, tearing away limbs and muscle, soaking their tunics red with life-giving blood. Man upon man fell to the ground mortally wounded or dead. Horse's followed their riders tumbling down into the dirt never to get up again, many dying an agonising death as the blood drained from their wounds into the sand.

The battle raged for more than three hours before the signal was hoisted from the Lieutenant General for the Australians to join the fight. The twenty-nine New South Wales Lancers together with the Queen's Royal Lancers dashed towards the hidden foe. It was also time for the

THE PLOUGH, THE GUN AND THE GLORY

colonial infantry to join the fight. On the left flank the colony of Western Australia waited anxiously for the order to proceed from the imperial officer in command. He gave the signal to Major Moor. The major held his sword above his head as he yelled, 'FIX BAYONETS!'

The nervous, sweating men withdrew the long steel knives from their scabbards and attached them to their rifles, making sure they were properly secure. Moments later the major brought his sword swiftly down yelling simultaneously, 'FORWARD!'

The West Australians moved towards the enemy in the kopjes. Soon, mounds of earth were exploding all around and bullets went whizzing past their heads. They were puffing hard now as they made their way between smashed wagons, dead and wounded horses. British soldiers were crying out in agony, covered in blood, while others lay still and lifeless. Some had lost a leg or an arm while others were dying from chest and head wounds.

The imperial captain and the Australian officer steadily led the men towards the kopje, as bullets kicked up clumps of earth and grass around them, lacerating the men's faces and drawing blood. As they neared the base of the kopje the imperial officer shouted the order, 'CHARGE!'

The men ran towards the Boer positions screaming at the top of their lungs as a barrage of lead came in their direction. The Boers were now beginning to panic; their weapons weren't equipped with bayonets. One at a time they started leaping up from their shallow trenches. The Australians closed in on them yelling and screaming at the tops of their voices. Through the swirling black-smoke a young Boer suddenly appeared in front of James. The Afrikaner raised his rifle to take a shot at him. The Australian leapt forwards thrusting his rifle at the same time. The bayonet pierced through the young man's bandolier. With a sheer look of terror on his face the blade sliced through his chest, dissecting his heart and then continued on through his torso, before protruding from his back. His eyes were large and bulging as he gave a blood-curdling cry, before blood gushed from his mouth.

For a moment James stood frozen. He was trembling violently. He felt the weight of the man's body on the end of his rifle, as the Boer's knees gave way and he sank to the ground. James struggled hard to pull the bayonet out and then he had to place his boot on the man's chest. He gave a hard pull and the bayonet finally came out covered with a crimson-coloured liquid.

James saw a movement to his right out of the corner of his eye. Another Boer was aiming his rifle at him. There was an explosion and something painful nicked the side of James' neck. The Boer began to reload his rifle. Without hesitating, James ran straight at him yelling his head off. The Boer quickly lifted his rifle to take another shot. James hurled himself at the man. The bayonet caught him under his chin at an upward angle. It entered his jaw and then went through his tongue. After piercing the roof of his mouth it drove through his brain and came out the back of his skull. The man went limp. James withdrew the bayonet as the Boer fell lifeless to the ground. James looked up and saw Lieutenant Darling approaching him through the smoky, grey haze.

'Mitchell!' the officer called out.

'Sir!' James replied trembling.

'Move forwards and rejoin your section! ...Move it! Move it!'

'Yes sir!' James started towards the kopje through the smoke filled air, still trembling with shock. The Boers from the abandoned shallow trenches had joined the others amongst the rocks and were firing from higher ground. James noticed Billy and George over to one side and made his way towards them. He soon arrived alongside and took cover behind a boulder while he caught his breath.

Moments later Corporal Vernon joined them from somewhere out of the confusion. 'Mitchell! ...O'Reilly!' he yelled above the noise of gunfire. 'And you Gleniste! ...Follow me!'

They took off after him, in and out and between the moss-covered granite boulders. It was hard going climbing the kopje and having to fire the rifle upwards at the enemy. Bullets ricocheted off the granite rocks sending showers of stone splinters in a thousand directions. Several struck George in the face. He dropped to his knees, letting go of his rifle and covering his face with both hands.

Billy stopped to check on him. 'Are you... okay... mate?' he asked breathlessly.

THE PLOUGH, THE GUN AND THE GLORY

George looked at both of his hands and saw they were covered in blood. Then he looked up at his friend. 'Well, I can still see you're ugly mug, so I reckon I'm not dead yet.'

'You stay here mate. I'll come back for you later.'

'No-way, I'm coming,' the wounded man replied. 'Help me up.'

Billy assisted him onto his feet. Then, something hit Billy in the shoulder with incredible force. It sent him reeling backwards down the slope of the kopje. He finally came to a halt against several rocks. George went chasing after him hardly able to see anything, calling out, 'Billy! ...Billy!'

Billy clutched the pain and the raging fire in his shoulder. He had never experienced such agony before. Not even when a spear was thrust through his thigh by an elder of the tribe, for sleeping with another man's wife. This was far worse. This felt as though a fire stick had been shoved inside his body. He mumbled something about a snake-serpent having bitten him.

Meanwhile, James and Corporal Veron were still fighting their way up the kopje. James had to take cover while he reloaded the empty magazine on his rifle. He was wondering what had happened to George and Billy when a Boer suddenly sprang at him from behind a thicket of bush. He took James completely by surprise. The Boer was wielding a large knife and he thrust it wildly at James. He caught the man by the arm and they wrestled for a few moments. The Boer suddenly went limp and then let go of James. He then fell heavily to the dusty ground, his back covered in blood. James looked behind him and saw Corporal Vernon standing a little way off, still pointing his rifle in his direction. 'Come on Mitchell!' he called out, 'keep moving!'

James picked up his rifle and rejoined him.

'Stay close to me this time!' he told James with authority.

James nodded. He tried to explain that he had stopped to reload, but the Corporal had taken off, so James went after him. Moments later they reached the top of the kopje. The noise from the Boer's mountain-guns was deafening. They could see the smoke bursting from the barrels through the bushes. There were four Boers manning each of the guns.

The Corporal quickly looked over his shoulder to find there was no one else but James. He turned to him saying, 'Where the hell are O'Reilly and Gleniste?'

'I don't know... they just vanished... on the way... up here!' he replied trying to get his breath back.

'Christ sakes! Okay Mitchell! You shoot the men manning the nearest gun. I'm going to move around behind the second gun and pick off those Boers. After that, we will both need to try and get the men on the third gun, before they get us. Give me a few minutes before you start shooting. Good luck.' He vanished amongst the scrub and rocks.

James waited a couple of minutes and then took careful aim. The Boers were busy loading another shell into the breach of the nearest mountain-gun. James squeezed the trigger. The rifle kicked hard against his shoulder. Instantly, one of the Boers went reeling to the ground. James pulled the bolt back ejecting the empty casing, and then shoved the bolt forwards again. Another bullet was loaded from the magazine into the breach of the rifle. He took quick aim as one of the Boer's turned around to see what was going on.

James squeezed the trigger. He hit the man in the shoulder and he tumbled backwards into the other two. They made a grab for their rifles while James loaded another bullet. He took quick aim and fired and another Boer dropped.

The corporal had just managed to reach a good position when he saw the first Boer go down. He took quick aim and shot one of the four men manning the second mountain-gun. He managed to get another before they realised what was happening. They immediately took cover behind the mountain-gun and returned fire. Cronje's men appeared to be everywhere now as bullets rained down on the two Australians, who quickly dived for cover behind the rocks.

Moments later, the Naval Brigade arrived and forced the Boers to retreat. Shortly after, James was thankful to see the West Australians arrive with Major Moor leading the charge. The fighting greatly intensified with bullets blasting away in all directions, sending rock shrapnel and sand hurtling through the air. A bullet struck James' bush-hat snapping the chinstrap and sending it flying through the air. He ducked his head instinctively. He then felt his head with his hand to see if there was any blood. At that moment Major

Moor ordered a bayonet charge and the Australians swarmed forwards once more.

The Boers retreated further amongst the rocks but continued fighting back with a barrage of rifle fire. James and several others dived for cover behind the mountain-guns as bullets whizzed and ricocheted dangerously around them. They in turn, sent a rain of lead towards the enemy as the battle raged on. Moments later, a runner arrived alongside Major Moor with a message. The officer opened the document and read it to himself. 'You are to immediately retire from the kopje. Fall back to our lines. Reform your men and wait for new orders. Lieutenant General Methuen.'

'Damn it!' the major cursed to himself in disbelief. He wiped the sweat from his brow as he looked over towards the bugler. 'Sound the retreat!' he reluctantly ordered.

'Sir?' The youngster wore a surprised look on his face.

'Sound the retreat!' the officer yelled again.

The bugler put the mouthpiece of the brass instrument to his lips and blew hard, and the order was blasted out over the kopje. Major Moor could see the utter look of disbelief written on the men's faces. He felt their disappointment as much as they did. 'Fall-back!' he shouted to a man near him. 'Move it!'

The other men, including James, having heard the retreat were staring towards the officer with blank expressions. The officer signalled again for everyone to fallback. Some of the men made their way over to him crawling on their stomachs with bullets singing past their ears.

'We have been ordered to fall back!' he told them. 'That's an order! Move it! Move it!'

The men reluctantly began to move off and made their way back through the rocks and scrub. Once the major could see no more of his men around he also retreated from the area. James suddenly remembered he had left his hat behind and ran back for it. He found it lying between the rocks and placed it back on his head. He looked over at the mountain-guns one more time and was just about to leave when he heard someone calling for help. He brought the rifle up as his eyes surveyed the immediate area. He could see the bodies of several seamen lying around. They appeared to be dead. James then heard the call for help again. He crept forwards to where the sound was coming from. An Australian was lying amongst the rocks.

James crawled over to him. He had been wounded and looked in rather a bad way.

'You're darn lucky I came back for my hat,' he said as he got to his feet. James quickly lifted the man up onto his shoulders. Grabbing his rifle with his free hand he headed off in the direction of the others, with bullets whizzing around them.

It was hard work descending the kopje carrying a wounded man on his back plus a rifle in one hand. The perspiration poured from him and his lungs felt as though they were on fire. While James was weaving his way between the boulders he lost his footing. The weight of the wounded man across his back brought him down. They both hit the ground hard and then rolled a few feet. James was winded and he just lay there gasping, sucking in the hot, dusty air. Once he had recovered sufficiently he got to his feet. The wounded man was a few feet away. James hauled him onto his back once again, picked up his rifle and then continued on down the slope.

40   At last he reached the foot of the kopje. James sank to his knees from sheer exhaustion and placed the man onto the black, burnt grass. For the moment all he could do was try and get his breath back. Once he had recovered slightly he then said, 'Okay, you just take it easy. I'm going to do my best to stop the bleeding. After that, I'll try and find you a field doctor.'

James pulled the field dressing kit off his shoulder and then undid the buttons on the man's jacket. It was soaked with blood. His trousers were the same. James pulled the jacket open and removed his braces. He then opened his blood-soaked shirt to find he had two bullet holes in his stomach. James tried to wipe the blood away with some wadding. Next, he sprinkled sulphur powder onto the wounds. He then took a handful of wadding and placed it over each of the bullet holes. With some difficulty he was able to get the bandage around the man's lower torso, but found that he had to pull the man's trousers down to enable him to get the bandages to stay in position. James did this by wrapping them around the top half of the man's thighs. Once he had finished, he then pulled the man's trousers up to also help keep the bandages in place.

'There,' he said, a little relieved that he had finally finished, 'that should do until we can get you some proper help.'

The man stared up at him. His vision was partly blurred and his face distorted from the pain. He felt around his stomach area with both hands. Then he looked at the blood on his hands saying, 'The buggers did a good job, didn't they?'

'Yeah. Try not to talk you need to save your strength.'

The man licked his dry lips. 'I've forgotten your name?'

'James Mitchell.'

...'Oh yeah, now I remember... It was me who stole your money onboard ship.'

James had always suspected him, but it was no longer of any importance. People were dying all around him and the last thing he had on his mind was money.

'You can have it back,' he continued, 'I think there's still fourteen quid, seven shillings and sixpence left. You'll find it in my kitbag.'

'It's not important. Don't worry about it now, Timothy.'

He frowned. 'How come you know my name?'

'I've know who you were ever since I saw you on the platform in Perth, the day we were departing for South Africa.'

Timothy appeared to find some hidden inner strength. 'Ah, you were the bloke I saw with Veronica? I knew there was something familiar about you, but I never quite figured it out.'

James didn't reply.

'Where do you know her from?'

...'That's my business.'

'She's still legally my wife, you know?'

'She ran away from you Timothy... She told me everything... how you would come home late at night drunk and savagely beat her and the boy.'

...'She never told you why though, did she?'

James didn't reply.

...'No! I thought not!' The man took hold of James by the arm. 'Did she ever tell you that Samuel was fathered by another man, a secret lover? Did she ever mention her many other secret love affairs?'

James said nothing. He was too stunned by what he was hearing.

'No! I didn't think she would!' he added, seeing the disbelief on James's face.

James' heart was racing. He still couldn't believe what he had been told. His mind was spinning. He wiped some sweat from his forehead with the palm of his hand.

The man on the ground coughed. It was painful and a little blood trickled from the corner of his mouth.

'You shouldn't be talking. You need to try and save your strength.'

The man let go of James' arm. He licked his dry lips once again. 'Can you give me a little water?'

James removed the water container from over his head. He pulled the cork out and poured a little into the man's mouth. A moment later Timothy passed out. James looked about to see if anyone was nearby. Moments later he caught a glimpse of George and Billy through the swirling smoke. He got to his feet and hurriedly made his way towards them.

THE PLOUGH, THE GUN AND THE GLORY

George's face was covered with blood. He was supporting Billy. The left side of Billy's jacket was covered in blood and his arm hung limply at his side. When George saw James he gasped out, 'Billy's coped... one in... the shoulder.'

James was relieved to hear that is wasn't something far more serious.

'We have to... keep on moving,' George puffed out. 'The Boers... could be right behind us... to finish us off.'

James glanced towards the kopje. There was no one that he could see. He turned to the two men again. 'One of our blokes is also over there.' He pointed in the general direction. 'He's been badly wounded. I've patched him up, but he needs a doctor.'

'Grab him mate, and let's keep going,' George replied anxiously.

Lieutenant Darling suddenly appeared from out of the swirling smoke. 'Come on you lot keep moving! ...And get that man to a field hospital,' he said pointing to Billy. 'Then reform into your sections.' The swirling grey-black haze swallowed him up again.

James went over to the wounded man and lifted him onto his back. Then, the three friends slowly made their way towards the British laager. The battlefield was strewn with smouldering debris, dead and wounded troops of the imperial army. Carcases of horse's and those that were still dying lay scattered around the field like mounds of anthills. In-between them, horse drawn ambulances with white flags fluttering in the light breeze, filtered their way through the carnage. Cape-carts followed behind collecting the dead, piling their bodies one on top of the other until the carts could hold no more.

James stopped near a wounded horse. He could plainly see that it was in terrible agony. The animal had been shot several times in the upper part of its legs and neck and was covered in blood. A young imperial cavalry rider lay lifeless nearby. James placed Timothy down on the ground and then he put his rifle close to the horse's head and pulled the trigger. He lifted Veronica's husband onto his back again and the three men continued staggering their way across the smouldering, blackened veldt.

41   General Cronje watched attentively through his binoculars as his commandos were pulled back. The man next to him was doing the same. 'Look sir!' he said excitedly, 'the rooineks are withdrawing from the field.'

'I have observed that Van.'

'I think we have made a blunder sir. We should have pushed forward now. We could win a glorious victory here today, bigger even than Stormberg, sir!'

'Who is in command here Van, you or me?' the general snapped back with an annoyed tone.

'You are, sir!'

'Then why are you questioning my decisions?'

The captain remained silent, which further annoyed the general.

'Damn it man, listen to me! ...If we try to defeat the British here we will have to take hundreds of wounded prisoners. I have only got two thousand men. I can't have my army tied up guarding prisoners... Besides, how many times do I have to remind you of our tactics? You know as well as I that our objective is to strike the enemy as hard as we can, then withdraw from the engagement before they can regroup. Our mobility is our strength, that's the only way we will win this war, Van!'

'Of course sir... the general is quite right. I apologise, I became excited when I saw the British retreating from the field, sir.'

'I want our wounded taken care of and our dead buried. Then, as soon as humanly possible, I would like to press-on to Belmont without delay.'

'Yes sir.'

'And captain.'

'Sir.'

'If you ever question my decisions again I will have you removed from your post. Is that understood?'

'I understand sir.' Captain Van der Merwe saluted and then rode off.

The general placed the binoculars to his eyes and surveyed the retreating British. He lowered the glasses and then dusted his bottle-green jacket as he said quietly to himself. 'We will meet again Lord Methuen, but, before that you will do battle with General Prinsloo.'

42

James stopped to rest for a moment due to exhaustion. Carrying the wounded man had sapped him of his strength. George and Billy joined him on the smouldering grass.

'You look buggered James,' George commented. 'I'll carry the bloke for you. You take Billy.'

'Thanks mate... I sure would... appreciate that,' he puffed out.

The three men sat in silence for a few moments trying to get their breath back.

'Listen!' James suddenly said, 'have you noticed how quiet it has gone?'

George got to his feet. He looked around the battlefield and then over towards the kopjes on either side of them. 'Well, bugger me,' he said scratching the back of his head.

'What's going on?' James asked.

'No idea mate, the Boers have withdrawn from the field,' he replied, almost in disbelief.

'Hey?' James couldn't believe it.

'They've all gone I tell you.'

At that moment a horse drawn ambulance pulled up alongside them. One of the medics jumped out of the carriage and came over. 'Is he dead or alive?' he asked looking down at the man lying on his back covered in blood.

'He's alive,' replied James, 'but only just.' He was relieved that help had at last arrived.

The medic knelt alongside the man. He opened his jacket and after a brief examination said, 'There's nothing anyone can do for him, except give him a proper burial.'

James looked over at Timothy's body. Then, he looked up at the medic. 'I carried him from the top of the kopje. I tried my best to patch him up and get him help.'

'He probably would have died anyway, he's been shot through the stomach and also the kidneys.' The medic turned his attention to Billy and George. 'You two can get a ride in the ambulance.' He looked across at James. 'You'll have to make your own way back.'

The ambulance left James standing alone watching them through the smoke-filled air. Moments later a Cape-cart pulled up. Two orderlies jumped off and came over. Without saying anything they picked Timothy's body up, placed it onto a stretcher, then carried it over to the cart. They threw it on top of a pile of other corpses and then left.

James picked up his rifle and then continued making his way towards the British laager. He looked up at the sky. It was rapidly growing darker with the setting sun. There were also heavy purple-black clouds on the western horizon and he wondered if it was going to rain during the night.

43   Once James arrived at the laager he found that everyone had been stood down for the night. He was told to go and sort out his kit before it got too dark. George had been attended to at the field hospital and was now making his way towards the place, where he and the others had left their kit that morning.

James spotted him and called out to him from a little distance. 'George! ...Hey George!'

George stopped walking and looked behind him. James was hurrying towards him. In the pale afternoon light James noticed that his face was orange from the iodine used to treat the cuts. The two men embraced one another. 'How's Billy doing?' James asked after a moment.

'The surgeon was still busy digging the bullet out of his shoulder when I left the hospital.'

'Well at least that's good news.'

'One of the nurses said we might be able to see him later tonight.'

'That would be nice... How are you feeling?'

'The iodine is stinging like mad but I'll live.' He looked at the wound on James' neck. 'You should have that seen to,' he said pointing, 'it could become infected.'

James felt the wound with his hand. 'It's just a nick. It should heal alright I've already put on some sulphur powder.'

George nodded. 'While I was at the hospital a young cavalryman was having his leg amputated at the knee. The poor bugger was screaming blue-murder. One of the nurses told me the surgeons have run out of chloroform. All they gave him was a few swigs of brandy. The nurse said it will take three days before they get re-supplies from Port Elizabeth.'

James shook his head. 'Let's pray that we don't get shot tomorrow.'

'There are badly wounded limeys by the hundreds over there, James. We got off lightly today. Only about twenty of our blokes were wounded. I think the only bloke that was killed was the one you were carrying.'

'He was Veronica's husband by-the-way.'

'Hey?'

'Yeah.'

'How do you know that?'

'He told me... He also confessed to stealing the money onboard ship... Somehow, I had always suspected him.'

'You never ever said anything to Billy or me about it.'

'I wasn't completely sure, George. I could have been wrong, you know. What if it had been someone else?'

'Mmm, I suppose so.'

'He said I would find the money in his kitbag. Fourteen quid seven shillings and sixpence.'

'Hey?' George couldn't believe the amount. 'Fourteen quid, seven shillings and sixpence?' he repeated. 'Hell, that's a lot of money mate. Prize fighting sure pays well. Maybe I should do that after the war when I get back home? I sure can't make that kind of money working as a jackeroo.'

'That's for sure.'

'How are you going to find it... the money?'

'I don't care about the money any more George.'

'Jesus, James, that's at least eleven weeks pay. Besides, it's the principle of the thing. You won that money fair and square. In my books it rightfully belongs to you and you should get it back.'

James gave a sigh. 'I suppose so.'

'If you don't someone else will, you can bet your last shilling on that. I'll bet you that someone's already going through his stuff this very moment.'

'Probably... Albert was the name of the bloke that was with him that night. If we can find him we will probably find the money.'

Shortly, the two men came across their kit, which was still piled together in a heap where they had left it earlier. Moments later someone came out of the darkness. It was Corporal Mc Whirter. 'Have you blokes eaten yet?' he asked.

'No corporal,' James replied shaking his head.

'Well you had better hurry over to the cookhouse or you won't get anything tonight.'

'What's for tea corporal?' George asked eagerly, 'anything exciting?'

'Yeah, bully beef, biscuits and a mug of tea or coffee, if you are lucky.'   'Bloody great!' George muttered. 'So where do we find this delicious meal?'

The corporal pointed. 'Follow those blokes.' He walked off into the semi-darkness.

They grabbed their plates and mugs from their kitbags and then scampered after the others. When they arrived they joined a long queue. At last it was their turn. Three biscuits and a lump of bully beef were plonked onto their plates. A muddy-colour tea was poured from large jugs into their mugs. They made their way back to their kit where they sat on the ground and began eating their supper.

George took a mouthful of his tea and then spat it out. 'Jesus, this tastes awful! ...I can't drink this muck.' He poured the tea onto the ground.

'James took a mouthful and also spat it out. 'What the hell did they make this with?' he asked pouring the foul liquid from his mug. 'We'll just have to drink water tonight. Tomorrow, we'll get ourselves organised and make our own tea in the billy.'

'And where will we get tea leaves from?' George asked.

'The cookhouse.'

He laughed. 'We couldn't get a rotten tomato from those darn limeys... Hell, and I was really looking forward to meat and vegies tonight... I'm damn famished I tell you.'

'Me too.'

'I've already lost weight, look how loose my uniform is.' He showed James. 'If I wasn't wearing braces they would be down around my ankles.'

THE PLOUGH, THE GUN AND THE GLORY

'If there is no war tomorrow, I'll try and catch us a rabbit or something for us to eat.'

'Do they have rabbits over here?'

'This is Africa George, the place must be crawling with animals of one type or another.'

'I suppose so, but I sure haven't seen anything around.'

'That's because we have been a little busy today... And anyway, if you were a wild animal would you hang around here with all the racket going on?'

'I suppose not.'

'They probably hide somewhere during the day and only come out at night once all the noise has stopped?'

'Yeah, I suppose so... Should we go and see Billy now?' George suggested getting to his feet.

'Okay.'

They headed off in the direction of the field hospital. When they arrived they found the place a hive of activity. Surgeons, doctors and nurses were running around in all directions, their aprons covered with blood. Most were carrying lanterns in order to find their way between the rows of wounded and dying men.

A putrid, sickly smell of singed hair and flesh from the cauterised wounds, hung heavily in the still air. Other odours like vomit, urine and excrement were mixed with sulphur-powder, carbolic acid and peroxide, with the stench of death everywhere. Men were crying out in agony begging to be relieved from their pain. A young man had lost both his arms from the elbows. Several others had lost a leg or a foot or had half of their face blow off. A number had lost their eyesight.

They continued to search for Billy and eventually a nurse told them to look outside the tent as many of the men had been taken there due to lack of space. They were both glad to get out of the marquee and into the fresh air. They found him shortly afterwards in the dim light of a lantern. The bullet had been removed, but he had lost a lot of blood and was delirious. He was mumbling something about Rambling Meadows and snake serpents.

James knelt down next to his face and said softly, 'What about Rambling Meadows, Billy?

'I see the snake serpent going there. It will bite somebody, the same as me.'

'You were shot by a damn bullet Billy, you superstitious bugger.'

He mumbled something else that James couldn't make out. James got to his feet. 'He's delirious. I think his Aborigine blood is coming out well and truly now. We'll have to come back tomorrow and see him, if we can.'

They left making their way through the myriad of wounded and dying men, and made their way back to their kit. 'We're going to need our greatcoats tonight, George. It's going to get cold out here later on, and to make things a little more unpleasant I think it's going to rain.' James was looking over at the lightning in the distance.

Someone approached them out of the dark. He was dressed in a tattered British uniform covered with dried blood. 'There's an empty tent going spare tonight,' he said with a strong cockney accent. 'You two may as well make use of it, if you like?'

'Hey, that's great. Thanks mate.' James put his hand out. 'I'm James Mitchell.'

The stranger refrained from shaking hands. 'Thomas Robson,' he said standing a little way back from them.

'This is George Gleniste,' James added.

'Bring your kit and follow me... I'll show you the tent.'

They grabbed their things and tagged along behind the stranger. The tent was only a short distance from where they were bivouacked. 'This is it,' Thomas advised, pointing it out.

'How come no one's using it tonight?' James asked out of curiosity.

The soldier gave a sigh. 'Two are dead and the other two are lying over there.' He pointed in the direction of the field hospital. 'They will most probably be dead by morning.'

James swallowed hard. 'I'm sorry to hear that.'

Thomas told them he had to go as he was very tired and wanted to go straight to bed. The two men watched him as he vanished into the dark.

James turned to George. 'That was pretty good of him offering us the tent, hey?'

'Yeah. He seems like a nice bloke, even if he is a limey. There was something a bit strange about him though, especially his eyes, don't you think?'

'As you said, he's a limey, so that would account for that.'

The two of them laughed heartily for a few moments. Then James' expression became more serious. 'Do you realise that this is the first time we have laughed since Joseph was killed?'

George nodded. 'So it is mate... It felt good... I have a feeling that it won't happen again for a long time.'

'Yeah... Well, I don't know about you, but I am also ready for bed. This is going to be pure heaven tonight,' said James before giving a yawn. 'It's sure been a long day.'

'Yeah, it sure has... We can sort all our gear out tomorrow when we can see what the heck we are doing in this place.'

They took their kit and threw it inside the tent, and then crawled in one at a time, together with their rifles. There were four bedrolls plus lots of kit lying around. James found a lantern. 'Hey, this is just what we need,' he said feeling pleased with his discovery.

'Well, I hope there are matches to go with it?'

'Yip, there sure are.' James struck a match and a small bright flame produced a soft glow. He shoved the naked flame onto the wick of the lantern, which burst into life throwing light into the interior of the tent. 'Now this is what I call living,' he said looking around the tent.'

'Damn right mate.'

They both pushed the other men's kit over to one side and then rolled out their bedding. James removed the bandolier first and let it drop to the ground. After that he undid the buttons on his jacket and removed it. 'Ahhh, that feels better, I can tell you.' He looked at it to see it was covered with dry blood. He threw it into the corner of the tent. Next, he pulled the braces off his shoulders and let them hang down the sides of his trousers. Then, undoing the buttons of his shirt he took that off. He then sat down and undid the putties and laces on his boots, and then slowly pulled his boots off. 'Oh, God, that feels so good,' he said with a sigh of relief.

Next, James carefully peeled off his socks as they were stuck to his feet with congealed blood. He threw both the bloodstained socks and boots outside the tent. He then examined his raw, burning feet in the flickering light of the lamp. 'I've got darn blisters the size of half-a-crowns,' he said glancing over at George.

'Me to.' He was also busy examining his feet.

Having removed his trousers James lay back on the blanket in his underwear. 'I sure could do with a nice hot bath tonight.'

'Fat chance of getting that around here mate.'

'I would even settle just for a wash.'

George blew air with his mouth onto his blisters. 'Maybe we could steal some hot water from the cookhouse?'

'That would be great. The only problem is I don't have the strength to do it. I've never felt quite so buggered in my whole life.'

'Me neither... I reckon it's because we haven't eaten properly for days mate. All we've had is bloody biscuits and tea, and we couldn't even drink that muck. I could sure do with a good chunk of beef or mutton right now. I can smell it in the air. I'll bet you someone out there is roasting meat over a fire.'

'Oh God George, don't torture me any longer.'

'Sorry mate, it's just that I can't seem to get the thought of food out of my head.'

James was exhausted. All he really wanted to do now was get some sleep. 'Night George.'

'Night mate.'

George blew the lantern out and darkness filled the tent. Now and then a flash of lightning would light up the interior for a brief moment. James tried to go off to sleep but was unable even though he was utterly exhausted. After awhile he sat up and stared out of the opening of the tent. He could see the flickering lights of several lanterns out on the battlefield as hospital staff continued their search for the wounded and dead. Every so often, the sound of gunshots would confirm the killing of another horse. A flash of lightning lit up the ink-black sky just as someone walked closely past the tent. James crawled his way over to the opening and peered out. He watched the man for a few moments before he was swallowed up in the dark. James crawled back to his bedroll. 'I'm sure I just saw that bloke who let us use the tent,' he said. 'He looked as though he was going towards the hospital.'

'I thought he said he was going straight to bed?'

'I guess he changed his mind.'

James lay back on the blanket staring at the top of the tent. Slowly, the numerous small fires dotted around the camp, grew smaller, eventually, only one or two flickered weird dancing shadows onto the tents. Later, James thought he saw the face of the young Boer that he had killed with his bayonet. It troubled him and he felt sick in his stomach and the sweat broke out on his forehead. He called out George's name.

'What?' The sound of James' voice had startled him as he was almost about to fall asleep.

James was relieved that he was still awake. 'Did you kill anyone with your bayonet today?'

…'Yeah... You?'

James gave a sigh. 'Yeah.'

'If you want to know, it was the worst feeling I have ever had mate.'

… 'I know what you mean.'

They were both silent for awhile until James said, 'So much has happened during the last few days.'

'Yeah.'

…'It's still hard for me to believe that Joseph's dead.'

George sighed but said nothing.

…'And now Billy is also lying wounded over at the hospital.'

'Yeah.'

…'And you were darn lucky that you didn't lose your eyesight today, mate.'

'Damn right,' George replied with relief.

...'We could have all died out there today George... You! Billy! Me!'

'Yeah mate... we sure could have.'

'I don't think this war is going to end as soon as everyone thinks it will George. Look what happened today... Look what happened at Stormberg. Half a British regiment were practically wiped out. Methuen's advance towards Kimberley has been held up for three days now... God knows what will happen tomorrow.'

'Try not to even think about it mate.'

The two men fell silent once again. Moments later there was a loud crack of thunder overhead, making both of them jump. The sound of heavy raindrops began falling on the tent.

'I'm sure glad we are sleeping in here tonight,' said James thankfully.

'Me to.'

Both men closed their eyes and listened to the rain, finally falling into a deep exhausted sleep.

44   James was woken early the next morning with someone shining a lantern into the tent. At first he had to shield his eyes from the flickering light and then he made a grab for his rifle. George had also woken. Still half asleep he stared wide-eyed at the lantern. He was a little bewildered and was trying to think where he was.

'Well bugger me!' the familiar voice of Corporal Vernon bellowed. 'I've been looking for you two blokes everywhere!'

The two men relaxed after realising they weren't under attack from Boers and released the grip on their rifles. James yawned and then shielded his eyes again from the lantern.

'Who gave you permission to sleep in here?' the corporal asked with an annoyed tone of voice.

'Some limey,' answered George, still half asleep.

…'Thomas Robson,' James added while scratching around his groin. He yawned again.

'Thomas Robson?' the corporal repeated sarcastically.

'Yeah, that's the bloke corporal,' George confirmed.

'Well it must have been his damn ghost! For your information, Robson happens to be listed on the death register notice. He and another feller from this tent were killed yesterday. The other two men who occupied this luxurious accommodation also died during the night in the hospital.'

'Hey?' James and George sat-up simultaneously. The two men were speechless with their hearts racing in their chests, both experiencing icy-cold shivers down their spines.

'How come I know all this, you might well ask yourselves?' the corporal continued, 'so, I'll tell you. Earlier this morning when I couldn't find you two and nobody knew where you were; I checked the hospital register to see if your names had been listed. As they weren't, I then thought to myself that maybe you had absconded during the night... However, as it had been raining I thought that I would check the vacant tents... And bingo whom do I find? ...I have a damn good mind to lay charges against you two. You are supposed to be bivouacked down there with the rest of the men so that we can find you when we need you! ...Now, get dressed, you have both been detailed for burial duties. Hurry up and fall-in outside! And bring your valise (bag containing entrenching tools) with you.'

The two men dressed as fast as they could. James grabbed his boots and socks from outside the tent. They were soaking wet and he muttered to himself for having left them out in the rain. He first wrung out his socks and started to pull them on, his blisters stinging like mad while he cursed under his breath. Both men grabbed their greatcoats and valises and then left the comfort of the tent. It was still dark and they were greeted by a cold damp morning with puddles of muddy water everywhere. A number of other men were standing around huddled together shivering.

Corporal Bishop arrived. 'Don't worry,' he said, 'you won't be feeling cold for long. You are going to be digging graves, lots of them. One hundred and thirty-eight in-all so that should give you plenty of time to get warm.'

A few of the men muttered something amongst themselves, which the corporal ignored. Then he said, 'I trust that all of you have brought along your entrenching tools?'

A few of the men hadn't.

'Everyone was told to bring valises'!' his voice had increased in volume and had an annoyed tone to it. 'Now, hurry up and get them!'

The men hurried off as the corporal then turned his attention to the remainder of the group. 'Right, I need twenty volunteers to go over to the hospital to start fetching the bodies.'

The men were slow to respond.

The corporal pointed to some of them. 'You lot over there have been volunteered.'

They were shown where the carts were and then went off in the direction of the hospital. The corporal then turned his attention to the remaining men. 'Come on you lot let's get going, and bring those stakes with you!' He pointed to a pile of wooden stakes lying in the mud.

The men followed behind him and once they reached the selected area the corporal brought them to a halt. He then commenced to pace-out each grave at approximately three-foot intervals. After that a sharpened wooden stake was knocked into the ground to mark the position. Once a grave was marked the men began digging. James and George were amongst the first to get started. The ground was hard despite the rain, which had fallen during the night and they soon discovered another problem, it was full of small rocks.

'Bugger me!' George complained after his pick had struck rock, hurting his wrist and sending sparks flying. 'This is going to be much harder than we thought.' He wheeled the pick again and struck more rock.

The first cartload of bodies arrived and a corpse was dropped off like a sack of potatoes alongside each of the marked gravesites. After half-an-hour James took the shovel from George and he started to scoop out the soil and rocks. Eventually, they had both completed two shallow graves and were taking a breather before starting another two.

The corporal came around checking on the progress. 'Come on you two there's no time to hang about!'

George glanced over at James. 'Did we actually volunteer for this, or were we press-ganged?'

'You volunteered!' the corporal butted in, 'so get on with it, we haven't got all day there's a war to be fought!'

The morning sun had broken through the clouds and the perspiration began pouring from the men's bodies. One after another they stripped down with their braces hanging loosely down the sides of their drill trousers. The warmth had produced another menace with flies beginning to swarm around the corpses. They also pestered the men digging the graves, attacking their eyes and biting the bare skin on their backs and arms. During the digging, one of the corpses suddenly sat upright. A couple of the men nearby fled from the scene in panic yelling, 'Corporal! Corporal! This bloke's still alive!'

The corporal went over to the upright corpse. He placed his one boot on the legs and then with his other foot he pushed the body down onto its back. A loud groaning sound expelled from the mouth. 'Now he is dead again,' he said looking at the two men who were standing a little way off. 'Now come on, and get back to digging!'

The two men approached the corpse cautiously. 'Are you sure corporal?' one of them asked nervously.

'You have my word.'

The two men, not yet fully convinced, picked up their tools and continued digging, keeping one beady eye on the body at the same time.

Finally, the graves were ready to receive the fallen men who had died for the glory of the Empire. The corpses wrapped in blood-soaked uniforms were placed, one at a time, into the newly excavated holes. Once that was done a British army chaplain gave a short service and then the closing-up of the graves began.

James started shovelling sand over one of the corpses when he noticed the eyes open and close. He stood back for a moment with his heart thumping in his chest. 'Bugger me, that gave me a darn fright!' he said aloud.

George looked across at him. 'What's that?' he asked.

'I just saw this blokes eyes open and close.'

George came over. 'Damn spooky all these corpses, if you ask me... What about the one that sat up?
I don't like things like that... I'll be glad when we have finished this job and get the hell out of here.'

'Me to.'

George was returning to the other grave as James scooped another shovel of soil over the body. He saw the eyes open and close again. 'Oh Jesus!' he said loudly jumping back from the grave for the second time. 'There! ...You see? It did it again! ...Maybe this bloke's still alive or something?'

'Well he looks pretty dead to me!'

James wiped his sweating hands on the back of his pants. Then he knelt down next to the side of the grave. He touched the corpse lightly on the hand and then on the face. The eyes sprung opened again. 'Oh, God!' he hollered, clambering back to his feet with his heart racing wildly. 'This bloke's still alive I tell you!' he said looking over at George.

'Pack it in James, you're starting to give me the damn creeps!'

This time James saw the eyes blink several times. 'George! Quick, give me a hand to get the body out of the grave.'

'This is going too far now,' he protested as he came over. He looked down at the body for a moment. 'Can you imagine being buried alive? The thought makes me go cold. I suppose it has happened, hey? I mean it's not imposable, is it?' He looked up at James.

'Another thing,' James continued without answering his question. 'I touched him and he doesn't feel very cold to me. Not like the other corpses we touched.'

'So how can we tell if his dead or not?' George asked rubbing the whiskers on his chin. He looked down at the body again. 'Maybe I could stick my bayonet in his foot or something?'

James shook his head. 'I think we should get him out so we can have a proper look, don't you?'

'Well come on then. I'll take the legs you take the arms.'

They lifted the body out and placed it onto the ground. James knelt down and placed his hand under the man's neck. 'Now, you feel how warm that is.'

George crouched down and did as James had asked. The eyes opened again and he quickly scrambled away falling onto his backside. 'Jesus! This is horrible!' he complained. 'Don't ask me to touch it again!'

Suddenly the corpse croaked out, 'W…water.'

Both men jumped to their feet with fright.

'By God! He's…he's alive! George! He's alive!' James shouted. He fetched his water bottle and placed it to the man's lips. 'Here mate,' he said pouring a little into the man's mouth. The man spluttered and coughed a little. James got to his feet and shouted for the corporal to come over.

'What the hell is going on with you two?' he asked sarcastically. 'Don't tell me we have another corpse that has miraculously come back to life,' he added.

'This bloke has he's still alive,' James said excitedly, 'I swear it!'

'Yeah, like that other stiff that sat bolt-upright and scared the living daylights out of those two clowns,' the corporal replied sarcastically.

'Well, this bloke's definitely alive I tell you,' James argued.

'Mind out of the way and let me take a look.' He knelt down and lifted the man's one eyelid. The corporal looked at the eye for a moment and then he placed his hand over it casting a shadow. He wasn't sure if the pupil enlarged or not. Then he lifted the other eyelid and repeated the procedure.

'How can tell if he's dead or not by doing that, corporal?' James asked.

'I was told when you are dead that the pupils of your eyes don't enlarge or contract with variations of light.'

'What are his eyes doing then?'

'I'm not sure... well I'm not a darn doctor Mitchell! Besides, it's difficult for me to tell in this kind of light. There's also another way. If you place your hand on the neck just below the Adam's apple you should feel a heartbeat.' The corporal felt his neck for a pulse. He wasn't convinced if there was one or not. The corpse suddenly croaked out for water again. The corporal got such a fright that he ended up landing on his backside. The men standing around burst into boisterous laughter, more from nerves than anything else.

The corporal got back to his feet feeling a little embarrassed and brushing the back of his trousers. 'I think maybe you are right Mitchell.'

'I knew it!' James replied joyfully.

'Get the cart over here and let's take this feller back to the hospital in double-quick time. Let them have a look at him... Now move it! Move it!'

The two men ran off for the cart, standing a little way off. They hurried back and the man was loaded on to it. Together, with two other men, James and George set off towards the hospital. When they arrived James called out for one of the doctors. Eventually, someone came over and James explained the story briefly to him as calmly as he could.

'Very well then, get him off the cart,' the doctor said in a disbelieving tone of voice. 'Take the body over to that table,' he pointed, 'so that I can take a proper look at him.'

James and the others soon had the bloke laid out on the blood-soaked wooden table for examination. The doctor carried out a routine check by using his statoscope. Then, he looked over at James. 'This man is quite definitely alive, but I don't know for how long.'

James and George were both given a pat on the back by some of the other men. Then it was back to filling in the remainder of the graves. Finally, the loose rocks, which had previously been dug up were piled on the top. The weary men then collected up their clothing, rifles and entrenching tools and then made their way back to camp.

As they arrived Lieutenant Parker approached them with new orders. 'You men, get your kit sorted out, we are moving out within the hour.'

'Aren't we going to get any breakfast, sir?' James asked in protest. 'I'm starving.'

'There's only biscuits and coffee this morning. You had better move it before the kitchen packs up.'

James and the others rushed over to the cookhouse. As they arrived, one of the cooks, a large overweight sergeant, who was sweating profusely looked over at them. 'What do you lot want?' he asked rudely.

'Something to eat and drink, we are famished, mate.'

'Mate?' he repeated sarcastically. 'First of all private, you will address me as sergeant. Is that quite clear?' he said with some arrogance.

'Right sergeant,' James replied. 'Please may we have something to eat and drink?' he asked as politely as possible under the circumstances.

'May we have something to eat and drink?' the sergeant repeated sarcastically looking them up and down. Then he looked over at the other cooks. 'Did you lot hear that?' He looked back at the men. 'Well now, I regret to advise that you are one hour too late. We have closed this restaurant for the day. At this moment we are preparing to pack up. In case you don't know it we are moving this fine establishment in the direction of Belmont.'

'Look sergeant,' James continued, 'we were told we could get biscuits and coffee. Now surely, that can't be all that difficult, can it?'

'Why didn't you lot come at the proper time, like everyone else? Do you think we are running a luxury hotel here for you Australians or something?'

James could feel his temper rising. 'Listen, we have been out digging graves since four 'o-clock this morning burying the dead! Your dead! British soldiers who were killed on the battlefield or died overnight in hospital! ...Now! Do you think we could possibly have the biscuits and coffee?'

'You lot had better bugger off before I get annoyed with you!' the arrogant sergeant replied, making a two-fingered gesture with his hand.

That was it. George had enough of the limey cook. He made a rush at the overweight man grabbing him around the throat. He then punched him on his nose sending him reeling backwards into the other cooks. They in turn fell against pots and pans, which went crashing to the ground.

'Now! Let's have those biscuits and coffee before we demolish the rest of this damn place!' he yelled at them.

'Okay! Okay!' One of the other junior cooks said rushing to get the biscuits.

Coffee was quickly made and the biscuit ration handed out. James then grabbed the whole box of biscuits and dished them around. They ate with a ferocious appetite and gulped down the coffee. When they were finished James said to the sergeant, 'Now what was so difficult about doing that! Hey?' Without waiting for a reply the men started to make their way back towards their bivouacs.

'I'm going to have charges laid against you lot!' The sergeant yelled after them, wiping the blood from his nose. 'I know who you are! You Australian bastards! ...Bloody convicts the lot of you!'

'Yeah, good on yah, mate!' George yelled back. 'You do that you limey bastard!' He looked across at James hunching his shoulders. 'Why are we fighting for this bloody lot, hey? It's enough to make anyone join the damn Boers.'

Everyone laughed heartily. It felt so great to have a good laugh.

45   Lord Methuen paced the floor of his tent while his generals stood around nervously watching. His arms were behind his back and that was not a good sign for those who knew him. After awhile he stopped and looked at each officer in-turn. 'Cronje may think he has us beaten gentlemen! But, I can assure you all here right now that I will soon bring him to heel! That I promise gentlemen! ...Henceforth, we will no longer play at the Boers game! Instead, we will dictate the terms! ...We will choose the ground where and when we fight!'

The generals shuffled their feet but remained silent.

Lord Methuen continued, 'Cronje's retreat yesterday was a tactical error. He has now afforded us the opportunity to turn the tide gentlemen. He has unwittingly left the door wide-open for us to move swiftly onto Belmont.'

One of the imperial generals raised his white-gloved finger.

...'You have something to say, General Colvile?'

'Yes sir... If I may interrupt the Lieutenant General for a moment, with your permission, sir?'

Lord Methuen gave a sigh then nodded his head. 'Very well if you must! What is it?' he asked impatiently.

'As you are aware sir, one of our foremost problems has been with our scouting. This has been mainly due to Rimington's Tigers having been reduced in numbers. In addition, many of the scouts who have gone out have not been heard of since. We can only presume that they were either killed by Boers or the kaffirs or perhaps deserted altogether, sir.'

...'Where is this all leading to general? We don't have all night!'

'Quite right sir... I believe that we need to replace the missing men sir. Perhaps increase their numbers? We need them to be well ahead of our columns while on the march. This would greatly reduce the risk of surprise attacks by the Boers sir.'

Lord Methuen stroked his moustache looking thoughtful. 'Very well, I see no reason why we should not entertain the idea.'

'Thank you sir, I will see to it personally.'

THE PLOUGH, THE GUN AND THE GLORY

'Where will these additional scouts come from general?'

'From the cavalry sir, I happen to know of a number of good men who would make excellent scouts sir.'

'I am sure that you do general... However, as you are aware the cavalry has already been stretched to the limits. Besides, they are far too valuable to be used as scouts, therefore you will have to look elsewhere.'

...'Yes sir.'

'Furthermore general, I don't think these additional scouts of yours should be drawn from the British regulars. Instead, they should be selected from amongst the colonial regiments, preferably the Australians.'

General Colvile was rather surprised by this decision. 'May I be so presumptuous as to ask the Lieutenant General why, sir? After all, the Australians are mere civilian volunteers. They still have much to learn about the art of warfare, sir.'

Lord Methuen continued to stroke his moustache. 'That maybe so general... However, both the New South Wales Lancers and the infantry contingents have been highly praised by several imperial officers after yesterdays action.'

'So I am led to understand, sir. But scouts, well, I really think that is quite another matter all together, sir?'

Lord Methuen's face became a little flushed as his blood pressure rose. 'You have presented your opinion general, and I have given the matter my consideration. Nevertheless, my decision still stands.'

'Very well sir... May I presume that the Lieutenant General intends these additional scouts to be drawn from the New South Wales Lancers, sir, as they already have the necessary equestrian experience?'

Lord Methuen looked thoughtful for a moment before replying, 'Well you have presumed wrongly General Colvile, that is not my intention at all... First and foremost, there are only twenty-nine Lancers; therefore I would like to keep them intact. We can make far better use of them on the battlefield. Instead, I want you to draw these new scouts from amongst the infantry contingents. You may select two men from each of the six Australian colonies. Find men who already possess the necessary equestrian experience, stockmen and drovers, that kind of thing. Men who are used to long hours in the

151

saddle and also to the harsh conditions experienced in the outback.'

'Very well sir, as the Lieutenant General pleases.'

'Good! ...Then let us not waste any more valuable time general. We have a long and hard ride ahead to reach Belmont before sundown!'

46 Corporal Vernon was making his way through the West Australian Contingent, with the men busy packing their gear in preparation to move out. He spotted James from a little way off and called out his name loudly. 'Mitchell! ... Mitchell!'

James looked up and watched him approaching. He wondered what lousy task the corporal had planned for him this time.

'Mitchell! I have some good news for you,' he said with a big smile as he arrived. 'You've been volunteered for a new task.'

'Oh yeah! By who might I ask? Or is that a stupid question?'

'Never mind who!'

...'What is it this time?'

'How many times do I have to tell you that you are to address me as corporal?'

...'What is it this time, corporal?'

'I am sure that you will be more than happy to know that you will be leaving the infantry.'

James said nothing.

'Major Moor has requested your immediate presence. So, I suggest that you leave your kit here and come with me.'

'I've only just put it all on.'

'So, take it off again. Just bring your rifle.'

James undid the straps and pulled the heavy pack off his back and dumped it on the ground. He followed the corporal to the officer's tent. The corporal announced their arrival. James was then called into the tent. Major Moor and Lieutenant Parker were seated at a small table. James came to attention and saluted both officers.

'Thank you Corporal you may leave now,' the lieutenant advised him.

The corporal saluted, turned and left the tent.

James' heart was racing. 'What was going on?' he wondered, feeling the sweat under his armpits running down his torso.

'During our short time together Mitchell,' the major began, 'I have received a number of reports with regards to your behaviour. Firstly, you were involved in a bar brawl during the train journey from Perth to Albany. Secondly, whilst onboard ship you were placed in the brig for prize-fighting no less. More recently, a sergeant from the British catering division claims that you were involved in an incident at the cookhouse, when apparently the sergeant was punched in the nose. Furthermore, you have been in conflict with a number of corporals on more than one occasion.'

'Yes sir.'

'On the other hand however, you certainly impressed Mr Churchill with your accurate shooting whilst proceeding to De Aar. And during battle yesterday you almost single-handedly captured no less than three Boer mountain-guns. You then carried a wounded man down from the kopje and attended to his wounds. Early this morning you plucked a British Dragoon from a certain early grave.'

'Is he going to be alright sir?'

'I understand he's doing rather better than the surgeon first expected. He will likely be shipped back to England within a month or so.'

'That's good news sir.'

'The reason I had you brought here private, is that I understand from our enlistment records that you possess good equestrian skills having worked as a jackeroo.'

'Yes sir, on my father's property near Wickepin.'

'Lord Methuen has requested for a number of Australian infantrymen to be transferred to Rimington's Scouts. Each of the six colonies' will select two suitable men for the position. As you appear to have the required background the general is presently seeking, you have therefore been considered as a suitable candidate.'

'Thank you sir, I am very pleased to learn that.'

'Don't be so eager Mitchell you haven't heard all the conditions yet. Firstly, scouting is an extremely dangerous job. Should the Boers regrettably catch you they will shoot you on sight. The kaffirs will also kill you. You may be required to operate alone on some occasions, perhaps for a number of days on end.'

'That's fine sir, I have no problems with that.'

'Well, you may change your mind after awhile?'

'I doubt that sir.'

'You will carry few provisions with you. More-than-likely you will be required to live off the land for much of the time.'

'I understand sir.'

'From nightfall to daybreak you will live in the dark without the comfort or warmth of a campfire. You will have to sleep on the ground in the cold and the rain. There are highly poisonous snakes, scorpions and even wild animals that could harm you. Another thing, should you become wounded you will have to patch yourself up, if you are able. And, should you not be in a position to make it back to our lines you could die alone out there on the veldt. Perhaps a slow and agonising death... Still interested?'

James nodded. 'Yesss sir,' he replied keenly.

'All right then, your task will be to ride well ahead of the advancing columns. You will need to survey the landscape for positions that could possibly be used by the Boers to attack our advancing columns. If thought necessary, you should make rough sketches of suspect areas of terrain. Most importantly, you are to report back the movements, positions and strength of the enemy, things of that nature.'

'Yes sir... May I ask the major who will provide the horse and saddlery, sir?'

'The British will provide you with everything you require. They will also explain your duties in greater detail. Lord Methuen is apparently under the impression that we can probably do the task as efficiently as the present scouts... What do you think Mitchell?'

'I think the Lieutenant General is an extremely wise bloke sir.'

Both officers smiled at James' description of the most senior British officer.

'Well then, you had better not let the Lieutenant General down,' Major Moor added.

'No sir.'

THE PLOUGH, THE GUN AND THE GLORY

'When you leave here you are to report to Major Rimington's Tigers.'

'Yes sir.'

'There's one other thing Mitchell. Your name has been put forward by Lieutenant Parker recommending you for promotion.'

James couldn't believe what he was hearing. 'Sir?'

'You are to receive the rank of corporal.'

James swallowed hard as he thought, 'What's going on, am I going to wake up and find out that I'm dreaming?

'Both the lieutenant and myself believe that you rightly deserve the promotion in recognition of your outstanding courage shown under fire during the battle on the kopje.'

'Thank you major, and you to lieutenant... May I have permission to say something sir.'

'You may.'

'It was Corporal Vernon who led the attack on the Boer guns, not me sir.'

The major nodded. 'That's very honest of you Mitchell. However, if it eases your mind any I can assure you, that both myself and the lieutenant are well aware of the corporal's invaluable contribution to the battle.'

'Yes sir.'

'Just for the record Mitchell, it was Corporal Vernon who praised the accuracy of your marksmanship and also your courage under fire.'

James was surprised to hear that. 'I see? ...Thank you for telling me sir.'

'Naturally, your pay will be adjusted accordingly. By holding the rank of corporal you will receive four shillings and nine-pence per day, of which half will be deferred until your arrival back in Australia.'

'Thank you sir.'

'We require one other suitable man for the position. We were considering another man in your section, Private O'Reilly. However, as he is in hospital with a shoulder wound we need to find someone else.'

'Then sir, may I recommend Private Gleniste?'

The major smiled. 'Is he the right man for the job though?'

'Yes sir, I have known him for a long time and can highly recommend him to the major.'

'Very well... In that case have him sent to me corporal.'

'Yesss sir.'

'Good luck corporal.'

'Thank you sir.' James saluted, turned smartly and left the officer's tent.

He almost ran back to tell George the exciting news. At first, George thought James was pulling his leg, but finally he accepted that James was telling the truth, and then he raced off towards the major's tent. James then made his way over to the water cart to refill his bottles. While proceeding there he came across Corporal Vernon. There was a moment of awkward silence between them. Corporal Vernon was the first to speak. 'Well Mitchell, I can't exactly say that I am sorry to see you leaving us.'

'How come you put a good word in for me with the major?'

'You deserved it. Besides, I was only doing my duty and don't think for one moment that I have gone soft on you Mitchell.'

'Yeah, well thanks all-the-same.'

'Anyway, congratulations on your promotion to the rank of corporal.' He stuck his hand out and they shook hands.

'Thanks.'

Corporal Vernon walked off with James watching him. He then thought to himself, 'He's not such a bad bloke when you get to know him I suppose.' He turned and then proceeded towards the water cart to refill his bottles.

47 Sometime later, James and George said goodbye to the blokes whom they were friendly with, picked up their kit and made their way over to the Rimington Tigers stables. When they arrived they met the eight other Australians. From there they were quickly shown their horses by a couple of stable-hands.

'That one's yours corporal,' one of them said pointing out a big chestnut gelding to James. 'He's from England. His name's Wellington and he hasn't been ridden for awhile... not since the surgeon took a few bullets out of him. The rider was killed.'

James patted the horse on the snout as he talked to him. 'G'day Wellington, my name's James... you and I are going to be spending a lot of time together. So, I hope that you're going like me?'

The horse snorted and then gave a little whinny, nodding its head at the same time, as though it understood him.

'I'll leave you two to get acquainted,' the stable-hand said giving James a wave with his hand.

'Thanks mate.' James turned his attention back to the horse. 'You and I have something in common, you know... Both of us are in a strange land fighting a war far from our homes... I have a horse over in Australia. His name's Thunder... I miss him a lot.' James walked around him brushing his coat with his hand at the same time. He liked the horse. He then checked his hooves one at a time. After that he looked at the scars left by the bullets. There were four in total. There was also another large scar that ran along the horses' upper right leg. James wondered what had caused that. After awhile he left Wellington and went over to George. His horse, also a chestnut, was called Norwich.

'So what do you think of him?' James asked.

'He looks good... I think he will do the job just fine... And yours?'

'I like him.'

Shortly after, a sergeant took the men across to a large marquee where several imperial officers were waiting for them. The men were told to sit down on the canvas floor.

Once everyone had settled down Major Rimington addressed the men.

'We are not normally in the habit of sending untrained men out into the veldt to become prey for the Boers, kaffirs, wild animals or vultures,' he said with an Oxford-English accent. 'However, as you have been thrust upon us at rather short notice we are obliged to make the most of you. As you know we are breaking camp shortly and advancing towards Belmont. Therefore, we have less than two hours to teach you some of the basic scouting requirements, and then also get you prepared.' He looked the men over one at a time. 'I trust you are all acquainted in the art of map reading?'

The men appeared to have blank expressions on their faces.

'If any of you are not then this is the time to raise your hand.'

All hands went up with the exception of one man.

The major shook his head. 'I trust that you can all read and write? Those who cannot raise your hand.'

This time no hands were shown.

'Well, thank God for that,' he said with a relieved tone of voice. 'I have decided that as you are untrained in the art of scouting, each of you will be temporarily attached to a regular scout. You will travel in pairs. Hopefully for your sake neither the Boers, kaffirs, snakes or other wild animals will get you. You will take your orders from your appointed scouts. You will observe and learn the skills of scouting from them in as short a time as possible.... Good luck gentlemen.'

48   Wellington steadily plodded between the dry scrub, almost in a trance like state, while following the horse in front. The South African scout was heading towards several distant kopjes as they made their way across flat, open veldt. Every now-and-then he would stop his horse and point out something to James that he thought he should know about.

They had been travelling for the best part of three hours and were gradually nearing two small isolated kopjes. The man at the front stopped his horse and then half turned in the saddle to enable him to see James. 'You see those kopjes ahead?' he asked, pointing his finger in the general direction.

'Yeah,' James replied, peering towards them through the shimmering heat.

'Keep your eyes fixed on them. There could be Burghers (Boers) observing us from there. I suggest you un-sling your rifle from your shoulder and carry it across the saddle. That way you can use it quickly if need-be.'

'Right.' James did as instructed. He liked the man up-front even though they had only met some hours earlier. His name was John Smith. He had told James that he had migrated from England to Grahamstown, in the eastern Cape colony, as a young boy with his parents and two younger sisters. Before the war he worked with his father in the family hardware business. His oldest sister, Gwendolyn, had joined the South African Medical Corps to serve as a nurse.

It was extremely hot as they proceeded towards the semi-barren kopjes. Flies pestered him the whole time. James could also feel the sun burning his arms and legs through his uniform, and the sweat from his armpits was wetting the shirt under his jacket. The sky overhead was growing darker though, as huge purple-coloured-clouds began building-up. And then occasionally they would block-out the sun bringing some temporary relief from the heat.

James looked upwards at the swirling masses of dark cotton wool. A rainstorm would sure be a welcome, he thought. Once again his eyes fixed on the kopjes ahead. He wondered if they would be able to find shelter for the night, because, as hot as he was the thought of being soaking wet the whole night wasn't all that appealing. Still, if he were in the infantry things wouldn't be any better. He was glad to be in the saddle again and he felt completely at home. He leaned forward slightly and gave Wellington a pat on the side of his neck.

The kopjes gradually grew larger looming up from out of the scrub and flower-covered veldt. Now that they were closer, James could see that there were a number of trees and bushes amongst the rocky outcrops. Finally, the kopjes towered above the men on horseback.

John half turned in the saddle in order to look at James. 'We'll leave our horses here and climb the larger of the two kopjes. From up there we'll be able to scan the area for miles around.'

'Right.'

'Take your rifle, water, map and compass with you,' John added as both men dismounted. 'Another thing, you had better remove your spurs. We don't want to be advertising ourselves up there.'

Once they were both ready they made their way up the side of the small hill with John in the lead. It was hard going and both men puffed for air as they weaved their way between the rocks and bushes. Once or twice both men almost lost their footing on the loose sand, which concealed the smooth rock surface underneath. Sometimes they stopped to catch their breath and take in the view.

Finally, they made the last few feet onto the top of a large overhanging rock. The view far below them of the shimmering veldt was quite spectacular. James took a few gulps of his water as his eyes scanned the horizon. 'Ahhh, that's better,' he said wiping his mouth with the back of his hand.

'Take small sips only to conserve your water,' John advised. 'At this point in time we have no idea when we will next be able to replenish our bottles.'

James nodded and replaced the cork.

'Just remember that you may also have to give your horse water if we don't find any by sundown.'

James nodded again and then he looked up at the ever-darkening sky. 'I think we'll be lucky and get rain tonight.'

'Maybe... But James never ever gamble on the unpredictable. Out here, it could cost you your life.'

James nodded.

THE PLOUGH, THE GUN AND THE GLORY

'I'm now going to give you a basic lesson in map reading. I want you to open the map and then I'll point out several features of the landscape to you.'

James opened the flap of the canvas bag, pulled out the map and then unrolled it.

'You will also need the compass.'

James removed it from the canvas bag.

'Firstly,' John continued, 'using the compass, I want you to locate north for me.'

James placed the navigating instrument onto a flat surface of the rock. He then rotated it until the needle pointed to the north.

'Good.' John was pleased. 'One important tip to remember is that large rocks can interfere with the compass reading and give you a false north position. Your rifle can do the same so make sure that it's not close to the compass. John pointed towards the horizon. 'Now we know the direction of magnetic north. If you look at your map you will also find that the north point is also indicated.'

James quickly found it printed on the bottom left-hand side.

'This time I want you to place your compass on top of the map. Then, line-up both the compasses north point with that shown on the map.'

It took a moment for James to do that.

'Good. Now that we have both map and compass pointing in the same direction, we are ready to find out where we are.'

John then pointed out on the map, several prominent features of landscape surrounding them, items such as kopjes and rivers. He then showed James where those features were in reality, using the binoculars to get a good view of them. Then, he got James to show him on the map which kopje they were standing on by taking bearings. He did that without any difficulty and John was pleased with his progress. The lesson continued for another half an hour with John going over the more important aspects of navigating the land.

'There may be a time when you have neither compass nor map for some reason,' John continued. 'In that case you'll need to use the sun to give you east and west directions. At night you can also use the moon for the same purpose. Better still, if it's not too cloudy, make use of the Southern Cross. If you are lost and you are on foot, travel at night and rest during the day. That way you'll conserve both your strength and prevent dehydration. Remember that rivers run downhill and will eventually reach the sea. By following a river you will have a constant supply of drinking water. You may also be able to catch fish for food.'

James was also given a quick lesson in scouting methods, and received some handy tips on how to cover his tracks. Finally, John felt that James had learned enough for his first day and told him to pack his things away. John was also interested in hearing a little about Australia. James tried to explain how vast the colony of Western Australia was. He also told him about Rambling Meadows and his parents, and about his brother and sisters, where he went to school, and so-forth.

Eventually John said, 'I think we should be on our way now as we still have quite a bit of scouting to do today. In-case you have forgotten there is a war going on down there.'

After placing the compass and map into the canvas bag they began making there way down the kopje with John leading the way.

49   About a third of the way down the kopje, John suddenly stopped and surveyed the ground around them.

'What is it?' James asked as he caught-up with him.

John pointed to the sand. 'Footprints. They weren't here on our way up.'

'Are they Boers?' James asked a little nervously.

'No. They're kaffir's footprints. See how broad the foot is. Only kaffir's have got feet like that mainly because they go bare foot.'

'Will they be a threat to us?'

'Maybe… depends on whose side they are on.'

'What do you mean whose side they are on?' James had heard that the blacks were reasonably neutral, as this was essentially a white man's war, which the blacks were staying well out of. But then, you couldn't always believe what you hear.

'They could be renegades,' John advised, 'they will kill any white man no-matter who he is. Sometimes I think they hate the British more than the Boers. They could also be scouting for the Boers or perhaps out hunting for rock dassies.'

'What are those?'

'Rock rabbits?'

'Oh.' James' eyes surveyed the surrounding area, and then they returned to John. 'How would we know that?'

John smiled. 'That, my Australian friend, is the big question. If we come across any kaffir's and they start shooting at us then we'll know. Stay extra alert until we are well away from here. The last thing I would want is for you to get yourself killed on your first day out as a scout.'

'Me to mate, believe me.'

'Can you imagine what Rimington would have to say to Lord Methuen?'

James didn't reply but he had a good idea.

John waved a fly from his face. 'I can assure you that he wasn't very happy with this whole arrangement. In-fact he was damn annoyed. He wanted trained men as scouts not a bunch of Australian farmers or whatever you blokes call yourselves over there.'

James still didn't say anything. He was far too busy looking around checking for any signs of immediate danger. They continued down the slope of the kopje making their way between large overhanging rocks and thick bushes. A sudden, loud clap of thunder overhead gave James a fright. He lost his footing and went tumbling to the ground. He rolled over once or twice before coming to an abrupt stop against a small rock. As he looked up he saw John stagger slightly and then he dropped from James' sight.

Next thing, two black men were seen running over the rocks in front of him. They were both armed with guns. The adrenalin kicked in and James felt his heart skip a beat. He lifted the rifle and took a quick shot at the leading man. He reloaded and then saw another to his left. James fired a round in his direction. The man shot back. James ran for cover behind some rocks. Once there, James reloaded while sweeping his eyes across the rocks looking for the attackers. His heart was racing wildly. He wondered if John had been badly hurt. He needed to get to him. James looked over to his right. There was a gap between the rocks, which appeared to be just wide enough for him to squeeze through. He took off in the direction of the opening.

Gunfire broke out kicking up the dust and sand all around him. Bullets ricocheted off the rocks producing high-pitched noises, and sharp fragments of stone stung his face and arms. James squeezed through the narrow gap and then made his way towards the shelter of an overhanging rock. A black man wielding a spear suddenly appeared from nowhere. James pointed the rifle at him and pulled the trigger. Blood exploded from the man's chest and he went reeling backwards. The Australian quickly reloaded before coming out from under the rock. There was a man running across the top. James took quick aim and shot at him. He hit him in the side of his torso and he was catapulted from the rock.

Once again the rifle was reloaded before James set off in search of John. Moments later he saw his body while jumping over a gap between two rocks. John was lying about fifteen feet down on a narrow ledge. It appeared that he was wedged between the rocks. He was lying awkwardly on his side with his right arm facing upwards. His head was twisted to one side and James could only see the right half of his face.

His eye was closed. James called out to him, 'John! ...John! ...Can you hear me?'

There was no reply and no visible signs of life. James knelt down to have a closer look. At that moment he heard something go whistling past his head. The hairs on the back of his neck stood up. He glanced up and saw a spear ricochet off the rocks. He turned, standing up at the same time. A black man was about to launch another primitive weapon in his direction. Quickly aiming the rifle James put a hole in the centre of the man's forehead. His brains blew out of a larger hole at the back of his skull. Instantaneously, his body went limp and then he fell lifeless to the dusty ground.

Again, the rifle was reloaded as James' eyes surveyed the surrounding area. After a few moments his attention returned to the stricken scout. He called his name out several times with no response. James wondered what he could do to get down to John. He knew there was a length of rope down by the horses. If, he went and fetched that he could use it to lower himself down to John, and also to hoist him up the rock. Apart from that there wasn't much else that he could think of at the time.

James surveyed the area with his eyes. There were several small trees and also bushes that he could possibly anchor one end of the rope. They looked strong enough to hold his weight, but were perhaps a little too far away. He then wondered if the rope would be long enough. James peered down at the wounded man again. Then he noticed that his right-hand was twitching. One of John's eyes, the one eye that James could partly see from where he was, had opened.

'John! ...John!' James called out with his heart racing. He thought he heard a faint reply. James quickly lay down on the rock in order to get closer to him and called out, 'John! John! Can you hear me?'

'James,' a soft reply came back.

'Thank God!' James said with a sigh of relief. 'I want you to listen carefully to me. I'm going down to the horses to fetch the rope and also the Red Cross field-bag. I won't be long. You just hang on. I'll soon have you out of there, mate.'

50 James quickly got to his feet. After checking the area first to make sure that the coast was clear he set off down the side of the kopje. In his hurry he would often slip on the loose sand and land on his backside. Finally though, covered in dust and scratches, he reached the two horses. He was out of breath, puffing and gasping for air. A loud clap of thunder overhead scared the horses and James had to calm them down. 'Whoa! You two! Steady! Steady! ...That's only thunder, not cannon fire!'

James hurriedly removed the length of rope off John's saddle and then decided to also take the panga with him. He opened the saddlebag and removed the field-kit. James was feeling the heat and the perspiration poured from his forehead. He decided to get rid of his army jacket. 'Oh God, that's much better,' he said with relief as he let it fall to the ground. He replaced the bandolier and then his hat. Next, he had a long drink of water from the spare bottle. Slinging the field-bag over his shoulder and then the rifle next, he grabbed the rope and panga, and then headed up the kopje. Twice on the way up he had to stop for a few moments to get his breath. Then he pushed on as hard as he could go.

Once James had reached the rocks where John was lying, he first let him know that he was back before laying out the rope. James had previously suspected that the rope was going to be a little short, especially after tying a few knots in it. It would never reach down to John. Looking around the area James wondered what he could do. Closer than the trees was a large rock, which was split in two. If he could somehow attach the rope to that, it would be more than long enough to reach John, even with all the knots. James then thought of using one of the black man's spears, as a brace between the rocks, to secure the rope. It was lying over near his body. James ran over to it and picked it up. Then, he realised that the shaft was not strong enough to support the weight of a man's body. He dropped it to the ground wondering what else he could find to do the job.

James then looked at his rifle where he had left it leaning up against a large rock. If, he could wedge it between the rocks that would probably do very nicely. He ran over to it, grabbed the weapon and then went over to the split rock.

The rifle however, proved to be too long to wedge between the gaps. He was also unable to get into a good enough position due to other rocks being in the way. Instead, he would now have to cut a thick branch from one of the trees to exactly to the right length.

James then found a suitable branch and began hacking away with the panga. At the same time keeping one eye open in case any unwanted intruders pitched up. The tree however, was a lot harder than he had expected, reminding him of when he used to cut Jarrah and Karri trees back home in Australia. Eventually, the branch parted company from the trunk and it fell to the ground. James then began to cut it to the required length. He carried it over to the split rock and wedged the branch into place. He was happy with that now, but there was no time to waste, every moment counted if he was to save John's life. He grabbed the rope and tied it to the branch. Then, he tied several knots along the length. Once that was done he pulled as hard as he could, applying all of his weight, to ensure that the branch wasn't going to slip out of position. Having done that, he took a quick gulp of water to quench his intolerable thirst.

A loud thunderclap overhead gave him a fright and he instinctively ducked his head. James looked upwards at the rain-threatening sky. As desperate as he was for it to rain he certainly didn't want it to rain now. Not now, that he was trying to rescue a wounded man from a difficult place. James lowered the end of the rope over the side of the rock and then placed the water bottle over his left shoulder. James straddled the rope before he picked it up. He took hold of it firmly with both hands and then he climbed over the edge of the rock.

He first had another quick look around the area and hoped that there weren't going to be any more surprise attacks. Then, using one hand at a time he lowered himself down, using his feet to cling to the rope at the same time. As he lowered himself James could feel the muscles in his biceps bulging under the strain of his weight.

John was lying further down the crevasse than James had first though, and when glancing upwards he wondered how he was going to haul him back up. As he got nearer James could see that John was badly wounded. The front of his jacket around his waist was saturated with blood, which he hadn't been able to see previously from above.

167

'John! ...It's me,' he called out, as he got closer, still clinging onto the rope.

There was no response from the scout. James lowered himself onto the narrow ledge. There was also another problem. The ledge was too narrow for him to stand on without continuously holding onto the rope. He would have to find a foothold on the other side of the gap. There were several tiny crevices in the rock-face, which he could possibly use. Keeping his left foot on the ledge while still hanging onto the rope he then spread his legs wide and shoved his other foot into a small crevice. When he was sure that he had a good foothold he slowly let go of the rope. James bent forwards and gently touched John on the side of his face. 'John, can you hear me? It's James,' he said softly.

John slowly opened his eyes.

James was relieved. For a moment he had thought that perhaps he was dead. 'I'm going to get you out of here now, mate. Then, we can take care of that bullet wound.' He could tell John was in agony, it was written across his face. 'I'm going to tie the rope around your body under your armpits. Then, I'll have to climb back up and then hoist you up next.'

James realised that not only had the ledge broken John's fall, but there was also a tree trunk lodged between the gaps in the rocks. This meant that John wasn't actually wedged into the rocks as James had first thought. At least that was some relief. James carefully fed the rope under John's body and then he tied it off. 'I'm going back up now, John.' He gave him a gentle pat on the head. 'You need to drink a little water first though.'

James removed the water bottle from his shoulder and pulled out the cork. Then, with some difficulty he poured a little water into John's mouth. John gave a slight cough.

'Try and swallow as much as you can mate,' said James pouring a little more from the container into his mouth.

The problem was, the awkward angle John was lying at, almost face down with his head twisted over to the one side. This made it difficult, if not impossible to get much water to go down. 'Once I get you up to the top I will give you more.'

James hauled himself back up the rope, the knots he had tied proving extremely helpful, and he was glad that he had put them in. Once he reached the top he climbed onto the rock. Then, he took up the slack in the rope and began to heave on the rope. John was extremely heavy and James could feel every muscle in his body straining. Worse than that however, his boots were not gripping on the smooth rock. After slipping once or twice he sat down and pulled off his leggings, boots and socks.

James tried hauling up John again. His bare-feet were gripping with a little more success, but still not as well as he would have liked. To make matters worse, large raindrops were beginning to fall from the darkening sky. This wasn't what James needed right now. 'Don't you think I have a difficult enough job here, Lord, without sending the rain now?' he puffed-out under his breath.

Drops of rain were leaving neat round holes in the sand surrounding the rock. James' feet were also sweating and the rainwater wasn't helping. Soon, his feet lost their grip altogether and then skidded over the smooth rock. John was rapidly returned to the tree trunk landing with a heavy thump, knocking the breath out of him. James was now exhausted. He sat down while recovering his breath.

51   James slowly regained his strength while thinking about what to do next. Trying to haul a wounded man up the side of a rock-face was proving to be far more difficult than he had first thought. He had also encountered a few unexpected problems. The first difficulty was that John was unable to assist him in any way. The other was the lack of a good grip on the smooth rock. James tried to think of some other-way to raise John. Another problem was that he needed to be able to stop for short rest-breaks in between hauling on the rope. 'How could he possibly do this?' he thought, while looking around for clues.

James then looked across the gap to the other side. 'Maybe there was something over there that would shed some light?' He jumped the narrow gorge to the other side and then looked around for something that would help. Anything would be better than nothing at this stage. There were several shallow holes in the rocks, no bigger than a side plate used on a dining table, sculptured over thousands of years, the rainwater having washed the softer parts of the rock away.

'Footholds!' James bellowed. 'Yes! This is it!'

He would now be able get a far better grip with his feet by using these. But, how was he going to be able to take the necessary rest-break while pulling up John? He then decided to check along the edge of the rocks. There were numerous places where the rock-face had cracked leaving narrow gaps. If they could be used to jamb the knots of the rope into, he could probably do it. James became excited shouting down to John, 'I'll have you out of there in a jiffy mate, you just hang in there!'

James crossed over to the other side. He hurriedly untied the end of the rope, which he had originally attached to the branch of the tree, wedged between the split rocks. Next, he quickly pulled on his boots and tied the laces. Slinging the rifle over his shoulder and then taking the rope in one hand he sprang across the opening between the rocks to the other side.

This time James was confident he could do it. He selected two suitable footholds and began to pull with all his strength. When he could heave no longer he lowered a knot in the rope, into one of the cracks in the rock-face. The knot wedged itself and held tight. James relaxed and sucked the air into his lungs. Then he also took a drink from the water container.

Once his breath had returned he hauled on the rope again. The raindrops had increased in numbers now and a light steady rain was falling. It didn't bother James. In-fact, he was pleased because it helped to cool him off and he also had more energy.

Again he rested briefly to regain his breath and also to drink water. Then he continued to haul on the rope. At last, John's head appeared. James jammed the knot into a crack and then carefully let go of the rope. Then, he bent down and took hold of the rope tied around the wounded man. He took a deep breath first and then with all of his strength, he hauled John up and onto the rock. James lay next to him for a moment exhausted.

Once he recovered his strength he got to his feet calling, 'John! ... John! Can you hear me?'

A faint moaning sound came from his lips. James grabbed the water bottle and poured a little into John's mouth. He swallowed it down so James poured a little more and that too was swallowed.

'That's right mate, you just keep getting some of that down you.'

Once James thought he'd had given John enough water for the time being, he crossed over to the other side to collect the field-kit. He returned to John and then carried him over to a small alcove in the rock that he had noticed on his way down to the horses. At least this would give them shelter from the elements. James carefully removed John's bandolier, and then he undid the buckle on the gun-belt and carefully removed the holster and gun. He placed it on the ground. After that he unbuttoned John's blood-soaked jacket and pulled it open as wide as wide as possible. The sight underneath wasn't pleasant. The bottom half of John's shirt was saturated with congealed blood. James then undid the buttons attaching the braces to his trousers. Next, he pulled John's trousers down as far as he could. James then ripped open the blood soaked cotton shirt.

For a moment he stared at the bleeding wound and then he opened the field-kit and searched through it. There was a small roll of wadding, two cotton bandages, a tourniquet (cord with wooden rod), a tin of sulphur powder (for sterilising wounds), a small Liston knife and also a bullet extractor. The instrument was about eight inches in length. On one end was a thin spoon-shaped section that could be opened and closed, similar to a pair of tongs, this was done by sliding a rod up and down through the inside of an external shaft. At the top end of the shaft were two half loops. These were finger and thumb holds of your left-hand to enable the operator to hold the instrument firmly when covered with blood. There was also a small knob at the end of the sliding rod. This was also for gripping purposes with your right-hand.

James turned to John. 'This is going to hurt like hell, mate, but it might be your only hope.' He took the bullet extractor and then carefully inserted it into the hole in John's stomach. James looked at John's face. His expression hadn't changed. 'Well, at least if you are out cold you won't feel this thing inside you.'

James then tried to locate the piece of lead with the end of the instrument. The job was made more difficult with all the blood, making the extractor slippery and difficult to control. The perspiration began to pour from James' brow. He also couldn't feel anything that resembled a bullet. He then tried wiggling the extractor from side to side in the hope of locating it. Without any success he then pushed the extractor deeper into John's stomach. After a few moments James had to stop in order to wipe the blood off the handle of the extractor. He used a piece of the wadding but the cotton wool stuck to the shaft of the extractor and also his hands.

'Damn!' he cursed while wiping his hands on his shirt. At least now he could hold the extractor a little more firmly. After a few moments he thought that he felt something hard at the end of the instrument, but then he lost it again. The perspiration was running down his nose. When it reached the end it hung like a raindrop for a second, then it fell landing on John's stomach. James then used his shirtsleeves to wipe the sweat from his forehead.

At last he found something hard again. This time he closed the extractor and slowly removed it. He felt the end to see if the bullet was there. There was nothing. James wiped more sweat from his forehead with his sleeves. Then he inserted the extractor back into John.

Shortly afterwards he located something hard. James carefully and gently closed the instrument and removed it.

This time the extractor was gripping a hard lump. James wiped the blood off it and looked at it. It was the bullet. 'Yes!' he bellowed with relief. 'Got you, you bastard!'

James now had to try and stem the flow of John's life-supporting liquid. Firstly, he thought he had better sprinkle sulphur powder over the wound. He then grabbed a handful of wadding and shoved it over the hole. After that he wrapped the cotton bandages as tightly as he could around John's stomach. Using the Liston knife he gut the end of the bandage and tied a knot. James then threw the medical things back into the field-kit bag. There was nothing he could do now but wait and pray for John's fever to break. That would most probably only be tomorrow. He got to his knees and said a short prayer. 'Dear Almighty and most merciful Lord... I humbly kneel before your presence to ask you to heal John's wounds and spare his life. I have not known him for long, Lord, but I believe that he is a good and honest man. I ask this in Jesus' name... Amen.'

52   James left the alcove to find large patches of blue sky peeping though the clouds. It had stopped raining which pleased him. He then thought he would gather firewood and make tea in the billycan. The only drawback was, he would first have to go down to the horses and fetch what he needed from the saddlebags. James thought that he would collect the wood first. A quick hunt around the surrounding area soon provided enough wood for a small fire. Once that was blazing away, James washed his hands in the small pools of rainwater.

After that, he walked over to the edge of the rocks and peered outwards over the vast flat veldt below. The horizon was still shimmering despite the shower of rain that had fallen. James wondered how George was doing and whether he was anywhere nearby. Then he thought of Billy and hoped he was recovering well at the field hospital. Major Moor's words came flooding back to him. He had warned James about the hazards and risks of becoming a scout. If he should be wounded, he could possibly die out on the veldt alone. James' thoughts returned to John again. John knew the dangers involved in scouting. He knew the consequences far better than James. John was well aware that he could die out here in the middle of nowhere. He was in God's hands now. Only God could save his life. Only God could create miracles.

After awhile, James thought that he had better go and check on his patient and see how he was doing. He returned to the alcove and looked at the wounded man lying wrapped in the blood-soaked bandages. John looked more peaceful to James than before. The signs of pain that had previously distorted his face had now gone.

James knelt down next to him and looked closely at John. Then he touched the side of his face, which he thought felt cold. James placed his ear to John's nostrils to try and hear if he was breathing. Then, he licked his finger and placed it against John's nostrils. He couldn't feel any breath on that either. He remembered the corporal opening the eyelids of the man that James had saved from being buried alive. He did the same. John's eyes were soft and watery. James moved his hand across his eyes to see if the pupils altered in size or not.

There was nothing. They were fixed in position staring blankly up at the roof of the alcove.

Once James was fully convinced that John was actually dead, he then dug a shallow grave in the alcove using the panga. After that he redressed John as best he could. James was about to close up John's jacket when he decided that he had better go through his pockets first. He found an opened envelope. Inside, was a photograph of an attractive young woman. James turned the photograph over and read the writing on the back. 'To darling John with all my love, Heather.' He returned the photograph to the envelope and then placed it in his shirt pocket.

Apart from that there was nothing else of any importance. James then laid John's body in the shallow grave. Firstly, he covered it as best he could with the sand from the hole. Then, he searched around the area outside, for several smallish rocks to place on the grave, to prevent wild animals from digging it up. The stones were hard to find despite the rocky nature of the area. Eventually though, he had found enough to cover the grave to his reasonable satisfaction.

James made a crude cross, using two pieces of the wood that he had previously gathered for the fire. After shoving it into the ground he placed John's hat over it. He then said another short prayer. Having thrown sand on the fire James collected up all the things and then made his way down the kopje to the horses.

At first, James thought of unsaddling John's horse and letting it go free. But, seeing as it belonged to the British army and the fact that they were desperately short of horses, he changed his mind. He would take the horse with him for the present time and would hand it over when he made his first report in to the army.

'Come on Bullet, you're coming with us,' James said taking hold of the reins. After mounting up James looked upwards towards the top of the kopjes where several vultures were now circling. They would feast themselves on the corpses of the blacks.

53   It was a long hot ride towards the small river in the surrounding area. John had pointed it out when giving James a short, but important lesson in map reading. He had also mentioned that normally it would be dry, as it was only a seasonal spruit (stream). However, the water would now be flowing quite rapidly due to the good rains in the area.

The rain-clouds had dispersed having rolled back to the distant horizon. Once again it was scorching hot and the sun burnt James' hands and also the left side of his face. He decided to unhook the clasp holding up the left side of his brim hat, and then pulled it down flat, to try and give that side of his face a little shade. He was perspiring profusely and parts of his uniform were damp with sweat. Flies were pestering him and he continuously tried to wave them away with his hand. And now-and-then he would have to lift the braces across his shoulders to enable the air to get under them.

James was also struggling to keep awake and every-so-often he would doze off in the saddle. Wellington was having a similar problem. Several times his front hooves would catch on rocks and he would half stumble, or he would step into a small hole in the ground, and both horse and rider would then wake with a fright. For a few moments their eyes would remain open and then slowly they would become heavy once again and close.

At last though James caught a glimpse of water in the distance amongst the earth colours, and by the time he reached the river the sun was already setting. He let both horses have a good drink first, before leading them over to a more secluded spot for the night. He unsaddled them both. Once he had removed the bridal and reins he left them to graze. Later, before retiring, he would rope them to a small tree, as the last thing he wanted was to wake at daybreak and find both had strayed.

James was hungry and he decided that he may-as-well look through the remainder of John's things in his saddlebags. He would take whatever there was instead of leaving it to go to waste. The first thing James found was a parcel. He opened it up to find a bundle of what appeared to be the roots of trees. He smelt them and then realised that they were sticks of dried meat. James sliced off a small piece and chewed on the meat.

It had been seasoned and salted and he liked it, thinking that it tasted far nicer than beef jerky, so nice in-fact that he ended up eating the whole lot. After that he was quite thirsty and drank down several gulps of water.

Other items that James found were a bag containing tealeaves, a small box of biscuits and four tins of bully beef. There was also a pipe and a tin of tobacco. James didn't smoke so he returned them to the saddlebag. He was still hungry though having lived only on biscuits and tea rations for the past few days, so he opened the tin of bully beef. He dug a chunk of the meat out with his knife. James shoved it into his mouth, chewed on it for a moment and then swallowed. Bully beef had never tasted quite this good before. He devoured the remainder of the contents in the tin.

After that he began to feel a little better. Then he thought of making himself tea in the billycan. However, as it was now getting too dark to make a fire he decided to settle for water. He would be up early the next morning and make tea, which he was looking forward to more than ever. James also knew that he would have to go easy on the food, which was supposed to be only used for emergencies. He was really expected to find something to eat off the land. That could be almost anything including snakes and lizards. He thought of the river next. There would be fish in there and wondered what types they were.

One thing he wanted though, even more than food, was to wash himself and also his uniform, which was covered with John's dried blood. He got to his feet and then after having had a good look around the surrounding area James made his way over to the river. The water looked inviting. Further up from him there was a small waterfall. The temptation to strip off and plunge in was almost overwhelming, but he would have to be patient and wait until tomorrow.

He returned to his camp and settled down on the bedroll. Later, the stars were out and he soon found the Southern Cross hidden amongst the Milky Way. He thought it was marvellous that he could see the exact same stars as at home in Australia. James was tired though and soon he closed his eyes and fell asleep.

54 Later, something woke James. He sat up and stared around at the darkness and then pulled the pistol from the holster. Wellington and Bullet seemed a little unsettled and were making snorting noises. James got to his feet and went over to the horses. 'What is it, boy?' he said quietly, rubbing Wellington comfortingly on the snout. He then gave the other horse several comforting pats on the neck. The distinct smell of wood-smoke came strongly to James' nostrils. The hairs on his neck prickled him as he peered into the darkness. Something orange was flickering not far off. His heart pumped a little quicker. 'I wonder who that could be?' he whispered. 'Boer scouts, perhaps?'

James watched the dancing lights of the small fire for a few moments. 'They couldn't possibly be scouts,' he whispered again. 'They wouldn't be foolish enough to be sitting around a campfire advertising their whereabouts... So who were they?'

He gave both horses another rub on the snout. Moments later a strong unmistakable fragrance of barbequed meat came drifting through the air. James took a deep smell filling his lungs to capacity. 'Oh God, that smells so, so good Wellington,' he whispered.

The last time he had smelt anything as good as that was before he left the farm. James stood staring in the direction of the orange flickering-glow and wonderful smell coming from there. The temptation to sneak up on whoever was there and take a look was beginning to overpower him. He glanced at Wellington, then at John's horse. 'You two had better be quiet while I go over there and take a look.'

Wellington horse shook its head as though he didn't approve of the idea.

'Oh, that's all right for you, you don't eat meat. Besides, you have had nice lush grass for supper. Unlike you, all I had was a stick of beef jerky and a tin of bully beef.'

James crept off as quietly as possible. It took him longer to get there than he had first expected. Firstly, he had to make his way through several thorn bushes, receiving a number of scratches to his hands, arms and face. Then, a long spiky thornbush almost took out his eye. There was also a donga (gully) to be negotiated, which he didn't see until the very last minute and almost fell into it.

Finally though, he was close enough to see what was happening. There were three black men sitting around the fire. There eyes were large and bulging and they talked loudly and excitedly. James wished he knew what they were saying. His eyes then surveyed the perimeter of the fire searching for weapons, but he couldn't see any. Naturally, that didn't mean they weren't armed and he wondered if they had been part of the group that had attacked John and him on the kopje.

They were busy cutting meat from the carcase, which appeared to be a small type of buck. The meat was then pushed onto sticks and held over the fire. Each man had several sticks with meat on them. Now and then they would remove a stick and blow furiously onto the burning meat. Then they would pull the meat off and shovel it into their mouths. James could feel his stomach rumbling and the smell of the cooking meat became too much for him. He hoped they were friendly and that they wouldn't mind sharing their meal with a starving white man. He pushed his way past the last few thornbushes.

One of the black men suddenly saw him. His eyes almost came out of their sockets. He sprang to his feet with terror written on his face. He yelled something at the others. They turned around, saw James and then bolted into the darkness screaming their heads off.

James called after them, 'Hey! Come back! Come back!'

He stared in their direction for a few moments with the sound of the fire sizzling and crackling. Strange shadows were dancing everywhere. James looked down and saw that the meat was burning. He bent down and quickly pulled several sticks from the flames. He blew them out and then tried to pull bits of the meat off the stick. They were extremely hot and burnt his fingers. James had to keep blowing on them to cool them off. Hunger overcame the pain however, and he wrenched the meat from the stick and pushed it into his mouth.

James chewed a few times and then swallowed. The taste of the meat made him roll his eyes back, making sounds of satisfaction at the same time. 'Thank you Lord,' he mumbled, 'for providing this delicious meal. This is definitely the best food I have ever eaten.' He pulled more meat off the stick and shoved it into his mouth.

After awhile he picked up the knife lying in the sand and wiped it off on his trousers. Then he cut several slices of meat from the carcase and pushed them onto the stick. James put the stick back over the fire and removed another. Once his stomach could hold no more he stopped. He licked the fat off his fingers and then wiped them on his trousers. James looked all about him and wondered if the blacks would come back or not. After a few minutes he decided they probably wouldn't, so he threw sand onto the fire and watched it slowly die. Without the light of the fire it was extremely dark again and it took several minutes for his eyesight to readjust. As soon as he was able to see again he made his way back to his camp.

Wellington was lying down. He lifted his head when he heard James approaching. James went up to him and gave him a pat on the head. 'I have just eaten one of the best meals in my life,' he said rubbing his stomach. 'I think we should get some sleep now as we have a long day ahead of us tomorrow. Goodnight, Wellington.'

James then went over to John's horse and gave him several comforting pats on the side of his neck saying, 'Goodnight, Bullet.'

After that, James lay on his bedroll feeling a lot more satisfied with life now. He closed his eyes and was soon sound asleep.

55 Alanna had collected William, Elizabeth and Bridget from school and they were now on their way home. About a mile from Rambling Meadows Alanna noticed that there were two men on horseback up ahead. They appeared to be riding in the middle of the road so she started to slow the cart down. The two men heard the horse and cart approaching from behind. They glanced around to have a look and then pulled their horses over to the side of the road. They stopped and waited for the cart to pass.

'Thank you!' Alanna called out politely, giving a wave of thanks at the same time, and continued on her way. However, while passing them she had felt uneasy about them. Something about the men worried her. It wasn't so much that they appeared rough and unshaven. She was used to the farmhands looking like that. It was something else that she saw in their eyes. One of them, who had piercing blue eyes, also had a nasty scar on the side of his cheek. It started at the side of his mouth and ran up to his right-hand ear. It was clearly visible even though he wore a short beard. Then Alanna thought that she was just being a little paranoid. They were obviously just a couple of swagmen who had probably been on the road for a while and were down on their luck.

Moments later one of them rode up alongside the cart on Alanna's side. He drew level with her. 'G'day miss,' he called out, raising his wide-brimmed hat at the same time.

Alanna politely greeted him back, noticing it was the man with the horrific scar. She looked straight ahead again, hoping he would drop his horse back and leave them alone.

'Where you lot from, miss,' he asked, and then glanced at the two younger girls in the back of the cart.
Alanna realised now that she may have a problem on her hands. He wasn't going to simply ride away as easily as she had hoped. 'We're from a nearby farm.'

'What's it called miss?'

She gave a sigh and reluctantly replied, 'Rambling Meadows.'

'Well, what do you know!' he said boisterously, 'that's exactly where me and me mate were heading! Weren't we Bert?' he asked looking back at the other man riding behind them.

'That's right Harry!' the voice from behind called out, 'that's the place!'

'Well in that case, perhaps I can save you the journey?' said Alanna. 'If you are looking for work I'm afraid that I have to disappoint you. What with the drought and everything we aren't taking on any hired hands these days.'

The cart bumped and shook over the rough dirt road.

'Are you the land owner, miss?' the man with the scar asked.

'No, but my father is.'

'Well then missy, how can you tell me there ain't no work? How would you know being a woman and all? A very pretty one at that, I might just say.'

Alanna encouraged her horse to pull a little harder and increase the speed. The rider with the scar did the same, spurring his horse on to keep up with the cart. Alanna was becoming more anxious with every passing moment and her heart started racing in her chest. While she was still in town she had heard stories about a couple of swagmen who were robbing farms in the area. She wondered if these might be them. She wished that James, George and Billy were still on the farm. The other rider suddenly drew level with the cart on the opposite side. Alanna didn't look his way; instead, she concentrated on keeping the horse moving as best she could along the narrow, twisting dirt road. William was seated next to her and although he was only seventeen he sensed something was going on. He felt the sudden urge to assist his older sister. He looked at the rider who had just pulled up next to him and yelled, 'Is there anything else we can help you with?'

'And who might you be?' the man on horseback asked with a gruff voice.

'That's of no importance!'

'I like to know who I'm talking to!'

'Well, I am sorry but I am not telling you!' William answered.

'Cheeky young bugger! ...I have a damn good mind to belt you one around the lughole!'

'Don't you dare touch him!' Alanna yelled back at the man, while coming to the aid of her younger brother.

She had angered Bert and he yelled back at her. 'You damn bitch! Who the hell do you think you are, hey? I'll teach you a lesson that you won't forget in a hurry!' He spurred his horse on and caught up with Alanna's. Leaning far over he grabbed the reins, near the bit, and pulled hard. The horse began to slow and was soon brought to a rapid halt. Dust and stones were sent flying into the air from the horse's hooves and the wheels of the cart.

The rider with the scar had already dismounted. He went up to the cart and grabbed hold of Alanna, wrenching her violently from the seat. She landed heavily onto the ground knocking the wind from her lungs. Without hesitating, William dived off the cart and landed on top of the man. They went tumbling down into the dirt. They both scrambled onto their feet and William immediately went for the stranger again. Alanna had just got to her feet when Bert grabbed hold of her from behind. She struggled wildly to free herself from his grip, but he was much stronger than her and hung on. Alanna was desperate to get rid of him, twisting and turning and trying to elbow him in the stomach.

William was punched hard in the face, splitting his upper lip and breaking a tooth. He went reeling backwards and then down onto his backside in the dirt. The two younger girls, Elizabeth and Bridget, were petrified. They crouched in the back of the cart scared half-to-death. Elizabeth could see the old rifle lying near the seat. Her heart was thumping madly in her chest as she took hold of the gun and got to her feet.

'Stop! Stop! All of you!' she yelled as loudly as she could.

The man with the scar turned to face her. Then he said calmly, 'If you point that at me little missy, you are going to have to use it... Do you think you can do that?' he asked with a smirk on his face.

Elizabeth was trembling violently. 'If you make me!' She then turned the gun on the other man. 'Now you! ... You let go of my sister!'

Bert looked at the gun. It was pointing it directly at his head. He was however, reluctant to let go of Alanna.

'I'll pull the trigger on the count of three!' the fourteen-year-old girl threatened. She began to count. 'One! ... Two! ...

Bert released his grip and Alanna moved away from him as she called out, 'Good girl, Elizabeth!' She then ran over to William and helped him to his feet. 'Come, let's get you onto the cart.' They walked towards it with Alanna keeping one eye on the two men. 'If one of them makes the slightest move, Elizabeth, shoot him!'

'I will, don't worry!' she replied confidently.

Bert glanced towards the man with the scar. He was thinking of drawing the pistol hidden from view by his jacket. But, even he had never shot a child before. It didn't seem right somehow. Maybe, if he drew his gun she would freeze up and do nothing?' What's more, he couldn't bear the thought of a prize such as Alanna slipping through the noose so easily. Should he draw his gun or not? He watched Alanna and William climb aboard the cart. They were about to leave when he finally went for his gun.

Elizabeth had been slightly distracted by William and Alanna climbing onto the cart. But, she noticed the man make a move. She saw a gun appear in his hand from under his jacket. She pulled the trigger and there was a loud bang. The sound of the gun spooked the horses. Alanna's horse took off sending Elizabeth reeling backwards into the cart. She hit her head on the wooden tailboard and was knocked unconscious. The man with the pistol staggered as he clutched at his left arm. The pain was excruciating and his knees buckled under him and fell to the dusty road. Harry rushed over to his horse. He pulled the rifle out, placed through the saddle belt, and after loading a round he took quick aim and squeezed the trigger. He saw the boy slump over to one side and topple into the back of the cart.

Alanna looked down and saw blood gushing from William's back. She let out a blood-curdling cry of horror, but she kept the horse going as fast as she could. Finally, they reached the entrance to Rambling Meadows. Alanna continued to race the horse and cart down the twisting dirt road. The dogs had heard the cart and came running out barking to great them. Once Alanna had reached the house she brought the horse to a halt next to the verandah. The dust from the wheels and horses hooves went swirling into the air. The wind carried it over the verandah as Alanna screamed for both her parents.

Her mother was first to come running out of the house with her father close behind. Alanna carrying William up the wooden steps. Lily saw William's battered and bloody face.

She placed her hands to her cheeks. 'Dear God, what happened?' she cried out.

Charles pushed passed his wife and took William from Alanna's arms. His heart was racing as he turned and went towards the screen door. Lily pulled it open for him and he entered the house. He went straight over to the settee where he placed William down.

'What happened?' he asked anxiously looking up at Alanna.

She burst into tears before crying out; 'We were attacked by two swagmen on our way home. We managed to escape but they shot William in the back.'

'Oh God no!' her father cried out in anguish. 'Quick Lily, we have to stop the bleeding. Get the first-aid box.'

Lily hurried as fast as she could. At first she couldn't find it amongst all the other items in the pantry cupboard. Then she spotted it. It was under a pile of sewing that she had placed there on one of the lower shelves. She grabbed it and raced back to the lounge. Meanwhile, Charles and Alanna had removed William's shirt and had turned him over onto his side. His blood was everywhere. Charles took the first-aid kit from Lily and opened it up. He then looked up at Alanna with desperation on his face as he said, 'Get a dish of hot water from the stove.'

Alanna hurried off to the kitchen.

'I need to clean around the wound first,' he said to Lily, 'then I'll place a dressing over and try and stop the bleeding. After that I'll go for the doctor.'

She nodded in agreement.

'Ask Elizabeth to go quickly and saddle my horse,' he said with urgency.

Lily looked around the lounge. Elizabeth wasn't there and neither was Bridget. She thought that strange and hurried off out onto the verandah. Bridget was sitting in the cart.

'Bridget!' she called out, 'where's Elizabeth?'

Bridget looked towards the verandah. 'She's right here mother! ...Come quickly!'

Lily arrived alongside the cart. 'What happened?' she asked her eight-year-old daughter as she saw Elizabeth lying in the bottom.

'I don't know mother, but she has a large cut on her forehead!'

Lily opened the tailboard of the cart and looked at Elizabeth. Then she called out her name while gently patting her face at the same time. Elizabeth slowly opened her eyes. She recognised her mother immediately even though her vision was blurred. 'My head hurts mother... What happened?' she asked after a moment or two.

'You must have knocked it on the cart somehow.... Here, let me help you out.' She turned to Bridget. 'You can help me.'

They got Elizabeth to her feet and then slowly took her up the steps. 'William was shot in the back,' Lily advised her before entering the hallway.

'Oh God!' she cried out loudly.

They entered the house. Charles and Alanna were busy bandaging William. Charles looked over at his wife and two daughters. 'What's wrong with Elizabeth?' he asked with concern.

'I think she must have knocked her head on the cart,' Lily replied. 'She has a large cut on her head and a huge bump.'

'Sit her down in one of the chairs.' Charles got to his feet and then had a quick look at Elizabeth. 'Can Alanna and you please attend to her? I have to go and saddle the horse and go for Doctor Redmond. Pray to God that I can get him back here in time.'

'Yes, we will be fine... Go now! ...And be careful Charles, those men might still be waiting along the road.'

'I'll be taking my pistol with me so don't fret, Lily. You and Alanna take good care of William for me.'

He rushed off to his office where he strapped the holster and gun around his waist. Then, Charles hurried off to the stables. At the last minute he decided to take James' horse, Thunder, instead of his own. He was a much bigger, stronger horse and this was going to be a gruelling ride to Wickepin and back.

56   James woke with bright sunlight streaming onto his face. For a moment he had forgotten where he was and he sat up with a fright. Then he looked around at the surroundings and saw the two horses. They were both grazing near a tree. James had roped both of them to it the previous evening so they didn't wander off somewhere.

The scout rubbed his hands through his hair while giving a large yawn. Next, he pulled on his boots and then got to his feet. He replaced the pistol into the holster and after strapping it on he walked over to the horses. 'Did you two sleep well?' he asked, patting them one at a time on the side of their necks.

Wellington snorted, nodding his head at the same time.

'Good because we have a lot of ground to cover today.'

James untied them so that they could find another patch of grass to feed on. Then he made his way over to a bush to relieve his bladder, which was about to burst. He then returned to where his kit was lying, running his tongue over his teeth at the same time. They felt furry. James could hear the river nearby and thought it was time to clean his teeth and have a wash. He scratched through the saddlebag, found the small tin of baking soda, his toothbrush and a small bar of soap.

Having surveyed the surroundings to make sure it was safe, James then made his way over to the pools, which he had seen the previous evening. After another quick glance around James removed the holster and gun, which he then placed on a flat rock. Next, he pulled off his boots and then his socks, removing them carefully so that he didn't start the blisters bleeding again. After that he stripped naked. He dipped the toothbrush into the water first, sprinkled a little baking soda onto the brush and brushed his teeth.

James then waded in up to his waist. The water was colder than he had expected, taking his breath away for a few seconds. He went under a few times and then washed his hair with the soap. After that he washed his body, the soap stinging the blisters cuts and scratches on his hands and face. Once he was finished washing he fetched his uniform and socks from the riverbank. Having first soaked them he then placed them onto a smooth rock and rubbed the soap into them. James then kneaded them against the rock several times with a muddy, brown coloured-dirt oozing out from the garments. They were then given a thorough rinsing. James climbed out of the water shivering a little. He picked up his things and made his way back to the camp. Apart from being cold he felt much better having washed and cleaned his teeth. James hung his clothes over several branches to dry and then he sat on a log.

57   Later, once his uniform was dry, James saddled Wellington and then led both horses down to the river. Once the horses had both had a good drink, James climbed into the saddle and made his way towards a small kopje, about four miles north of the river. Once there, James continued to ride up the side of the hill, until he felt the going was becoming too hard on the horses. He dismounted and then led both horses by the reins for a short distance before stopping next to a small tree. Having first secured the reins to the tree and removing his spurs, James slung his rifle over his shoulder and then made his way further up the kopje.

He eventually came to a crop of rocks where he then removed the field glasses from the case. James placed them to his eyes and after adjusting them slightly he brought them into focus. In the distance was a trail of dust that caught his eye and he concentrated on that for a moment. A short time later the dust discontinued. James then swept the glasses over several kopjes for any signs of movement. He couldn't see anything and so he looked northeast towards the railway line. The small town of Belmont was in the far distance. James then surveyed the valley to the south. A huge cloud of brown dust hung in the air in the distant horizon. Methuen and his troops were on the move.

James next had a look at his map and then he marked the kopje that he was on in pencil. He also marked the position, on the other kopje, where he had buried John the previous day. After that he folded the map and put it away in the bag. From there he made his way further up the kopje to flatter ground, having passed through several crevices and also gone around gigantic boulders. Once again James placed the field glasses to his eyes and swept them across the veldt far below. He was wondering where George and the other scouts were. It seemed to him that he was the only one out here. Where the heck was everyone else? For the first time in his life James felt totally isolated and alone.

Suddenly and unexpectedly someone behind him shouted something in Afrikaans. It totally startled James. He swung around and saw a Boer pointing a rifle at him. The man wore a shabby khaki-coloured uniform with a large wide-brimmed hat. Two bandoliers of ammunition were draped over his shoulders and across his chest. James' heart was pounding wildly in his chest. He thought of trying to unsling the rifle from his shoulder and taking a pot shot at the man. But he decided against that. Perhaps he could draw his pistol, which would be much easier and a lot quicker?

The Boer came a little closer. He was shouting something, which James didn't understand. At the same time, he was also gesturing with his rifle for James to put his hands up. James then noticed two other men hurriedly approaching from higher ground. He gave a sigh and raised his hands above his head. The two new arrivals joined the first man. They were dressed in a similar fashion and were very excited. One of them wore a large bushy beard and looked a little older than the others. They began talking at the same time with James wondering what they were saying.

The one with the beard then came closer. 'Keeps your hands in the sky, where I can sees them,' he said in broken English with a strong Afrikaner accent. He came even closer up to James and then, very cautiously; he removed the rifle from James' shoulder. After first handing it to one of the others he then took the pistol from James' holster. Then, he stepped back while saying something to the others in Afrikaans. One of the other men then ran off while the other two kept their guns trained on James. Moments later the man reappeared carrying a length of rope. The bearded man told James to put his hands together and then they were bound tightly.

One of the men also took James' binoculars and also the bag containing the map and compass. The other man began searching through his pockets. He found the envelope

189

containing the photograph, which James had removed from John's clothing. They each looked at the photograph in-turn. Then, one of them made some sort of remark while looking at the picture. They all laughed and then a discussion broke out amongst them for a few moments. After that, the same man continued to search through the remainder of James' pockets. Inside his jacket pocket they found another envelope. After opening it they removed the photograph of James' aunt and uncle together with their three children. It was the photograph that James' mother had given him the day he left the farm for Perth.

All three men studied the photograph for a short time. Then, the bearded man turned it over and read the writing on the back. Although it was in English he was able to recognise the names. He read them aloud, 'Aunty Ruth, Uncle Jacobaas, Piet, Haans and Freda.' He then read the address on the envelope that James' mother had written down in case he was able to pay them a visit sometime.

The Boer with the beard then looked over at James. 'Why do you have these peoples picture and address?'

'They're relatives of mine. My mother was hoping that I might be able to pay them a visit sometime.'

The man nodded. 'I know these peoples... they are farming not far from my place.'

James' heart raced a little harder. 'Would it be possible to get a message to them for me?' He was hoping that they weren't going to execute him on this lonely, isolated kopje.

'What kind of a message?'

'Tell them... that their family in Australia are thinking of them all, and that we hope that they are all well and safe... and that the war will end soon... and that my mother also wrote a letter to them.'

The man sucked in a lung-full of air before saying, 'I can't promise you anything, but I'll see what I can do.'

'Thanks, I would very much appreciate that.'

The Boer then turned his attention to the first photograph. 'Who's this woman's?'

'She was the fiancée of another scout.' James then briefly told him the story of how John was killed and that was the reason why he had the photograph on him. The three men then had a long discussion in Afrikaans. Now-and-then they would all stop talking and look over at James. Then, they would continue their discussions again. Even though James didn't understand one word of what they were saying, he could tell by their actions and tone of their voices, that they weren't having a friendly chat.

After awhile they stopped talking. The man with the beard went over to the edge of a rock and gazed south towards the horizon. He looked at the huge, brown dust-cloud rising up from the veldt. Then he spoke to the other two men for a few moments. Afterwards he turned his attention to James. 'Those verdommed rooinek's,' he pointed south, 'are in for a big frights when they gets closer to Belmont.'

'Why?' James asked out of curiosity.

He smiled. 'Do you thinks that I am really that stupid, hey? Do you thinks I would tell you that?'

'Why not? I'm not going anywhere. I'm not going to be able to tell anyone, am I?'

The big man scratched his beard several times while wearing a frown on his forehead. Then he said, 'Nooo, I suppose that's true.' He glanced over at the other two men first, before looking back at James. 'General Cronje has two thousand Burghers ready and waiting just over there,' he pointed, 'behind those kopjes.'

James could feel his heart racing wildly. How could he possibly escape from these men? How could he possibly warn the advancing British columns that they were marching straight into hell? He felt angry and frustrated with himself for having been captured in the first place. The bearded Afrikaner interrupted his thoughts when he suddenly asked, 'Where did you leave your perd?'

James had no idea what that meant. 'My what?'

'Perd! Perd!' he repeated loudly. 'I forgets how you says the word in English.' He then made actions as though he was riding a horse.

'Ah, you mean horse?'

'Yah, horse,' a broad beam spread across his face.

'I left him further down the kopje.'

'You are lucky I doesn't just shoots you right here. That's what they wants,' he pointed to the other two men as he spoke. 'That's what we do with rooinek scouts. We doesn't even bury them. We leave the hyenas and vultures to feeds off them. They leave nothing but bones.' He stroked his beard a few times. When he thought the message had sunk-in he said, 'Now listen. I'm going to takes you down to your perd. Then, we are going to General Cronje's laager. If you try to run away I will kills you dead... Do we thinks the same way?'

James nodded. 'Yeah, mate. We understand each other perfectly.'

'Good.' He smiled. 'Let's go.'

They began to make their way down the kopje between the rocks and crevices. It was much harder for James with his hands tied together, and while going between two large rocks he slipped on the loose stones and fell heavily. He then went rolling down part of the slope cutting his knees and elbows. The Boer came chasing after him. He practically shoved the pistol into James' ear as he yelled, 'Dom kop! (Dimwit). If you try's anything stupid. like that again, I'll just shoots you right here and be done with it!'

James spat some sand and grass from his mouth. He was sore and he was also angry. 'I lost my darn footing you idiot!'

'Come on! Gets up now!' the Boer said harshly while hauling up him to his feet.

They continued on down the slope.

Shortly afterwards, the Boer saw the two horses. 'Halt!' he called out to James.

The Australian did as ordered.

The Boer surveyed the area with his eyes, sweeping them across the rocks and small bushes. 'Why does you have two perds?' he asked after a short time.

'I've already told that! The other horse belonged to the scout that was killed.'

The Boer thought about what James had said. 'Why did you brings it up here, man? Why doesn't you just sets the thing free?'

'Because it belongs to the British army, that's why!' he replied a little agitatedly.

The man looked thoughtful for a moment before saying, 'Keeps on going now!' He gestured with the handgun simultaneously.

The two men continued on down the sloping ground. James could see Wellington patiently waiting for him. He tried to think of a way of escaping, but decided this wasn't the time or place. For one thing, his hands were bound. And, even if he were able free himself he wouldn't be able to ride out of here. It was far too steep and much too dangerous. Wellington could easily slip and lose his footing and go down. He would just have to be patient and wait for the right moment and then take his chance.

Once they reached the horses the Boer said, 'Now gets on! ...And no funny business this time!'

James shook his head in annoyance. He then went to untie the reins attached to the tree.

'Leave those! ...You just gets on the perd likes I told you.'

James struggled to get his left foot into the stirrup. Once that was done he grabbed hold of the saddle horn and with a little difficulty, he then hauled himself up and onto the horse. He could immediately feel that Wellington was uneasy. The Boer took the reins of the other horse first and then tied them to James' saddle. After that, he took hold of Wellington's reins and led the way along a narrow rocky path. Sometime later, they came across a very sharp cliff-face on their left with a sheer drop on the right. The Boer looked over his shoulder and upwards at James. 'This is not the place to does anything's stupid.'

James could see that for himself. He really didn't need to be told. He looked down on his right. If anyone fell down there, he thought. No one would ever find you. Wellington sensed this was a dangerous place and was reluctant to continue on, holding back slightly. The Boer pulled harder on the reins. Wellington didn't appreciate that. He shied up at the same time almost throwing James off, but he just managed to hang onto the saddle. He tried to pat Wellington's neck to help calm him, which was extremely difficult to do with both his hands tied together. 'Whoa boy, steady, steady!' he called out while trying to comfort the horse. 'You and I don't really want to end up falling down there believe me.'

Wellington soon settled down after hearing James' voice, and he continued walking again with Bullet following closely behind. After awhile, they met up with the other two men who were now waiting for them on flat open ground. The Afrikaner who had been leading Wellington then mounted his own horse. With one of the Boers leading the way, James followed next, and then the two remaining Boers. John's horse was tagging along at the back. From there they proceeded to slowly make their way down the side of the kopje.

58 Lord Methuen was pushing hastily forward. He was extremely eager to reach Belmont before nightfall forcing his weary troops to march at a gruelling pace. Not only was this exhausting on the infantry, but extremely taxing on artillery horses, mainly due to the recent rains, which had softened the topsoil, and the wheels of the heavy field guns sank into the ground.

Wagons carrying stores and ammunition that were being pulled with bullocks, fell even further behind with each passing minute. So did the field ambulances and hospital staff who were also unable to keep up with the rapid pace. The Lieutenant General wasn't overly concerned about them though, they could catch up later once he had reached Belmont and made camp for the night. The imperial officers under his command were anxious at the forced-pace that he had set the troops and made known their concerns for both men and horses. They were however, rebuffed by the Lieutenant General and ordered to continue pressing on as hard as they could.

59　　　The Boer scouts, who had captured James, had now reached General Cronje's laager located on a maize farm. Thousands of horses and men were preparing to ride out. Over to one side James could see dozens of field guns. Horses were being in-spanned in readiness for the guns to be hauled away at a moments notice. They arrived outside the brick building used for the storage of farm implements. After dismounting James was placed into a small storeroom with a guard posted outside the door.

The young Australian removed his hat and then knocked the dust from it, bashing the hat against his one leg. He threw it into a corner. He was still angry with himself for having been captured and was frustrated by the fact that he hadn't been able to escape while en-route from the kopje. James glanced around the room noticing it was practically empty, apart from several sacks of maize, a damaged wagon wheel and a wooden cask. On one wall there was a small barred window but it was too high for him to see out of.

James sat on the hard cement floor with his back against the wall. He brushed his damp, sweaty hair back with his hands. His mind was busy. He was thinking of how he could escape so that he could warn Methuen's advancing columns of Cronje's ambush plan. He got to his feet and went over to the door. There were several cracks in the wood where it had split over a period of time. He placed his face against the door. Using one eye he peered between the gaps. There wasn't a great deal that he could see though, apart from horses and men. James then looked over at the wooden cask. That would be ideal to stand on to enable him to could see out of the window. All he had to do was move it and place under the window. James went over to the cask and then tried to roll it. It was extremely heavy though and wouldn't budge an inch.

'What the heck have they got in here?' he thought scratching his head.

The lid appeared to be loose so he removed it.

'No wonder,' he whispered, seeing that it was chocker-block full of horseshoes. He would either have to empty it or think of something else. He looked over at the sacks of maize. These would be far easier to move. James took hold of the top sack and lifted it onto his shoulder. It was heavy and caused his breath to expel as his body took the full weight. He carried over to the window and placed the sack down onto the floor. He was puffing for air as he went for a second one. After placing that on top of the first one, James them climbed onto them, using his knees first and then carefully getting to his feet. He was puffing for air as he peered out between the iron bars. Looking downwards and over to his left he could see the brim of the guard's hat. Looking upwards and straight ahead he saw that the Boers had now formed into sections and were almost ready to move out. 'Damn!' he cursed to himself, feeling helpless at being held a prisoner.

James then noticed a big man approaching on horseback from over on his right. The man walked the animal slowly past the ranks of mounted infantry. He was speaking to them in Afrikaans. James realised that this must be General Cronje, and his heart beat faster as he was only a matter of twenty yards from him. Once the general had finished addressing the men they broke into song (Boer Anthem The Volkslied). Although James couldn't understand the words he could tell by the passion in their voices, and also the way in which they sang with pride in their hearts, that it was of great importance to them. When the multitude of voices had died down the men raised their rifles in the air and gave the general three cheers. He saluted them back and then he turned his horse towards James' direction. The Australian could see the look of determination in his eyes, and yet, he also appeared to have the face of a desperate man.

James watched the two thousand mounted infantry following General Cronje away from the laager. Once they had all gone James climbed down from the maize bags. He was disillusioned. There was nothing he could do to warn the British. He sat down on the floor and leaned his back against the wall. He hoped that the other scouts would spot Cronje on the move, and have enough time to warn Methuen's columns.

60   General Cronje's men took-up their positions along the western side of the advancing British columns. The area had been carefully selected by the Boer General and offered him a number of advantages over the enemy. Firstly, the setting sun was behind his commandos. This meant that when they attacked the enemy, the British troops would be facing westwards into the blinding sunlight. Secondly, both men and horses were well hidden from view down in a donga (gully), which provided the opportunity for a surprise attack.

    Cronje also knew from his scouts, that the British troops and horses would be exhausted from their gruelling march. His men and horses however, were fresh and ready for battle. Lastly, but no less importantly, his men had open ground behind them in which to make good their retreat. The Boer Generals objective, being seriously outnumbered, was simply to hit the imperial army as hard as he could and then withdraw from the engagement, before the British had a chance to regroup.

    He watched patiently through his binoculars until the time was just right, then he gave Captain Van Ne Kerk the order for his artillery to commence firing. The Long Toms, which had been stealthily camouflaged with brush, sent their shells hurtling towards the marching British columns. By the time Rimington's Scouts had seen the large movement of men on horses it was too late. As the troops neared Belmont a force of about two thousand Boers suddenly attacked Methuen's flank. They caught him totally unprepared and inflicted heavy casualties on his troops. The Australians were lucky. They had got off lightly but the British regulars paid a heavy price losing over three hundred men, plus they had hundreds seriously wounded.

61 The sound of distant cannon-fire brought James scrambling to his feet. He hurried over to the sacks of maize and climbed onto them. He peered out of the barred window with his heart racing in his chest. This was the sound he knew was coming and which he had dreaded. It only lasted for about an hour and then it faded away. James climbed down from the sacks of maize and went over to the door. He looked between the cracks in the timber. The guard was still there. He wondered how many Boers were still around. Maybe the guard was the only one? He doubted that though. He could also tell by the lengthening shadows on the ground, that the day was drawing to a close.

Looking up, James studied the pitched roof. It was high and there was no ceiling. It was constructed from wooden poles and thatch. If he could somehow get up there he might be able to dig his way through the thatch, guessing that it was about a foot thick. However, he would have to wait until nightfall and the cover of darkness. The walls on either side were gabled, but the two opposite walls were only about eight foot high. He thought that they were possibly his best bet, as he could use the sacks of maize to give him enough height in order for him to reach the lowest part of the thatch. That was his plan, and as soon as it was dark enough that's what he would do. James sat down on the floor again with his back against the wall. He was exhausted and closed his eyes.

62   Later, James woke to find that it was now dark except for a beam of moonlight streaming through the barred window. He stiffly rose to his feet and then yawned. After that he stretched his aching body and wondered how long he had been asleep. He decided to climb onto the sacks of maize and have another look out of the window. Golden moonlight flooded the surrounding area. The place now appeared to be deserted. At that very moment though he saw two crouching figures moving quickly across the open ground. He watched them approaching for a few seconds, and then jumped down from the sacks. He quickly removed one of the horseshoes from the cask and waited over by the door. Moments later he heard muffled voices then the padlock being removed. He waited in readiness to strike with the horseshoe with his heart pumping loudly in his ears.

The door opened slightly with a creek. 'Hello!' a female voice called out softly with a strong Afrikaans accent.

James remained silent wondering who it could possibly be. The door opened wider and the light from a lantern spilled into the small room. 'Are you there, James?' the softly spoken voice asked.

He instantly relaxed and then he stepped out from behind the door into the lamplight. The figure of a woman was standing in the doorway. She was wearing a dookie (scarf) over her head and he was unable to fully see her face. His sudden appearance from behind the door had given her a fright, momentarily taking her breath away. She quickly recovered. 'It's me James, your Aunty Ruth.' She removed the headscarf, revealing her face.

The light from the lantern washed over her and James recognised her immediately. She was the spitting image his mother, although a bit shorter and with a more rounded, portly type figure. 'When I got your message,' she continued, while smiling up at him, 'I couldn't believe my eyes... Thank the Lord that you didn't come to any harm.'

'You look so much like mother its uncanny, Aunt Ruth.'

They hugged one another for a moment before she said, 'We must hurry. It's not safe here, there are commandos everywhere.'

'Where are we going?'

'To our farm... it's a two hour ride from here.' She blew the lantern out and they were left standing in the pale moonlight. 'Come,' she said as she turned and went outside.

James followed her. A young man was standing in the shadows waiting for them. James also noticed that he was armed. 'This is Haans, James, your cousin,' Aunt Ruth advised.

James shook his hand firmly as he said, 'Hi, Haans, it's good to finally meet you, mate.'

The young man smiled shyly, his teeth white in the moonlight, but he didn't reply.

'He doesn't speak any English James,' his aunt advised.

James nodded. 'No problem, mate, I can't speak your language either.'

'We have horses waiting over there,' she pointed into the darkness. 'Come on, we have to hurry!'

They set off in the direction his aunt had indicated until James suddenly stopped and said, 'Just hang on a moment, Aunt Ruth! ... I've left my hat behind.'

He was about to go back for it when his aunt took hold of him by the arm. 'Leave it James!' she said anxiously, 'there's no time for that we must keep going!'

James hesitated for a moment and then nodded his head in agreement. They continued on with Haans leading the way. Once they reached the horses James recognised Wellington immediately and was pleased to see him again. His aunt then removed a cape from her saddlebag and handed it to James. 'You must wear this in case we are stopped... And remember, only to let me or Haans do the talking.'

James threw the cape around his shoulders. After mounting up the three riders and horses left in single file with James at the rear, the moonlight guiding Haans in the direction of home. James looked up at the Southern Cross and noticed they were travelling in a north-easterly direction.

Twice en-route they had to stop, dismount and lead the horses behind the bushes, after Haans had spotted several riders approaching. The third time while nearing a bridge, they were suddenly challenged by a group of Boers who had mounted a roadblock. They surrounded the three riders shouting excitedly in Afrikaans while pointing their rifles at them.

James' aunt spoke to them for a few minutes. Another Boer suddenly approached James. He prodded his leg with his rifle and then asked him something in Afrikaans with James' heart racing wildly. James' aunt half turned in her saddle and said something to the man. He went over to her and they spoke for a few minutes. James could tell by the sound of their voices that it wasn't a friendly chat they were having. The man returned to James, said something and then walked off. James could feel the sweat running down his forehead. After a few minutes the Boers let them go and they continued on their way.

A mile or so later, they crossed over a railway line and after another three or four miles they entered the Free State. They continued east along several twisting, turning roads until they reached a wooden gate. Haans dismounted and opened it, the iron hinges creaking and groaning in protest. After the horses had passed through they were closed again. The riders then continued on with the strong fragrance of lilac trees in the air. James could hear several dogs barking in the distance. His aunt brought her horse back alongside of his. 'This is our home. Welcome to Rooi Fleig James,' his aunt said with the moonlight dancing on her face.

'Thanks, Aunt Ruth.'

'I only wish it was under much happier circumstances James.'

'Me to aunt, believe me... What does the name of the farm mean?'

Aunt Ruth frowned for a moment. 'Sometimes it's difficult to translate an Afrikaans name into English. Rooi fleig means something like the red veldt or red earth.'

'Well, it's certainly a good name for a farm around these parts, seeing as the earth is so rich in colour.'

'Jacobaas' late father actually named the farm.'

They rode on towards the house. 'I'm curious to know what those Boers said to you back at the road block, Aunt Ruth?'

...'They wanted to know what we were doing out at this time of night. I told them that we had been visiting a dying relative of mine, and that we were now returning home.'

'Oh.'

... 'The one that spoke to you wanted to know why you weren't serving with the commandos, and why you didn't answer him when he spoke to you. I told him that you had the misfortune of having being born both deaf and dumb.'

'Oh... that was good thinking.'

'We were just lucky tonight not to be shot.'

63   Shortly, they arrived at the homestead. The entrance and interior of the house was lit up with lanterns producing a warm welcoming sight. Several dogs were running around excitedly barking and sniffing at the horses. Wellington wasn't used to dogs and he shied away whinnying at the same time. James patted him on his neck. 'It's alright boy, they're just dogs they won't harm you.'

Two black males appeared out of the darkness. They came running from the direction of the stables. After dismounting James' aunt spoke to them in Afrikaans. They took the reins of the horses and led them away. James' aunt turned to face him. 'The boys will unsaddle your horse, feed and stable him for the night.'

'Thank you.'

'Let's go inside.'

The three of them entered the house through large wooden double doors into a wide passageway, and from there they went into a large parlour. Haans said something to his mother and then he left the room while James glanced around at the furnishings. One of the walls had a zebra skin another buckskin. But, most impressive of all was a trophy of a lion's head. James approached it. This was the first time he had ever seen a lion apart from a photograph, and he was amazed at how large the head was.

'Jacobaas shot that many years ago near the farm,' his aunt advised, seeing him admiring it. 'It's a black-mane lion.'

'It's quite magnificent,' James replied while gazing at the trophy. He turned to face his aunt. 'Where is uncle Jacobaas, by the way? ...And Piet and Freda?'

'Freda's here, she will be joining us shortly... Your uncle's away,' she sighed. 'So is Piet. They are both serving with General De la Rey's commandos.'

'Oh.' A sudden feeling of guilt came flooding over him. These people were part of his family. The woman standing in front of him was his mother's sister, and yet he had come half way across the world to help the British wage war against them.

'I sincerely hope that you are feeling hungry?' his aunt asked interrupting his thoughts.

'To be honest, I'm more thirsty than hungry.'

'What a pity, Freda cooked her favourite dish when she knew you were coming.'

'Oh... well that was very kind of her.'

'It's oxtail stew. I'm sure you must have eaten that back in Australia?'

'I don't recall ever having it.'

'Freda will be very disappointed, she has been cooking most of the afternoon for you.'

'In that case I am definitely very hungry.'

'Good... Would you like to wash your hands and face first?'

'That would be nice, thanks.'

James followed his aunt down the passage where she showed him the bath area. 'There's a clean towel and soap for you,' she said. 'Once you have finished, come through to the dining room. It's through that door,' she pointed.

Once she had left James closed the door behind him. There was a small fireplace on one wall. But, as it was now summer there was no need for it. There was a large bathtub in the centre of the room. On the floor next to it was a mat. A wooden table with a bowl and a jug stood against one wall. There was also a chair with the towel neatly folded on the seat. Above that on the wall was a mirror. James looked into it. His face was dirty, sunburnt and unshaven. He felt his beard with his hand. It was hard and rough. Suddenly he felt very scruffy and untidy which he hadn't done out in the bush.

He removed his jacket and shirt and placed them over the chair. Then he poured the hot water from the jug into the bowl. He placed his hands into the water and then had to quickly remove them as the water burnt him. After weeks of only using cold water he wasn't used to hot water any longer.

He slowly placed his hands back into the water. It felt good, very, very good. After a few minutes he splashed the water over his face. Then he took the soap and washed it. Then he washed his arms and hands next. The water turned to a brown muddy colour. He dried himself on the towel, noticing that he had also made that dirty.

James pushed the door open, which led into the dining room. There was a large table and eight chairs. The table was laid for three persons. In the centre of the table stood a silver candelabrum. The candles flickered and danced from the movement of the air surrounding them.

His aunt suddenly appeared through another doorway. 'Ah, you're all done and ready to eat then,' she said cheerfully.

'Yeah. I sure needed that wash though. I'm afraid that I've made the towel very dirty.'

'Don't worry so much James, there are plenty of other clean ones.'

The pleasant aroma drifting from the kitchen reached James' nose. He couldn't help but take a huge lung-full of the pleasant smell causing him to close his eyes for a second.

'After supper you can take a nice hot bath,' his aunt continued, 'I'm sure that you would enjoy that?'

'That would be very nice, thanks. I haven't had a bath since leaving home… I mean a hot bath.'

'That's your seat over there,' she indicated with her hand. 'Jacobaas usually sits there.'

James sat down. It felt strange for a moment. He hadn't sat in a chair since leaving Rambling Meadows. His aunt rang a small silver bell. Moments later a black maid appeared carrying a tray. She placed a large bowl of steaming soup in the centre of the table. Aunt Ruth picked up a ladle and scooped it full of soup then poured it into a bowl. The maid then brought it over and placed it down in front of James. His aunt then filled another bowl and the maid placed that next to one of the empty seat. After pouring herself half a bowl the maid was told to take the remaining soup away.

'Haans and Freda will be joining us shortly,' his aunt said. 'Meanwhile, you can say grace before everything goes cold.'

James obliged and said a short prayer. After that, his aunt cut several slices of freshly baked bread. James spread a thick layer of butter over a slice and then bit a large chunk out of it. He had forgotten what it tasted like and ate the whole slice. After that he took a mouthful of his soup. 'Mm, this is delicious,' he said after swallowing it down.

'Good... When did you last eat a proper meal?'

'Not for a while,' he answered buttering another slice of bread, 'not since leaving home.'

When they had both finished their soup Aunt Ruth rang the bell again. The maid returned and cleared away the empty plates. The main course was then placed on the table. A large bowl contained the oxtails in gravy. Other dishes were laden with a variety of vegetables. James' aunt dished up a large plate for him and the maid brought it over. His aunt then said something to the maid and she left the room. 'I told Mavis to go and find out what has happened to Haans and Freda,' his aunt advised.

James nodded. 'This smells fantastic,' he said picking up his knife and fork. He pulled a chunk of soft meat off the bone and shoved it into his mouth. James hardly chewed on the meat it was so tender. He swallowed it down. 'Mm, I see what you mean, this is absolutely beautiful.'

'Freda will be pleased to hear that.'

James ate another few mouthfuls.

'I must be honest with you James, that after receiving your mother's letter I was more than shocked to learn that you had joined up with the army and come over to South Africa. I could hardly believe that one of my own family, were actually willing to help the British take our land from us. Have the British not stolen enough from us James? ...First, Cape Colony, and then they annexed Natal, and now the Orange Free State and Transvaal... I can understand the Redcoats greed for our country James, but I can't for the love of God understand that one of my own relatives are willing to help them... You are going to have to fight for every inch of it. We will never give up. You will have to kill every one of us, women and children included.'

James placed his utensils down on the plate. He had suddenly lost his appetite.

'Eat James, you need to keep up your strength.'

'I'm sorry Aunt Ruth, I just can't.'

'Is there something wrong with the food?'

'No,' he replied shaking his head. 'There's nothing wrong with the food, it's delicious, it's just that I'm feeling kind of full.'

'Full? ...Nonsense! Even Haans and Freda eat more than that! You're a grown man you need a good plate of food.'

'I'm just not used to eating a big meal any longer. I've been living on biscuits and bully beef mostly since we got here.'

At that moment a young girl entered the dining room. She had long blonde shoulder length hair and was tall and slender. Her resemblance to his sister Elizabeth was quite remarkable. He got to his feet as his aunt said, 'This is your cousin, Freda.'

'Hi, Freda, I am very pleased to meet you at last. You remind me very much of my second youngest sister, your cousin Elizabeth.'

Aunt Ruth repeated in Afrikaans, what James had said, and she smiled shyly.

Then his aunt said, 'Ever since we received your mother's letter with the photograph of you all, she has been looking forward to meeting you. Like Haans though, she doesn't speak any English. Her father doesn't allow it in the home.'

Freda approached James. She placed her arms around his waist and gave him a big hug. She then glanced at his plate of food and said something in Afrikaans to her mother. His aunt looked at him as she said, 'Freda has asked if there's something wrong with the meal, as you don't appear to be eating much.'

'No,' he replied glancing at her, 'tell her that the meal is excellent.' James immediately sat down at the table. He picked up his knife and fork and continued eating.

Finally, Haans joined them. He spoke to his mother for a moment while she dished up for him. She looked over at James. 'Haans has asked me to give you his apologies for being late to the table.'

'Tell him that's fine,' James replied with a smile.

Haans was hungry and began to eat as if there was a race to see who could finish first. James stopped eating for a moment and looked up at his aunt. 'By-the-way, I would like to thank both Haans and you for coming to my rescue tonight.

I want you to know that I greatly appreciate what you have done.'

'That's what families are for James, helping each other out in time of need,' his aunt replied.

James nodded. 'I suppose so, but I know that you risked your lives for me tonight and I won't ever forget that.'

'We had God's help tonight... You can praise the Lord that you weren't shot on sight when you were captured. Another thing, you were very lucky to have been carrying that photograph of us, and that those commandos knew us.'

James nodded. He then ate another mouthful of food. Once he'd swallowed it down he said, 'My mother gave it to me the day I was leaving for the army.'

'What are your plans now?' his aunt asked.

...'I'll need to make my way back to our lines tomorrow.'

'You will be travelling through very dangerous country, James.'

...'I know... But, I have no choice, I must get back to my contingent.'

The remainder of the evening was spent in the lounge with James telling Aunt Ruth about the family back in Australia. She in-turn would translate to Freda and Haans. Then, they would ask her questions and she would have to translate to James. Finally, Freda and Haans said goodnight and made their way to bed. James and his aunt had another coffee and it was quite late when James eventually went for his bath. The houseboy, Moses, had previously filled the bathtub for him and the water was still more than hot enough for James.

64   James woke with the sun streaming into the bedroom through a gap between the curtains. He could hear the sound of chickens clucking outside the window and for a moment he thought he was back home at Rambling Meadows. He got out of bed naked and then went over to the window and peered out. He could tell that it was quite late in the morning, by the angle of the sun. James then went over to where he had left his clothes the previous night, to find them missing.

There was a note, which he picked up and read. 'Dearest James, don't panic if you wake up and find that your uniform and underwear are missing. Haans collected them for me early this morning to have them washed and ironed. We can't have you returning to your contingent looking shabby, can we? Aunty Ruth.'

James sat down on the bed with his mind racing. A feeling of guilt came washing over him, as it had done the previous night. 'What a dilemma?' he thought, 'these are good people, part of his family, how could he continue helping the British take their country from them? Yet, there was nothing he could do, he had taken an oath to serve Her Imperial Majesty Queen Victoria.

There was a knock at the door, disrupting his thoughts, and then his aunt called out, 'James! ...James, are you awake?'

James quickly pulled up the sheet over himself. 'Yeah Aunt Ruth.'

'May I come in for a moment?'

'Please do.'

The door half opened and her face popped around the corner. 'I'm just returning your things.'

'Thank you.'

'Did you sleep well?'

'Like the dead... I'm sorry I overslept this morning, I usually wake early.'

'Never mind.'

'What time is it, Aunt Ruth?'

'Shortly after ten o'clock.'

James couldn't believe it. 'I haven't slept this late since I was at school.'

'I'm afraid that we went to bed far too late. You were tired and obviously needed a good nights rest. Anyway, your uniform looks much smarter now.'

'I honestly don't know how to thank you.'

'Don't worry about it. Oh, and Moses will bring your boots shortly, they are being polished at the moment... I also left you a new toothbrush and baking soda to clean your teeth. You'll find them in the bathroom together with a razor and shaving brush. When you are ready come to the kitchen for breakfast.'

She left and closed the door behind her.

James got to his feet and walked over to his clothing. They smelt fresh and clean and it was a good feeling when he dressed. Once his boots arrived he went to the bathroom. He washed his face with warm water and then lathered up with the shaving brush. James took the cutthroat razor, sharpened the blade on the leather strop first, and then began shaving. When he was finished he washed his face and then brushed his teeth.

After that he found his way to the kitchen, which was easy due to the excellent smell coming from that direction. Breakfast consisted of fruit juice, toast, fried eggs, bacon, boerworse (sausage) and tomatoes washed down with a large mug of tea.

'Where are Haans and Freda this morning aren't they joining us for breakfast?' James asked after a short while.

'They had to go off to school early this morning.'

'Oh... That's a pity, I was really hoping to say goodbye to them before leaving.' He buttered more toast.

'They told me to give you their love and that they hope that you will make it safely back to the British lines. They also asked if you would send them each a boomerang once you return to Australia.'

James felt a lump in his throat. 'Of course... You have two wonderful children, Aunt Ruth. I think very highly of them both... How old are they now?'

'Freda's thirteen this year. Haans is sixteen.'

'And Piet?'

She gave a sigh. 'Piet is now eighteen. I pray to God every night to spare his young life.' She took a handkerchief out the sleeve of her blouse and wiped her eyes.

James gave her a moment before saying; 'I shall never forget your kindness shown to me or the risk that you took to bringing me here to your home.'

'You take care of yourself and come back one day to visit us all when this war is over.'

'I will, I promise. Besides, I still have to meet Uncle Jacobaas and also Piet.'

'Yes... They will both be disappointed when they learn that you were here and they missed you.'

Once James had finished eating he asked his aunt to thank the servants for doing his washing and ironing. Once she had done that she said to James, 'I found one of Jacobaas' old hats in the passage cupboard this morning. I hope it fits... Come, let's go and see.'

They went to the cupboard where his aunt removed the hat and handed it over.

James placed it on his head. 'Fits perfectly,' he said with a smile.

'Good, you will be needing that today out on the veldt.'

Then she took him to the front of the house where Wellington was already saddled and waiting for him. James hugged his aunt and then gave her a kiss on the cheek. 'Thanks for every thing, Aunt Ruth.' He could feel moisture in his eyes.

'Oh yes,' she said, 'I nearly forgot. Haans also gave me this to give you.' She took a revolver out of her apron pocket. 'He said it was far too dangerous for you to travel without it. It's an old gun that belonged to Jacobaas. He doesn't use it any longer. These go with it.' She handed him a box of bullets.

James couldn't believe that they were actually giving him a gun to protect himself from their own countrymen. 'May God bless you and your family, Aunt Ruth.... Please thank Haans for me, and also Freda for the beautiful supper last night. I'm sorry that I can't stay longer with you all.' He kissed his aunt on the cheek and then gave her another big hug. James then took hold of the reins and climbed into Wellington's saddle.

'Oh James, there's one other thing that I've forgotten,' she said, handing him a folded piece of paper. 'It's a rough sketch of how to get to Belmont from here.'

James took the paper from her and placed it into his jacket pocket. 'Thank you… You have all been very kind. I hope that one day I will be able to repay you.'

'May God go with you James,' she said waving her hand with tears in her eyes.

He gave her a salute. Then, Corporal James Mitchell rode off up the road with the dogs chasing after him. Halfway along he stopped and turned the horse around. His aunt was no longer standing there. James glanced around at the farm with its fields of green maize stretching as far as he could see. He turned the horse and then he continued along the jacaranda tree-lined road, with the pleasant fragrance of the jacaranda trees heavy in the air.

65 James more-or-less headed west with the warm morning sun on his back. Over to the southwest he could hear the sound of cannons booming amongst the distant kopjes. After a short time he came across several black farm-workers. They were riding on the back of a rickety-cart pulled by a pair of moth-eaten looking donkeys. James gave them a friendly wave as he rode on past them, but they ignored him and looked the other way. He continued on his way until he reached a small river, which Piet had marked on the sketch as the Reit River.

There was a wooden bridge over. The name Waterval Drift was engraved into a signpost. According to the sketch he was to cross over and then follow the river south until he reached the ruins of an old farmhouse. He turned left after the bridge and trotted Wellington through the short grass while keeping a sharp eye open for any signs of Boers. It was a beautiful day with a cloudless blue-sky and James filled his lungs with the clean fresh air. Wild flowers were growing in abundance everywhere and as the horse parted them hundreds of colourful butterflies scattered into the air.

Later, James stopped alongside the river at a secluded spot, to let Wellington have a drink. He was thirsty himself and decided to have a drink from his canteen. As he gulped down a mouthful of the cool, thirst quenching liquid his eyes surveyed the surrounding area. When he had finished he wiped his mouth with the back of his hand.

James' heart suddenly gave a skip as the adrenalin kicked in after spotting a large column of Boer commandos heading southwest. He froze for a second and then instinctively crouched down. He quickly took hold of Wellington by the reins and led him into a thicket of bush. He waited, holding onto his breath with his heart pounding wildly, with James not believing that he hadn't been spotted.

A moment later he exhaled through his mouth as he gave a sigh of relief. Then, he quickly removed the pistol and loaded it with six bullets. After that, he watched from his clandestine position, as hundreds of horses and men rode on past. Several times, James noticed Boers glancing in his direction, making him hold onto his breath each time. He counted their numbers and took note of their artillery, etc, writing it down on the back of the sketch.

Once the last of the Boers had gone, and James was sure that there were no stragglers he backed Wellington out of the bushes. After remounting he rode up the riverbank and then followed in the Boer's tracks. The landscape was relatively flat apart from a range of kopjes in the near distance, and only a few isolated trees were dotted here and there. The lack of good cover worried James as the last thing he wanted was to be spotted out in the open by Boer scouts. Over in the distance the roar of cannon fire seemed closer. A large snake suddenly slithered across the ground in front of Wellington. He reared up whinnying. James held on tight yelling, 'Whoa, boy! Whoa!' The snake soon disappeared amongst the grass and stones and Wellington soon settled down with James comforting him. 'It's alright, boy, it's gone now.' He gave the horse several pats on the side of his neck to reassure him.

Midday was approaching and it was starting to get very hot. James was beginning to perspire and his sweat attracted the flies, which pestered him, and he had to continuously wave them away from his eyes. The Boers tracks were now heading directly west and after about an hour James came to a narrow ravine, between several low kopjes. At first, he was a bit sceptical of continuing on. His mind was busy thinking, 'What if the Boers had left scouts to keep watch in-case anyone was following? ...And, what if he became trapped in there, there would probably be no means of escaping?'

THE PLOUGH, THE GUN AND THE GLORY

James removed the pistol from his jacket pocket and checked it. Then, he proceeded into the narrow gorge with the sweat trickling down his forehead. Rocks and trees overhung on either side with thick green bush growing abundantly as well as tall wheat-coloured grass. Under the circumstances, it was an eerie type of place, which sent prickles up James' neck. To add to the tension Wellington seemed a little nervous. James patted his neck and spoke to him in a soothing manner, but he suspected that the horse had sensed there was danger in the air.

After half an hour James suddenly brought Wellington to a rapid halt. On either side of him two men were pointing rifles at him. Both shouted something in Afrikaans, which James guessed meant he was to dismount. His heart rate increased as his mind began racing. He was going to have to act swiftly if he was to avoid being captured again. As he dismounted he quickly drew the pistol from his jacket, turned suddenly and shot the nearest man in the chest, as the gun exploded in his hand James ran towards him. When he reached the body he grabbed the man's rifle and then scrambled for cover behind large boulders. Bullets were kicking dust and sand up all around him as others ricocheted off the rocks.

It took a moment for James to recover his breath and then he tried to see where the other man had got too. The top of a hat was just visible above some rocks. James waited with his heart racing as he took careful aim. As soon as the man showed himself James was going to take a shot at him. Sweat was running down his forehead and getting into his eyes. He quickly wiped it away with the sleeve of his jacket then concentrated once-again on the hat. After a few moments James suspected something wasn't quite right. No one he ever knew sat that still for this long.

His eyes started surveying the surrounding rocks on either side of him. What if the Boer had moved from that position? But why could he still see his hat? And what if there had been more than two of them? James' eyes continued to roam the area as the questions went through his mind. He then decided to move to another position, but while on his way a Boer suddenly appeared in front of him. Both men pointed their rifles simultaneously and pulled the triggers. James felt a bullet go whistling past his face as the other man went reeling backwards. James quickly reloaded another round into the breach, and then he slowly moved forwards in a crouched position.

The man was lying face down between two rocks and was very still. James thought he would check to see if he was dead or not. In order to do that, he had to drag the body by the feet onto some flatter ground. James turned him over and looked down at him. He was only a young boy of about seventeen or eighteen. His hair was long and blonde and his face was covered with freckles. James knelt next to the body. He brushed the boys hair away from his forehead as he said, 'Dear Lord... I ask that you take this young boy's soul so that he may find peace in Heaven. His life was taken from him, not in anger or rage, Lord, but in self defence only.'

James got to his feet and then returned to the first man he had shot. He was a little older than the other boy. After that, James looked for a suitable place to bury them both, as he didn't want to leave their bodies to be ravaged by animals or vultures. He dug two shallow graves using the butt from one of the rifles. Then he scooped the sand out using both of his hands. Once that was done he dragged the bodies one at a time, over to the graves. After covering them with the sand he then placed as many stones as could find over them. Next, he took the one rifle and drove it into the ground between the graves. As he picked up the younger boy's weapon he noticed a name carved into the butt.

James wiped the sand off first and then read the name aloud. 'P. Vorster.' The sound of his own voice stunned him for a moment as a horrible cold feeling came over him. His heart skipped a beat and he dropped to his knees. 'Oh God, no!' he cried out. 'No! No! Nooo!' He was trembling as he brushed his hand through his hair while thinking of what had happened. James shook his head several times in disbelief as he repeated, 'God forgive me! God forgive me!'

Sometime later he got to his feet and looked around at the surrounding bush. The hat was still visible above the rock. James approached it without caution. He found it sitting on a piece of driftwood. James removed it and went back to the two graves where he placed the hat over the rifle protruding from the ground.

66 It was approaching nightfall by the time James reached the railway siding of Graspan approximately eight miles north of Belmont. Once closer to the town he was suddenly challenged by several pickets (guards) from the 2nd Battalion Royal Canadian Regiment. Later, James learned that Lord Methuen had left Belmont early that morning and that the Boers had again attacked the British columns inflicting heavy casualties. Lord Methuen had now pushed on towards Enslin approximately ten miles further north.

After a quick meal provided by the Canadians James pushed on towards Enslin in order to catch up with his contingent. As it was now dark, he followed the railway line, which ran along the border between Cape Colony and the Orange Free State. He kept to the Cape Colony side of the track as he thought it would probably be a little safer. He arrived on the outskirts of Enslin at 11.45pm. Four pickets challenged him from the Tasmanian contingent. A lantern was lit and James recognised one of the men he had fought onboard ship, whose name he recalled was Fredrick.

He approached James. 'Un-sling your rifle and drop it to the ground!' he said gruffly. 'And be very careful how you do it!'

James reluctantly did as requested.

The rifle was picked up and looked at. Then, the big man asked one of the others to lift the lantern higher so he could see what had been engraved into the butt. He read the name out aloud so that the others could hear. 'P. Vorster... Well now me mates, it seems that we have captured ourselves a Boer!'

'I'm no Boer Frederick! And you darn well know it!' James replied feeling somewhat annoyed as the man knew full well who he was.

Frederick gestured with the rifle for him to dismount.

James obliged.

'Now, what would you be doing out here in the middle of the night armed with a Mauser and all?'

'I'm now attached to Rimington's Tigers. I have been out scouting,' James replied.

'Scouting?'

'That's what I said.'

'So how do you explain this?' He pointed to the rifle.

'It was taken from a dead Boer.'

'Is that so?'

'Yeah!'

'Well anyway, we weren't told of any scouts coming in tonight masquerading as Boers, were we mates?'

They agreed that they hadn't.

'I could shoot you right here,' Frederick continued, 'and say that we thought you were the enemy sneaking into our camp. Especially as you are carrying this.' He held the rifle up.

'Yeah, I guess you could... But, on the other hand you have already recognised me and you know who I am.'

'Ahhh, but no-one else knows that, do they?'

'They do.' James pointed to the other men.

'They do what I tell them! If I say you are a Boer, then you're a Boer! If I said you were a bleedin wallaby, they would agree! Handcuff him mates, he's going to spend the night in the lock-up!'

James' hands were brought behind his back and the cuff's applied to his wrists.

The Tasmanian then pushed his finger hard into James chest. 'I still think you had something to do with ripping me off of me money!'

'You mean my money... I won the money fair and square, remember?'

The big man suddenly punched James hard in the stomach and then in the face splitting his lip. The blood shot out over his fist. He wiped it off onto James' jacket. Then, he punched James again and he sank to his knees.

'How do you like that hey, big boy?' The Tasmanian punched him a third time on his ear. The blow stunned James numbing the side of his head. The man then struck him again under the jaw. James' eyes rolled back and he toppled onto the dirt. After that, he was savagely kicked several times in the ribs and head. Once Frederick had enough he looked at the others. 'Lock him up!' he growled at them. James was then dragged off towards a cage on wheels. The handcuffs were removed and then he was thrown into the cage where he lay unconscious on the dirty wooden floor.

67   James woke to find it was daybreak. He was cold and every muscle in his body ached with pain. His lips were sore and swollen and his one ear was throbbing. As he tried to sit up, sharp stabbing pains shot through his ribcage causing him to wince. After awhile he slowly and stiffly got to his feet and then peered out between the bars. The surrounding area was covered with hundreds of tents. Smoke from campfires, hung in the still morning air like a thick misty-cloud. Over to his right Wellington was standing a little way off, together with several other horses. Wellington was still saddled and was eating hay from a nosebag. James patted the side pocket of his jacket feeling for the gun. He gave a sigh of relief when he realised it was still in there. Next, he checked the other pocket for the box of bullets.

About twenty minutes later he noticed that someone was approaching. A large bunch of keys were attached to his belt. James' heart gave a little jump in his chest. When the man arrived the prisoner said, 'I am Corporal James Mitchell of Rimington's Tigers. I demand to be taken to a senior officer immediately.'

The overweight man sniffed loudly. Then, he made a noise at the back of his throat and spat some mucus out of his mouth onto the sand. 'Is that right?' he asked sarcastically, 'well that's strange because I heard you were a Boer.' He came up closer to the bars. 'I've brought you breakfast.' He pushed a bowl of sickly looking porridge through the bars.

James moved quickly and grabbed him by the arm. At the same time he pulled the gun out of his pocket and shoved it into the man's face. 'Now, listen very carefully and you won't get hurt. I want you to open the lock and I want you to do it quietly.'

The man had suddenly become very nervous and he hesitated. James cocked the hammer on the revolver. Hearing the distinctive click the man hurriedly removed the bunch of keys from his belt with his free hand. Then, he fumbled with them awkwardly trying to find the correct one.

'If you drop them I'll kill you,' James threatened. 'So, I suggest you think very carefully about doing that.'

The man nodded with his eyes bulging in his head. 'This is the one,' he said showing it to James.

'I hope so for your sake. Now, place it into the lock and undo it.'

The man did as he was told. As soon as the lock turned the door sprang opened slightly.

'Good,' said James. 'Now, I am sure that you don't really want to die here this morning, do you?'

The man shook his head. He was perspiring profusely and the sweat flicked from his thinning hair.

'I want you to enter the lock-up. Just remember that I can't possibly miss you from this distance.'

James let go of his arm and the man came through the barred door. Once he was inside James swiftly struck him across the back of his head with the gun and he dropped to the floor. James looked around to see if anyone had seen what was going on. A few men were standing around chatting outside their tents, while others were stretching and yawning. None of them had noticed anything-suspicious taking place. James calmly closed the door behind him and locked it. Then, he walked as normally as possible over to Wellington. 'So far, so good,' he thought as he removed the nosebag. He dropped the keys inside the bag and placed it down on the ground. James took hold of the reins. He then placed his left foot into the stirrup and hauled himself up and into the saddle.

A couple of the men glanced his way for a moment and then they looked away again. James turned Wellington slowly around and walked the horse away from the others not to draw attention to himself. He greeted two men who were close-by and continued on his way towards the perimeter of the camp.

Someone suddenly shouted, 'The Boer's escaped! The Boer's escaped!'

James' heart jumped wildly in his chest.

...'Stop him! ...Stop him!' someone else shouted.

James spurred Wellington hard saying loudly, 'Let's go, boy! Go! Go! Go!'

The big horse took off with James skilfully guiding him between the rows of tents and sleepy-eyed bewildered men. As he galloped through the camp bullets whistled past his head. Several times troopers would appear ahead of them and James would have to bring Wellington almost to an abrupt halt, with dust and stones flying into the air, before heading off down another row of tents.

THE PLOUGH, THE GUN AND THE GLORY

Dozens of men were now running in all directions taking pot shots at both horse and rider. James turned the horse left and then galloped between rows of tents, with more bullets whizzing past his head. Finally, he reached the edge of the camp only to find pickets blocking the way out. James spurred Wellington harder as he headed straight for the two men. The pickets panicked and dived out of the way as Wellington leapt into the air and over their heads. Other pickets guarding the camp perimeter fired several shots at them, but luckily none of them found their target. James kept Wellington going at a full gallop heading north, knowing that there would already be mounted infantry hot on his heels. After awhile he slowed the horse to a canter and without looking back he kept on heading north towards Enslin.

James reached his destination shortly before midday where he immediately reported to Major Rimington. He explained how he was beaten-up and thrown into the lock-up by the Tasmanian pickets at the Graspan laager.

'I'll have a message of protest immediately dispatched to Captain Cameron and demand that he take disciplinary measures against the men involved,' the major advised. Then, after listening briefly to James' story of how John Smith was killed and also of James' capture by Boers, the major arranged for James to complete a report sheet of the whole incident, including what happened at Graspan.

'Once you've finished your report corporal, proceed onto the medical corps and have your wounds treated. From there report to the quartermaster stores and draw your replacement kit.'

'Yes sir.'

'Once you have done that, go over to the armourer and draw another rifle.'

'Yes sir.'

'You will be reattached to another scout and will probably be sent out on reconnaissance this afternoon.'

'Yes sir.'

After completing the report James did as previously instructed and was now making his way over towards the cookhouse for lunch, when a familiar voice called out, 'Hey James! ... James!'

He turned to see George hurriedly approaching.

'George!' he said loudly brandishing a big grin. 'Boy, am I glad to see you.'

The two men shook hands and then embraced one another. They spoke excitedly about the past few days, catching up with each other's news, as they made their way towards the cookhouse. Throughout lunch they both chatted in-between swallowing their food and gulping tea down. George told James of the dissension amongst the troops and even several officers, that Lord Methuen was trying to advance too quickly towards Kimberley. 'The success of the Boer attack at Belmont,' he continued, 'could probably have been avoided if Methuen would only slow down. Thirty-three horses had died purely from exhaustion between Orange River Station and Belmont. Another twenty-eight were killed during the battle. Over three hundred troops were killed.' George swallowed a mouthful of tea. 'It was the same thing at Graspan,' he added wiping his mouth. 'The cavalry were unable to halt the retreat and take-on the Boers because there just weren't enough of them, and also because their horses were too exhausted.'

'You know what one of the big problems is here, George?'

He looked at James a little puzzled. 'What?'

'The high altitude.'

George's expression didn't change.

'Look, we are at least 6000 feet above sea level. We are using horses that haven't been acclimatised to the conditions. We need local horses that are used to the high altitude and the tough conditions, like the Boers have, that would even things up a little.

'The Whalers from New South Wales are damn good horses.'

'I'm not saying that they aren't, George. The British have also got good horses, but they've all come from sea level. Up here the air is much thinner. That's why we've all been finding it so hard to breathe.'

George nodded. 'Hey, do you remember the twenty-nine New South Wales Lancers who were on the train with us?' George suddenly asked changing the subject.

'Yeah... the ones that came to Orange River Station with us?'

'Yeah. Well anyway they did really well at Graspan.'

'Yeah?'

'Yeah... At one time they were cut off from the British lines when the Boers retreated. Everyone thought they were done for, that the Boers were going to get them, but they held steady under fire and drove the Boers off in another direction.'

'Good on them.'

'The limeys have nick-named them the Fighting Twenty-Nine.'

'Yeah? That's excellent.'

'The infantry haven't faired too well though. Just about all the units have got blisters on their feet as large as two-bob pieces. They practically wore the soles off their boots getting here. Many have also fallen sick from dysentery and also sunburn, and hundreds are weak from the lack of proper food.'

James shook his head as he gave a sigh. 'Our infantry units need horses George, that's the only way we're going to beat the Boers.'

'Hey, another thing, have you heard that General Methuen's pulling out of here this afternoon?'

'No. ...You're the first bloke that I have spoken to since I arrived.'

'He's heading for the Modder River with only over half of his troops.'

At that moment they were interrupted by someone who asked, 'Are one of you blokes James Mitchell by any chance?'

James looked up at him. 'Yeah, that's me.'

'I'm Frank Jones. You have been assigned to me by Major Rimington.'

James extended his hand and the two men greeted one another with a firm shake.

'If you've finished your lunch we'll go and prepare our kit and horses to leave within the next half an hour.'

'Right.' James got to his feet. 'This is a mate of mine, George Gleniste.'

The two men shook hands. James then said a quick goodbye to George and then left with the other man.

68   Sergeant Frank Jones peered northwards through his binoculars from the height of a small kopje. He was looking towards the tree-lined Modder River. He surveyed the railway bridge and saw that the Boers had destroyed it. On the east side of the damaged bridge there was a fork in the river where both the Modder and Reit Rivers joined one another. General Del la Rey had dug-in his commandos along the south bank. Further along the river bank General Cronje had done the same. East of the bridge General Prinsloo was dug-in towards Rosmeads Drift. The sergeant took the glasses away from his face and passed them over to the Australian. 'These Boers know how to fight a war when they're outnumbered by professional soldiers,' he commented to James.

James placed binoculars to his eyes and then scanned the riverbanks first and then surveyed the bridge. He could see the debris lying everywhere. 'I see what you mean. They're well prepared and waiting to welcome Methuen.'

'I'll mark their positions and approximate numbers,' said Frank unfolding his map.

James placed the glasses back to his eyes. 'I wonder what General Methuen's plan will be this time?'

Frank hunched his shoulders. 'Who knows? ...All we can do is give him the best information we can, the rest is up to him.'

After writing the relevant information down the two scouts then headed back to the British lines where Sergeant Jones made his report to Major Rimington. He then took the information to the Lieutenant General's operational tent.

Later, James, Frank and a few other scouts, including George Gleniste, who were not already out on reconnaissance duties were attached to the mounted infantry to help bolster their numbers. After first studying the information the two scouts had provided, General Methuen set out towards Modder River. His plan was to make a bold frontal attack against De la Rey's men. Then, General Colvile was to attack Cronje on the eastern flank, while General Pole-Carew attacked Prinsloo on the west flank.

As they closed in on the two rivers General Methuen brought his army to a halt. A short while later the balloon corps launched a hot air observation balloon attached to a wagon by a winch cable. The balloon carried a signaller, who after surveying the Boer positions provided information back to the ground using signal flags, confirming what the scouts had previously reported.

Boer scouts had also reported the arrival of British troops and once the balloon was sighted aloft, the order for the field guns to commence firing was given. Within moments the German manufactured Creusot 155mm (Long Toms) boomed loudly as they sent their 94-pound shells hurtling towards the British lines. The air was suddenly filled with a yellow, grey smoke as bursting Lyddite shells fell amongst the troops, killing and maiming both man and horse.

The Royal Field-Artillery answered back, their 15-pound shells exploding along the banks of the river, hurling clumps of earth and grass skywards. Methuen then ordered the 9th Brigade and Guards Brigade forward and they surged towards the Boers. They opened fire from their trenches sending a rain of lead in the direction of the cream of the British troops. The imperial army were out in the open and without cover. Bullets kicked up the dirt and sand around them, as they pushed forward in close formation. Brave men fell to the ground dead or mortally wounded, while others continued surging towards an encounter with certain death. The cavalry bravely galloped their horses through the barrage of lead and exploding shells, as machine guns killed and wounded horses and riders.

James was galloping towards the hail of lead when Wellington's left ear was blown off, spattering James with blood. Next thing, the horse went down from under him. James hit the ground hard landing on his back, knocking the wind from him. For a few moments he lay there trying to suck the air back into his lungs. He was about to get to his feet when he was again knocked violently to the ground. This time, it was due to a horse jumped over him, which collected him with its hind legs. James lay on the ground grabbing hold of his side in agony. Eventually, he was able to get to his feet. He looked in dismay at Wellington. He was badly wounded. Most of his snout had been shot away on one side, including the eye, and blood was pumping from the gaping wounds. 'Noooo!' he cried out as he made his way over and knelt down next to the dying horse. Wellington was whinnying in agony while trying to get to his feet at the same time.

'Oh God noooo! ...I am so sorry boy! I am so sorry!' James reluctantly picked up the rifle and placed it to Wellington's head. 'Forgive me boy. Please forgive me.'

He pulled the trigger and the rifle kicked in his arms. Wellington's blood sprayed out over James' face and uniform. He then turned and hurriedly made his way towards the river. Bullets were whizzing past his head kicking up the dust around him. James no longer cared for his safety. He continued firing his rifle at the enemy until he ran out of ammunition. James then hurriedly attached the bayonet to his rifle and then he pressed on. At last he reached the trenches. They were abandoned apart from a few wounded men and boys, and blood-soaked corpses. James looked up through the swirling smoke to see the Boers were crossing the river to the other side.

He gave chase. Once he reached the river James waded into the bloodstained water. The bodies of dead Boers were intermingled with British troops, together with the carcases of horses, which were floating slowly downstream. Wounded men and horses were trying to stay afloat and swim to the safety of the riverbank. There was a man near James, a Gordon Highlander, also forging his way across the river. His head suddenly exploded with his blood, bone, brains and hair sprayed into the air. James pushed on with the adrenalin pumping through his veins. Finally, he reached the opposite bank.

Crawling out of the blood-soaked water he then got to his feet. A Boer was directly opposite him. James rushed towards him with the bayonet out in front. The steel blade drove into the man's chest, travelling through his torso first it then protruded out of his back. James struggled to remove the steel blade from the body and eventually it came out. There was another Boer nearby. James ran towards him. The man saw him coming and quickly drew a panga from its sheath. James lunged at him with the bayonet. The Boer was quick to move out of the way. He struck viciously at James with the large blade.

The Australian was lucky though, the blade missing him by inches. James tried to plunge the bayonet into the man's stomach but he missed. The Boer struck out at James with another vicious blow from the panga. James placed the rifle overhead and the blade struck the steel barrel with a shattering blow. This time, James let got of the rifle and punched the man square on the nose. He went down onto his back still holding the panga in his one hand. James quickly grabbed the rifle and as the Boer was getting to his feet he drove the long blade into the man's chest. He immediately fell to the ground.

James looked up and saw that many of the Boers were mounting their horses. He ran after the fleeing men on horseback screaming his lungs out, but they galloped away to the north. James stood staring at them while gasping for air. The tears were running down his cheeks as he turned around and then looked across the river, and then up over the battlefield. Amongst the swirling clouds of black gun-smoke lay hundreds of bodies… the bodies of the men who had died for the Empire. Other wounded and dying men lay scattered across the veldt. Many, were crying out in agony while others waited patiently for ambulances to come to their aid. Mingled amongst them, were the carcasses of hundreds of horses. Animals that had survived the slaughter whinnied with pain waiting to be put out of their misery. Death and destruction was everywhere.

James waded into the bloodied water and slowly made his way across the river. Once more, pushing between mutilated carcases and the bodies of men. From there, he made his way back to where Wellington lay. When James arrived alongside the dead horse he knelt down and gently stroked his neck several times. James then waved several flies away and after that he decided to remove the saddle, which he placed on the ground.

Cape-carts and horse-drawn ambulances were moving through the veldt collecting the wounded and dead. The carcases would be left for the ants, flies, wild animals and the vultures to feast on. James tried to lift Wellington's saddle onto his shoulder but he was unable due to the pain in his ribcage. He suddenly felt light-headed. His knees gave way under him and he fell to the ground. He lay there without attempting to get onto his feet, staring into the eyes of a dead Highlander. The multitude of tiny wild flowers growing abundantly everywhere swayed in the gentle breeze. Butterflies, were precariously perched on the petals, while others fluttered around unaware of the death and the bloodshed surrounding them. James' vision went blurry and finally the pain dissipated and a calm blackness took over.

69 'Corporal! ...Corporal! ...Are you awake yet?' a female voice asked softly with a friendly tone of voice. James slowly opened his eyes. For a moment he thought an angle was standing by his bedside. Although his throat was dry and parched he managed to ask softly, 'Am... am I dead?'

'No,' she replied with a smile while shaking her head.

His eyes roamed the surroundings and then he realised that he was in a field hospital. He looked back at the nurse. There was something familiar about her face. She reminded him of someone but he couldn't think who it was.

'How are you feeling?' she asked, smiling down at him.

'Sore... What happened? How did I get here?'

'You were brought in from the battlefield in a concussed state. You also have a badly bruised ribcage, plus multiple lacerations about your torso.'

It suddenly came to James in a flash. He now realised who she was. Somehow though, she looked different from how he had remembered her. 'Christina?' he asked with a little uncertainty.

'Yes James, it's me... I'm so glad that you have regained consciousness at last.'

He was still a little confused. 'What are you doing here?'

'At the present moment I am nursing you, plus a dozen other wounded men.'

'I meant...'

'Shhh!' she said softly placing her finger to her lips. 'You should rest. I'll tell you all about it some other time.'

James tried to sit up, but a sharp pain in his ribs made him wince and he lowered himself back onto the pillow. 'How long have I been in here?'

'Three days.'

'Three days?' he repeated with disbelief. 'What's the date?'

THE PLOUGH, THE GUN AND THE GLORY

'There are only nine days left till Christmas.' She gave a little smile.

...'How did we do... in the battle, I mean?'

She shook her head. 'Not good... four hundred and sixty men were killed and many wounded. General Methuen was also wounded in the thigh...Colonel Northcote died from his wounds. Over a hundred horses perished. Many of them dropped dead under their riders from sheer exhaustion.'

James suddenly thought of Wellington lying out on the veldt and a lump came to his throat. After three days out in the open the vultures and other animals would have left very little of him.

'We did even worse at Magersfontein,' Christina continued. 'General Methuen's 1st Division Highlanders were totally defeated and failed to relieve Kimberley. They were forced to retreat here to the Modder River. I'm afraid the Boer Generals, Cronje, Prinsloo and De la Rey, proved to be too good.'

James shook his head in disbelief.

'It gets worse... are you sure you still want me to continue?'

James nodded. 'I may as well hear it from you as anyone else.'

'Lieutenant-General Sir Redvers Buller and Lieutenant-General Sir Francis Clery lost the battle at Colenso. Ladysmith is still under siege by the Boers. The imperial army has been severely beaten by a collection of farmers in only seven days... It's such a monumental military disaster that the British army have named it Black Week.'

'Black Week?' James sighed. It was difficult for him to believe that this could have happened to Her Majesties Army, the greatest and most powerful army in the whole world.

'The doctor will be coming to see you shortly. If you are strong enough you will have to relinquish your bed as we are desperately short.'

'That won't be a problem.'

'I have to leave you now, James... I'll come back and see you later.'

He nodded.

Christina left his side and James slowly closed his eyes. His mind drifted back to the small schoolhouse in

Wickepin where he first saw Christina. She was a new girl at the school and was placed in the seat near James. And, even though he was only fourteen at6 the time, and she only twelve, his heart had skipped a beat and he had fallen in love.

It took him two weeks to pluck up the courage to talk to her during break time, and only with help from his older sister Alanna. From that day on though, Christina and he became good friends. Later, they became childhood sweethearts and when he was sixteen, he and Christina made a promise to each other to marry once they were older. Sometimes after school, they would secretly meet down at the river. The only other person to know about this was Alanna. She would often call around to Christina's house and ask her mother if she could come out and play. Although they all knew it was deceitful it was the only way they could think of getting Christian's mother to allow her out of the house. Christina's parents were very strict and would never let her out to play with the other kids, especially boys.

Everything had been going fine until one afternoon when Christina told James that her father had been transferred with the bank, and that they were moving to Melbourne. It was the last time they saw each other. Christina promised to write every week, but he only received one letter from her despite him writing several letters to her. Some years later, he heard from a friend in Wickepin that Christina had married a wealthy banker in Melbourne. James was heartbroken and it took a long time for him to get over her. Now, after all these years she had suddenly come back into his life in the middle of a war in South Africa.

70   When Charles Mitchell and the doctor from Wickepin arrived at Rambling Meadows Lily was waiting anxiously out on the verandah for them. She didn't have to say anything to her husband. Her hopeless sad face and swollen red eyes, told him everything that he had feared. Without saying anything he raced inside. Alanna and the two other girls were standing in the parlour. They were crying into handkerchiefs and their faces were ghostly white as they tried in vain to dry their tears.

Charles slowly approached the large leather-covered couch. William's blood covered the entire area including parts of the immediate floor area. He lay there white-faced cold and stiff, his young body without life. Charles got down on his knees next to his son's body. Tears were running down his cheeks as he gently touched William's face. Then, he broke down sobbing. The girls tried to comfort him without success.

Later, Charles slowly got to his feet and looked over at Alanna. 'What did these two men look like?'

Alanna wiped her eyes. 'One of them had a large scar on his face, from his mouth to his right-hand ear. He had blue eyes. He was unshaven and rough looking.' She sniffed loudly then blew her nose.

'His name was Harry,' Elizabeth added, 'he was tall with blonde hair.'

'And the other?' Charles asked Alanna again.

'He was unshaven and also rough looking... I think his eyes were a dark brown.'

'Yes they were,' Elizabeth added, 'almost black father.'

'I think his name was Bert,' Alanna added.

'Which one of them shot William?'

The two girls glanced at one another for a moment and then looked back at their father. 'We don't know,' they both answered.

'I do,' said Bridget. 'It was the one with the scar on his face.'

'Are you sure?' her father asked.

She nodded. 'I saw him run over to his horse. He quickly removed a rifle and then shot at us. After that I saw

William lying in the cart with blood over his back.' She started to cry.

Charles Mitchell tried to offer them all a little comfort while the doctor examined William's body. After a short time the doctor turned to face Charles. 'I'm afraid that William was shot through the lung. There was nothing anyone would have been able to do to save his life.'

Charles walked over to the window and starred out over the verandah. Then, he said aloud, 'I swear, God is my witness; the man who killed my son will also die for this foul deed! ...I will hunt him down like a wild animal and I will kill him myself!'

The doctor approached him. 'Perhaps you should leave that to the local constabulary, Charles.'

'No! That's easy for you to say, doctor! That's not your son lying dead on the couch! That animal must die in the same manner that he killed my boy! ...Nothing else will satisfy me! ...Nothing else will let me rest until that has been done! ...Nothing, I tell you!'

'You have to think of your own health Charles,' the doctor advised, 'remember that you have a heart condition.'

'My heart will do me just fine doctor, just fine!'

71   The following day James was moved from the hospital into a smaller tent together with two other wounded men. Two day's later he was up and about, but still had to take things easy. Later in the day he saw Christina. She was on her lunch break and they went for a short walk together.

'How come you ended up here in South Africa?' James asked as they made their way between the seemingly endless rows of white tents.

'It's a long story James.'

'I'm not in a hurry... Besides, you did say you would tell me.'

She gave a sigh. 'I suppose I did... After leaving my husband I worked in a Melbourne hospital as a nurse. Later, when I read about the war here in South Africa I volunteered to join the Army Nursing Services. I was amongst the first nurses from the colonies to sign up. I even had to pay for my own passage to Cape Town, although I was reimbursed later.'

'Why didn't you ever write to me like you promised you would?'

...'I did try, James, believe me. As a matter-of-fact after my first letter to you I then wrote several others... I just never posted any of them.'

'And why not?'

'I don't know... I suppose it was because I found myself caught up in a circle of new friends at finishing school, and then later Melbourne society life.'

'Obviously I was no longer good enough for you then?'

She shook her head. 'It wasn't that, James... It's just that... well... my mother and father always had such high aspirations for me. Ever since I can remember they have always wanted me to marry a lawyer or a successful businessman... Anyway, six months after I was introduced to a banker, Stephen Davidson, he asked me to marry him. He was twelve years older than me. At the time, I thought he was the most dashing man in the whole of Melbourne society.'

James spotted several large flat rocks over to one side and asked Christina if she would like to sit down. She was feeling a little tired and said that would be nice. James first dusted the rocks down with his hat before Christina sat down.

Further away, over to their right, were the new graves of the young men who had died at Modder River. The mounds of fresh earth were marked with small wooden crosses with a serial number carved into them.

'So, you just forgot all about me?' James said, picking up the conversation where they had left off

'Oh James... You're still that unspoilt, almost naive, fresh-faced farm boy that I once knew and loved so dearly. But, you have to realise that going to Melbourne changed me. I'm not the same little girl you once knew in Wickepin. I could never have gone back there and been happy. I would have been a miserable wench, pining the whole time for the social life and the hustle and bustle of the big city. I would have missed the fancy parties, the art galleries, operas and museums. I would have been like a fish out of water... Don't you understand that?'

James looked towards the graves and then over at the flower-covered veldt. 'Well, I don't see any fancy parties, art galleries, operas or museums around here... And, I don't see the hustle and bustle of city life either.'

She sighed. 'I had no choice, James... At the time I was desperate to get away from Melbourne and that so-called husband of mine... let alone my parents... I needed time to myself so that I could think of what to do with my life... The war in South Africa offered me that opportunity.'

'Why did you leave your husband?'

She gave another sigh. 'I have never told anyone about this before James, not even my parents... You must first promise me that you will never ever repeat what I am about to tell you.'

'You have my word.'

She knew she could trust him. 'I returned home early from a tea party one afternoon. Usually I would only arrive home around five o'clock. However, on this particular day I got home shortly after three o'clock. As it was a Wednesday afternoon, the maid was off duty and so there was no one at home. Anyway, I made my way up to the bedroom where to my horror I discovered my husband in bed with someone.'

'I'm very sorry to hear that,' he said shaking his head in sympathy.

...'It was a young boy James. Well, he was practically a boy. He worked at the bank.'

'Oh God Christina! ...That must have been a terrible shock for you?'

She nodded. 'At first I didn't know what to do. I was in such a state that all I could think of was to get out of the house. I fled downstairs in panic and then I hurried over to the park opposite the house. I sat on a bench until darkness. It was cold and starting to rain, but I had nowhere else to go, so I went back to the house.'

'Why didn't you go to a friend's house or over to your parents home?'

'I needed time alone to think. In any-case I didn't want anyone to know, especially my parents... Anyway, perhaps if it had been the maid or even another woman, I might have been able to deal with it... Maybe over a period of time I would have been able to forgive him... But, I could never accept the fact that he was sleeping with a young boy.'

'I'm sorry, Christina. I apologise, I should never have pressed you to tell me your private business.'

She wiped her eyes. 'It's not your fault... I was bound to eventually tell someone, so it may just as well be you... Anyway, after that I couldn't stand being anywhere near him. In-fact the very sight of him made me feel quite ill. I moved out of our bedroom and into my own room. I even ate my meals alone. For awhile I thought that perhaps there was something wrong with me. But, the more I thought about it, the more I realised that our marriage had been nothing more than a charade from the very beginning. It was simply a sham, a front, for him to hide the fact that he was homosexual.' Christina waved a fly away from her face. 'When we had to attend parties and also bank functions the other guests noticed our apparent coolness towards one another. I started to get the feeling that they were gossiping about us and laughing behind my back. I began to wonder if they knew that Stephen was homosexual and that he had been sleeping with a boy from the bank. God only knows how many other young boys he has slept with.'

James shook his head. 'God! Christina! That must have been a terrible time for you?'

'You have no idea James. I even questioned our maid to try and find out how much she knew. At first she denied knowing anything. Then, one morning she broke down and told me that before Stephen married he used to have a number of young boys calling around to the house... To make matters worse he started openly inviting the boy home. He would stay overnight and the two of them would get drunk and then sleep together... I suppose that I should have confided in someone at the time, maybe a close friend, but I was too ashamed and too embarrassed, and I couldn't bring myself to do it. After some months I knew that I had to get away from Stephen or go insane.'

'Surely though, you could have at least told your parents?'

'Oh God James! You knew what my parents were like. The scandal and embarrassment of the whole sordid matter would have destroyed them both. My father would have probably resigned his position at the bank. They would have left Melbourne. God knows what would have happened to them after that.'

'So, you just ran off without any explanation to them whatsoever?'

'It seemed like the only sensible thing I could do at the time.'

James shook his head as he placed his hand to his brow. He then brushed his hair back several times. 'You must have felt desperately alone?'

'Yes... Anyway, I am sorry that I have burdened you with my personal problems.'

'I did ask, remember? Anyway, I'm sure you will feel a little better now. Sometimes it helps to talk about these things.'

'Oh James, you're still so kind and sweet... I am terribly sorry that I hurt you.'

He nodded. 'I eventually got over it.'

'Listen. I have tomorrow night off and the nurse that I share the tent with will be on duty. Would you like to come and visit me? I have a bottle of South African brandy.'

He smiled. 'Now that sounds like a bribe to me?'

'So, what do you say then?'

'Yeah, that would be nice... very nice. What time?'

'About seven o'clock.'

'You'll have to show me your tent on the way back so I that I'll know how to find you.'

'Well then, let's go now and I'll point it out, as I have to be back on duty in five minutes.'

72   After washing himself using a bucket and a flannel, and then brushing his teeth, James dressed into clean clothes. He then made his way over to the tent, which Christina had pointed out the previous day. Along the way he picked a small bunch of wildflowers. When he arrived at her tent there was a lamp burning inside and he could see Christina's silhouette against the canvas wall. For a moment he hesitated and thought of returning to his tent, but then he changed his mind and announced his arrival. 'Christina... it's me... James.'

'Come in,' she replied in a jolly sort of way.

He entered the tent to find her dressed in a silk nightgown. The soft fragrance of her perfume came to his nostrils. It was a pleasant smell and James inhaled it deeply. Christina's long hair hung loose over her shoulders and down her back. It reminded him of when she was much younger. James had always thought that she had the most beautiful mouth and smile he had ever seen on any woman. 'Am I too early?'

'Nooo! ...Heck whatever gave you that idea? Take a seat.' She pointed to a folding wood and canvas chair.

'These are for you.' James handed her the flowers.

'Oh James, that's so sweet of you. Thank you.' She gave him a peck on the check. 'I'll have to place them into a drinking glass, it's all I have.'

He watched her while she poured the water from a canteen into a glass. Then, she artistically arranged the flowers. James sat down in the chair. 'You nurses are living pretty well,' he said, pointing to the two folding beds on either side of the tent.

Christina glanced in his direction. 'Well, compared to the field troops I suppose we are... And, I have absolutely no idea how four grown men fit into such a confined space, and then still manage to get a nights sleep.'

'Well believe me you are usually so exhausted that you don't care... and sleeping in any kind of shelter is a real luxury.'

'I suppose so... Brandy?'

'Thanks.'

Christina poured a good measure into a glass and then handed it to him. Then, she poured herself a similar amount and then held her glass up. 'To our most unexpected and very pleasant reunion.' She clinked her glass against his. 'Cheers,' she said before drinking a mouthful.

James did the same. The alcohol burnt his throat before sending a glowing warm feeling down into the pit of his stomach. He gave a little cough. 'This is very good brandy, but I'm afraid I'm not really used to drinking spirits.'

She smiled softly. 'Of all the people I had to meet in Africa, it had to be you, James.'

'Yeah,' he replied smiling. 'It's funny how life works out, don't you think?'

Christina sat down on one of the canvas beds. 'After I left Wickepin, I missed you so much that I used to cry myself to sleep at night... But, as time passed, Wickepin and all of its beautiful memories faded away. ...I suppose that was only natural?'

'I never ever forgot you... Not even when I found out that you had married a fancy Melbourne banker.'

...'It was different for you, James.'

'Why?'

...'You were still surrounded by familiar things... things that you had grown up with and were used to. You still had your brother and sisters, your same bedroom, the farm and the house... the river and the boathouse... the same school friends. Nothing had really changed for you excepting that I had left. ...I, on the other hand had moved to a strange place. I moved into a new house... went to a new school... met new people and had to make new friends and start a new life.'

James swallowed a mouthful of his brandy without replying.

Christina gave a sigh. 'Please don't judge me so harshly, James.'

...'I'm not judging you.'

'Yes you are... you're still angry with me, I can tell.'

'You did hurt me deeply, Christina, more than anyone has ever hurt me... After you left Wickepin you just forgot about me and all those promises that we made to each other.'

'We were both just kids, James... kids say a lot of things they forget when they grow up... we grew up... time and distance changed us and our childhood dreams.' She handed him the brandy bottle.

James took the bottle and poured half a tumbler of the dark liquid into his glass. After he had placed the bottle down on the floor Christina said, 'I was worried that you might change your mind and not come here tonight.'

...'I almost didn't.'

...'So why did you then?'

...'I'm not sure.'

She smiled softly. 'When I first recognised it was you lying there in the hospital bed, my heart almost jumped out of my chest... For a moment I actually lost my breath and I had this tight feeling in my chest.'

James drank from his glass without saying anything.

...'Do you still remember the first time we ever made love, James?'

'Yeah, of course... I'll never ever forget... it was in the old boatshed.'

'I have never forgotten either... Oh God, I was so nervous that afternoon.' She gave a little laugh. 'Do you remember how we were both shaking and were scared-stiff that someone would come along and find us?'

He smiled while nodding his head. 'You were always nervous with me.'

'Somehow, I feel a bit like that tonight... I know it's silly, but look how I am trembling.' She held out her hands to show him. 'And my heart is racing wildly like it did that day.'

'It's probably just the brandy? I believe it can have that effect on some people.'

'What's yours doing, your heart? I bet it's doing the same?'

'A little.' He swallowed another mouthful of his drink. 'Okay, it's pounding.'

Christina got up from the folding bed. She then kissed him gently on the lips. 'When did you last make love, James?'

He looked into her blue eyes. They were sparkling in the soft lamplight. 'Sometime ago... shortly before I left home to come over here.'

'Is she beautiful... the woman that you made love to?'

...'Yeah I guess so.'

'Are you in love with her?'

...'I'm not sure... maybe... why?'

'I'm just curious... is she in love with you?'

'I think so... well, that's what she said.'

'Where do you know her from?'

...'Her father bought the old Two Valleys property after Mr Fieldman died... You must remember the place?'

'Sort of I suppose... Can I ask what her name is?'

'Yeah... it's Veronica.'

Christina picked up a hand-brush and started brushing her hair. After a few moments she said softly, 'James.'

'Yeah.'

'I am so pleased that we have met one another other again after all these years... and that you also came here tonight. I can tell however, that something is deeply troubling you?'

He drank from his glass. 'Yeah, I guess there is.'

'Is it something to do with me?'

...'No,' he replied shaking his head, 'it has nothing to do with you. Why do you think that?'

Christina gave a sigh of relief. 'Would you like to talk about it?'

James shook his head. 'Not really, well not tonight... perhaps another time.'

Christina came forwards and then kissed him gently on the lips. 'I want you to forget all about the war tonight... promise me?'

He nodded.

'Make love to me James.'

He stared into her eyes. 'I have bruised ribs which are still very tender, you know?'

'I know... We can do it gently, like the very first time we ever made love.' She kissed him lustfully on his mouth. James kissed her back sensually, his heart pumping quickly, and the earlier memories of her went flooding through his mind. 'Oh, James, the truth is I never ever truly stopped loving you.'

They kissed intensely. James could now feel something stirring in his groin area. He stopped kissing her and said, 'I've never made love on a folding bed, have you?'

'No.'

'Somehow, I don't think it will be strong enough,' he added.

'Then, we will just have to use blankets on the floor like we used to do.' Christina went over to the lamp and turned the flame down until it was almost dark in the tent. 'There, I think it's more romantic in here like this, with the flowers and everything, don't you?'

'Yeah, it's great.'

'Fancy another brandy?'

'Yeah.'

She poured them a glass each. Then she took the blankets off her bed and laid them out on the floor. 'There, at least that's done.'

James had a drink from his glass while watching Christina in the soft flickering lamp light. She was truly a beautiful woman and he knew that most men would be very proud to be seen out in public arm in arm with her. If anything, she was more beautiful now than ever, if that was at all possible?

There was a loud rumble of thunder in the background. 'Sounds as though we might be in for a storm tonight,' James said softly.

'Oh, I do hope so... I love thunderstorms and when it rains hard during the night, don't you?'

'Not when I have to sleep out in it.'

'No, I suppose not... let me remove your boots for you, so that you can relax?'

'That would be nice.'

Christina removed the putties first, then undid the laces and pulled his off boots one at a time. 'There, that's better isn't it?'

'Much better thanks.'

'I might as well take off your socks too.' She pulled them off and then gently massaged his feet. 'How does that feel?'

'Very nice.'

After a few moments Christina stopped. 'Why don't you come and lie down on the blanket next to me?'

James got out of the chair and joined her.

'That's much better,' she said. 'How about another brandy?'

'Well just a small one or I'll get drunk and pass out on you.'

Christina poured them and then handed James his glass. She placed her glass down and then kissed him on the cheek. James lowered his glass to the ground and then they kissed more passionately. James then kissed her neck and then pushed the tip of his tongue into her ear. She giggled like a young girl, who he remembered so vividly, as the shivers ran along her spine.

After a few moments James placed his hand inside her gown and gently massaged her right breast. Her nipple was erect and surrounded by goose bumps. James did the same with the other breast. Christina started breathing a little heavier. James gently stroked her stomach and then he lowered his hand to her vagina. Her pubic hair was damp. For a few moments he rubbed the inside of her thighs and then he slowly started to massage her clitoris.

Christina's legs slowly began to move apart as she became more aroused. James kissed her on the neck again and then on her breasts. He sucked her nipples while gently massaging her down below. Then, he began kissing her stomach, slowly moving his way down till he reached her vagina. Christina opened her legs a little wider and James inserted his tongue into her warm moist cavity. She gave a little moan. He massaged her tiny, erect penis with his tongue and then he started sucking it. Christina was breathing much heavier now and she was arching her back slightly. 'Oh James,' she moaned softly.

James' penis was throbbing as the blood surged through the multitude of tiny veins, swelling it, making it larger and harder. When Christina was ready for him he inserted his erection into her and began a slow rhythmic pumping action. Christina was breathing harder now as she moved her bottom up and down in rhythm with his thrusting. She could feel him deep inside her and the memories of the boathouse and Wickepin came swirling back.

Heavy rain now began falling on the tent and the almost non-stop booming of thunder rolled across the heavy black-sky, almost drowning out Christian's constant moans of sexual pleasure.

73   After William's funeral, Charles Mitchell prepared a few things for himself in order to go in pursuit of his son's killer, despite his family's continued pleading for him not to go. He then brought the horse around to the verandha. The family were there to see him off.

'You all know that I have little choice,' he told them. 'I shall never find peace in my heart, knowing that my son's killer is somewhere out there... that he still has life in his body, while my son lies cold and lifeless in his grave, years before his time. He has taken our lives and imprisoned us in grief and sorrow. The only thing that will relieve the pain in my heart will be the taking of his miserable worthless life, and letting the devil claim his soul.'

'I don't have to remind you that it's a sin to kill, Charles,' Lily repeated to him.

He turned to her. 'What would you have me do woman! Let William's killer go scot-free? No! That will never do! ...Besides, I may also take this opportunity to remind you that it says in the Bible, an eye for an eye and a tooth for a tooth.'

This time Lily sighed but she didn't reply.

'The Lord will judge me dear, no one else... and most certainly no one in this family... May God take care of you all until my safe return.'

Charles then spurred the white stallion and Thunder galloped away from Rambling Meadows, leaving a trail of dust behind him. An hour later Charles Mitchell arrived in Wickepin. Charles was well known in the village and after asking around he was soon given a lead. It came from a friend of his, Bill Davis, who owned a gunsmiths and saddlery. His friend described both men in detail to him. They had been in his store a day earlier buying bullets and other items. After leaving, they had set off in the direction of Kulin a small village east of Wickepin. Charles rounded up a few swagmen by offering a reward for the capture of both men. Once everyone was saddled up and ready, the eight men set off down the dirt road heading east.

74   Following the succession of military disasters labelled 'Black Week' a sense of gloom and doom now prevailed over the British Empire. Rumours were spreading throughout the camps that Lieutenant General Sir Redvers Buller was to be replaced by Field-Marshal Lord Roberts, who was apparently on his way to South Africa from England.

James decided to make good use of his few days at the hospital to write home. This was the first real chance he'd had to tell them any news, since his arrival in South Africa. Christina lent him a writing pad and pencil and he found himself a quiet secluded spot under the shade of a wagon. Firstly though, he had to lay a canvas sheet over the ground to sit on and also keep his things clean, and then he began writing his letter.

By the time he had finished he had written eleven and a half pages. Although he felt there was still a lot more news he could tell them, he thought perhaps some was best kept for later, such as the unfortunate and tragic killing of his cousin, Piet Vorster.

After that, James began a letter to Veronica. He was however, having difficulty getting started, mainly because he was no longer sure how he felt about her. Not only because he had met Christina again, but also because of what Timothy had told him about Samuel being fathered by a lover. Somehow, it had cast serious doubts in his mind about Veronica sincerity. And after all, he hadn't known her for very long either. Had Timothy lied though about not being Samuel's father? And, if so, why? ...Why would a dying man have told James something like that? It just didn't make any sense. But then, nothing really seemed to make much sense any more.

Each time James tried to write something down on paper he would scratch it out and then crumple the page into a ball. He glanced around at the canvas sheet and noticed that there were at least seven altogether. After another poor attempt he decided to leave it for another day. Perhaps then he would have a little more inspiration?

While James was taking his letter over to Christina at the hospital, as she had previously said that she would post it for him, he met Billy. It was an unexpected meeting and both men were surprised to see each other. The left sleeve of Billy's tunic was folded up and for a moment James thought that his arm was in a sling.

Billy had noticed James starring at the sleeve. 'They took it off at the shoulder,' he suddenly blurted out.

James was a little stunned for a moment at hearing the news. 'Oh God Billy... I am so, so sorry, mate.'

They embraced one another with James saying, 'I thought that your wound was healing the last time I saw you in hospital at Orange River Station?'

Billy stood back. 'It became infected with gangrene after you'd left.'

Again James said how sorry he was. Apart from that though, they were both happy at meeting up with one other and spoke for almost an hour. Billy also congratulated him at having been promoted to corporal. He then told James that he was returning to Australia shortly, and that he would call-in at Rambling Meadows to see the family.

'That will be nice Billy, they will all be so happy to see you again.'

'Yeah, I'm looking forward to seeing them all.'

'Father might even be able to give you a job as there are always so many things that need doing around the farm.'

'He won't have a need for one armed farmhand.'

'Don't be silly that won't matter to him.'

'And if the drought hasn't broken there won't be no work anyway, will there?'

'Well, let's think positively, hey?'

'I suppose so... What will you do once you're released from hospital?'

He shrugged his shoulders. 'Continue scouting I suppose. Mind you, everything's up in the air at the moment after Black Week... I wish we could form our own mounted infantry Billy. We need to be more mobile, like the Boers, that's the only way we will win... I reckon if we were provided with horses we could give the Boers a darn good run for their money.'

'Maybe when this new bloke... what's his name?'

'Lord Roberts.'

'Yeah, that's the fella... maybe when he gets out here he'll do that?'

'Let's hope so.'

There was a pause in the conversation while both men thought of what to say next. Then, James raised his finger. Waving it he said excitedly, 'In-fact, Billy O'Reilly, you have just given me a brilliant idea.'

'What's that mate?' He wore a surprised expression on his face.

'I'm going to write a letter to Lord Roberts and suggest the very idea.'

Billy frowned. 'Are you crazy, James? Do you think a posh fella like him is going to listen to the likes of you, a jackeroo from Wickepin?'

'Why not?'

'I'll bet you the damn fella doesn't even know where Wickepin is?'

'Maybe not... but listen Billy, the Boer commandos are mostly farmers and up till now they have beaten the most powerful army in the world. The way I see it the British have nothing to lose by providing us with horses, do they?'

Billy scratched under his chin. 'I guess not. But, you had better watch out that you don't get yourself into a lot of trouble or something.'

'What for?'

'For going over everyone's heads... I mean how will the officers feel about you doing that? You could get yourself into a heck of a lot of trouble... And what if this Roberts fella takes offence to a corporal telling him how to fight the war? ...Maybe you won't be a corporal no more after that?'

James sighed. 'Well I suppose that's just a risk I'll have to take. It'll be worth it if we get given horses. I know that if we become mounted infantry we can turn this war around, and sooner we do that the sooner we all get to go home.'

After agreeing to meet later, James then hurriedly wrote his letter. Once he was finished he made his way over to the hospital. Christina was sitting outside with a few other nurses having a break. She excused herself from their company when she saw James approaching. When they met he handed over one of the letters to her.

'My, but you have been a busy boy,' she said when she saw how bulky it was, 'this feels as though you have written a book.'

He told her how many pages there were. Christina had noticed that he was holding another letter in his hand. 'Is that also for posting?'

James replied excitedly, 'It's for the British Field-Marshal Lord Roberts. There are rumours going around amongst the men that he's going to be relieving Sir Redvers Buller of his duties shortly.'

Christina frowned. 'Why on earth would you be writing to a British Field-Marshal?'

James quickly explained his idea of converting Australian foot soldiers into mounted infantry. Then, he said, 'The problem is I'm not sure how I'm going to have it delivered to him.'

'Well that's a lot of good, James.'

'I was thinking of asking Major Rimington to forward it on for me.'

'Mm, if you like you can leave it with me. I'll ask matron to pass it onto the chief surgeon and see if he would kindly make sure that it reaches Lord Roberts?'

'Thanks.' He handed it to her.

James was about to leave when Christiana said, 'Come over for a brandy tonight I'll have the tent to myself?'

'That'll be nice.'

'Come early... say, about half past six.'

He nodded. James turned and walked off.

Christina watched him for a few moments. She gave a sigh, turned and walked back to the hospital.

James went to see Billy again as agreed. They chatted for another hour and then it was time for the two men to say goodbye. 'Take care of yourself Billy O'Reilly, and don't forget to give my love to everyone back home. And write to me sometime.'

'I will... cheers, mate.'

The two men embraced one another. Both men had a lump in their throats.

'You take care of yourself too... and try not to end up like me, if you can,' Billy said with a smile.

James nodded. They shook hands and then James walked away. Once he had gone a little way, he stopped and looked back to wave to Billy, but he had already gone.

75   Two days later James was discharged from the field hospital. He only had a few minutes to say goodbye to Christina as she was on duty, and the hospital was extremely busy. 'I'm going to miss you,' she said once they had reached a secluded spot.

…'I'll miss you too.'

'Will you try and come and see me whenever you can?'

'What do you think?'

…'I don't know.'

James placed his hand to her cheek and gently rubbed it. Her skin was soft and smooth. A tear broke free from her eye and went rolling down the side of her face. He wiped it away with his hand looking into her soft blue eyes. 'You know I will whenever possible.'

'Promise me.'

James nodded. 'I promise.'

He placed his lips to hers and they kissed each other lovingly. Afterwards, Christina wiped the tears from her eyes. 'I have to go now, James, the hospital is very busy. Fifty wounded men arrived early this morning.'

They kissed once again. Then, Christina said goodbye and also told him to take care of himself. She turned and walked briskly towards the hospital with James watching her. Twenty minutes later, James reached the area where the Rimington's Scouts were bivouacked and then he reported to Major Rimington. The officer explained to him that due to a chronic shortage of horses the other Australian scouts had been returned to their original contingents. James was now required to report back to Major Moor.

Having first collected his kit and rifle, James then made his way over to the West Australians, now encamped along part of the railway line, half a mile further south of Modder River Station. James reached the camp as the lunch gong rang out. He was hungry and thought that he may as well get something to eat while he had the chance. Once he had retrieved his eating utensils from his kitbag he joined the long queue.

When it was his turn, James slowly walked down the line in front of a long, wooden trestle table. He held out his plate and a cook dumped a pile of stew onto it. As he proceeded along the line another cook gave him a slice of bread and another poured a muddy coloured tea into his mug. From there, James made his way over to several wooden boxes. After first placing his food and mug down, he un-slung the rifle from his shoulder and placed it against one of the boxes. He then sat down on another and began eating the meal. The stew smelt fantastic and tasted even better. James consumed the lot mopping up the dregs with his bread. He then sipped his tea while watching hundreds of small black ants swarming over a little spilt stew that had fallen to the ground, when James noticed someone walk up to him. George was wearing a large grin on his face. 'I heard on the grapevine that you were rejoining us today.'

The two men shook hands firmly. 'It looks as though we've ended-up in the infantry again George?'

'Yeah, the British are short of horses... Norwich collapsed and died from exhaustion during the battle at Modder River.'

James nodded sympathetically.

George waved a fly away from his face. 'What happened to yours?'

...'Wellington was badly wounded... I had to destroy him.' A lump came to his throat.

George nodded in sympathy. 'That must have been tough on you?' He was well aware of James' passionate love of horses.

James nodded.

'Well, I hate to be the one to tell you this, mate. But that's what you've just been eating, horse stew.'

'Ah God don't tell me that!' James blurted out.

'It's all we have had for several days now.'

James suddenly felt ill. He got to his feet quickly, feeling something rising-up from his stomach. Vomit sprayed from his mouth splashing onto the ground, some of it landing on his boots. When there was nothing left, James had a long drink of water from his canteen bottle. After that, he poured water over his boots and washed the vomit off.

George waited until James had finished. 'Sorry about that, mate... you would have found out sooner or later?'

James cleared his burning throat. 'Yeah, I suppose so.'

The two men then spoke in general for a few minutes, catching up with each other's news and then James said, 'Hey, guess who I saw the other day.'

'Who? ...Don't tell me Billy O'Reilly?'

'Yeah. They're sending him back home... he lost his arm.'

'Ah God no! The poor bugger! How did he take it?'

'As well as can be expected, I guess.'

They spoke for a little longer and then James said that he had to go and report to Major Moor.

76   The following day the Australian infantry moved to Enslin where they took up positions along the western railway line. However, it wasn't long before a sense of despondency set in amongst the troops of the six colonies. Guarding a lonely section of railway track wasn't exactly what they had volunteered for, and they certainly hadn't come all the way from Australia to be left out of the real war. Arguments and fisticuffs soon broke-out amongst the men as their frustration and discontent got the better of them. To try and break the boredom cricket matches were organised between the colonies. On Christmas day, Colonel Hoad paid a visit to each tent, a monumental task when you consider that there were approximately two hundred and forty tents strung out along many miles of railway track.

The letter that James had written to Lord Roberts had now found its way onto the desk of Colonel Pilcher, commander of the garrison at Belmont, approximately 40 miles south of Enslin. He was reading the name written on the back of the envelope while he rapped his fingers on his desk. He was thinking, 'What would an enlisted man from the Western Australian Contingent possibly have to say to the most senior imperial military commander?'

He then lifted a glass from the desk and took a mouthful of scotch. After that he puffed vigorously on a large cigar. Moment's later; he summoned one of his staff members over to his desk. When the captain approached him he said, 'I want you to send a telegraph message to Enslin for me Frank.'

'Yes sir.'

THE PLOUGH, THE GUN AND THE GLORY

'Make it for the attention of a Major Moor care of the Western Australian 1st Contingent.'

'Right sir.'

77   James and three other men were doing guard duties in one of the bunkers along the railway line. It was already hot although it was only 9am, and the flies were beginning to pester them. All four men continuously waved them away from their faces cursing the foul insects at the same time.

On the other side of the railway line a young male piccaninny was herding a number of donkeys and goats. Behind him, were five young females no more than ten or twelve years of age. Some of the girls were carrying large pots of water precariously balanced on their heads, the others bundles of firewood. A short time later they disappeared into the shimmering heat. James' thoughts turned to home and he was wondering how everyone was doing. Moments later he heard his name being called. He turned around to see Sergeant Hensman approaching from a little way off. He had a private accompanying him.

'Your presence is required by Major Moor,' the sergeant advised James when he got closer. 'And, if I were you I would get myself over there in a hurry, the major isn't in a very good mood. I wonder why? Austin here,' he pointed to the man standing next to him, 'will take over your guard duty until you return.'

James climbed out of the bunker. 'I'll see you blokes later,' he said to the other three men. He dusted his uniform down and then he and Sergeant Hensman made their way in silence towards the major's tent. After first announcing their arrival they were then asked to enter. The major first thanked the sergeant, and once he had left, Major Moor turned his attention to James.

'The reason I sent for you Corporal Mitchell, is due to a rather disturbing telegraph message that I have received from Colonel Pilcher at the Belmont garrison.'

James listened attentively with his heart pounding in his ears, wondering what it was all about.

'Apparently, for some reason best known to yourself, you took it upon yourself to write a letter directly to the most senior imperial officer, with neither my consent nor my knowledge of the matter.'

James' heart beat harder in his chest. 'Yes sir... it's not quite like that, sir... I can explain. At the time of writing the letter I was at Modder River hospital. I was still under the command of Major Rimington. I was going to hand the letter into Major Rimington, but then someone who I knew at the hospital, a nurse, kindly offered to pass the letter onto the chief surgeon instead.'

'Let me explain something, Mitchell... It is quite improper and most certainly against army regulations for an enlisted man to write a letter to a senior imperial officer.'

'Yes sir.'

'What was the intention and nature of this letter?'

James explained his idea about converting Australian foot soldiers to mounted infantry. When he had finished the major said, 'Well, for your sake private, I am rather relieved that your letter wasn't a criticism of an imperial officer or of a callous nature. Somehow, I don't think that's in your nature though. If it's of any consolation to you, I happen to agree with the idea. In-fact, I have rather been contemplating the very idea myself. However, that doesn't mean for one moment that I condone what your actions.'

James swallowed the lump in his throat.

'Furthermore, I fear the worst maybe still to come, as both you and I have been ordered to proceed to Belmont to explain the purpose of your actions directly to Colonel Pilcher... Have you a clean uniform to change into?'

'Yes sir.'

'Good... Well then, get yourself washed and dressed and then return here.'

'Yes sir.'

'And make sure that your boots are highly polished.

'Yes sir.'

'Make it quick Mitchell. We have over an hours ride to Belmont and I want to be back here well before sundown.'

78   The ride to the small town south of Enslin was pleasant enough despite the heat and the dust. Four mounted infantrymen accompanied Major Moor and James in case they ran into Boers. Once they had reached the garrison they made their way over to the Hotel Belmont, which had been commandeered by the army for Colonel Pilcher's headquarters. After a short wait Major Moor was taken upstairs to Colonel Pilcher's office while James remained downstairs. Once the formal introductions were over the major was shown a chair and offered a cigar. The colonel stroked his moustache several times while the major lit-up puffing clouds of smoke into the room.

'May I also offer you a brandy major?'

'No thank you sir.'

'Then, let's get down to business, shall we?'

'By all means sir.'

The major puffed on his cigar sending more clouds billowing up to the ceiling. A gentle breeze coming through the open windows made the lace curtains flutter sending the smoke swirling around the room.

The colonel reached forward and picked up James' envelope off the desk. He held it up for the major to see. 'It is yet to be opened. I wanted you to be present before doing that.'

'Thank you sir.'

The colonel took a paper knife and inserted the point into the ear of the envelope and sliced it open. He removed the letter and read the contents aloud, which were exactly as James had explained it to the major. When the colonel finished he threw the letter onto the desk. 'The damn audacity of the man!' he said aloud. 'Who does he think he is by writing such a letter? ...Is he trying to make fools of us all, old boy?'

'I honestly don't believe that was his intention, sir.'

The colonel stroked his moustache in an agitated manner... 'We cannot tolerate enlisted men severing the chains of command major, by writing letters to the highest of British military commanders!'   'I understand sir... May I have permission to speak frankly sir?'

'Very well if you feel you must.' The colonel picked up his cigar from the ashtray and puffed vigorously on it.

'In Western Australia, Corporal Mitchell works on his father's sheep farm as a jackeroo. They're a rough tough breed of men and are not afraid to speak their minds sir. However, I believe that Mitchell meant no malice by writing this letter. He was simply frustrated by the apparent easy victories the Boers have enjoyed over us. If I may also say sir, the idea does carry merit. It's one that I have personally given thought to myself and we are certainly in desperate need of a victory sir. The mounting of Australian foot soldiers will vastly increase our mobility to great benefit. I think the idea should receive some consideration, sir... May I add one other thing, sir?'

The colonel gestured with his hand for the major to continue.

'I believe that the first imperial officer to convert foot soldiers to mounted infantry will be rewarded with a superb victory over the Boers.'

The colonel puffed vigorously on his cigar. 'Alright major, you have made your point... And, I cannot say that I disagree with the idea. However, as you are aware at present we haven't the horses... Next week however, should see the arrival of the 1st Contingent Queensland Mounted Infantry. Perhaps then, we could implement this plan?' The colonel placed his cigar down in the ashtray looking thoughtful for a moment. 'Alright, old boy... under the circumstances I am prepared to overlook the incident of Corporal Mitchell's apparent lack of military edict. Nevertheless, I do believe that he should be given a severe reprimanding and will leave that to your better judgement.'

'Thank you sir.'

'However, I'm sure that you realise that this type of outspokenness amongst the colonial ranks must be discouraged major. Believe me, nothing good can come out of it. If we allow this kind of behaviour to go unchecked it could spread amongst the British regulars like the plague. The entire discipline of Her Majesties military machine could break down.'

'I fully understand your concerns sir.'

'Dismissed.'

Major Moor got to his feet, saluted the colonel, turned and left the room.

79   On the 1st January 1900 Colonel Pilcher led an attack on a laager of Cape Colony rebels at Sunnyside, northwest of Belmont. His troops comprised of two hundred Queensland Mounted Infantry, one hundred Canadian and forty British Mounted Infantry, plus artillery support. The colonel sent five Queenslanders ahead of his troops to act as scouts. They were however, ambushed by the Boers. Lieutenant Adie and Private Jones were killed along with their horses. Colonel Pilcher then began his attack on the laager sending the Canadians and British in a frontal attack, while the Queenslanders carried out an enveloping movement on the Boer's right flank. A third member of the Queensland contingent, Private McLeod, was also killed before the artillery was able to bring the battle to a conclusion. With the Boers in retreat the Queenslanders surged forward and captured forty-one prisoners.

This small, but decisive victory at Sunnyside was the turning point in the Boer war. Henceforth, the use of mounted infantry was seen as a vital key to winning, and the morale of the imperial army was lifted to new and greater heights. Two days after the victory at Sunnyside Corporal Mitchell received a promotion to sergeant after Major Moor received a telegraph message from Colonel Pilcher. No one was more surprised than James himself.

When Lord Roberts took command in South Africa in mid January 1900, orders were immediately issued to convert as many foot soldiers to mounted infantry as possible. Volunteers were called for amongst the Australians and four hundred and fifty men responded out of eight hundred and fifty. Later, the remaining 400 also volunteered. And while the Australian Regiment waited for suitable horses to arrive from Australia, many of them practiced their horsemanship on mules and carthorses while based at Enslin. From there, the 1st WAMI (Western Australian Mounted Infantry) were moved to Slingersfontein in the Colesberg area in an attempt to try and clean out the Boers, in preparation for the drive north into the Free State.

80   On February 4th, James received his first letter from home. He was extremely happy and was trembling with excitement as he carefully opened the envelope. As he unfolded the pages he could tell straight away by the handwriting that it was from Alanna.

'My dearest, darling brother James,' he read softly to himself, 'I pray to God that nothing has happened to you and that you are safe and well. I wish this letter was good news from home, but sadly that is not the case. I have been trying to gather my thoughts together in order to tell you in some easy manner, but unfortunately I find that I am unable, so please forgive me.'

James noticed that the ink was smudged in several places as though drops of water had fallen onto the pages. He continued reading. 'Whilst returning home from school with William, Elizabeth and Bridget, we were stopped on the side of the road by two swagmen. They said they were looking for work, but when I told them we had none they became troublesome. After a short scuffle we managed to break free of them. During our escape though one of them shot William in the back. He died later at home. We have buried him next to grandfather and grandmother.'

The news stunned James. His heart was racing wildly as the grief whelmed up from within his chest and then burst from his mouth. He walked briskly away from the men nearby him until he reached a rocky outcrop. James wiped the tears from his eyes as he tried to carry on reading the letter, but was unable.

After awhile he started reading the letter again. 'Father was so grief stricken that he hired a few men in Wickepin and they took off after the two swagmen. When it grew dark they had to make camp overnight. The following morning one of the men found father dead when he went to wake him. As you know father had a heart condition for some years. The doctor said that his heart simply gave up with grief. We buried him alongside William.'

James was unable to contain his grief and he cried bitterly, wiping his eyes and sniffing loudly. Several times he had to wipe his nose on the sleeve of his jacket. Once he had recovered slightly he continued reading the remainder of the letter. 'I don't know what else to say to you James, to help relieve the pain that I know will now exist in your heart. We pray daily that no harm will come to you and also for your safe return to Australia. God bless you. All our love, Alanna, mother, Elizabeth and Bridget.'

81

'Sergeant Mitchell... Sergeant Mitchell,' the voice called out just above a whisper.

James stirred in his sleep. Moments later the voice called again, 'Sergeant Mitchell it's time to wake up.'

James opened his eyes with a fright and then immediately grabbed for his rifle lying next to him. He relaxed once he realised that he was in his tent. 'What is it?' he asked still half asleep.

'It's almost four o'clock.'

'Oh God,' he sighed. He couldn't believe it. James felt as though he had just gone off to sleep. He sat up and then shielded his eyes from the glow of the lantern. 'Thanks, I'll be fine now.'

The man left and the blackness closed in once more. James then groped around nearby for the matches. Finding them he then struck one against the side of the box. The tiny flame brought light to the darkness and then he lit the lantern. A warm yellow glow filled the tent. James gave a yawn stretching his shoulders and arms at the same time and then rolling his head from side to side, as his neck was sore and stiff. After that, he quickly pulled on his boots and then wrapped the putties around the bottom of his trousers and ankles. He had gone to bed fully clothed except for his jacket, knowing he would be up early this morning. Once he had finished dressing he grabbed his rifle, bandolier and field-kit and then left the comfort of the tent.

It was very cold outside and still dark except for the moon and stars, and it took a moment for James' eyes to adjust from the light of the lantern. From there he made his way over to where the horses had been rounded up for the night. Most of the other thirty-seven men of the WAMI, were already saddling their horses. After James had saddled his horse he then walked him over to where Major Moor, Lieutenants Parker, Darling and Hensman (the latter having been recently promoted from sergeant) were waiting. He greeted the officers saluting them at the same time. Once everyone was ready they made their way over to the bivouacs of the 6th Inniskilling Dragoons who were also ready. When Captain Haig (OC Slingersfontein Camp) arrived the one hundred Dragoons and the WAMI left the camp heading south along the Resburg Road.

After travelling about three miles the dawn had broken with a pale weak sun giving birth to a new day. With the advent of daylight the troops discovered that they had entered into an area of kopjes resembling the shape of a horseshoe. Between the two ends at the opening and almost in the centre there was a smaller kopje. Next to this was another smaller one. Captain Haig quickly realising that his troops were in a vulnerable position for an ambush, gave the orders to turn around and move out of the area, when a barrage of gunfire broke-out from the kopjes surrounding them. Two horses immediately fell from under their riders hurling them to the ground.

Captain Haig turned to Major Moor yelling, 'Take your men to that kopje!' He pointed to the small hill near the mouth of the horseshoe. 'Keep the enemy in check and hold the kopje at all cost!'

The major turned his horse and then after realising that his men were spread to far out to hear his commands above the noise of the gunfire, he started galloping towards the kopje signalling for them to follow him.

James saw what was happening and was about to follow when he noticed a horseless rider getting shakily to his feet. Without hesitation, he galloped towards him as hard as the horse would go. Bullets were raining down from the surrounding kopje's sending sand and stones flying. Once James reached the stranded man he shouted, 'Hop on the back, mate!' At the same time he reached down. The man took hold of his hand and James pulled him up onto the back of the horse. From there they galloped towards the kopje with bullets singing past their ears.

THE PLOUGH, THE GUN AND THE GLORY

Major Moor had meanwhile ordered Lieutenant Darling to take four men over to the smaller of the two kopjes, on their left, and hold the position in order to prevent the enemy outflanking them. By the time James reached the base of the kopje Major Moor and twenty men had climbed up and were hurriedly building small walls from lose stones to give them some protection. Once James and the other man reached them they did the same. No sooner had James taken cover, when several bullets ricocheted off the stones sending rock splinters flying through the air. From his position James saw about a hundred Boers moving up through the kopje opposite him. He looked over to his right towards Major Moor. 'Boers on the right flank, sir!' he called out.

'Thank you, sergeant! ...We need to keep our nerve and hold our fire until I give the word! ...There must be at least three or four hundred of them! So, it's most important that we don't waste our ammunition!'

'Right sir.' James turned his attention to the Boers with bullets flying all around him. Five minutes later the first of the Boers were only about eighteen metres away when the major gave to signal to open fire. At that moment the Australians sent a hail of lead towards the enemy. After quickly reloading they sent another volley of bullets towards the Boers, whose rifles flew into the air as they clutched at their chests. Others cried out in agony as they fell to the ground and then were silent. Other Boers kept surging forward and the Australians kept on firing, the wooden stock covering the barrel, burning their hands from the intense heat. After a few hours the left flank of the Australians were running low on ammunition and a resupply had to be obtained from the men safeguarding the horses further down the kopje.

James volunteered to go.

'Good luck Mitchell,' Lieutenant Hensman said, as James scrambled over the rough ground crawling on his stomach. Once he was well clear he got to his feet and continued on down the kopje in a semi-crouched position. After collecting what ammunition the men could spare he then made his way back to the others.

'Well done sergeant,' Major Moor said once he arrived back.

During James' absence Lieutenant Hensman had been shot through his right thigh and when Corporal Conway went to his assistance, he was shot through the head and died instantly. During the course of an hour Lieutenant Hensman was then hit in the right leg by another three bullets. Later, another grazed his temple and finally a fifth made a large cut across his stomach. The volley of fire coming from the Boers prevented another attempt to reach him and the lieutenant lay in the blistering heat with bullets flying all around him. James tried more than once, but was forced back behind the stones as a hail of lead came in his direction. When Private Bird tried to reach him he was wounded in the right breast. He was lucky enough to be able to crawl back to the relative safety of the low makeshift wall. Private Krygger made the next attempt and he was able to build a wall of rocks in front of the lieutenant before being forced to take cover himself.

After that, Major Moor then decided to send five men, Sergeant-Major Edwards, Corporal Trathan and Privates Murray, White and Messer, back to Captain Haig's lines to request permission for his men to retire from the kopje. Permission was denied however and the five men were ordered not to return to the kopje. During the remainder of the battle another two men were wounded, Private Ansell and Private France. On at least two separate occasions the Boers came close enough to call out to the Australians to surrender. The major then gave the order to fix bayonets and then yelled, 'Come and get us if you dare!' Hearing this the Boers decided to pull back some distance.

Towards the end of the day when it was starting to grow dark artillery support arrived from Slingersfontein Camp. They immediately began to shell the surrounding horseshoe shaped kopje. As the shells began bursting amongst the enemy they started to retreat. The Australians were then able to gather the wounded and dead and make a break for the British lines as the sun dipped on the horizon.

At Slingersfontein Camp James was unsaddling his horse when one of the men approached him. He recognised him as the bloke he had rescued after his horse had been shot from under him.

'I didn't get a chance to thank you before, serge,' he said as he came closer. 'I reckon you sure saved my life out there today.'

'No worries... I was glad to be able to help out.'

THE PLOUGH, THE GUN AND THE GLORY

...'I didn't think that we were going to come out of that today... on the kopje. Did you?'

...'No.' James removed the saddle from the horse and placed it down on the ground. Then he took the blanket off. 'What's your name by the way?' he asked throwing the blanket on top of the saddle.

'Alexander Krygger.'

'Well, that was a very brave thing you did today, building those stones around the lieutenant like that. I reckon you very likely saved his life.'

'He's in a bad way serge. I sure hope he lives.'

'Yeah... He's a tough bugger though, and I'm sure with God's help he will make it.'

* * *

Later, it was learned that Lieutenant Hensman had died in hospital after his leg was amputated, due to gangrene having set in. The kopje which had been so gallantly defended by the twenty-one men, against almost four hundred Boers, was renamed West Australian Hill. For the remainder of the time spent in the Colsberg area, the WAMI, fought in a number of skirmishes and small battles as did the Victorians, New South Wales and Queensland contingents.

With the imperial army now under the command of the charismatic Lord Roberts they had found a new strength in his leadership. Both Kimberley and Ladysmith were soon to be relieved. Roberts had been mustering a huge force of forty-five thousand troops at Enslin in readiness to cross into the Free State. But first, he had to deal with General Cronje and his army of six thousand strong at Paardeberg.

82   On March 20th sixty one WAMI, plus thirty-six South Australians, under the leadership of Major Moor departed from Donkerpoort near Colesberg. Having first crossed over the Orange River they headed in a northerly direction. The Boers had mostly withdrawn from the area in order to defend Bloemfontein, the capital of the Free State, and only relatively small groups of between two and three hundred were known to still be operating.

While enroute to Fauresmith the Australians were moving through a small village called Waterkloof when they suddenly came under a surprise attack. Initially, the streets of the town had been almost deserted apart from several men and women, who at the time appeared to be going about their normal daily chores. The attack was initiated when one of the men in the street removed a concealed rifle from under his coat and fired it at one of the troops, hitting the man in the leg. Within moments hundreds of Boers appeared from between the gaps in the buildings, others fired their rifles from windows, doorways and from behind carts.

In order to escape from the ambush area as quickly as possible, the Australians spurred their horses hard while firing their rifles towards the enemy. James' horse was killed outright throwing him heavily to the dusty ground. For a moment he just lay there trying to get the air into his lungs. His left foot was also trapped under the weight of dead horse. Once he had recovered his breath slightly he tried to free himself. James pulled as hard as he could with bullets kicking up dust and sand all around him. He quickly decided the only way to free his foot was to get rid of his boot. He hurriedly pulled off the putties first, undid the laces and then after a good hard pull he was free. Using the horse for cover he began returning fire at the enemy. Moments later, James clutched at his left arm in agony. It felt as though a bolt of lightning had struck him. With his arm feeling as though there was a raging fire inside he continued to engage the enemy with his rifle, although loading and unloading was extremely difficult, painful and slow.

A Boer ran up from behind James and struck him a savage blow to the head with the butt of his rifle rendering him unconscious. Meanwhile, the Australians had initiated a counter attack. The Boers retreated from the battle and after mounting their horses they rode off with the Australians giving chase.

Shortly afterwards James was dragged over to a livery stable. When he came around there was a young female kneeling by his side. She was no more than sixteen or seventeen years of age. She was very attractive with long blonde hair worn plaited on both sides of her head. An older woman then joined them and removed the bullet from James' arm, which was extremely painful. The young girl then cleaned and dressed the wound. As she worked she glanced into James' eyes from time to time, then she would shyly look away again.

'What's your name?' he asked, trying to smile at the same time despite the pain in his arm.

She didn't understand him as she only spoke Afrikaans, and yet somehow she knew what he had asked her. 'Theresa,' she answered softly with a friendly smile.

'I'm James.'

She smiled softly again as she repeated his name in a whisper.

At that moment two Boers came into the stable. They spoke to the older women for a moment and then James was hurriedly loaded onto a cart along with two other wounded Australians. From there they were taken to a railway siding where they were placed inside boxcars and then chained to them. Later on, a train arrived and the boxcars were added on. When the train pulled out of the station James peered between the gaps in the wooden sides. He saw the name Springfontein on a sign overhanging the platform. He turned and looked back at the other two men with him. 'I wonder where they are taking us?' he asked.

The South Australian came across and also peered between the cracks in the timber. 'I have no bloody idea, mate... No bloody idea.'

James starred between the gaps again. 'It looks as though we are travelling north... Maybe they're taking us to Bloemfontein? ...Unless, we manage to escape first.'

'Escape? ...How for God's sake? ...For one thing, how will we get out of these chains? ...And that bloke over there,' he pointed, 'ain't going nowhere, mate.'

James looked over at the other man. He had been wounded in the stomach and didn't look so good. He certainly wasn't going to go anywhere unless he was carried. James looked back at the South Australian. He had taken a bullet through the leg and could hardly walk. Then there was James himself. His arm was extremely painful and felt as though it was on fire, plus he had chains around his feet and wrists. James sat down on the wooden floor leaning against the end of the wall of the boxcar. He looked up at the South Australian. 'Well then, I guess we'll just have to be content at being burgher prisoners for now.'

The South Australian nodded and without saying anything he hobbled over to the other side of the boxcar, where he sat down with his back against the wall. James closed his eyes. His mind turned to thoughts of William's tragic death and also that of his father. The words in Alanna's letter were still fresh in his memory and his heart was heavy with grief. After a few moments he wiped the moisture from his eyes with the palm of his hand.

The gentle swaying motion of the boxcar from side to side, and the click-clacking sound of the wheels as they ran over the joints in the rails, made his eyes heavy, and he soon fell into a deep exhausted sleep.

83 James woke when the train came to grinding shuddering halt. He sat up and looked at the other two men. They were still sound asleep. He got to his feet wincing from the throbbing pain in his left arm. Once again he peered between the gaps in the wooden sides. He could see that they were at a large station with armed guards everywhere.

He then crossed over to the other side of the boxcar and looked out. Across from them, were railway wagons carrying field guns. James wondered where they were going. James also had something else on his mind though, far more pressing at the time. His bladder was bursting. There were no toilets in the boxcar and the only thing he could do was to kneel down and pee through the gaps in the floorboards. After undoing the buttons on his trousers and then his underwear, James aimed his penis between the gaps in the floor and let go. The relief was instantaneous and he gave a sigh as his bladder emptied the contents onto the ground below. 'Oh God, that feels much better,' he said with great relief.

James got to his feet and buttoned his fly. He then heard the train across from them pulling out. He peered out of the boxcar and watched. As the wagons rolled past he counted at least twenty-five field guns. Other boxcars were carrying horses and there were also carriages packed with Boer commandos. Once the train had gone James could see across the tracks over towards a large platform. It was swarming with Boers. He then decided to sit down again. After a few moments the South Australian woke. He stretched and yawned before realising the train wasn't moving. 'Hey, we've stopped!' he blurted out with surprise. 'Where the hell are we?'

'No idea.'

Mumbling sounds were then heard coming from the direction of the other man, but nothing of what he said made any sense. James went over to him to take a look and found that he was burning up with a fever.

'Do you think this bloke's going to make it?' the South Australian asked looking over at him.

…'I don't know,' James replied shaking his head. 'I think perhaps I should say a prayer for him.'

When James finished the two men sat in silence. Their minds were busy going over the many things that were swirling through their thoughts. After a few moments the South Australian suddenly asked, 'You really believe in all that stuff then? ...You know, prayen to God and all that?'

...'Yeah... Well, I wouldn't be praying if I didn't, would I?'

'I guess not... I don't... I recken if there really was a God there wouldn't be no wars... would they?'

'Man creates wars, not God.'

'Is that so... and what about all the diseases then, mate? Who makes them, hey?'

James sighed. 'Some say they're the work of the devil.'

'The devil?' He laughed sarcastically. 'You people have an answer for everything... Tell me something. Doesn't it say somewhere in the Bible that you should not kill?'

...'Yeah, in the Ten Commandments, why?'

'So, what are you doing over here then? Why are you killing people who have done absolutely nothing to you? Why have you have come all the way from Australia to kill them?'

That was a good question... why had he come here? 'For the same reasons as you,' he answered, 'to fight for the Empire.'

...'That's not answering my question, mate... and besides I'm not religious.'

Suddenly, the sliding door of the boxcar opened with a crashing sound startling both men. Three armed guards appeared. One of them was carrying three metal plates, a small bucket with a ladle, and a loaf of bread. He then said something in Afrikaans to the prisoners who didn't understand a word. Then he dished up a pile of stew into each of the plates and broke the bread into three pieces. They were about to leave when James said, 'This man needs urgent help!' He pointed to the West Australian. 'He needs a doctor! ...Please fetch a doctor!'

One of the guards went over to have a look at him. He said something to James in Afrikaans and then they left. As starving as he was James was unable to eat. The South Australian ate with a ferocious appetite. When he had finished he wiped his plate with his bread. Then he looked over at

James' plate. 'Aren't you going to eat that tucker, mate?' he asked wiping his face with his hands.

James shook his head.

'I may as well 'ave it then, no sense in wasting good tucker, is there?'

James gestured with his hand for the man to help himself. Then, he got to his feet and went over to the West Australian. He tried to feed him a little of his food but was unsuccessful. The door of the boxcar suddenly opened again with another loud crash. James turned to see a man with a white apron entering. He went straight over to the wounded man and had a look at him. After a few moments he said to James in English, 'I will see that this man is taken to hospital immediately.' He spoke with a strong Afrikaans accent.

'Thank you,' James replied with some relief. 'What's the name of this place by-the-way?'

'Bloemfontein,' the doctor answered. He then turned to the guards and spoke to them in Afrikaans. After a few minutes a stretcher was brought in carried by two Indian men. After placing the man onto the stretcher they left. The door was slammed shut with a loud bang and the locking-bar dropped into place.

A moment later the South Australian went over to where the plate of leftover food was lying on the floor. He picked it up. Looking at James he said, 'No point in letting this go to waste either.' He picked up a handful of food and shovelled it into his mouth. The food squelched between his fingers with some falling to the floor. He bent down and picked it up and pushed it into his mouth.

Ten minutes later both men were almost knocked off their feet when the boxcar suddenly jerked violently backwards. Then, after several shuddering jolts it began moving forwards again.

84   The following evening the train pulled into Johannesburg and then after an hour it continued on its journey. Once again James peered between the gaps of wood trying to see what direction they were travelling in. He decided it was still north.

Around midnight the train ground to a screeching halt. The men were then taken off the train and made to climb onto a wagon. Fifteen other men in chains were already seated. From there, they were then taken to a high-walled building. As they entered through the heavily guarded gates James looked up at the signboard. The name was written in Afrikaans in large capital letters. Underneath those in much smaller letters he read the name quietly to himself, 'Pretoria State Schools Prison.'

They were then taken to the infirmary to have their wounds attended to and remained there for a week. After that they were placed into prison cells. The following Sunday morning the prisoners were let out to attend a church service in the exercise yard. James thought that he had recognised someone and approached the man from behind. Once he was close enough he tapped him on the shoulder. The man turned around.

'Hello Winston, I thought it was you,' said James with a big smile.

Churchill stared blankly for a moment. Then he said with a big grin, 'I never forget a face, old chap. But, I'm afraid that I'm terrible with names.'

'James Mitchell... We met on the train going to De Aar... I removed several splinters from your forehead.'

Churchill's face lit up. 'Of course, forgive me, now I remember.'

'How did you end-up in here?' James asked out of curiosity.

'I was travelling from Durban to Ladysmith onboard an armoured train when the darn blighters captured us. I have been here almost a month now.' He looked around to make sure no one else was listening, and then he turned back to James. 'Listen, we can't talk here it's too risky... Follow me.'

He walked off with James following in his footsteps. They came to a wall where no one else was standing.

Churchill turned to James. 'The Boers have planted spies amongst us so don't trust anyone in here'.

James nodded.

'I will be escaping from here on Wednesday night,' Churchill said quietly.

'How?'

'I'll explain the details later... Do you want to come with?'

'Yeah, too darn true I do.'

'Are you going to be able to travel with that shoulder of yours?'

'No problems,' replied James without hesitation.

'Good... Meet me tomorrow morning when we come out to the courtyard for exercise.'

Churchill walked off and joined the congregation with James doing the same as inconspicuously as they both could.

85 The following day James met Winston as agreed. They found a quiet spot where it was safe to talk. 'I've told one of the guards that you will also be going with me.'

James was surprised and frowned while saying, 'Guard? What... what did he say?'

'I gave him another two pounds and he was quite happy.'

'Thanks... I'm not in a position to repay you... well not now anyway.'

'Don't worry old chap. You can buy me a few brandies one of these days.'

James nodded. 'How many of us will be escaping?'

'Just you and me... otherwise it will be far too risky... On Wednesday night after supper, we'll slip away from the others before returning to the cells.'

'Surely the guards will see there are two men missing when they do the head count?' James protested out of concern.

'Don't worry. The guard that I bribed will be on duty. He will give the correct total... When we slip away from the others we'll make our way over to the woodshed and stay there until later. From there, we'll climb onto the roof and then go over the wall.'

'Are you sure we can trust the guard though?'

'We'll soon find that out on Wednesday night, old chap,' he replied smiling.

86

Once it was dark enough the two men crept out from the woodshed. James rubbed the palms of his sweating hands together as he looked up at the corrugated-iron roof. Then he said, 'Climb onto my shoulders. Once you're on the roof you can give me a hand up.'

From there it was over the wall and a bit of a drop to the ground. They both landed on their feet and then fell onto their backsides. 'Darn!' Winston complained while getting onto his feet. 'It's darker than a black man tonight.'

James got to his feet dusting his off backside. 'Which way from here?'

'Follow me,' Churchill advised leading the way.

They crossed over the road and entered the sanitary lane between the buildings.

'There should be a couple of jackets and hats for us here somewhere,' said Winston. He soon found them in a hessian bag stashed inside a small crevice in the wall. 'Here James, take off your army jacket and put this on.' He handed James the garment.

James tried on the jacket.

'That looks fine,' Churchill said pulling on his own jacket. 'How about mine?'

'It looks good.'

'You had also better remove those putties, old chap. They're an absolute dead giveaway,' said Winston pointing down at James' feet.

While James was busy removing the leggings Winston searched through a second small hessian bag. 'We also have a little chocolate to eat and also a canteen of water.'

'Great... How much did this little lot cost you?'

'One pound four shillings and sixpence.'

'I guess we'll have to take good care of the jackets then,' James remarked, 'that must be the most expensive chocolate in the entire world.'

'Yes... the results of war, I'm afraid.'

Once they had stashed their discarded clothing into the empty hessian bag, Winston placed it back into the crevice in the wall. 'Well, we had better be on our way,' he said looking apprehensively in both directions of the lane.

'I'm ready.'

As they placed the hats on their heads Winston said, 'Now we really resemble a pair of sorry looking burghers.'

James laughed softly. 'Where to now?'

'Well, as we have neither map nor compass old chap, I thought of stowing away on a freight train going to Delagoa Bay. That's in Portuguese East Africa (Mozambique). From there we will catch a ship to Durban.'

'I don't have any money to pay for the passage on the ship.'

'Neither do I... well not much anyway... Don't worry, I'll arrange for the Morning Post, that's the newspaper I represent, to pay for them. Now let's get going.' He started to walk off, then he stopped and turned around as he said, 'Another thing, we will be travelling through town in order to locate the railway line to Delagoa Bay, so keep a sharp eye open for sentries.'

87   It was early evening and the streets were busy with horses and carriages going to and fro, and the pavements were crowded with pedestrians. Winston and James blended in rather well and made their way through town without a problem. Once on the other side, people and buildings became fewer until the two men were alone once again. Over in the distance, on the side of a kopje, was a magnificent looking building which James had never seen the likes. 'What the heck is that place over there?' he asked gazing in the direction of the structure.

'That old chap; is the seat of government for the republic of the Transvaal.'

'Very impressive.'

... 'Mmm, yes, I suppose it is.'

'Someone must be working late look at all the lamp lights?'

'President Kruger and his cabinet perhaps?'

'Imagine that,' James said excitedly.

'What's that old chap?'

'Us, being so close to Kruger and yet so far... The next time I see this place will be when we ride in on horseback and capture Pretoria... Wouldn't it be great to take your horse right up those steps and then inside the building and demand President Kruger's surrender?'

Winston smiled. 'That old chap would make history and a jolly fine story for the morning papers.'

The pair chatted on as they left the Houses of Parliament behind, and once safely on the other side of Pretoria the two men became a little more relaxed. They still had to be careful though as guards were posted at bridges and culverts. After two hours of walking along the railway line, they came to a small junction where the rails branched off in two directions.

'Now which way do we go?' asked James. He had no idea of what direction they were travelling in. If it had been a clear night he would have been able to navigate by the stars, but tonight the heavens were hidden behind heavy rain clouds.

'That way.' Winston pointed to the right-hand side. 'The other way goes to Southern Rhodesia.'

THE PLOUGH, THE GUN AND THE GLORY

They started off again and about an hour later they heard a train approaching from behind. Both men turned around to see a bright light in the distance. 'Let's hope that's our ride to Delagoa Bay,' said Winston excitedly. 'We'll hide in those bushes.' He was pointing. 'When it passes us we'll jump on.'

They didn't have very long to wait and fortunately the train was also going up a steep incline at the time, and travelling quite slowly. They let several carriages go past before Winston said, 'This is it, old chap. Good luck.'

The two men bolted out from the bushes and started running alongside the train. Several times, they almost tripped and fell due to rubble and other debris lying on the side of the track. Winston threw the sack containing the water and chocolate into the boxcar first. Then, he made a grab for one of the handrails and tried to board the train. But, as he went to get a foothold on one of the steps his foot slipped, and he was left clinging to the handrail with both feet dragging behind him.

James only just managed to climb onboard after almost falling himself. Then, he quickly went over to Winston and grabbed him by both his wrists. He pulled with all his strength with Winston trying to help by placing his feet onto the steps. After a few moments he managed and James was then able to pull him onboard. Both men lay on their backs gasping for air with James holding onto his wounded arm.

Once Winston had recovered his breath slightly he said, 'Is that wound playing up, old chap?'

James nodded.

'Let's take a look, shall we?' Winston got to his feet and came over to James. Together they removed his jacket. Winston could see there was blood on the bandage. 'I think you may have opened it up. You'll have to take it easy on that arm until we can get it redressed. The last thing you want is for it to get infected.' He helped James to replace his jacket. Then he said, 'We had better find a suitable place to hide for the remainder of the night, in-case the carriages are searched.'

They looked around the boxcar. To their disappointment it was half filled with coal sacks. 'I suppose they will just have to do,' said Winston looking somewhat forlorn. 'At daybreak we will have to jump train and hide somewhere.'

James agreed and they buried themselves under the sacks. Once or twice during the night, when the train had stopped somewhere, they could hear voices and footsteps on the wooden floorboards of the boxcar.

88 Shortly before dawn Winston woke James. 'Time to hop off!' he said to the sleepy-eyed Australian.

James got to his feet brushing the coal dust from himself with his hat. 'So-much for taking care of our priceless jackets,' he said with a grin. He yawned giving a shiver at the same time from the cold morning air. His left arm was still painful and he rubbed it gently. When they were both ready Winston climbed down the short steps on the side of the boxcar. Holding onto the handrails with his feet on the steps, he waited a few moments until a suitable spot was seen, then jumped.

James threw the sack out containing the water and chocolate, and then followed shortly afterwards. He landed on his feet before tumbling head over heels down an embankment, finally coming to rest puffing and panting for air. He got to his feet and then made his way into several bushes. Once the train had gone, and James was sure no one had seen him, he walked the short distance to retrieve the sack. After that, he made his way over to Winston. As he approached he saw that Winston had his trouser leg pulled up and his knee was bleeding.

'I'm afraid that I must have landed on something rather sharp old chap,' he said looking up at James. 'A stone perhaps?'

'Let's take a look.'

There was a large gash but luckily it wasn't deep. James washed it as clean as he could using a little of their drinking water. After that, he tore the bottom off his shirt and bandaged the knee as best he could. 'There,' he said getting to his feet, 'that should do for now.'

'Thanks old chap.' He gave James a pat on the back. 'I must say it feels much better already.'

'You'll be walking a little stiff legged... And running after trains will be difficult.'

THE PLOUGH, THE GUN AND THE GLORY

'I'll manage,' he replied with a grin... 'Well, I suppose we had better find somewhere to spend the day,' he said looking around at the surrounding veldt.

'What about over there?' James was pointing to a culvert under the railway line.

'Take a quick look old chap and see what you think.'

James made his way over and peered under the small concrete bridge. It was certainly large enough to sit comfortably under, and it would also give them shade from the hot midday sun. James thought the place was ideal and went back and told Winston. Then, the two men made their way over to it. Once they were comfortable they ate a little of the chocolate and had a mouthful of water. When James was finished he wiped his mouth with the back of his hand. 'Can I ask you something, Winston?'

...'By all means old chap.'

'What were you doing before coming out to South Africa?'

He gave a sigh. 'Trying to become a Member of Parliament. My late father, Lord Randolph, was in politics for many years.'

'Your father was a Lord?'

'Yes... anyway, I stood for the conservative seat of Oldham. However, regrettably I was defeated by some fifteen hundred votes... Before that, I was earning a meagre living trying to write books.'

'Really? ...What kind of books?'

...'The first was a text book titled "The Story of the Malakand Field Force." I wrote that while I was with the army in India.'

'Really? So you were a professional soldier then?'

'Yes... I held the rank of Second Lieutenant with the 4th Queen's Own Hussars. We were garrisoned at Bangalore.'

James listened attentively, fascinated by the young man who seemed not a lot older than himself and yet had accomplished so much. He guessed Winston's age to be no more than twenty-four. 'What made you leave the army?'

...'Ahh, yes you might ask. I missed the social life in London and naturally all of my friends. Believe me, old boy, eighteen months in India is more than sufficient for any virile young man.'

'I can well imagine... Did you ever write anything else?'

'Indeed,' he sighed, 'a seedy novel titled "Savrola" a sort of romantic thriller that took place during the revolution in Cuba.'

'Yeah? That sounds very intriguing.'

'Mm ...to be quite honest with you, I'm trying very hard to forget that I ever wrote it.'

James nodded, sensing that Winston no longer wished to discuss the subject. After that, he gazed out of the open sides of the culvert, one side at a time. There was a gentle breeze coming through one end, which was pleasantly cool. It was already quite warm outside even though it was still early morning. After a few moments James looked back at Winston who at the time appeared deep in thought.

'Winston,' he said softly.

The sound of James' voice in the relative quietness of the culvert broke his thoughts and his mind came racing back to the present. 'Yes old chap.'

'How did you become a war correspondent?'

Winston smiled. He didn't really mind James asking him questions. In-fact, he rather enjoyed the company of the inquisitive, sometimes almost boyish Australian. He looked his way. 'I once worked as a war correspondent in Cuba. That's where I got the idea to write "Savrola." When I heard of the war out here in South Africa, I decided to approach the Morning Post. Somehow I managed to convince them to give me the position.'

The two men then spoke at length with James telling Winston about his family in Australia and the untimely deaths of his younger brother and father, and then all about Rambling Meadows. Between the chatting they caught up with a little sleep, as they were both tired. When they woke they ate a little more of the chocolate and drank another ration of the water. James had been doing a little thinking of his own and needed to discuss his thoughts with the man next to him. 'There's something I need to tell you, Winston.'

'What's that old chap?'

'I hope you won't be offended with me, but I have decided not to continue onto Delagoa Bay. Instead, I am going to try and make my way back to my contingent... When I was captured, we were making our way towards

Bloemfontein. Going all the way to Delagoa Bay and then onto Durban will be much too far out of my way. By the time I rejoin our troops the war will have very likely ended.'

Winston brushed his hand through his hair. 'Well of course that's entirely up to you old chap.'

'You're not angry with me... or disappointed I hope?'

Winston smiled. 'Not at all... However, I do think that you will be taking a great risk as you have neither compass nor map, and nor are you familiar with the countryside. Nor do you have water. The route you will be travelling could possibly be crawling with Boers... You could find yourself back in Pretoria prison much sooner than you think.'

James gave serious thought to what Winston had said. 'I agree with everything you said, but I think I'll still take the chance.'

'Then, I can only wish you all the very best of luck old chap, and I'll certainly miss your company.'

'Thanks Winston, I'll miss your company too... I'll help you to board the train tonight before I leave.'

'There's no need for that old chap. I should be alright on my own.'

'I would feel a lot happier having seen you onboard the train first.'

'Alright, as you wish.'

Once darkness fell the two men came out from under the culvert and made their way up the embankment. When they found a suitable place they lay down and waited for the train. About seven o'clock James sat up as he said, 'I hear a train coming.'

Winston had also heard it. He took the remaining chocolate out of the bag, broke it in half and gave it to James. 'This is for later-on until you can find yourself something to eat.'

James felt a lump in his throat. 'Thanks.' He placed the chocolate into his pocket.

'Would you like a drink of water?'

'No thanks... Besides, there's not much left.'

'That's alright I'll have to find more from somewhere, sooner or later.'

'I'm okay for now, thanks.'

As the train approached the two men crouched down in the grass and once the engine had gone past they got to their feet. With James in the lead they ran alongside the wagons, and as soon as he was able, James grabbed hold of the handrails and jumped onto the steps. With some difficulty he opened the locking bar and then slid the door open. After that, he quickly climbed into the boxcar. Once on his feet he pushed the door further open, put his hand out to Winston, and took the hessian bag from him.

By now Winston was starting to drop back from exhaustion. His knee was excruciatingly painful and he was beginning to think that he wasn't going to make it. James realised that he was tiring and made a desperate grab for his hand. Taking hold of his wrist he then hauled Winston up into the boxcar.

Both men were so exhausted that they just lay on the floor trying to get their breath back. After awhile James got to his feet. 'If I don't jump... off this train soon... I will be going all the way... to Delagoa Bay,' he puffed out.

The two men shook hands. 'Good luck James.'

'You to Winston.'

James made his way down the ladder and without hesitation he jumped. He landed heavily onto his feet before going head over heels and rolling several times down the embankment. He finally came to rest and then clambered to his feet. He watched the coloured lamps at the rear of the guards van growing smaller. Once the train had gone the silence of the veldt rushed in, and for a brief moment James suddenly felt desperately alone. After dusting himself down he then started walking. 'I sure hope you've gone and done the right thing James Mitchell,' he said softly to himself.

89 Every so often, patches of broken, soft golden-moonlight danced on the railway lines between breaks in the clouds as they swept across a stormy sky. Now and then James could feel drops of rain falling. There were also periodic flashes of lightning on the distant horizon. He was also wondering how far they had travelled from Pretoria. About two hours later he came over the top of a rise. He could see the twinkling lights of a small town in the distance. He continued to follow the rails and as he got closer he came across a signpost. James waited for the moon to break through the cloud and then read the long and almost unpronounceable name of Bronk-horst-spruit.

The name didn't mean anything to him and he continued walking towards the twinkling lights. He was feeling hungry and so he decided to eat the piece of chocolate that Winston had given him. He removed it from his pocket and peeled the greaseproof paper from it. There wasn't much and James soon devoured it, thanking Winston afterwards.

Sometime later he reached a small railway station. James approached the building with caution keeping to the shadows. He went around the back and peered through a window. There were two armed guards sitting around table playing cards and talking loudly in Afrikaans. James left them and went to another window. He looked inside and saw a wooden table with four chairs. What really caught his eye though, were two plates of half-eaten food that had been left there. He was starving and would give anything to get hold of food, and after thinking about it for a moment he decided the risk was well worth it.

James crept around the side of the building. After first checking to make sure that no one else was about, he stepped onto the platform. He hesitated for a second before walking the short distance to the closed door. With his heart pounding in his chest he placed his hand on the handle and gently turned it. Then, he slowly pushed the door open. The hinges creaked slightly, which made him stop. He then waited for a moment before pushing it any further open.

Once inside he went over to the table. James picked up half a sausage and shovelled it into his mouth and began chewing. It tasted good and he swallowed it down almost whole, which gave him a pain in his chest. There was a jug standing over to one side. James looked inside. It was milk. He lifted the jug to his lips and gulped several mouthfuls down. Not only did this help quench his thirst, but also relieved the pain in his chest.

There was another piece of sausage on the other plate and James also ate that. Over to one side was a pot containing a thick porridge like substance. Next to that was a bowl with gravy, which looked as though it was made from fried onions and tomatoes. James scooped up a handful of the solid porridge. He then rolled it into a rough ball and dipped it into the gravy. He pushed it into his mouth and chewed for a moment, then swallowed it down. It tasted good and he continued eating until his stomach was full. After drinking another few mouthfuls of milk he left the building and returned to the dark.

James decided he might as well continue following the railway line and set off again. After awhile dawn began breaking on the horizon and when he came across a culvert he decided he had better hide and also get some sleep.

90

Late morning the following day a terrific rumbling sound shook the entire culvert, which woke James from a deep sleep. The loud thundering noise overhead had given him a fright making him sit upright causing him to bash his head against the underside of the concrete above. Realising it was only a train he sat rubbing his head gently, feeling the fine grains of sand which had fallen into it from above. He continued to doze on and off for the remainder of the day and once darkness had fallen he climbed out of the culvert and stretched his sore aching body.

After first urinating onto the ground he then rubbed his painful arm. Then, he set off along the rails once more. After about an hour, James came across a signboard saying Pretoria 39 Miles. 'Woohoo!' he said aloud, not that he wanted to go there, but at least now he had some idea of where he was. James decided it was time to leave the railway line and he headed south and so he then made his way across the dark, lonely veldt.

During the night it rained hard soaking James to the bone but he kept on walking, mainly to keep himself warm and because there was nowhere to shelter anyway. Several times, he fell into dongas (gullies) that were full of rainwater, frogs and scorpions. Other times, James tripped over rocks or fallen branches scratching his face and arms. Sometimes he walked into unseen objects, such as fencing wire or tree stumps, etc.

At last though, the first signs of daybreak broke on the horizon, creating a beautiful orange, grey colour cloud-laden sky. James was pleased to see from the direction of the early sun that he was heading roughly south. After an hour he came across a farm in the distance. He then made his way towards it. As James got closer he could hear a cockerel crowing and then the sound of chickens, and knew there would be fresh eggs to eat.

91   Having first surveyed the area to make sure that no one was around, he then made his way over to a barn. He opened the door and peered inside. Several chickens were squatting on bales of straw. James entered the barn and made his way towards the hens. He chased one off from a bale and found three eggs. He took one, cracked it open and swallowed it whole from the shell. Then, he ate the other two. After that he found another four and ate those. He was wiping his mouth with his hand when he heard a young male voice behind him say loudly in English, 'Put your hands in the air, mister!'

James did as asked.

'Now turn around nice and slowly! And, don't try anything funny or I'll blast you to kingdom come!'

James obliged. Standing a little way from him was blonde headed boy. He guessed his age to be around twelve. He was dressed in a nightgown and was pointing an old musket at James. 'What are you doing here mister?' The boy asked.

'I was hungry... I have eaten a few of the eggs.'

'Stealing huh?'

...'I suppose so.'

'Well you'll have to pay for them mister, or my mother will get the constable!'

...'I don't have any money.'

For a moment the boy looked a little puzzled. Then he called out loudly for his mother. He waited for a few moments, but when she hadn't come he said to James, 'Walk slowly this way towards me, mister.'

Once again James obliged, with the boy walking backwards keeping the old musket pointing at him. Once outside the barn the boy told James to walk towards the farmhouse. As they approached a young girl, about eight years of age came out of the back door. She was dressed in a nightshirt. For a moment she just stood there staring at James wide-eyed and then she yelled, 'Mommy! Mommy! There's a strange man here!'

Within moments a woman also dressed in a nightgown came bolting out the back door with a worried expression on her face. She saw James standing there, dirty and scruffy, and the woman quickly told the girl to go back inside the house. Then, she said to the boy, 'Give me the gun, John!'

He reluctantly went over to her while still keeping the musket pointing in James' direction. The woman took the gun from him and pointing it at James she asked, 'What do you want here?'

Before James could reply the boy said loudly, 'I found him in the barn, mom! He's been stealing our eggs!'

The woman looked back at James. 'Is that true?'

'I'm afraid so, mam.'

The boy tugged at her skirt. 'Should I go for the police, mom?' he asked eagerly.

'Just a moment, Johnny!' she replied sternly. She then turned her attention back to James. 'Apart from stealing my eggs what are you doing on my property?'

'I was passing through... I'm on my way to Bloemfontein, mam.'

She surveyed the area behind James from left to right. 'Bloemfontein, you say?'

'Yeah mam.'

'Where's your horse then?'

'I'm travelling on foot, mam.'

...'Hmm, I'll have you know that Bloemfontein is well over one hundred and sixty miles from here. No person in their right mind would walk that distance unless he was desperate or perhaps running from the law.'

'I think he's an escaped convict mom!' the boy bellowed, 'maybe even a murderer? I'll go for the constable!' he begged.

The woman's eyes ran over the cuts and scratches on James' face and arms. He was filthy dirty with his clothes in a disgraceful condition. 'Well, are you?'

James shook his head. 'No mam.'

'Well, I must say that you certainly look like a convict on the run.'

'I have been walking all night in the rain. It was very dark. I fell into ditches and things along the way.'

'What name do you go by?'

'James Mitchell.' He was reluctant to offer too much information. The fact that she spoke English didn't mean that she was automatically on the side of the British. There were thousands of English speaking people living in South Africa who didn't agree with what the Empire was doing. Many, had joined the side of the Boers in the conflict. Her husband could even be a Boer commando for all he knew.

'Should I go for the constable now, mom?' the boy called out.

She glanced his way while keeping one eye on James. 'I think you should be getting yourself ready for school young man,' his mother replied a little harshly.

The boy put his head down and then he reluctantly went inside the house.

'Don't be too hard on him, mam. He was only trying to protect you.'

The woman didn't reply.

The wound on James' arm was giving him a lot of pain. 'May I lower my hands my arms are beginning to ache?' he asked trying to smile. 'Or are we going to stand around here like this all day?'

The woman indicated with the musket for him to lower his hands. James was relieved as he dropped them to his sides.

'Whereabouts have you come from?' she asked.

James was exhausted and his whole body ached. In addition he was also feeling cold. He decided to take a gamble and tell her a little of the truth and then see what happens. He told her how he had been captured and then imprisoned in Pretoria, and how he had escaped. While he was talking she appeared to become a little more relaxed. After a few moments she lowered the musket. 'I'll call one of the kaffirs to start the boiler so that you can have a hot bath. After you have eaten you can go on your way again.'

'Thanks, mam, I appreciate that very much.'

The woman rang a bell which was suspended from the verandah roof. Moments later a middle-aged black man came running towards the house doing up the buttons on his shirt. He looked in James' direction with large bulging eyes. When he arrived the woman told him to place wood on the fire and to make sure there was also water in the boiler. The black man ran off to carry out his tasks. The woman then turned her attention to James. 'You can wait over in the barn. When the water's hot enough the boy will bring over to you. I will also provide you with a towel and soap.'

James thanked her and then he turned and started walking towards the barn.

The woman watched him for a few moments then she called out, 'When you have bathed and dressed mister, come up to the house!'

James stopped walking. He turned around to thank her, but she had already gone inside. When he got to the barn he went over to the bales of hay and sat down with his back against them. Then, he closed his eyes.

92 Later, James woke with a fright when someone shook him by the shoulder. The black man was standing over him and he quickly stood back when James sat up. He was holding several items of linen and clothing over one arm. Behind him, steam was rising from a small wooden tub.

James got to his feet as the black man placed the items onto a hay-bale. Without a word, he then turned and walked off. James went over to the bale and looked at the things. There was a towel, a scrubbing brush with a long handle, and a bar of soap. There was also a pair of trousers, a shirt and a long sleeved undergarment plus a pair of socks. Next to them was a hand mirror and cutthroat razor.

James removed his tattered, dirty garments and stepped into the hot water. He slowly sat down in the small round tub, which he was barely able to fit into. The water went gushing over the top and onto the barn floor. The warmth of the water sent a shiver through his cold, aching body and for several moments he just sat there enjoying it. Once James had bathed and shaved, he dressed and then made his way over to the house. As he came closer there was a strong smell of cooking in the air that made his tummy rumble. He knocked on the door and moments later it opened.

'Come in sah,' a large black maid said with a big smile.

James thanked her and then entered the kitchen. It was nice and warm in there. On the far side of the kitchen another huge black woman was working over by a wood stove. James was shown into the dining room. The table was laid for four persons. Moments later the woman arrived. She was dressed in a long black skirt with a white blouse. Her blonde hair was brushed out and hung down her back to her waist. James thought she was extremely attractive and guessed she was probably a lot older than him.

She was pleasantly surprised by James' refreshed appearance and commented, 'I wasn't sure if the clothes would fit, especially the trousers and jacket.'

'The legs are a little on the short side, mam,' he replied with a smile, 'but otherwise they are perfectly thanks.'

'You can sit down there, mister,' she said pointing to one of the chairs.

'Thank you... and please call me James. Mister, sounds, well, very formal.'

'So does mam... My name's Susan.'

He nodded... 'Will your husband be joining us for breakfast, Susan?'

'No ...actually my husband's deceased.'

'Oh, I am sorry.'

Susan had noticed James looking at the other two table settings. 'The two children will be joining us any moment.'

'Oh,' he nodded with a smile, 'that will be nice.'

They soon arrived, both dressed and ready for school, and took-up their places at the table. Susan introduced the girl as Emily. James already knew the boy's name. After that, Susan rang a small brass bell and moments later the maid entered the room carrying a large tray. A dish containing sausages was placed onto the table followed by a bowl of cooked tomatoes. Then, there was a bowl with bacon and mushrooms and lastly a dish containing six fried eggs. By this time James' stomach was rumbling rather loudly. He was feeling a little embarrassed and gave Emily a wink which made her giggle, but her mother soon put a stop to that. Susan dished up a plateful of food for James, which the maid then placed in front of him. He waited patiently while Susan prepared the children's meals and after that she said grace.

James could hardly wait for her to finish. Then, he quickly sprinkled salt and pepper onto his food and began eating. Emily watched with large staring eyes. Susan noticed her and told her to eat her breakfast or she would be late for school. John ignored James throughout the meal. He didn't trust the stranger that he had caught red-handed stealing their eggs, and who his mother had now invited into their home.

THE PLOUGH, THE GUN AND THE GLORY

Once breakfast was over the children climbed onto a horse-drawn buggy waiting for them outside the front of the house. The middle-aged black man, who had brought James the water and clothing, was seated in the driver's position. Susan waved goodbye to the children and then the buggy left. She turned around and made her way back to the verandah.

James had been waiting there while she attended to her offspring. 'You have two fine children,' he said as she approached.

She smiled as she said, 'Thank you... Would you like a cup of coffee out here on the verandah before you leave?'

'That would be very nice thanks. Are you sure I'm not overstaying my welcome?'

'If you were, I wouldn't be offering you something to drink... Would you like to sit down over there?' She pointed to several chairs placed around a table further along the verandah. 'If you'll excuse me for a moment while I go and instruct the maid to prepare the things.'

After she had left James made his way over to the table and chairs and sat down. He wondered how the war was going and hoped that Winston had made it safely to Delagoa Bay. He also thought himself lucky at having come across the farm and meeting such a kind-hearted woman as Susan. He wondered what had happened to her husband. When Susan returned James got to his feet. Once she was seated he sat down again. 'You have a very lovely place here from what I've seen.'

'Thank you.' She sighed. 'Yes... I suppose in many ways I have been blessed.'

'What do you mainly produce on the farm?'

'Maize mostly... but we also grow deciduous fruits, peaches, apricots, plums. I'll get one of the boys to pick some for you.'

'Thanks very much you are very kind.'

'You're welcome.'

'You don't happen to have any wadding and disinfectant handy, do you?'

'As a matter of fact I do... Are you requiring some?'

He nodded. 'I need to change the bandage on my arm. I was wounded before being captured.'

'I'll get the maid to bring you some.'

'Thanks.'

Susan rang a small bell and after a short wait the maid came hurriedly along. Susan told her to go and fetch the first aid box from the pantry. She returned with it and left again. Susan opened the lid and then looked at James. 'I'm afraid that you'll need to remove your jacket.'

'That's okay, I'll change it later myself,' he replied with a surprised tone, 'I really didn't expect you to have to do it.'

'It will be far easier for me to do it than for you.' Susan waited patiently while he removed the jacket and then hung it across the back of the chair. 'Now, roll up your sleeve.'

James did as asked but the sleeve was still in the way. 'I might have to take off my shirt.'

She nodded. 'I think so.'

James removed the braces from his shoulders and let them hang down by the sides of his trousers. Then, he undid the buttons and pulled off the shirt. His good physique and hairy chest didn't go unnoticed. Susan quickly directed her attention to the bloodstained, grubby bandage. 'How long have you had this on for?'

'A few days.'

She shook her head. Susan then took a pair of scissors and carefully cut off the bandage. She had a look at the wound. 'This could be infected. I'll need to get hot water to wash it first before we place anything on. You take a seat I won't be long.'

Susan got to her feet with James doing the same thing and after she had left he sat down again. About five minutes later Susan returned with a bowl of boiling water. 'This is strait off the stove,' she said, 'so it's going to be extremely hot.' She took a handful of wadding off the roll, dipped it into the hot water and began washing around the wound. Susan repeated the exercise several times. Once all the dried blood had been removed she bathed it with carbolic acid. James gritted his teeth without saying anything. Susan then soaked some wadding with carbolic and then placed it onto the wound. After that, she wrapped a cotton bandage around the whole thing and tied it off. 'There,' she said, 'you can replace your shirt now.'

James thanked her and redressed. When he was finished he sat down. Susan rang for the maid to take everything away. Then she left him for a few moments while she went to wash her hands. When she returned she said, 'So, James, whereabouts is home?'

He told her about Rambling Meadows and of his family, and how his late brother William had been tragically killed and also the death of his father. When he finished he said, 'You mentioned previously that your husband was deceased.'

...'Yes... He was killed two years ago in a freak mining accident near Johannesburg.'

'I'm sorry to hear that.'

'My late husband made a substantial sum of money from gold mining and then later from diamonds in Kimberley. He sold his claims to Cecil Rhodes when he left the mining business. After that he purchased commercial properties in Johannesburg and also this farm amongst other things.'

At that moment the maid arrived with a silver tray containing the tea and coffee items. Once she had left Susan continued with her story while pouring James' coffee. 'A close friend of my husbands discovered a new gold mine near Carletonville and asked Brendan, my late husband, to take a look at it. Although he had reservations about returning underground he agreed to do it as a special favour.'

Susan poured tea for herself and after dropping a sugar cube into the cup she daintily stirred it with a spoon as she said, 'There was a cave-in... Brendan and five other men lost their lives... Their bodies have never been recovered.'

James shook his head in sympathy. 'I am sorry.'

'Thank you... I learned later that we had in-fact very little money. Unknown to me at the time, Brendan had gambled most of it away. He had even sold off his commercial properties in Johannesburg in order to repay his debts owed to the bank. Fortunately, we still had the farm otherwise I don't know what the children and I would have done.' Susan sipped more of her tea. 'Brendan was a lot older than me. He was, by no stretch of the imagination, an affectionate or loving sort of man, but he was a good provider. I first met him at a garden party when I was sixteen. After a short courtship of six months we were married.'

As much as James was enjoying listening to her, it was a job for him to keep his eyes from closing, and even harder for him not to yawn. The hot bath and huge breakfast, plus the lack of sleep had caught up with him. He was thinking of excusing himself so that he could go off somewhere and get some sleep, and hoped that Susan wouldn't be offended.

Susan had noticed that he was having problems staying awake. 'You look tired, James?'

'I apologise... I hope you don't think I'm being rude?'

'Not at all... Why don't you get some much needed sleep?'

'That would be very nice.'

'I have been thinking that perhaps you should stay overnight in order to get proper rest. You can leave tomorrow instead, if you wish?'

He was surprised. 'You don't mind me staying on?'

She shook her head. 'Not at all.'

'Would you mind if I use the barn?'

'There's no need to do that. I have a spare bedroom that you can use.'

...'That's very kind of you, but you have already done quite enough for me. The barn will be more than adequate and compared to the army and prison, it's a luxury.'

'As you wish... I'll send one of the boy's over with some blankets and a pillow.'

'You're very kind. Thank you.'

James made his way over to the barn and moments later a young black man brought the bedding. James thanked him and then laid them out on top of a bed of straw. He lay down and put his head on the pillow.

93   James slept for the remainder of the day and was woken at five o'clock by the maid. She had brought a bucket of hot water for him to wash his hands and face. She told him that once he was ready he was to go up to the house where he would find Mrs Swanepoel waiting on the verandah. When James arrived he was surprised to see her dressed in a stunning frock.

'Did you sleep well James?' she asked as he came up the steps.

'Like a log thanks, and I feel a lot better.'

'Good... would you like something to drink... perhaps a brandy?'

'That would be very nice, thank you.'

Susan began pouring him a drink while he sat down in a chair opposite her.

'I hope you don't mind me saying how very nice you look this evening, Susan.'

'Thank you.' She enjoyed the complement. 'This is the only time of the day that I have to wear something nice. Well, there's no point in having lovely clothes if you leave them hanging in the closet, is there?'

'I couldn't agree more.'

Susan finished pouring his drink and handed the glass over to him. 'Well James, here's to a safe return to your contingent, wherever they may be.' She lifted her glass.

James did the same and they clinked them together. They both said cheers and placed the glasses to their lips. James swallowed a mouthful of the neat liquid. An immediate feeling of glowing warmth travelled down through his body to his stomach. 'Ah, this is an excellent brandy.'

'I'm glad you like it.' Susan sipped her drink delicately as she gazed out of the verandah at the fiery orange-ball slowly sinking on the horizon. 'This is the part of the day that I love the most.'

James glanced westwards. The sky was a brilliant pallet of colour comprising of orange, pinks and purples, as the sun reflected off heavy rain-filled clouds. 'Yeah, it's also a favourite time of mine.'

Susan gave a sigh and then her face hardened slightly. She looked deep in thought as she said, 'Do you think Britain will win this war, James?'

He nodded. 'I'm sure they will... They should do, they have the numbers.'

Susan swallowed a mouthful of her brandy and then placed her glass on the table. 'My parents were both from England. I however, was born in a little dorp (village) called Newcastle. That's in the colony of Natal. My father and mother once owned a small hotel there until they sold it and returned to England. So by birth, I'm a South African. Naturally though, I still have strong ties to Britain.'

James nodded. He could understand that, after-all his situation was similar.

'Brendan, my late husband, was Afrikaans,' she continued; 'therefore, both my children have Afrikaans blood running through their veins.'

They both drank from their glasses.

'If I was to tell you that I believe what Britain is doing to the Afrikaners is very wrong James, what would you say?'

...'I don't know... I suppose you have a right to your own opinion.'

'Does it make me a traitor to Britain?'

...'I guess you have to be on one side or the other. Who you choose is entirely up to you.'

She smiled. 'Do you really think it's that simple? ...How much do you know about this war James, or even about the history of this country?'

...'Not much... well very little to be honest.'

Susan nodded. 'Let me tell you something... This war is about expanding the British Empire. It's a war of pure greed. A war to gain control of the huge wealth of gold and diamonds in the Transvaal and Orange Free State... Britain never cared a hoot about this part of Africa until the discovery of gold and diamonds. The Boers on the other hand are farmers... farmers who are fighting for their very existence. They are fighting for their land and their whole way of life. They won't give up easily, you know?'

James nodded. He had tasted a little of the war and he knew she was probably right.

THE PLOUGH, THE GUN AND THE GLORY

'So, I'm sure that you can see my dilemma? ...Whom do I give my loyalty to? ...Which side do I choose to be on, James?'

...'I can fully understand your problem. And, I can sympathise with you. Believe it or not I have a problem not unlike yourself.'

'Really?'

'Yeah.'

James told her about his Aunt Ruth and his Uncle Jacobaas who were farming in the Free State, and of his cousins Piet, Haans and Freda. How he was captured by the Boers and later rescued by his aunt together with Haans. And, how later, he had killed Piet with a gun that his aunt had given him, and that he would somehow have to return to the farm one day and tell them. Then he would have to take them to the place where he had buried Piet and the other boy's body.

'Oh James, that is such a tragic story.' Susan wiped the tears from her eyes with a lace handkerchief.

Shortly after, the maid arrived and told Susan that dinner was ready. They finished their brandies without further conversation and then went to the dining room. The two children joined them for the meal. They started with mushroom soup, followed by roast beef, roast potatoes, pumpkin and a variety of other farm grown vegetables, topped off with a rich creamy gravy. Then, there was a mouth-watering pudding. The whole meal was finished off with coffee, cheese and biscuits.

After supper they all sat in the lounge discussing the days events until it was time for the children to say goodnight. Susan excused herself and took them off to bed. When she returned to the lounge she poured James and herself another brandy and offered him a cigar, which he politely declined. Susan sat down at the piano and played a selection of her favourite classical pieces, which brought many memories of Rambling Meadows flooding back to James.

Shortly before ten o'clock James thanked Susan for the excellent meal and a very pleasant and entertaining evening. After saying goodnight he returned to the barn, stripped off and climbed under the blankets. He blew out the lantern and laid his head on the pillow; moments later his mind turned to thoughts of Christina, and then also Veronica. He should really write and tell Veronica that he had met

Christina again and that he still loved her, despite that she was married? Finally, his eyelids grew heavy and then they closed.

94   James had been asleep when something woke him. He sat up. He could see a lantern over by the barn door and his heart quickened a little. Then, a female voice called out, 'James! ...James are you still awake?'

Realising it was only Susan and not Boers he relaxed slightly. 'Yeah Susan, I'm awake.' He wondered what she was doing outdoors this late at night. 'Is there something wrong?'

The lantern came nearer. 'No James, nothing is wrong.'

He could see her now in the soft glow of the light. She was in her nightshirt. She knelt down next to him and placed the lantern on the floor. 'I'm sorry if I disturbed you. I was unable to sleep. Then, I began thinking of you out here all alone in the barn.' She placed her hand on his face and gently stroked it. 'You're a very handsome young man James... I would think many young women would be very happy to become Mrs Mitchell... Is there someone special in your life waiting for you back in Australia?'

...'Umm, there was someone.'

'What happened, did she run off with another man and break your heart?'

'No nothing like that... The problem is that I'm no longer sure how I feel about her. I also promised to write to her, but I never have. Maybe she has given up on me by now?'

'Not if she really loves you James... A woman will rarely give up a man who she truly loves. Why don't you write to her before you leave here?'

...'I have tried writing once or twice to her. The problem is there's someone else who has unexpectedly come back into my life... someone that I knew from school and who was also my girlfriend. While I was in the field hospital at Modder River we met again. She's nursing out here with the army medical corps.'

'Oh... Well, I'm sure that in time your heart will give you the answer you are seeking... I brought the brandy along.'

She showed him the bottle. After removing the cork she had a small swig and then handed it to James.

He swallowed a good mouthful.

'The last few years have been a very long drought for me James... After Emily's birth, Brendan and I slept in separate bedrooms. We never made love again. He, however, had numerous affairs and had quite a reputation along with his drinking and gambling addictions.' Susan stopped talking for a moment. 'I'm not embarrassing you by telling you all this, am I?'

James shook his head. He couldn't help but feel sorry for her. He could tell she was lonely, otherwise she wouldn't be telling a complete stranger her innermost private and personal secrets. Her life was slipping away out here on the farm and she probably knew it better than anyone. 'Surely there must be a number of men in the district who would love to have a beautiful and intelligent wife such as yourself Susan?'

She was flattered by his comments and smiled. 'Thank you... You have a very kind heart James, and you know how to make a woman feel better about herself.'

'I meant every word.'

'As a matter of fact several men have approached me since Brendan's death. They were however, only interested in having seedy little affairs behind their wives backs. One man who said he would leave his wife and six children for me was the local priest.' She gave a sigh. 'It's not easy being a widow with two children. Most men see you as easy prey and their wives see you as a vulture.'

James swallowed the lump in his throat. He had never thought of things that way before.

Susan placed her hand on his youthful face. 'Will you end it for me... the drought? Will you make love to me James?'

His heart was racing slightly. 'I... If that's what you want... I would be very honoured.'

She smiled gently. 'Thank you.'

Susan sat on her knees and then pulled up her nightshirt and over her head. The light from the lamp highlighting her full, yet firm body. Her breasts were like those of a younger woman. Susan placed her hand on his chest and then rubbed it gently. 'It's been a long time since I did that.' She lent forwards and placed her lips on his and kissed him with wild passionate desire.

James kissed her back. Susan lifted the blanket and then slid under. She could feel the warmth from his body. His penis was hard and it pressed against her. She lay on her back and James kissed her sensually. Susan placed her arms around his shoulders and then pulled him closer to her. She opened her legs for him and he pushed his rigid organ into her soft, warm, moist vagina. She gave a slight moan and closed her eyes. Susan could feel him inside her and it felt sensually wonderful. At first, James began pumping his rigid gland slowly, but as their lovemaking intensified he increased the pace until it became more frenzied.

'Oh James,' Susan uttered with ecstasy. 'Uh! Uh! Oh God!' She dug her fingernails into his back. 'Please don't stop!' she begged as she continued to make sounds of sexual pleasure until she reached her second orgasm. They were both sweating and moments later James ejaculated. He rolled off Susan and they both lay gasping for air.

95 It was still dark when James was woken by one of the black farm workers. 'The madam says you must get dressed quickly boss! ...And then you must go to the house.' After he had left, James sat up and rubbed his eyes. He yawned, stretching his arms at the same time. It was cold in the barn and a shiver ran through his body. He got dressed and then made his way to the door. A light rain was falling. After a moments hesitation he ran through the rain to the house. When he arrived at the back door the maid was waiting and let him inside. She asked him to go through to the parlour. Susan was dressed and was sitting in one of the large leather upholstered chairs. They greeted one another cordially. 'I am sorry to get you up this early James. But, I am afraid it was necessary. One of the farm workers told my maid that the army were searching a near-by farm yesterday afternoon for two escaped prisoners, from the State Schools Prison in Pretoria. By the time they were finished it was too dark for them to come over here.'

James' heart began to thump in his chest.

'Apparently, they will continue searching here early this morning.'

'I'll have to be on my way then. You can't afford to be implicated in any way for harbouring an escaped prisoner.'

'I have already thought of a plan. We will take the children into school this morning instead of the driver. From there, we will proceed to Delmas and then onto Heidelberg. I have a very good friend of mine living there who I have known for many years. I would trust her and her husband with my life, if I had to.'

'Well, let's hope you don't have to do that.'

'From there you can make your way to Bloemfontein.'

'What if we are stopped along the way?'

'Then leave the talking to me.'

James shook his head.

'What's wrong?'

He gave a sigh. 'You are taking such an enormous risk for someone that you hardly know. Two days ago Johnny held me up at gunpoint for stealing your eggs.'

She ignored his concerns. 'I have a hamper packed with food and lemonade to take with us, plus a selection of fresh fruit... You will also need these.' She went over to a coat stand in the hallway and brought a raincoat and hat over to James. 'They were Brendan's. I took them out of his closet this morning.'

'I don't know what to say except thank you.'

...'I also found these amongst his things.' She handed him a map and compass. 'You never know they just might come in handy sometime.'

James was speechless. Her kindness and generosity were overwhelming and he felt a lump in his throat.

'I'll get the children ready for school and then we must leave.'

96   Susan and James proceeded along the winding dirt road towards the small village where the school was situated. When they arrived James waited in the buggy while Susan took the two children to their classroom. Parents of other children arriving stared at James as they walked past and he could almost read their minds. Their eyes told him they were wondering who this strange man was with Susan. A little further away was a group of men and women huddled together. James could tell they were gossiping by the way they were behaving. Now and then, one of them would look slyly in his direction, but when they saw him watching them they would quickly look away again. He was relieved when he saw Susan returning. 'You've got the whole village gossiping, you know?' he said as she climbed into the buggy.

She glanced towards the small group huddled together. 'Let them gossip all they like. If those pathetic women knew that their husbands tried to affairs with me they would soon loose that stupid smug look on their faces. They make me sick the lot of them.' Susan took hold of the reins and jeered the horse on.

The journey to Delmas was pleasant and without mishap. Apart from the odd passer-by the road was quiet. James and Susan chatted in a relaxed mood and soon reached the small village. Susan stopped at a drinking trough so that the horse could have water. A young boy was handing out leaflets in the street. When he saw Susan and James he came over to the cart. He handed a sheet of paper to James and said something in Afrikaans. Susan quickly replied in Afrikaans while taking the paper from James. She had a quick look at it. Then she rolled it up and pushed it into her blouse while saying, 'We need to get out of here.' She flicked the horse's reins and they headed out of the village.

'What's the big hurry?' James asked with the buggy bumping and swaying over the rough road.

'I'll explain when we get further away from the village.'

After a mile or so Susan found a suitable place to stop and pulled the horse off the road. Moments later they came to a halt under the shade of tree. She took the poster out of her blouse and after unrolling it she gave it to James.

He looked at it. 'I can't read this, it's in Afrikaans.'

Susan took it back saying, 'I'm sorry I forgot. I'll read it for you. It's from the Pretoria State Schools Prison. It's a reward for Twenty-five pounds Stirling offered by the sub-commission of the fifth division, on behalf of the special constable of the said division, to anyone who brings the escaped prisoner of war, CHURCHILL, dead or alive to this office. Signed; Lodk de Haas, Secretary.'

'My God! ...That's the bloke that I escaped with! His name's Winston!'

...'You didn't tell me that you escaped with another man!'

...'I didn't think it was important at the time. After that the subject never came up again.'

She frowned. 'When I told you this morning that the police were searching for two escaped prisoners from Pretoria, you didn't say anything about this other man... Are you sure your name's not Churchill? You're not this man are you?'

'No! ...What ever gave you that idea?'

She sighed. 'I don't know James... What happened to him? Why aren't you still together?'

'We split up... He went onto Delagoa Bay to catch a ship to Durban.'

'We will have to be extra careful from now on. Twenty-five pounds will have every vigilante for miles around looking for him.'

'Hopefully he's out of the country by now.' James smiled. 'He's probably sitting in a deckchair under a palm tree on a beach in Delagoa Bay, with a brandy and a cigar.'

'That may well be so, but the situation is still very dangerous for you though.'

'Why?'

'Because, if someone thinks that you are this man, Churchill, you could be shot on sight. The reward say's quite clearly dead or alive James... Dead or alive! ...Sometimes men don't ask questions until it's too late.'

James swallowed the lump in his throat as he brushed his hand through his hair. 'I never thought of that.'

...'Anyway, I think while we are here we should have something to eat. This place looks like a nice little spot to have a picnic lunch. I hope that you're feeling hungry?'

'Not really to be honest.'

They took the things out the back of the buggy and after James had spread the blanket out they sat down opposite one another. Susan opened the hamper and unpacked the things. There was a bowl containing boerwors with fried onions and mushrooms. Others had a variety of salads including avocado, sliced tomatoes, potato salad and coleslaw.

'Hey, this looks great, Susan,' James said enthusiastically having now smelt the food. All of a sudden he was feeling a lot hungrier than he had realised.

'Good... For a moment I was worried that I might have to throw most of it away.'

'I'll eat all of it, don't you worry.'

Susan dished up and they began their meal. Suddenly she stopped eating and said, 'I almost forgot something.'

James looked up from his plate. 'What?'

'The wine.'

'Wine? ...I thought we were only having lemonade?'

'I also brought a bottle of rose wine along.' She pulled it out the bottom of the hamper and unwrapped the damp cloth. She gave it to James to pull the cork out. After that she took two glasses out of the hamper and filled them to the brim. She gave a glass to James then lifted hers. 'Cheers,' she said and then they clinked them together.

James had a mouthful. 'Mmm, very nice.' He looked up at the trees and then at the surrounding veldt. 'It's hard to imagine sitting here and picnicking like this, that there is a war raging around us. People are dying in bloody conflict at this very moment.'

Susan sighed. 'Let's not talk about the war now James... Besides, you will soon be rejoining it.'

He smiled. 'I'm sorry, you're absolutely right. Trust me to go and spoil a perfect day.'

They continued their meal and washed it down with the rose wine. James had another helping of food, finishing off the leftovers. Susan also gave him the last of the wine. They were almost ready to start packing up the things when they heard the thunder of horse's hooves approaching. James' heart started to thump a little quicker and he got to his feet.

'I think you had better sit down, James,' Susan said calmly.

He glanced back at her sitting on the blanket. 'Don't you think we should try and hide or something?' There was a sense of urgency in his voice.

Susan shook her head. 'There's no time for that now. Just sit down and let's continue picnicking.'

James reluctantly sat down on the blanket.

'Perhaps you had better sit this side James,' she was indicating with her hand, 'with your back towards the road.'

No sooner had he done that and the horses came into sight. Susan watched as they came closer. They were Boer commandos and as they got nearer she recognised the leading rider. 'Well, well, we are indeed being honoured today,' she said calmly.

'What do you mean?' he asked a little nervously.

'General Louis Botha is no fewer than eighty feet from us.'

James turned his head slightly and looked over his shoulder. He saw a big man astride a white charger. He was clean-shaven apart from a moustache and a small beard on his chin, and he carried a bandolier draped across his left shoulder. The general had noticed them sitting and picnicking and had politely tipped his hat to Susan as he rode-on past. She in-turn had graciously smiled back. The general continued on his way with his mounted troops following. Horse-drawn artillery came next, then lastly, several covered wagons. After a short time the silence returned to the veldt and birds could be heard in the trees again. When the last of the dust had almost gone Susan looked over at James. 'Well, that was an unexpected surprise to say the least.'

'You can say that again... I would like to know where they are heading?'

'Maybe to Bloemfontein?' Susan replied.

'How many of them do you think there were?'

'I counted about eight hundred men on horseback. They also had four very large guns on wheels.'

'Long Toms... That's what they call the Creusot 155mm field guns.'

'How would you know that you had your back turned to them?'

James smiled. 'I caught the odd glimpse here and there over my shoulder.'

'There were also covered wagons,' Susan continued. 'Two of them had white crosses painted on the covers. Obviously ambulances. The others were probably carrying spare ammunition and food.'

James nodded.

Susan began placing the things into the hamper. 'We had better get going it's still a long way to Heidelberg.'

'What time will we reach there, do you think?'

'Not until after dark.'

'What will happen then... you can't travel back to the farm tonight? What about Johnny and Emily? Who will look after them? How will they get home from school?'

'Everything's been taken care of James. I made arrangements for them to be collected from school and stay overnight with friends of mine. I'll pick them up after school tomorrow.'

They packed the remaining things and James placed them into the buggy. After climbing aboard, Susan took hold of the reins. She gave them a couple of flicks while saying loudly to the horse, 'Gee-up Bronson! Gee-up!'

The gelding pulled hard digging his hooves into the dirt and the buggy set off on its journey once again.

97   When they reached the gates with two grand columns on either side, Susan turned the buggy into the driveway and they made their way towards the large double-story house. The horse was brought to a halt outside the front entrance. While James was assisting Susan down from the buggy the front door opened. A black maid was holding a lantern in one hand. After a few moments hesitation she recognised Susan and came hurrying outside. 'Good evening, Madam,' she blurted out, curtsying at the same time.

'Hello Molly... I sincerely hope that Mrs Beeton's at home.

'She is, Madam,' she replied with a broad beaming smile.

'Thank heavens for that.' There was a relieved tone to her voice.

The maid led the way inside with the lantern. Susan's friend, Bella, was waiting in the parlour. She was surprised to see that it was Susan. They greeted one other and then kissed each other lightly on the cheek. After that Susan introduced James. Then she said to Bella, while indicating with her eyes that the maid was waiting in the background, 'I will explain everything to you shortly.'

Bella excused herself for a moment while she instructed the maid to have two extra places laid at the dining table, and to also have the guest rooms prepared. Bella then rejoined her visitors. She was brimming with excitement to hear what news Susan had for her. Susan then explained the whole story of how James had arrived at her farm.

During the conversation Bella's husband, Richard, arrived home from work. He was both surprised and pleased to see Susan there. After the usual greetings Susan introduced him to James. Sherries were poured while they chatted away with everyone trying to talk at the same time. The dinner bell was rung and everyone made their way through to the dining room. During the meal Richard told James that he was the proprietor of a small newspaper 'The Transvaal Post.' He then gave James the latest news on the progress of the war. 'Have you heard that Kimberley has finally been relieved?'

'No! ...When was this?'

'General French took occupation of the town on the 15th February.'

'Well that's good news.'

'Yes.' Richard refilled the wine glasses and returned to his chair. 'Well, we certainly needed some sort of morale booster... Apparently Cecil Rhodes gave Lord Roberts an ultimatum to immediately relieve the diamond town or Rhodes would surrender it to the Boers.'

'Would he really have done that?'

'I think Rhodes is capable of doing anything when it suits him. He's the sort of man who's used to getting his own way, his type always are. If he was bluffing Roberts, it certainly worked. I suppose that's all that counted?' Richard swallowed a little wine. 'The bad news though is that the British army suffered another terrible defeat at Spion Kop in Natal.'

James shook his head in disbelief.

'Sir Redvers Buller has duffed it once again and General Botha and his commandos won the day. The British retreated across the Tugela River after having lost over fifteen hundred men. The rumour going around at present is that Buller has been nick-named Sir Reverse Buller.' Richard drank a mouthful of wine. 'The good news however, is that General Cronje surrendered his forces to Lord Roberts at Paardeberg.'

'Really?' James was pleased to hear that, at last things were beginning to improve.

'But not until after a terrible, bloody battle though. I'll tell you a little about it, if you like?'

'Not while we are eating thank you Richard,' Bella politely interrupted. 'If you don't mind dear, you can tell James later in the privacy of the drawing room?'

'Very well, as you wish,' he replied politely with a smile.

After the meal Richard and James excused themselves from the company of the ladies and departed for the drawing room. 'Would you like a brandy, James?'

'That would be very nice, thank you.'

Richard poured two glasses and then handed one to James. 'Would you also like a cigar?'

'I don't smoke thanks.'

THE PLOUGH, THE GUN AND THE GLORY

Richard lit a cigar, puffed vigorously on it several times sending a cloud of smoke spiralling towards the ceiling. That, plus the distinct aroma reminded James of his late father, and for a brief moment his thoughts turned to home.

'Now, let's see... I was going to tell you a little of the battle of Paardeberg, wasn't I?'

The sound of Richard's voice interrupted James' thoughts. 'Yeah that's right.'

They sat down in two enormous brown leather chairs. They were extremely comfortable, although a little on the cold side. Once both men were settled Richard continued, 'It was I suppose, inevitable that Roberts would defeat Cronje. Roberts troops outnumbered Cronje's by something like five-to-one.'

James knew the British and colonial troops outnumbered the Boers, but he hadn't known it was by such an enormous amount.

Richard had a mouthful of brandy and then puffed vigorously on his cigar. 'While Roberts was gathering his invasion force, forty thousand strong near Enslin, Cronje with his army of six thousand were sitting athwart the railway at Margersfontein ...Cronje believed that Roberts was preparing to advance on Kimberley. However, French's sweep northwards and then Roberts' drive eastwards towards Bloemfontien, perplexed Cronje, and during the night he moved his army towards the capital.'

James drank from his glass.

'The following morning Roberts discovered Cronje had slipped away and went in pursuit of him. His plan was to halt him by using mounted troops and then crush him with his artillery and massive infantry. Part of Roberts' invasion army, two thousand mounted infantry, was under a colonel named Hannay. Six hundred and twenty of those were New South Wales Mounted Infantry.'

'Were any West Australians involved in the battle?'

'Not to my knowledge,' he replied shaking his head... 'Anyway, Hannay attempted to engage Cronje's commandos as they headed up the Modder River. However, they soon encountered heavy opposition from the Boers and were forced to fall back. In their hasty retreat they accidentally plunged over a steep embankment and into the river. Many men and horses were injured... some even killed.'

303

James shook his head in disbelief. Then he had another mouthful of his brandy.

'Hannay's force hurriedly regrouped and went on the attack, but yet again they were driven back by the Boers. General French had now returned from Kimberley and Roberts sent French's cavalry to engage Cronje. It was another horse killing ride with scores of chargers dying under their riders. The men have named it French's milestones.' Richard took a drink from his glass and after that he puffed clouds of smoke from his cigar. 'French's cavalry was able to force Cronje to laager at Paardeberg Drift. This was mainly due to Cronje's convoy being held-up by Boer families, mostly women, children and old folk, who had attached themselves to Cronje for protection.' Richard stopped talking for a moment while he poured them both another brandy. 'Hannay then received orders from Kitchener to rush the laager.'

'Who's Kitchener?' James had not yet heard the name mentioned before.

'Lord Kitchener is Roberts' chief of staff... his right-hand man. Roberts, who was apparently ill with a fever, had handed over the reins to Kitchener.'

'Oh.'

'Anyway, the charge was cut short by the death of Hannay, who it's said, rode recklessly at the head of his men. From that point on the battle became an artillery and infantry affair as horses were of little use against a besieged enemy. Heavy rains had also raised the level of the river and it was no longer possible for Cronjes convoy to cross. He was trapped and although he and his men could have broken out and got away, Cronje would not abandon the women, children and old folk. He decided to stand and make a fight of it, something that went against his better judgement. After a heroic struggle lasting eight days Cronje finally had no option but to surrender. Again, it was for the sake of the women and children as they had taken a terrible hammering from Roberts' artillery. When the two men met later, Roberts extended his hand in friendship and said, "I am glad to see you, general, you have made a gallant defence, sir." They had breakfast together before Cronje and his men were dispatched to St Helena where they will be imprisoned for life.'

'Napoleon's final home,' James added before drinking from his glass.

'Quite right... The Boers have lost their most famous general, James. Paardeberg was a much-needed victory as was Kimberley. For the first time since the outbreak of the war we have turned the tide and have the Boers on the run.'

'Do you know if Roberts is advancing towards Bloemfontein?'

'Yes.'

'How long will it take you to find out where the West Australians are?'

'As I mentioned earlier it shouldn't be too much of a problem... a few days at the most.'

'I can't wait to rejoin them.'

'Yes, I can see that you are anxious to do that.'

At that moment the door opened and Bella entered the room. Both men got to their feet.

'It's getting rather late, Richard, and I'm sure that James must be feeling tired after his long journey?'

'Of course my dear,' he replied taking his pocket watch out and looking at the time. It was after ten o'clock. 'I must apologise James, I completely lost track of time.'

'Not at all, and I have really enjoyed listening to you... And, the brandies have gone down very well too.'

They left the room and rejoined Susan in the lounge. After a hot glass of milk and saying goodnight to Richard, James and Susan were shown to their separate bedrooms by Bella. 'You will find a jug of hot water and hand-basin, so you can wash before you retire,' she told them both. 'There are also clean nightshirts. Oh, and new tooth brushes and bicarbonate of soda in a dish.'

Both Susan and James thanked her, said goodnight and then went into their adjoining rooms. James stripped down naked and washed himself. After brushing his teeth he put on the nightshirt and then climbed into the large four-poster bed. He turned the lantern down low and lay there thinking about what Richard had told him. Then, he thought of Susan. He hadn't had the chance to thank her for everything she had done, and she would be leaving early in the morning. He wondered if she was still awake.

After about ten minutes he got out of bed opened the door to the passage and peered out. The house was already in darkness. He went quietly over to Susan's door. There was a light coming from under it. James gently knocked three times. A few moments later the door slowly opened and in the soft glow of the lantern he saw Susan.

'I wasn't sure if you were asleep or not,' James said, almost in a whisper.

She opened the door a little wider. 'You had better come in before you wake the others,' she whispered back.

James entered the room. 'I didn't get the chance tonight to thank you for all you have done for me. And, I wasn't sure if I would see you in the morning before you leave.'

She closed the door quietly while saying, 'Surely you didn't think I would have gone without saying goodbye?'

'No, I suppose not.'

'Anyway, saying goodbye tonight will be far nicer. Tomorrow morning would have been a rather formal sort of farewell, don't you think?'

He nodded. 'Absolutely.'

'Come,' she said, as she took him by the hand and led him towards the large four-poster bed.

98   James woke the following morning with sunshine streaming into the bedroom through the open curtains. At first he wasn't quite sure where he was and then he remembered. He looked around for Susan but she wasn't there. He climbed out of bed picked up his nightshirt from the floor and pulled it over his head.

James opened the bedroom door and peered out. He could hear voices downstairs. He made his way over to his bedroom where he had a quick wash in the hand-basin, and then hurriedly dressed. When he was ready he made his way downstairs. Bella was giving instructions to two of the servants. When she saw James descending the stairs she ushered them away. 'Good morning,' she said all bubbly with a pleasant smile.

'G'day, Bella.'

'Did you sleep well?'

'Very well thanks.'

'Breakfast is ready and waiting. Would you like to come through to the dining room?'

'Thanks, I'm starving.'

When he arrived he noticed that the table had been laid for one person only. Bella turned to him as she said, 'You're the last one to eat. Everyone else has had their breakfast. Richard has gone into work and Susan has already departed for the farm.'

'Oh.' He was disappointed at not having seen Susan before she left. 'I apologise for oversleeping.'

'Don't be silly. Besides, it was Susan's idea. She said that you ought to have a good rest before returning to the army... She also left something for you.' Bella went over to the sideboard and removed an envelope from one of the drawers. She handed it James. 'You can read it after breakfast.'

He nodded while glancing at the envelope.

Breakfast soon arrived comprising of two fried eggs, tomatoes, bacon, sausages, brinjal and mushrooms. James ate the lot. After the meal, Bella poured coffee for him in a large mug. He waited until she had finished before saying, 'The breakfast was excellent thanks.'

She smiled. 'I'm pleased you enjoyed it... Now, I suppose that you are anxious to open your letter, so I'll show you to the reading room where you can have privacy. You can take your coffee along with you, if you wish?'

James picked up the mug and followed her down a long passageway. Near the end they entered a room. The walls were covered with bookcases, which stored an array of fine leather-bound books. There were also four leather armchairs positioned around a coffee table. Sunlight was streaming into the room through a huge bay window. To one side was a writing desk, which had a globe of the world standing on it.

'This is one of my favourite rooms,' Bella said proudly with a smile, 'although it is rather on the masculine side I suppose.'

'It's certainly very nice, and I have never seen so many fine books before.'

'Yes, well both Richard and myself are compulsive readers... I suppose that's because we are childless and so we have more time to ourselves. Who knows?' She looked sad for a moment and then she smiled and said, I'll leave you to it then.' Bella left the room closing the door behind her.

James placed the coffee mug down on a tablemat and then he sat down in one of the armchairs. There was a paper knife lying on the coffee table. He picked it up and opened the envelope. After unfolding the page he began reading the contents softly to himself. "Dearest James, I trust that you enjoyed the extra sleep this morning and that you are not too disappointed at me sneaking off without saying goodbye. I am not very good with things like that. I wanted you to know that the past few days have been amongst my happiest in a very long time. You will always hold a special place in my heart. I know that Richard will do all he can to help you return to your contingent, and Bella will do her best to make you feel right at home. I pray that you make it back safely. May God go with you James, your's sincerely, Susan."

James slowly folded the letter and then placed it into the envelope as he said softly, 'God bless you too Susan Swanepoel and both your children.' James went over to the writing desk and looked at the globe of the world. He turned it slowly until Australia was visible. He studied Western Australia for a few moments and then he turned his attention to the writing paper, pen and ink lying on the desk. He sat down and wrote a long letter home. After that, he wrote a short letter to Veronica telling her of Timothy's death and that he had also previously given the army her new address. He hoped that she did not object. James also told her of William's murder and also of his father's death. He didn't however, mention anything about his feelings for her or say anything about having met Christiana.

99   That same afternoon around three o'clock, Richard arrived home. His face was beaming all over and he seemed quite excited as he said to James, 'Let's go into the parlour, shall we? I have some rather splendid news to tell you.'

James followed the tall, portly man who then closed the door behind them. He lit himself a cigar and puffed vigorously before saying, 'I received a telegraph message this morning from one of our field reporters. I am pleased to tell you that Roberts has taken occupation of Bloemfontein.'

'What? ...That's fantastic! ...When was this?'

'Yesterday the 13th of March. Apparently Roberts rode into the city without any opposition whatsoever.'

James couldn't believe it as he shook his head.

'President Steyn had fled from the capital two hours earlier, accompanied by President Kruger of the Transvaal. According to our field reporter Kruger had been there, trying to encourage Steyn to make a stand at Bloemfontein, but failed. Apparently, Steyn didn't want the capital destroyed by cannon fire. The Boer armies have been withdrawing from the area the whole day and are heading north.'

'North? ...That's this way... towards us... right?'

Richard nodded. 'De Wet tried to make a stand at Driefontein but was flushed out by Stephenson's 18th Brigade... But, listen to this, James... As Roberts entered Bloemfontein to the cheering crowds, the town council came to greet him and solemnly handed over the keys of the capital to him. Everyone was wearing tricolour flavours. Union Jacks were flying. The crowds were singing God Save the Queen and Rule Britannia.' Richard went over to the drinks cabinet and poured two brandies. He handed a glass to James. 'This is indeed a cause for some celebration.'

He clinked his glass against James' and the two men drank them down.

'Unfortunately, it's not all good news though.'

James frowned. 'What do you mean?'

'I am afraid the taking of Bloemfontein has come at a considerable cost. My field reporter described the condition of the Australian troops and horses as sickening and heart breaking. What horses remain alive are nothing but skin and bone. They have survived weeks on half rations of food, a mere two and a half pounds of oats a day, and whatever else they could find to eat on the veldt. Thousands have died from sickness, exhaustion or been killed. The men are not much better, they are pitifully thin having lived on three-quarter rations of two biscuits a day, plus a mug of tea. During the day they suffered from heat exhaustion and sunburn... at night, from the cold and violent thunderstorms without any shelter. Their uniforms are in tatters, some no better than beggars rags, and their boots no longer have soles to them.'

James shook his head as he gave a sigh. He felt extremely guilty drinking brandy in the comfort of a fine home. 'I have to try to rejoin them as soon as possible.'

'There's more,' Richard continued, 'they were so desperate for food many had to live off the dead horses. The lucky ones raided farms along the way, stealing whatever they could, eggs, chickens and ducks. Some were even able to shoot sheep or cattle.'

'The way I see it they had little choice... you said yourself they were starving.'

'I am not condemning anyone. I am merely telling you what hardships they endured. But, worst of all James, thousands of our troops are dying from enteric fever. The river water at Paardeberg was contaminated from the carcases of dead horses and human waste from Cronje's laager. The field reporter says Roberts could be delayed for weeks in Bloemfontein, maybe even longer. The whole town could become a hell hole.'

'I still have to rejoin my regiment and the sooner the better.'

'I know... and, I have thought of a way to get you safely through the Boer lines.'

'How?'

'Let's have another brandy first.'

James nodded in agreement. Richard poured them one each and handed James his glass. 'You will have to impersonate a female Boer.'

'What?' he gave a little laugh almost in disbelief.

'It's not such a crazy idea as you think. Bella and I will also dress as Boers. We will travel by wagon to the outskirts of Bloemfontein. There, we will meet my field reporter at a prearranged rendezvous. He will help you find your regiment. Bella and I should be able to return home without too much difficulty. If we are stopped we will say that we are fleeing from the British invasion.'

James shook his head. 'I can't let you and Bella do this. It's far too risky... what if we are stopped by Boer patrols enroute? ...And there are bound to be dozens of road blocks?'

'Listen to me! You have very little chance of making it on your own, James. What if you are stopped and questioned? You don't speak any Afrikaans they will arrest you. Both Bella and I speak Afrikaans fluently. We are your best chance of getting you through to Bloemfontein.'

There was no point in trying to discourage Richard, he was determined to do it his way. James also realised that what he was saying made a lot of sense. He nodded... 'Alright then, when do we go?'

'First thing in the morning.'

'Wouldn't it be a lot safer to travel under cover of darkness?'

Richard shook his head. 'Believe me, we'll be far less suspicious travelling during daylight. After all, it's the normal thing to do.'

100 The following morning both Bella and Richard laughed heartily when James came downstairs dressed in a long pleated skirt with a frilly white blouse and a bonnet on his head. 'You look the absolute picture of pure Dutch beauty James,' said Richard between spells of more laughter.

'Take no notice of him James, he's just jealous.'

Richard broke into hysterical laughter. When he recovered he said, 'We will have to be careful that some Boer doesn't take a fancy to you.' He then broke into more uncontrollable laughter.

Once Richard had recovered sufficiently they climbed onboard the wagon. Richard soon got the horses trotting along at a steady pace. Half an hour later they clopped their way down a quiet back street in Heidelberg. As it was still early morning only a handful of people were about. Richard gave them a friendly wave as they past them. When they reached the dorp of Vereeniging they were only about five miles from the Vaal River on the border of the Orange Free State. During the journey they had to pull over to the side of the road on several occasions to allow convoys of Boer troops to pass them. Each time, Richard would raise his hat politely to the generals and they would in-turn tip their hats.

After one of the convoy's had past them Richard said to James, 'That was General Christiaan De Wet, by-the-way.'

James was surprised. 'He looks too young to be a general.'

'Yes. He's one of the youngest... and one of the smartest.'

'Where are they all heading?' James asked.

'Bloemfontein I would say.'

'That's nice,' James replied sarcastically.

The wagon rolled across the bridge over the Vaal River and continued its journey along the winding dirt road. Bella opened the hamper and removed a large bottle of lemonade. She carefully poured three glasses trying not to spill any, and handed them around together with a few Ouma's tea koekies (grannies biscuits), which James thoroughly enjoyed.

THE PLOUGH, THE GUN AND THE GLORY

Later, Bella handed out sticks of venison biltong. She asked James if he'd ever seen biltong before. He told her that he had eaten it once when he was scouting with the Rimington Tigers, after finding it in a saddlebag belonging to a dead scout. He liked it that much that he wanted to know how to make it.

'It's easy,' said Bella.

'Nothing to it James,' Richard added.

'I'll give you a good recipe,' said Bella. 'Firstly, you take about seven or eight pounds of venison.'

'What's that?'

...'You mean you don't you know what venison is?'

'No.'

...'It's the meat from a buck.'

'Oh... we don't have buck in Australia.'

...'Then use beef instead.'

'We have kangaroos though. Could I use that?'

'I don't know,' Bella replied.

'I think venison's much better James,' Richard added.

Bella glanced sideways at him. 'James just told you that they don't have buck in Australia. Now stop interrupting me.' She turned to James. 'Use the hind leg from the thighbone down to the knee-joint. Cut the meat off the leg so that you have long tongue shaped slices. Firstly, soak the meat in a little brown vinegar in a metal dish. Then sprinkle it with salt and pepper and rub well in. After one hour sprinkle the meat with coriander and rub in.'

'Hang-on,' James interrupted. 'There's a heck of a lot to remember here.'

'I've nearly finished now... Cover the meat with a cloth and let soak overnight. The following day, hang it up with wire hooks to dry in a cool windy spot. Remember to place a net over to keep the flies off. Never dry it in the sun, only in the shade. After three or four days it should be ready to take down. That's it.'

James gave a sigh. 'You'll have to tell me again.'

Both Richard and Bella went over the instructions a few more times. About midday they stopped to relieve themselves on the side of the road and then continued on again, finally stopping in the early evening alongside the Rhenoster River near the town of Kroonstad. After unhitching the horses for the night Richard and James gathered some

313

driftwood and made a fire. Meanwhile Bella went for a wash in the river. When she returned it was the men's turn. Later, Richard was lucky and shot a rabbit, which he skinned and then braaied (barbecued). They sat around the fire eating with their fingers and talking in general. James told them about Western Australia and Rambling Meadows, and about William and his father.

'You miss home very much don't you James?' Bella said once he had finished.

He nodded. 'Yeah, I do... It will be good to get back there again.'

Richard fetched a bottle of brandy from the wagon and he and James had a few drinks. Bella had tea, which Richard made for her in a billycan on the fire. Finally, it was time for bed. Bella and Richard said goodnight to James and climbed into the wagon.

James threw more driftwood onto the fire and then climbed under a blanket. He watched the flickering, dancing flames, sending their orange-red sparks rising into the night sky, with the wood popping, snapping and crackling.

101

Early the following morning the wagon travelled the last few miles into Kroonstad. The town was swarming with Boer commandos. James was seated in the middle between Richard and Bella, in case they were stopped and questioned. As the wagon proceeded through town they came across four officers talking on the sidewalk. As the wagon past them they tipped their hats politely. Bella and James in-turn smiled back courteously returning the complement. Once they were well past, Bella gave a sigh of relief. 'Well, at least we know one thing for certain,' she said softly into James' ear.

'What's that?'

'Your disguise obviously works.'

All three laughed, feeling a little nervous and somewhat relieved.

'Do you know who those men were James?' asked Richard.

'No.'

'The two men standing on the left were Koos De la Rey and Piet Joubert. The other two men were Ferreira and Christiaan De Wet. We just rode right past some of the Boers top generals.'

'No-one's ever going to believe me when I tell them,' James replied.

As the wagon rolled on towards the end of town they noticed that the road was blocked off with overturned wagons. There were also field guns positioned either side of the road pointing south towards Bloemfontein. Richard pulled the horses up as two uniformed men approached the wagon. One of them asked Richard a couple of questions in Afrikaans and he gave them answers. The other one climbed into the back of the wagon and had a quick look around. After he had jumped off further conversation took place between them and Richard.

James felt the sweat trickling down his temples and then it went rolling down his cheeks. He also noticed that the Boer asking most of the questions was now looking at him. An argument appeared to break out between Richard and the one man. James could tell by their raised voices. His heart was now pumping somewhat faster than normal. Moments later, Richard backed the horses up. Then, he turned the wagon around and they started making their way along the road in the direction they had come from.

James was unable to contain his emotions any longer. 'Will someone please tell me what the hell's going on?'

Bella looked at him. 'The road south has been closed to all civilian traffic.'

'No civilians are allowed to proceed beyond here,' Richard added.

'Great! ...So what happens now?'

'We are going a little way out of town,' Bella advised, 'then we'll find a suitable place to stop somewhere and discuss the situation.'

James felt frustrated but said nothing. About half a mile further on they came across a reasonable spot and Richard pulled the horses off the road and brought the wagon to a halt.

'What did that one Boer say to you that made you so angry?' James asked Richard while removing the bonnet from his head and then jumping down from the wagon.

'He asked me who you were. I told him that you were my sister. He then said that he had never seen such an ugly woman in his whole life. I pretended that I was insulted and furious at his comments.'

Richard and Bella laughed heartily, more from relief than anything. After that, all three sat together in silence under the shade of the wagon drinking lemonade. James was deep in thought when Richard said, 'It looks as though you will have to make it to Bloemfontein on your own after all James.'

'Yeah. He waved a fly from his face... 'Anyway, you have both done quite enough for me. I don't know how I will every repay your kindness.'

'It was lovely having you,' Bella said with a smile. 'You make sure that you get back safely to your troops so you can help win this war.'

'You'll need to be extremely careful,' Richard added, 'and remember to stay well away from the roads at all times.'

'I will... Luckily Susan gave me a map and compass, they'll sure come in very handy now.'

'That was good thinking of her,' replied Richard.

'Yeah... Well, I suppose I had better get rid of this outfit and change into my clothes.' He got to his feet. After changing in the wagon he jumped down to the ground. James then extended his hand and shook Richard's firmly. 'Thanks for everything.'

'We have both enjoyed having you.'

James then turned to Bella and gave her a big hug. 'Thanks Bella, I really appreciate all you have done for me.'

She stood back and wiped the tears from her eyes. 'You take care now and God Bless you.' Then she remembered something. 'Oh, I almost forgot to give you some fruit and lemonade to take with you, and also a few sticks of biltong. I won't be a moment.' She climbed into the wagon. A few minutes later she said, 'Here we are.' She handed down a few oranges, a bottle of lemonade and four sticks of biltong.

'Thanks Bella.' James placed them into the bag.

'You had better take this along too,' said Richard, handing James a blanket. 'It gets mighty cold out here at night as you well know.'

James thanked him and then he knelt down and rolled up the blanket as tight as he could. He tied it up with a piece of rope that Richard gave him. James got back to his feet. 'Well, I hope that you both have a safe and pleasant trip home. May God go with you.'

James turned and then made his way into the scrub. A little later he stopped walking and turned around to give a final wave. The wagon had gone and all he saw was a cloud of brown dust. After that he placed the map on the ground together with the compass and matched up the north points. To get to Bloemfontein he needed to travel south at about 220 degrees. According to the map there were still about one hundred miles to travel. After folding the map and placing it back into the bag James put the compass into his pocket.

'Well, James Mitchell,' he said softly to himself, 'there's no point in wasting time hanging around here. You're just going to have to walk every darn inch of the way to Bloemfontein so you better get on with it.'

He picked up the bag and then the blanket, slung it over one shoulder, looked at the shimmering horizon for a moment, and then started out across the lonely, scrub-covered veldt. Many things were going through his mind. James looked up at the sky, dark storm clouds gathering overhead.

102   Every now and then, James would stop to take another compass bearing, fixing something in the distance as a marker for him to head towards. It was around midday when he came across a small spruit (water course). He dropped the bag and blanket to the ground, removed the compass from his pocket and then sat down. Next, he hurriedly pulled off his boots and socks and then stripped naked.

He waded into the cool water and then dived under. After surfacing he cupped his hands together and drank mouthfuls of water until his stomach could hold no more. When he'd had enough he made his way back to the riverbank and climbed out. After picking up his things he crossed over the spruit to the other side. James redressed and then sat down to replace his socks, which was quite difficult with wet feet. Once his boots were on he took another compass bearing. Picking up the bag and blanket he continued on his way towards the next chosen marker.

Along the way James had to lay low for a short time when he heard a loud rumbling sound, and then saw a Boer convoy heading south. At sundown there was a small dorp in the distance to his left, and after checking the map he decided it was Hennenman. He wished he could just make his way there and catch a train going to Bloemfontein, but none were running as the Boers had suspended all services in that direction.

Once darkness fell it was more difficult for James to keep heading south as he was unable to read the compass. Storm clouds covered much of the sky and very few stars were visible. The rising moon helped a little, but that too was darting in-and-out of the clouds. Most of the time it was completely hidden for long periods, making it very dark and almost impossible to see.

After almost falling down a steep donga (gully) James decided to quit for the night. In any case, he was exhausted, hungry and thirsty. He ate a stick of biltong and then one of the oranges, which helped quench his thirst. After first removing three or four rocks and then sorting the blanket out, he pulled it over himself. James lay with his head on the bag and once a few adjustments had been made he closed his eyes and fell into a deep sleep.

103 The following morning James woke to find a dark cloud-filled-sky overhead. An hour later a heavy rainstorm swept across the veldt and he had to turn his back towards it to stop it from stinging his face. Twenty minutes later the rain eased and James continued walking. Finally the rain stopped altogether and sunshine broke through the cloud bringing warmth to his body.

With the rain having gone, James was able to take a compass bearing and fix a point on the horizon to make for. When he finally reached it he found that the ground beyond sloped away and he could see for many miles around. To his left about five miles away, was another dorp, which he thought was probably the town of Whites. Some distance in front of him was a river, which according to the map was the Vet River.

James reached the river an hour later and after wading across a shallow section he came across a kraal. Women with babies on their backs were working in the fields. Piccanins of various ages ran around, weaving their way between them playing some sort of game. Over to one side, a small group of men were sitting around a fire laughing and chatting. Chickens, goats and donkeys meandered freely between the myriad of mud and thatch huts, haphazardly strung-out over the veldt. James then spotted something of far more interest. It was a donkey cart carrying bundles of maize. There were a couple of piccanins riding at the front and they were heading almost directly towards him.

'That's just what I need,' James thought while cleaning something out of his ear. 'I wonder if I could bribe those little blacks to take me, say, fifty miles? What could I possibly bribe them with though? I certainly haven't got very much to offer.'

Once they got closer James stood up so they could see him. He obviously gave them a fright, because their eyes popped out of their sockets and their colour changed to a pale shade of grey. At the same time they began yelling at the tops of their voices. James stood watching them as they fled leaving the donkey cart behind. The men sitting around the fire had heard the commotion and came running to see what was going on. The two piccanins were pointing in James' direction still yelling at the tops of their voices.

James started to walk towards the oncoming men, who by then had stopped walking and were now staring in his direction. Once James got nearer he asked if any of them spoke English, which afterwards he thought was a silly question anyway. He wasn't surprised when no one replied. A lot of chatter broke out amongst them. One of them then said something to one of the piccanins who then took off in the direction of several huts.

Five minutes later he was seen returning together with a lean grey-haired man. When they reached the others the grey-haired man approached James. 'Can I help you, boss?' he asked in English.

James was relived that there was someone who he could communicate with. 'I am on my way to Bloemfontein.'

'Bloemfontein?' He was a little more than surprised. 'Bloemfontein is very far from here, boss... Where is the boss' horse?'

'I don't have one.'

The grey-haired man told the others and there was a lot of jabbering. Finally everyone quietened down again as the grey-haired man said, 'In Johannesburg I have seen many white men without horses. But I have never seen one on the veldt without a horse.'

'I was hoping to hire that donkey cart,' James pointed, 'to take me part of the journey.'

...'How much will you pay, boss?'

'I don't have any money. All I have is what I'm carrying.'

The man nodded. 'Let me see.'

James showed him the bag and the blanket. The grey-haired man had a look at them both. There was a lot of jabbering coming from the others. After awhile he said, 'For the blanket and the bag I will take you to Brandfort, boss.'

'Brandfort? ...Let me see where that is first.' James opened the bag and removed the map. He quickly found Brandfort, which was about forty miles from the kraal and left roughly thirty miles short of Bloemfontein. He didn't really have anything else to offer the man, to be taken any further, as he wanted to keep both the compass and map. 'Alright, it's a deal.'

The grey-haired man smiled showing several missing teeth. 'First we must eat and drink. Then we go.'

James nodded thinking that was a good idea. He folded the map up and placed it inside his shirt. Then he took the biltong, orange and the bottle of lemonade out of the bag, before handing it over to the grey-haired man.

James followed the black man together with the others over to a mud hut. On the floor were a few goatskin mats and James was asked to sit on one of them. After a few minutes two bare-breasted young females brought a couple of clay pots. They placed them in the centre of the seated men. Other smaller pots were then placed near each man. They had water in them and the men washed their hands. Nothing was provided for drying them though.

The grey-haired man then dipped his hand into one of the pots containing a thick porridge-like substance (sadza; thick white porridge substance). It was similar to what James had eaten when he came across the leftover food at the small railway station. He rolled the porridge into a ball and then dipped it into one of the other pots containing goat meat and gravy. The others did the same with James following. He was hungry and the food was tasty although the goat meat was extremely tough to chew.

After the meal the men washed their hands, removing the sticky white porridge that clung to their fingers. Following that, goat's milk was then poured, by one of the females, from a clay jug into small bowls and the men drank it down.

The grey-haired man then got to his feet. 'We go now boss,' he said looking at James.

James stood up. 'I'm ready,' he replied, 'thanks for the meal.'

The donkey cart was brought closer having been unloaded and James and the grey-haired man climbed onto it. A piccanin hurriedly brought a water bag made from the bladder of a goat, and then the two men set off for Brandfort. The donkey trotted along, with a little encouragement of a whip, as they followed a well-worn path in the general direction south. Every so often James would try and take a compass bearing, more for something to do than checking the direction they were going in.

'My name is Samson boss,' the black man suddenly advised after a long silence. 'I used to work in the gold mines in Johannesburg. That's where I learned to speak English... It was terrible work but the money was good... I was paid one shilling a day boss. Uitlanders (foreigners) would get two shillings, some three shillings. When I heard there was going to be a war between the English and the Afrikaners, I left the mines and came home.'

The cart pitched and rolled over the bumpy ground disrupting the grey-haired man for a moment. 'When the white people first came here they fought against the black people for the land. Now, they are fighting against each other. Now, the blacks are caught in the middle of this white man's war, boss. Some of our people are siding with the British, others the Boers. It is dividing our people and causing many problems.'

James wondered why he was telling him all of this. After all, he didn't know James from Adam. 'So whose side are you on?'

...'Neither... I hate them both boss. The black people have fought both the British and the Boers and lost. But, if I have to chose between them I will choose the Boers.'

'The Boers?' James was surprised. 'Why not the British?'

He shook his head. 'You must understand boss. The Afrikaner's have been living here for a very long time, much longer than the British. Like us, this is their home. They have nowhere else to go. The British want to take the land from them and make it part of Britain... like they have done with the Cape colony and also Natal colony.'

James was thinking about what the black man had been saying when his heart skipped a few beats. Almost directly in front of them was a bearded man on horseback. He was pointing a rifle straight at James. The grey-haired man quickly pulled up the donkey and the cart ground to a halt. The man on horseback yelled something in Afrikaans. The black man replied. The man on horseback came nearer and said something else to the grey-haired man.

'What does he want?' James asked apprehensively.

'He asked me where we are going, boss... I told him. He then asked me who you were. I told him that I don't know, boss.'

THE PLOUGH, THE GUN AND THE GLORY

The man on horseback came alongside the cart on James' side, keeping his rifle trained on James the whole time. More conversation took place in Afrikaans between the black man and himself. The black man then turned to James. 'The boss says he thinks you have escaped from prison... and that your name is Churchill, boss. He said there is a reward of twenty-five pounds for you, dead or alive.'

James shook his head. 'Tell him that's not my name. My name is James Mitchell.'

'Yes, boss.' The black man spoke to the man on the horse. More conversation took place. Then, the man on horseback said something directly to James in a loud tone of voice. James asked the black man what it was that he had said.

'The boss says you are his prisoner now. He wants you to get off the cart, boss. He said that he will take you into Theunissen. If you can prove to the constable that you are not Churchill you will be set free, boss.'

'How will I be able to prove who I am in Thunissen? No one knows me there! ...Who will identify me?'

He screwed up his face and shook his head. 'I don't know boss,' he replied sympathetically.

James heart was racing in his chest. He had to do something quickly. He made as though he was going to get down from the cart, but instead, he took a flying leap at the horseman. He caught the man completely by surprise. His rifle went flying from his hand as both men went toppling to the ground.

The horseman was a little winded having landed heavily onto his back. James scrambled onto his feet first and then he threw a hard right-hand punch to the man's face breaking his nose. The man placed his hands over his nose in pain as the blood poured from it. James threw another right-hand punch to his abdomen. This time the man doubled up gasping for air. James was hoping that the Boer would give up now but he was mistaken. The man drew a knife from a scabbard attached to his bandolier and lunged at James. Fortunately, he was able to move out of the way in the nick of time. James threw a combination of left and right-hand punches to the man's face. This time he fell to the ground and lay there.

James picked up the rifle puffing and panting for air. He went up close to the man and placed the barrel near his face. 'I told you... I'm not the man... you are looking for... mate!' He then remembered the man didn't understand English. He turned his head slightly to speak to the black man to find him gone. James lifted his eyes. The donkey cart was bolting over the rough ground with a cloud of dust behind it, taking his meagre provisions with it.

James went over to the horse and removed the water canteen slung over the saddle horn. He had a few mouthfuls, replaced the cork and dropped the canteen on the ground near the man. James then mounted the horse and after unloading the magazine he threw it as far as he could. He then threw the rifle in the opposite direction. He turned the horse and then rode off at a gallop in the direction of south.

After a mile or so James pulled up the horse. He then removed the map out of his shirt. It was badly crumpled. James tried to flatten it out the best he could. Then, he searched his pockets for the compass to find that it was missing. He then realised that it must have fallen out during the fight. After studying the map and the surrounding landscape, James selected a small kopje in the distance to make for, and then he spurred the horse onwards.

104

Several times along the journey, James came across Boer scouts and sometimes even their laagers. Fortunately he was unseen. He usually managed this by keeping to lower ground wherever possible, travelling through dongas, etc. Sometimes, he would dismount and walk alongside the horse. Once or twice he had to get the horse to lie down in the knee-high grass, with him next to it, as a Boer patrol past ahead of him.

During another occasion James hid the horse amongst several huge rocks at the base of a small kopje, where he then watched a Boer army of some three thousand men, plus wagons and artillery going past. Once they had gone, and James was sure that there were no stragglers or scouts, he climbed the kopje. He found a ledge near the top and from there he could clearly see Bloemfontein nestled amongst the kopjes in the distance.

Using his map he identified several features on the ground, which would lead him straight to the capital. There was also another river to cross and according to his map it was a tributary of the Modder. Before that though, there was a smaller tributary that he would have to cross over. James decided as there were still forty miles to the capital he would find a spot by the river where he could spend the night. He made his way down the kopje, mounted up and then headed in the direction of the river.

By the time James reached the tributary the sun was sinking on the horizon. He soon found a sheltered spot with several weeping willow trees and decided it was a good place to spend the night. James unsaddled the horse and let it drink with him doing the same. He then decided that he needed a wash and so he stripped naked and plunged in. After washing and dressing he broke several branches off one of the trees to make a bed. He knew it would be cold during the night so he broke a few extra branches, which he would cover himself with. He had also thought of using the horse blanket but as it stank of stale horse sweat he decided against that.

James sat with his back against one of the trees as the last of the sun faded away in the western sky. He was beginning to feel hungry. Several times he saw fish jumping in the river, which didn't help. If he had some way of making a fire he would have tried to catch one or two. James even thought of eating them raw, but decided against that for now. Then, he thought of the biltong and lemonade that Bella had given him and wondered if the black man was enjoying it. James decided to put the thought of food out of his head and turned his mind to other things. After awhile he was feeling tired and decided to get some sleep. He piled the branches over himself and settled down for the night, and it wasn't very long before he fell into a deep sleep.

During the night he woke with a fright with the sound of gunfire nearby. He then realised it was across the river. James threw the branches off and got to his feet. He thought he had better grab hold of the horse in case it panicked and bolted, but he couldn't find it in the dark. 'Bugger it!' he cursed under his breath realising that he'd been too late.

The sound of gunfire grew louder and fiercer and so James decided to lie low in case stray bullets hit him. Gunfire continued on for what seemed like hours, but eventually it grew silent once again. It was bitterly cold now and James crawled under the branches of the weeping willow and tried to get a little sleep.

105

It was daylight when James woke and it took a few seconds before he realised where he was. He pushed the branches aside and got to his feet. His eyes surveyed the veldt across the river but he couldn't see anything over there. James searched around for the horse, which he was unable to find. He glanced at the river. It looked cold and the thought of having to swim across it this early in the morning wasn't all that appealing. He decided that he would walk along the bank for a short way and hopefully find a shallow section to cross. He walked up-stream, as the river would probably get narrower and hopefully shallower in that direction.

Sometime later, James came to a small weir where he was able to cross the river. After having a long drink of water he continued walking roughly south, making his way through tall wheat-coloured grass. Around midday James came across several damaged wagons where he decided to rest and take shelter from the blistering sun. He crawled under the nearest wagon into the shade. It was cool under there and a very welcome relief from the midday heat. He lay on his back and soon fell asleep.

Later, he decided to have a look around the wagons and see what he could find. He started with the wagon that he had sheltered under. Apart from a broken travelling trunk, which still contained soiled woman's clothing; there was only smashed timber and bits of junk. James made his way over to another wagon. This one appeared to be in a slightly better condition. He searched among the debris, but didn't find much there either, excepting a man's shoe with a hole in the sole, a few coat hangers and a broken lantern. Further rummaging produced a broken pocket watch, and then from under a pile of timber, a large round tin.

At first, it was a struggle to prise it open, but with a little perseverance James finally forced the lid off. He was surprised to find that it was full of biscuits. He took one out and looked at it. It didn't appear too bad so he thought he would try eating it. It tasted stale but he was so hungry he didn't care and ate another eight. James then foraged through the remaining wagons. He found a box of candles but no matches, a cooking pot without a handle and many other useless items. He was still hungry so he ate another six biscuits. The problem though, they made him thirsty. As it was getting late in the day James decided to remain here for the night and shelter from the cold under one of the wagons.

That night James was woken by thunder and lightning and was glad that he wasn't sleeping out in the open. Fifteen minutes later a heavy rainstorm swept across the veldt. This was his chance to get some drinking water. James got to his feet and raced over to the wagon, where he'd previously found the cooking pot, the lightning showing him the way. James stood the pot out in the rain and let it fill a little. Then, he quickly washed it out and placed it back in the rain, while he sheltered under the wagon. Once it was half full James drank as much as he could then placed the pot back in the rain. Half an hour later the storm had past over and the rain stopped.

James was a little wet and was now feeling the cold. He lay down under the wagon and curled up shivering. He thanked God for sending the rain and for providing the biscuits. Then, he fell into an exhausted asleep.

106

The following morning James placed the few remaining biscuits into his pockets. Then, picking up the pot containing the rainwater, he headed south through knee-high grass. Later that morning he came across the Modder River. It was a lot wider than the previous tributary and was flowing much faster. James wondered if he would be able to find a narrower section to cross over somewhere.

After walking along the bank for half a mile he then decided to take his chances and swim across. James sat down and removed his boots, which after tying the laces together, he hung around his neck. He also drank the last of the rainwater and also ate the few remaining biscuits. Then he waded in. The current was very strong and for a moment James wondered if he had done the right thing. He thought perhaps he should try somewhere else where the water was not running quite so fast. But it was too late now to turn back and he began swimming as hard as he could for the opposite bank, with the current sweeping him rapidly downstream.

James was a strong young man and an excellent swimmer, but he had no chance against the power of swift-flowing muddy water. He swam as hard as he could and it was a struggle just to keep from going under. As he kicked out with his feet his right foot struck something submerged, which was extremely painful, but he had to continue on swimming as hard as he could.

Further downstream the water became extremely rough as it entered a narrow gorge and James realised he was approaching rapids. The water tossed him around like a cork. One minute he was above the surface, the next, under the raging torrent. Sometimes, his head would break free of the surface and he would gasp for air before being sucked under again. Next, he was flying through the air as the water cascaded over a waterfall, plunging forty feet into white, foaming, turbulent water. Further down, James was able to grab hold of some rocks and after a great effort he managed to pull himself out of the water. He was gasping for air and had no strength to go any further up the bank.

He lay on the rocks like a rag doll while gasping for air and coughing up muddy river water. After that he fell asleep from complete exhaustion. When James woke he scrambled to his feet and then hobbled up the bank. His right foot was extremely painful to walk on. He sat down and had a look at it. The ankle was badly cut and his toes were bruised and swollen. He realised at that moment that he had lost his boots while crossing the river.

He got to his feet and then continued to hobble away from the river. James headed south with a hot scorching sun burning the sand under his feet. The horizon was nothing but a shimmering, dancing haze, and above him, vultures were circling waiting patiently for their next meal.

107 A mile from the river a patrol from the 1st Contingent Second Battalion Royal Canadian Regiment were searching for seven Boer prisoners who had escaped from their clutches. They had noticed the vultures circling ahead of them and decided to have a look and see what it was that was attracting them. Twenty minutes later, through the shimmering heat waves, one of the men thought he saw a man's body lying on the veldt. 'I've spotted something, lieutenant,' he called out to his senior officer. 'Over there, sir!' He was pointing in the general direction.

The officer raised his right hand and brought the patrol to a halt. He removed the field glasses from the case and then peered in the direction the private had pointed. A man's body was lying face down on the ground. It was motionless except for the shimmering air above him. 'Looks like we've found one of them,' he said a few moments later. He then gave the order to proceed on.

After ten minutes they slowed their mounts and then walked them towards the body. 'He looks done in, lieutenant,' one of the men commented.

'Take a closer look to be sure,' the officer replied.

The man dismounted and approached the body with caution. When he reached it he turned the man over onto his back. He had a quick look at him before turning towards the officer saying, 'He's still alive, lieutenant.'

'Is he one of the prisoners we're looking for?'

'I'm not sure, sir.'

THE PLOUGH, THE GUN AND THE GLORY

The officer removed his crowned felt-hat, wiped his brow with a handkerchief and then lastly the inside of the brim. He replaced his hat, saying with a little impatience, 'Well get someone who does then, man!'

'Yes, sir.' The corporal shouted for someone else to come forward.

A second man had a look at James. He wasn't completely sure either so they called a third man. After taking a quick look the man said to the officer, 'The men we are looking for wore beards, sir. This man has neither beard nor moustache.'

'He could have shaved it off, man,' the officer replied sarcastically.

'Yes sir, of course.'

'His clothing matches the type worn by the Boers,' the officer added. 'And who else would be out here in this damn, desolate, God-forsaken country?'

'You're quite right, sir.'

'Well, shove him into the cart and let's get moving, this heat is enough to boil a damn egg!' the officer ordered irritably.

The man was placed into the prison cart and the patrol continued on with the search. Finally, they gave up and returned to their camp on the outskirts of Bloemfontein as the sun was setting on the horizon. The man was taken to a field hospital where he received treatment for lacerations to his body, and also to his foot. The doctor advised him that it wasn't broken, just badly sprained. James then told the doctor who he was and requested that a message to be sent to Major Moor.

The following morning James was reunited with the 1st Contingent Western Australians much to his relief. He was however, shocked to see the state of everyone's uniforms, and how thin the men had become. Richard's field reporter certainly hadn't exaggerated their condition one bit. When he and George finally got together James hardly recognised him he had lost so much weight. They had many things to talk about and were both very happy to be reunited again.

James learned that new uniforms and boots were soon to be issued and that they would be camped at Bloemfontein for at least a month for rest and recuperation. Besides that, thousands of British and Colonial troops were lying sick in hospitals with enteric fever and other illnesses. The horses, which had survived the gruelling advance to Bloemfontein, were given a chance to recover and gain weight. Replacement horses were also being railed up from Cape Town after a long sea voyage from Argentina.

A few days later, James was sitting outside his tent writing a letter home, when out of the corner of his eye he noticed someone approaching. He could hardly believe his eyes when he realised it was Winston. He was dressed in uniform and carried the rank of Second Lieutenant. James got to his feet and saluted him. After that the two men embraced one another.

'I heard on the bush telegraph that you had finally made it back, old chap,' Winston said smiling while patting James on both his shoulders at the same time. 'I thought for awhile that perhaps the old Boer had got you, old chap.'

'No such luck for them I had a lot of good people helping me... you obviously made it to Durban?'

'Absolutely old chap, nothing to it.'

'How come you're dressed in uniform now?'

'Ah yes, well, after reaching Durban I was offered a commission as Second Lieutenant with the South African Light Horse. We were at Spion Kop. It was a blood bath I'm afraid, old chap. We lost seventeen hundred men. Still, I think Lord Roberts has made up for that now, don't you?'

James nodded.

'How would you like to attend a function with me on Saturday night?'

'Function?'

'Yes... It's nothing special I'm afraid. A number of war correspondents are getting together at the English Club to celebrate the imperial victory. It's really just an excuse to have a few drinks more than anything... So, what do you say?'

James wasn't sure. For one thing he had no uniform, as the replacements hadn't arrived from Cape Town yet. 'I'm afraid that I don't have anything to wear, and I certainly can't go anywhere respectable dressed like this.'

... 'I can lend you a uniform, we're much the same build, you and I.'

'I'll have to first request permission from Major Moor.'

'I'll organise that for you, if you like?'

'Well then, I can't think of any reason not to come.'

'Good... I'll have the uniform sent over tomorrow. Oh yes, and I'll also arrange a horse for you to get there.'

They said goodbye and then Winston walked off towards the Western Australian's administration tent.

108 On Saturday afternoon James had a hot sponge bath using water he had obtained from the cookhouse. After that he dressed into Winston's uniform. It was a little on the large side especially around the waist, but the jacket concealed the problem and his braces kept them up. When James left the tent he received a number of wolf whistles from the men outside. Several jokes were then made at his expense. James laughed them off with good humour. A trooper from the South African Light Horse arrived half an hour later with a spare mount for James, and the two rode off with more jeering and whistling.

A mile further on hustle and bustle filled the streets of Bloemfontein with people, horses and carriages travelling in all directions. Union Jacks hung limply from buildings in the breathless evening air. It was a strange feeling for James. He felt uneasy. It was as though the war had ended... no people dying, blowing each other to bits with guns and cannons... no horses whinnying in agony waiting to be shot to relieve them from the hell in which they had been plunged into.

Bloemfontein was much larger than James had thought it would be and the air was sweet with the smell of jacaranda trees. It reminded James of his aunt's farm and he wondered how they all were. The thought of having to go there one day and tell them that it was he who had killed their son, Piet, sent a cold shiver down his spine.

Shortly afterwards they arrived outside a huge double-story building. A sign said, "The Bloemfontein English Club." The military band of the Highland Brigade was outside blasting out patriotic marching tunes. The whole area was a hive of activity with carriages arriving endlessly discharging passengers. Photographer's flashlights were popping one after the other as various celebrities had their pictures taken. On the verandah, men and women sipped drinks from tall slender glasses with cigarette and cigar smoke spiralling everywhere.

'I'll be waiting over there for you sergeant,' the private advised, pointing to a large tree some distance away.

'Thanks... See you later.'

After dismounting James made his way up the steps of the verandah. He removed his slouch hat and then politely made his way through the crowd in order to get to the entrance. It was even busier inside. James glanced around the large hall with its heavy drapes bordering the windows. Banners and Union Jacks hung from the walls. Two large chandeliers hung from the highly decorated embossed ceiling, the light from the many candles, flickering with the movement of the air. James thought the whole place was very impressive. He then made his way inside and had to search for Winston's table before finding him seated together with several other men.

Winston had seen him. 'James!' he called out above the noise waving his hand.

James arrived. 'Good evening Winston... I thought you said this was nothing special tonight?' he said jokingly.

'I'm afraid it's rather like a snowball racing downhill, replied Winston. 'It just grew bigger. I think everyone in Bloemfontein must be out celebrating tonight. Take a seat.' He pointed to a vacant chair next to him.

'James sat down.

'Would you like a brandy old chap?'

'Thanks... Are you having another?' he asked seeing Winston's glass was almost empty.

'Of course.'

'I'm paying for them,' James advised, 'don't forget that I owe you money for the coat and hat that you bought for me when we escaped from prison.'

'As you wish, old chap.'

James ordered the brandies from a waiter.

'Let me introduce you to some of the opposition,' Winston said. He took a spoon and clinked it several times against his glass. 'May I please have your attention for a moment gentleman!' he called out above the noise. Once everyone was listening he said, 'I would like to introduce you to an Australian friend of mine. This is James Mitchell. He and I escaped from Pretoria together.' Winston turned to

James as he pointed to one of the men furthermost away. 'That fine looking gentleman seated over there is Bennet Burleigh of the Daily Telegraph.'

James and the war correspondent acknowledged one other with a smile and headshake.

'This is Edgar Wallace.' Winston indicated with his hand. The two men greeted one another cordially. 'And over there, we have Arthur Conan Doyle.' Again the two men acknowledged each other politely. 'And this gentleman is Rudyard Kipling.'

James smiled. 'Yes, I know. I met Mr Kipling before while onboard the train going to De Aar?'

'So you did old chap. My apologies. With all that's happened I've forgot about that.'

Rudyard and James shook hands. Rudyard remembered that James was a good shot and he had also removed several large splinters from Winston's forehead. The two men finished chatting and then Winston continued with the last introduction. 'This fine gentleman seated opposite you is Andrew Paterson of the Sydney Morning Herald.'

James' brow wrinkled and then his face lit up. 'Not Banjo Paterson who wrote Waltzing Matilda?'

He nodded.

James couldn't believe it. 'My mother loves your work. She plays all your ballads on the piano and knows them all off by heart without any written music. She also loves your poetry and stories. As a matter-of-fact so do I, especially Waltzing Matilda. She will be so envious when I write and tell her that I have actually met you,' James said enthusiastically.

They chatted for awhile longer with clouds of cigar smoke floating across the table, and in the background, the constant hum of voices and outbursts of boisterous laughter. 'Can I buy you a drink, Banjo?' James asked once their glasses were almost empty.

'Only if it's red wine thanks, mate.'

James asked the others at the table and then he ordered the drinks from the waiter. In the meanwhile, the laughter and chatting continued amongst the men who exchanged war stories and then jokes. Later in the evening, James asked Banjo if he would do him a very special favour. 'Would you be kind enough to come out to our camp and sing a few of your ballads for the boys one of these days? I reckon our blokes could really do with some cheering up right now.'

Banjo's face broke out into a broad smile. 'I would be very honoured.'

'Naturally, I'll first have to speak to Major Moor in order to obtain his permission.'

'Of course... and I'll also have to borrow a guitar from somewhere, but I'm sure that won't prove to be too difficult.'

'Thanks Banjo, I really appreciate this... Once I've spoken to the major, how will I get in contact with you?'

'If it's not too early in the morning you'll find me right here at the hotel.'

James was happy and he knew the blokes would be really pleased when he told them the news. Later, James was feeling tired and thought is was time that he went returned camp. In any case, his pass expired at midnight and he would have to be back by then. He thanked Winston for having invited him and for the loan of the uniform, said goodnight to the others and then pushed his way out of the club. There were a group of nurses standing over to one side of the verandah chatting. James thought that he recognised one of the voices and made his way over to them. When he was sure it was Christina he taped her on the shoulder. She turned around.

'Hello Christina.'

At first she just stood staring wide-eyed and then she let out a shriek of excited delight. 'Ahhh, James! What are you doing here?'

He couldn't help but laugh at her reaction. 'I was kindly invited by a friend of mine.'

She excused herself from the other nurses and they went over to a quieter spot where they could talk. They chatted excitedly catching up with everything since they had last seen each other. 'Oh God, I have missed you so much, James,' Christina said several times over during the conversation.

A carriage pulled up alongside the verandah. Christina looked rather disappointed as she said, 'I'm afraid that's for me and the other nurses. I'll have to be leaving shortly. Can you try and come and see me on Thursday evening it's my night off?'

'I don't know if I'll be able to arrange a pass.'

THE PLOUGH, THE GUN AND THE GLORY

'Promise me you'll try... Pleaseee!'

He nodded. 'I'll do my very best. Where will I find you?'

'Come to Langman's Hospital. Ask for me at reception. One of the nurses will give you directions to the nurse's cottages. We won't be able to stay there though. We'll have to go out somewhere.'

'That's alright, we'll think of something.'

She gave him a kiss on the cheek and then left as the other nurses were already in the carriage waiting. Christina waved to him as the carriage left. It was chilly and James rubbed his hands together as he made his way towards the tree where the private said he would be waiting for him. He found the two horses, but had to search around for the private. He found him lying under a carriage huddled-up with a blanket over him fast asleep. After waking him they rode off towards the outskirts of town and the West Australians camp.

James was feeling rather pleased with himself. Not only had he met the legendary Banjo Paterson, but he had also arranged for him to come and play for the blokes. And, just as importantly, he had unexpectedly met with Christina again, and hopefully they would spend Thursday evening together.

109   On the following Monday the long awaited replacement uniforms and boots arrived from Cape Town. They were issued to the men on the Wednesday, who were overjoyed at being able to discard their tatted torn-clothing and shabby worn-out boots. Thursday was payday and after collecting passes for the first time, the men headed off in small groups towards town. Although, it was over a two-mile walk no one complained. Everyone was in a good mood, talking, laughing and telling jokes.

'Yahoo!' George bellowed loudly as he and James plus a few other men neared the town, which was lit-up with a multitude of gaslights. 'I have a feeling that I am going to enjoy this evening like no other before,' he said excitedly.

Everyone agreed that was exactly what they were going to do. When they reached town the group split up, excepting for George and James, who had agreed to have a few drinks together at one of the hotels before James went off to meet Christina. They found a place called Chaka's Retreat. It was small but looked okay from the outside and the two men made their way through the swing doors. The hotel was quiet except for a few middle-aged men propping up the bar. James ordered a couple of brandies from a surly looking barman and then he and George sat down at a table.

'This place is deader than a darn cemetery,' George complained. 'Where's everyone? ...And more importantly where are the women, hey?'

'Good question... Maybe Christina has a friend she can introduce you to?'

George swallowed his brandy down. 'Ready for another?' he asked wiping his mouth with his hand.

'Yeah.'

George returned to the bar. After ordering the brandies he said to the barman, 'Where are all the women hiding in this town, mate?'

The barman finished wiping a glass and then placed it back on a shelf. 'This is a man's only bar,' he replied with a strong Afrikaans accent. 'No women's are allowed in here. If you want to meet single woman's you have to go to a saloon bar.'

THE PLOUGH, THE GUN AND THE GLORY

George nodded. 'Okay so where's this saloon bar then?'

'Up the road... the hotel is called The Owl's Nest.'

'The Owl's Nest,' George repeated. 'Thanks.' He returned to the table with the brandies and told James.

'So, I guess that's where you'll be heading then?'

'Too darn true, mate. It's been a long time since I had a bit of the other.'

They finished off their drinks and left. A few blocks up the road they found The Owl's Nest. There were a number of troops occupying the place and dozens of the fairer sex were milling around displaying their wares, receiving lots of attention and free drinks.

'This looks more like it, mate' George said excitedly.

'I'll leave you to enjoy yourself, then.'

'Yeah, see you back at camp later, mate.'

'Don't forget that you have to be back by midnight.'

George waved and then disappeared inside. James made his way over to the hospital. He asked for Christina at reception and was then told how to find her cottage. He made his way over there. When he arrived he knocked three times on the door. A few moments later the door opened and Christina was standing there. She was extremely pleased to see him. 'Oh James, I had this horrible feeling that you wouldn't be able to arrange a pass for tonight.'

'I think the whole of our contingent got passes. Luckily our replacement kit arrived from Cape Town on Monday.'

She kissed him on the lips. 'I am so happy that you are here you have no idea. Come, let's get away from here.' She took him by the hand and they walked along the road towards town.

'So, what would you like to do tonight?' James asked.

'Go somewhere secluded where we can be alone and make wild passionate love. Unless of course you would rather do something else?'

'Are you kidding? Who in their right mind would want to do something else with an offer like that from a very beautiful woman?'

Christina laughed. 'I was hoping you would say that... and, I just happen to know of a nice quiet little hotel that will suit us just fine. It's not all that far from here either.'

'And how do you just happen to know about this nice quiet little hotel, may I ask?'

'One of the other nurses told me about it. Her and a doctor are having a fling and they use the hotel.'

They put their arms around one another and walked on with streaks of white lightning, lighting up the sky. They reached the Hotel Jacaranda twenty minutes later and went straight to the reception. James booked a room and had to pay cash in advance. After that, he ordered a bottle of their best champagne and then Christina and him made their way upstairs. The room was quite pleasant and nicely furnished. There was a large double, four-poster bed, which looked comfortable. Christina sat down on it and bounced gently up and down. 'Thank goodness it doesn't squeak,' she said getting to her feet again.

'That's good. I would hate to have the people in the next room hammering on the walls.'

James went over to an ornate wood cabinet and removed two champagne glasses. He then popped the cork and then poured the champagne. He handed a glass to Christina and then he held his glass up high. 'To the Empire's victory!'

'Cheers!' Christina said, as she placed the glass to her lips. She drank a mouthful down. 'Mmm, this is very nice.' She licked her lips. Christina then raised her glass. 'To us.'

They drank from their glasses while staring into one another's eyes. When the glasses were empty James placed them down on the cabinet. His eyes returned to Christina. 'Did you know that one of things that I've always loved about you is your mouth?'

'No… what's so special about my mouth?' she asked inquisitively.

'It has the most beautiful shape as though it was made just for kissing.' James took Christina in his arms and kissed her lustfully. She kissed him back intensely until she was breathless. 'Oh James, I love you so much,' she gasped. Then she started vigorously undoing the buttons on his tunic, while he began undoing her blouse. She pulled off his jacket letting it drop to the carpet. James hurriedly removed her blouse and then he undid the button of her camisole. It came loose and Christina removed the straps from her shoulders and let it fall to the floor. James placed his mouth to her right breast and sucked gently on the nipple. Then he kissed the other breast and sucked on the nipple before moving up to her neck.

James then picked Christina up and carried her over to the bed where he gently placed her down. After removing her skirt with a little help, the remainder of her underwear was removed leaving her naked. James stripped off the remainder of his uniform and they hurriedly pulled the linen back and climbed into the bed. They kissed desirously again with James gently fondling her firm round breasts. Christina didn't need much foreplay; she was already highly aroused. She had been thinking of this moment ever since she had seen James on the verandah during the weekend. She was breathless and wanted nothing more than for him to penetrate the private part between her legs.

James' penis was throbbing as the blood surged into the veins. He too was ready and moments later he pushed himself inside her, his rigid gland meeting without any opposition, her vagina warm and moist. James drove his penis in as far as it would go and Christina closed her eyes with pure ecstasy.

110   Christina climbed out of bed and went over to her bag. She removed a bottle of perfume and then dabbed herself lavishly all over.

'Why are you doing that?' James asked inquisitively.

'To rid myself from that awful stench of death... don't tell me you can't smell it?'

James' brow wrinkled. 'I have no idea what you are talking about.'

'Can't you smell it?'

'No.'

'My whole body smells of it... my clothes... my bed... the hospital, everything. You can't get rid of it no matter how much you bath. Even carbolic soap doesn't get rid of it.'

'Christina, you smell just fine to me. I don't understand what you are going on about.'

'Only because I've dabbed perfume all over; otherwise you would smell it.'

...'Why don't you come back to bed... you must be freezing?'

She came over and climbed under the bed covers. He waited for her to settle down. 'Are you going to tell me what's going on, or not?'

'I told you... everything smells of death.'

He smelt her body and then her hair. 'Well, you smell very nice to me... it's all just in your mind.'

'Oh rubbish James. All the nurses say the same thing. Even some of the doctors have agreed that the conditions at the hospital are atrocious. It's overcrowded and there just aren't enough nurses. I overheard one of the doctors telling another that the surgeon, Major General Wilson, was incompetent and that Roberts should replace him as soon as possible.'

...'Have you any idea what you are saying?'

'Yes!'

James gave a sigh. He then looked at the bottle of champagne standing over on the cabinet. 'I'm going to pour us another drink.' He climbed out of bed and went over to the cabinet where he filled two glasses. She watched him admiring his raw, naked physique. He was muscular and strong. He walked back with her eyes fixed on him. After handing Christina hers James climbed back into bed. He took a mouthful of his drink and said, 'Ah, that's better.'

'Christina sipped hers. 'I will never ever forget the young men who have died here, or the endless procession of carts that keep coming to the hospital to take away their bodies. And, I'll never forget the stiff, blanket-shrouded shapes that had once been proud young men, or the overcrowded wards of sick, unfed, unwashed, unhappy men lying in their own urine and foul smelling excrement.'

James didn't know what to say to ease her mind. He too had seen the men with twisted, torn, mutilated bodies, their life giving blood draining away into the dry sand. He too had heard the cries of agony as men lay dying on the battlefield, as he tried desperately to patch them up and ease their pain... And, then there were the horses? If anything, they had suffered far more than the men who rode them to their unfitting and horrible, agonising deaths... And he, who was supposed to be a lover of horses, had proposed the idea of using more horses by mounting Australian foot soldiers. He had been a direct contributor to their cruel and bloody deaths. He had also killed his cousin and this still weighed heavily on his mind.

'You know something James?'

The sound of Christina's voice abruptly ended his soul searching. 'What?' he asked softly.

'I wish that I could just simply walk away from all of this and go back home... maybe back to the old boathouse by river where we used to swim naked and listen to the calls of the kookaburras... where we first made love... back to those sunny carefree days where everything was so peaceful and we were so happy.'

He gave a sigh. 'I thought you said you were a big city girl now... and after living in Melbourne, Wickepin would drive you mad if you had to return there?'

She took a mouthful of her drink. 'Maybe I should request a transfer to the New South Wales Army Medical Corps? Everyone at the hospital says they're the best... Do you think the British would let me transfer over to them?'

...'I don't know... I doubt it though, seeing as you are so short handed.'

343

'I'll make a formal request in writing tomorrow and see what happens.'

'Well, it's worth a try, I suppose.'

Their conversation fell silent for several moments until James said, 'Do you remember when we were still at Modder River, when you invited me over to your tent for the first time?'

'Yes... and we drank brandy and made love on the blanket.'

'Yeah.'

'Why?'

'You said I looked troubled and that you could tell that something was worrying me.'

'Yes... and you wouldn't talk about it.'

'Would you like me to tell you about it now?'

...'Only if you want to.'

James told her about the time he had been captured by the Boers and how his aunt and her son, Haans, had rescued him, and then taken him back to their farm where he spent the night. He told her about the pistol that his aunt had given him, when he left the following day to return to his troops. And, how he was ambushed and how he had killed two young boys, one of whom was his cousin. When he had finished Christina kissed him gently on the cheek. 'It wasn't your fault. You're fighting a war. He very likely would have shot you.'

'I don't know that though, do I?'

'It was just one of those unfortunate things that happens in war, James. You can't spend the rest of your life blaming yourself. Sooner or later you are going to have to put it behind you.'

'Before I return to Australia I'm going back to my aunt's farm. I'll try and explain to them what happened and then I'll take her and my uncle to the gravesite. That's the very least I can do for them.'

'Well do that then James, and maybe in time you will feel better about yourself.'

They both drank a little of their champagne and then they listened to the town clock chime 11pm. 'We'll have to get dressed soon... I have to be back at camp by twelve.'

Christina sighed. 'Make love to me again.'

He took the glass from her hand and placed it on the floor next to his. Then, they kissed sensually. Later, they both dressed in silence and then made their way quietly downstairs. From there they walked arm in arm to the hospital. Christina told James that her next night off was in two weeks time on a Wednesday, and asked if he would try and get a pass.

'We might be gone before then,' he replied. 'Roberts is keen to press onto Johannesburg as soon as possible.'

They kissed one another passionately and then parted company.

111

On Saturday afternoon Banjo Paterson showed up as promised. Other Australian contingents, also in Bloemfontein at the time, were also invited to attend. Over eight hundred men crowded around an open Cape-cart, which James had organised as a platform for Banjo to play from. Banjo was given a standing ovation as he climbed onboard the wagon, and it was several minutes before the men were quiet enough for him to address them.

'G'day to you all and thank you for your very warm welcome! ...I wish I could get audiences as large as this back in Australia.'

Laughter broke out amongst the men.

Banjo continued. 'The other night when James Mitchell asked me to come over and play a few tunes for the Aussie blokes, he forgot to mention just how many of you there were. I know that all of you are volunteers and I think the Australian colonies can be extremely proud of their contribution to the war effort.'

The men cheered and clapped.

'According to the dispatch records we now have over three thousand troops in South Africa, and more are on the high sea at this very moment on their way to join us.'

More clapping and cheering broke out.

Banjo paced the wagon looking at the men spread out all around him. 'I hope you fellas at the back can hear me?'

Hands went up from the back rows of standing men.

'Like many of you blokes here today, I was born and grew up on a station near Orange in New South Wales. Later, my father sent me to Sydney to finish my education where I graduated as a solicitor. However, music and poetry have always been my first love. I have never forgotten my childhood years growing up in the bush, and so, both my poems and music reflect those happy wonderful years of my life. However, since arriving here in South Africa I have written a new poem which I will recite at the end of this gathering.'

Banjo stopped talking for a moment while he took a drink of water from a glass. He looked over at James saying, 'I hope this was boiled I'd hate to get enteric?' He was only teasing and laughed at James when he responded defensively with, 'Yeah, I did it myself.'

The poet and musician turned his attention to the patiently waiting audience. 'Today, I'm going to start with a favourite ballad of mine which I wrote to the tune of an old marching song. Many of you will have heard it before.' He began playing "Waltzing Matilda" and a rowdy applause broke out from the men. Then they joined in singing the words as loudly as they could. After that he played "Clancy of the Overflow, The Man from Snowy River, A Bunch of Roses" and "As Long As Your Eyes Are Blue" plus several others. At the end he played "The Last Parade" a ballad that he had written and dedicated to all the Australian horses sent out to the Boer war.

James felt the tears come to his eyes as Banjo sang the words "Home to the Hunter River, to the flats where the lucerne grows… home where the Murrumbidgee runs white with the melted snows."

The men's overall favourite though was "Waltzing Matilda" and Banjo played it twice more. Finally, he had to stop when he started losing his voice, and he was given a rowdy standing ovation.

112
Once the horses from the Argentine arrived, which were still partly wild, the task of breaking-them-in began. This was something most of the Australians took too, like a duck to water. One morning James and a section of his men went over to the New South Wales Lancers paddocks to watch a bloke by the name of Harry Morrant, a bush-balladist and horseman, better known as Breaker Morrant, break-in several horses. They all agreed he was good, probably one of the best, except George who reckoned he was just as good.

As the days passed the troops prepared their kit, checked their weapons and took care of their horses. Some men received re-mounts brought back into service while others were issued Argentine horses. Others were issued with ponies captured from the Boers. And, while in Bloemfontein 'The Australian Regiment' was re-formed into 'The Australian Brigade.' They were then placed under the command of Major-General Hutton.

The imperial war machine under Lord Roberts was now ready to begin the advance northwards towards Johannesburg, by moving up the central railway line. Roberts' massive army included General Tucker's 7th Division, General Pole-Carew's 11th division, plus General Ian Hamilton's division, consisting of General Broadwood's Cavalry, Colonel Ridley's Mounted Infantry Brigades, General Smith-Dorrian's 19th Infantry Brigade, and also Major-General Bruce Hamilton's 21st Infantry Brigade.

The British force consisted of over thirty thousand men, eleven thousand horses, one hundred and twenty artillery guns, plus fourteen maxim guns. Amongst the artillery were two, twelve pounder Naval guns, which had been removed from the battle cruisers Terrible, Powerful, Monarch and Doris. These had been converted for field use at the suggestion of Lord Kitchener in answer to the Boer's Long Toms. Over twenty-two thousand mules pulled five thousand five hundred carts, and forty thousand oxen pulled some two thousand five hundred wagons, all driven by blacks.

On the 24th April the 1st WAMI together with four companies of Imperial Mounted Infantry, plus four companies of New South Wales Mounted Rifles were given three hours to prepare their kit and leave Bloemfontein. Consequently, James wasn't able to say goodbye to Christina, so, he hurriedly wrote her a short letter and handed it in for posting.

Apposing Roberts' army was General Louis Botha and Christiaan de Wet with a combined force of eighteen thousand commandos. Their artillery comprised of four Long Toms, four Vickers mountain 75mm guns, seven Maxim guns (pom-poms) and six Krupp 75mm guns.

The massive imperial army pressed northwards with the Boers sending their artillery shells hurtling at the British troops. Their commandos desperately tried everything to prevent the Empires unstoppable advance, defending farm after farm, kopje after kopje, river after river and town after town, and every mile of veldt. As they fell back they destroyed the bridges behind them in their attempt to slow the British advance.

British artillery shelled the Boers farmsteads and towns and the troops set fire to what was left. British troops who were half starved began looting livestock, feeding off pigs, chickens and geese, roasting them in the flames of victory. Some troops dug up potatoes and onions. Their horses were fed maize and oats.

The 1st WAMI on the right flank, under General Ian Hamilton drove northwards under constant attack from the Boers. Their route passed through the town of Thabaneliu on the 27th April reaching Winberg on the 5th, May. Both men and horses had been on three-quarter food rations for the entire ten days. Ventersburg was reached on 11th, May and Kroonstad the following day. The town brought memories of Bella and Richard flooding back for James. He wondered how they were surviving the war including Susan and her two children on their farm near Delmas, he had been helped by some extremely kind people and he would always remember them with gratitude.

By the time the imperial army reached Kroonstad they had lost two hundred and thirty-seven officers, plus six thousand four hundred and thirteen other ranks. The largest portion of men had died from enteric fever, exhaustion and other illnesses. Over eight hundred horses had perished either killed or had died from exhaustion. During the day soaring heat scorched both men and animal and at night they froze from the bitter cold.

THE PLOUGH, THE GUN AND THE GLORY

While in Kroonstad the 1st WAMI met-up with the 2nd, WAMI whom they thought would join them, but that wasn't to be, and the 1st WAMI left Kroonstad and pressed on northwards reaching Lindley on the 18th, May. From there it was onto Heilbron, which they reached on May 22nd. While there, General Hamilton received orders from Lord Roberts that he was to cross the Vaal River and then turn west. Later, having crossed over the central railway line he was to proceed to the town of Vredefort, which he reached on the 24th May. On the 26th May General Hamilton engaged in a frontal attack on a Boer position at Doornkop, using the Gordon Highlanders and the City Imperial Volunteers, losing twenty-eight men with one hundred and thirty-four wounded.

After several minor skirmishes with the enemy the 1st WAMI made camp near Florida and Roodepoort mine, about eight miles east of the Rand city (Johannesburg). Since leaving Bloemfontein both men and horses had lived on three-quarter rations of food for thirty-six days. At one time they went without rations for over forty-eight hours.

On the 31st May Roberts sent a message to General Hamilton. 'I am delighted with your success, and grieved beyond measure at your poor fellows being without their proper rations. A train with rations shall be sent to you today. I expect to get notice of the surrender of Johannesburg this morning and we shall then march into the city. I wish your column, which has done so much to gain possession, could be with us.'

Shortly before midday a troop of South Australian Mounted Infantry, under Lieutenant Peter Rowell, with Lord Roberts following shortly afterwards, occupied the city of Johannesburg to the jubilation of the Empire.

It wasn't all victory for the imperial army however, for on that day General Piet De Wet, brother of the notorious Christiaan De Wet, captured almost the entire 13th battalion of Imperial Yeomanry at the town of Lindley. Amongst them were Lords Longford, Leitrim, Ennismore and Donoughmore, together with the future Lord Craigavon, plus eighty troops had been killed. On the same day General Christiaan De Wet ambushed General Colvile's Highland Brigade at Heilbron, capturing fifty-six supply wagons and one hundred and sixty prisoners. Two days later he attacked the 4th Derbyshire's halfway between Johannesburg and Bloemfontein, killing thirty-eight men, wounding one hundred and ninety-four and taking four hundred and eighty-five prisoners.

113   That evening James and George were sitting around the log-fire with a few other men from the section. They were roasting a turkey that one of them had caught from a nearby farm. James got to his feet, turned the turkey over and then stood back from the heat. The smell from the roasting meat drifted to his nostrils. He took a deep breath and then rubbed his hands together before saying, 'I think we are really going to enjoy this, you blokes.'

'To damn true we are,' one of them replied.

'This is going to be the best bloody tucker we've ever had,' said another.

'What about the pig we ate last week?' asked another, 'when we were at...?'

...'Lindley,' one of them replied.

'Yeah Lindley, that's the place.'

'That was good,' the first one agreed.

Most of the others seemed to think so to.

After that the men fell silent as they listened to the sound of the wood cracking, snapping and popping. James sat on the ground again. Like the others around the fire he stared at it as though in a trance, seemingly mesmerized by the dancing, flickering flames. Many things began to race through his mind as he wondered how his mother and sisters were coping on the farm without his late father and brother. At times he still found it almost impossible to believe that they were both dead. He couldn't imagine the farm without them. After awhile his thoughts turned to Christina. Had he fallen in love with her all over again... and where would it all lead? She was a married woman who lived in Melbourne, and by her own admission wouldn't be happy living in Wickepin again. And what about Veronica, had he judged her too harshly? After all, he hadn't even given her a chance to tell her side of the story. What if her late husband had lied about not being Samuel's father... but then again, why would a dying man do that?

'Sergeant Mitchell!' a voice called out loudly.

THE PLOUGH, THE GUN AND THE GLORY

James' mind came rushing back to the present. He looked up to see Lieutenant Brown, who had been promoted from sergeant while still at Bloemfontein. James got to his feet and saluted the officer.

'Get your section together and join Sergeant Lesseys over by those wagons in five minutes.'

'We are just about to eat, sir. The men are starving.'

'You can eat later.'

James turned to the blokes around the fire. 'You heard the lieutenant. Get your gear and check your rifles and ammo.'

'What are we going to do with the turkey?' one of them asked.

'Take it off the fire; we'll finish cooking it when we get back. Place more wood on the fire to keep it going until we return.'

'Where the hell are we going now anyway?' another asked in a disgruntled tone of voice.

'We'll know soon enough.'

When they were ready they made their way over to the wagons, where they found four other sections including Lieutenant Darling. Once he was sure everyone was there he said, 'We are going to check the mine nearby. Some of the pickets have reported hearing strange noises coming from there.'

A bright half-moon was hanging midway in a cloudless, starry sky, which helped them find their way through the darkness. It was winter and freezing cold. Clouds of warm, steamy breath billowed from the men's mouths as they exhaled their stale breath. Small flashes of light suddenly appeared in front of them, followed by a succession of gunshots. The men spread out and hit the ground. They fired back in the direction of the flashing lights. The gunfight continued for about half an hour and then went quiet. The men were ordered to move forward, one section at a time, so as not to end up shooting each other.

They came to a large shed where they found a goods train. After several skirmishes with the enemy they took possession of the train and captured two armed Boers and fifteen unarmed railway staff. On-board the train they also discovered about sixty thousand rounds of Mauser ammunition. A section of track was then blown-up preventing the train from going anywhere. Afterwards the men returned to camp. The turkey was hurriedly placed over the fire again while the men huddled around it for warmth.

'You know what I would really like more than anything, you blokes?' James said after awhile of silence.

'A seductive blonde,' one of them replied followed by laughter.

'Yeah, and a bottle of grog to go with her,' said another.

James agreed that those would all be nice but that's not what he had on his mind. 'I would like our contingent to be the first troops to ride into Pretoria. I want to take my horse up the steps of the Houses of Parliament and go right inside and capture Paul Kruger.'

'You've had too much excitement for one day, serge,' someone said followed by laughter.

'It's the damn hunger, serge, it plays tricks with your mind,' said another... 'Some bloke once told me it can send a man mad.'

'Maybe... But, when I was escaping from prison there, with a war correspondent called Winston, I told him just what I've told you.'

'What did he say, this fella, Winston?' one of them asked.

'I forget his exact words. But I think he said something about making history and good reading in the morning papers.'

'Yeah, well somehow I have the feeling that Lord Roberts is reserving that privilege for himself, serge.'

James looked over at the man. He was dirty and unwashed and his face was shining brightly from the light of the fire, and also because he was sunburnt. 'For your information it was the South Australians who first rode through the streets of Johannesburg. Roberts only entered after them. That's why we should be the first into Pretoria.'

'Well, it's a nice thought I guess, James,' George added. 'But I'll tell you what I want right now and that's to eat some of this darn turkey before I drop dead from starvation.'

Everyone agreed, and they all thought it must be cooked well enough by now. James pushed his bayonet into it.

The meat was soft. 'Let's get it off the fire, you blokes, and get stuck in.'

There was no need to ask for volunteers for this task as several of the men helped remove the turkey and place it down on a flattish rock, which had previously been washed clean. The bloke who had caught the turkey got first choice taking a leg for himself. James was offered the other drumstick, which he then cut off. Then, the other blokes started carving off bits of meat for themselves and shovelled it into their mouths. The grease ran down from the corners of their mouths and they wiped it away with the backs of their hands. The meat was so tender and tasty and everyone agreed that it was the best meal they had ever eaten. Finally, the only thing left were the bare bones. They licked their fingers clean and then wiped them on their trousers. One by one the men drifted off to where they were going to bed down for the night. Some had chosen to sleep around the fire, others under wagons.

114   Two days after the surrender of Johannesburg the imperial war machine was ready to make the final thirty miles north to Pretoria. Ahead of them, strung out across the lonely veldt, the Boer armies of General's Louis Botha and De la Rey waited in anticipation. It was 4am, in the morning and James had just saddled his horse. He was checking the girth strap to make sure it wasn't too tight, so as not to restrict the horse's breathing when at the gallop. He looked up and saw Major Moor a little distance away. James approached him. 'G'day, sir.'

'Morning sergeant.' He was rubbing his hands together to warm them. 'Is your section prepared and ready to move out?'

'They are, sir.'

'Good.'

He was about to move off when James asked, 'Are we going to be the first troops into Pretoria, sir?'

The major smiled. 'That would be very nice, sergeant.'

'The South Australians were the first to occupy Johannesburg, sir. That's why we need to be the first into Pretoria.'

'I never realised there was a competition amongst the Australians, sergeant.'

'It's a matter of pride sir, and it would be a bigger victory than the of taking of Johannesburg.'

The major nodded. 'Then, perhaps that's what we should do, sergeant?'

'Yeah, sir, I reckon that's what we should do.'

Half an hour later the 1st WAMI and one Company of New South Wales Mounted Rifles departed for the capital of the Transvaal under General Hamilton. As the sun rose on that frosty cold morning they took-up the left flank of Roberts vast army.

As they reached the outskirts of the Boer capital they came under fierce attack. Major Moor gave the signal for his men to charge the enemy. The West Australian's spurred their mounts on and galloped towards the Boers position, followed closely by the New South Wales Mounted Rifles. Then, by a magnificent flanking gallop of five miles they turned the enemy around, and that evening they camped in full view of Pretoria.

That night Lieutenant Parker asked for eleven volunteers to accompany him to go and cut the railway line north of the capital that led to Delagoa Bay. Both James and George were amongst the first to offer their services. James took them to an ideal place that he had seen when he and Winston previously walked along that part of the railway line. They returned to their camp safely by midnight.

Before daybreak the 1st WAMI rode into Pretoria together with the New South Wales Mounted Rifles and took occupation of the Boer capital with little resistance. Major Moor together with Lieutenants Parker and Darling led the men through the streets. When they reached the steps of Parliament House the men dismounted and James led his section up the steps and inside the building. They searched through the many rooms and captured a number of staff, but learned from them afterwards that President Kruger had left two weeks earlier for Holland. President Steyn of the Orange Free State, together with Jan Smuts (Kruger's State Attorney), General Christiaan de Vet and General Botha had fled from Pretoria the previous day heading north.

As James came out of the building he began singing Waltzing Matilda as loudly as he could. The other West Australians joined in including the officers, and then the South Australians followed. Their voices were soon heard booming out over the grounds of Parliament House just as Lord Roberts' column arrived.

James ran down the steps to the grounds below and began pulling down the Transvaal flag. A British soldier came running up carrying a Union Jack, which was then hoisted to the top of the flagstaff. It fluttered gently in the morning breeze as a military band struck-up God Save The Queen. As the anthem finished the troops threw their hats into the air and cheered loudly, 'Hip, hip, hooray! Hip, hip, hooray! Hip, hip, hooray!'

Several British troops broke down and wept, while others stood in silence almost in disbelief that they were at last standing in the Boer capital. Most were just thankful that they were still alive and the war had virtually come to an end.

That same night James wrote a letter home dated the 5th, May 1900. "Dear Mother, Alanna, Elizabeth and Bridget,

I hope and trust that you are all keeping well. I am hurriedly writing this letter under candlelight so please excuse my writing. I have some very good news for you all. Today, we took occupation of Pretoria. We were the first troops into the capital ahead of everyone else. The British regulars couldn't believe it. Lord Roberts didn't even know we had gone ahead of them all. Everyone is rejoicing at our victory and say that this will be the end of the war. Thank God. I can hardly believe that we have been here almost seven months now. It seems like only yesterday that poor Joseph was killed on the train journey from Cape Town to De Aar. Since then so many men and horses have died here.

The British troops have had the worst of it. I understand that so far they have lost over eight thousand men and received twenty-four thousand casualties. The climate here is very harsh and is not unlike like Western Australia, which has taken its toll of the British. Enteric fever, dysentery and typhoid have killed many men including a large number of Australians. I pray to God that neither, George or I get any of it. I make sure that the blokes in my section only drink water that has been boiled. That is extremely difficult as we are constantly on the move. Firewood has also been a problem as trees are scarce. Most times we use the wood from wagons that have been smashed during battle. Other times we use whatever we can find in towns that we have occupied.

Once, we even burnt the pews and a pulpit from a church. The loss of horses has been very high. I hope that after this warhorses will never be used again for military purposes, although that's highly unlikely, as I can't think of how we could possibly do without them. I should be able to tell you soon when we are returning home, as I am sure that we will not be required to stay the full term of twelve months. I hope everything is going well with the farm and that the drought has at long last ended? George sends his love to you all. Has Billy been to see you yet? Please give him my regards when you see him. Well, I had better rush my letter over to the postal cart or I will miss them, as they are leaving shortly for Johannesburg. Love and God bless to you all, your loving son and brother, James."

115 After the occupation of both capitals, Bloemfontein and Pretoria, the Boers divided their commandos into smaller groups and began hit and run tactics against the imperial army. Lord Roberts soon realised that the war was far from over and that the farmers were not quite ready to give up the struggle for their land or their freedom. Many British and colonial soldier would still be required to spill their blood upon the veldt, and many a home was to become fatherless for the glory of the Empire.

The Boers struck back with a new vengeance hitting British supply wagons and trains, derailing them and blowing up the tracks. They attacked their garrisons and tore down the telegraph lines cutting Roberts' line of communication with his forces. He was rapidly becoming frustrated realising the war could drag on for years. He was nearly seventy years of age and wanted nothing better than to return home to England. Deep down in his heart he was still grieving the death of his son, Lieutenant Frederick Roberts, who had died from wounds received at the battle of Spion Kop.

At Lord Roberts Headquarters in Pretoria, on the 14th, June 1900, the Field Marshal and his staff were holding a council of war meeting. Roberts stroked his white moustache several times as he looked thoughtfully at the others. Then, he glanced in Lord Kitchener's direction. 'We must put a stop to these raids on the railways and telegraph lines, and the best way will be to let the inhabitants understand that there cannot be continued impunity. Methuen's troops are now available and a commencement should be made tomorrow morning by burning De Wet's farm, which is only three or four miles from the Rhenoster Railway Bridge. He, like all Free Staters fighting against us is a rebel and must be treated as such. Let it be known all over the country that in the event of any damage being done to the railways or telegraph, the nearest farm will be burnt to the ground.'

'What will we do with the occupants of the farms, the women and children?' asked Kitchener.

...'We will build prison camps and intern them.'

Kitchener nodded. 'And what of their crops and live stock?'

...'Burn the crops we can't use. Keep as many of the animals you can for our use, slaughter the rest. There must be nothing left for the Boers to eat... Nothing you hear! I'm going to starve every single one of them into submission!'

116 General's Hamilton and French were ordered to advance eastwards from Pretoria along the railway line towards Delagoa Bay, in pursuit of General Botha, who was waiting for them twelve miles away, along a string of kopjes know as the Donkerhoek heights. The most southern tip of these kopjes was called Diamond Hill and the 1st WAMI engaged Botha's commandos there. A fierce battle lasting two days took place before the WAMI occupied the hill. As usual the Boers withdrew from the engagement leaving one hundred and eighty imperial troops dead in the field. Private Corkill of the 1st WAMI was later awarded the Victoria Cross.

From Diamond Hill the 1st WAMI engaged with the enemy at Elands River station and Bronkhorst Spruit station, where James had passed through after escaping from Pretoria. After that they proceeded westwards to Irene on the outskirts of Pretoria where they were given a two-day rest period. Then, they moved southwards along the eastern side of Johannesburg engaging in a number of battles with the enemy. Firstly, at Springs, not far from Susan's farm, and James hoped that her and the children were alright.

Two days later they reached the outskirts of Heidelburg where a battle took place lasting until sundown. The following morning they rode into the town where James asked for permission to see someone he knew. Major Moor told him he could visit for half an hour and that he would have to take an escort with him.

James' heart was in his mouth as he and the other four men approached Richard and Bella's home. The columns to the gates at the entrance had been demolished to nothing but rubble. The once beautiful flower gardens had been trampled barren. Trees were stripped bear of their foliage and stood out of the ground like petrified crows feet. The house was in near ruins with half of the roof missing, and looked in a general state of near collapse.

James brought his mount to a halt outside the front entrance and ran up the steps to where the doors had once been. 'Bella! ...Richard!' he called out but there was no answer. He carefully ventured further inside clambering over the rubble where he called out again, 'Bella! ...Richard!' Again there was no answer. He looked at the staircase and saw that the first floor was almost totally missing. His heart sank and he turned around and made his way back outside. He looked up at George with dismay on his face. 'There's no sign of anyone in there. I guess they must have gone away somewhere?'

'Why don't you take a look around the back?' George replied.

James nodded. He then made his way around the side of the house to the back but couldn't find anyone around there either. He was just about to leave when he saw something a little distance away over by an outhouse. He cautiously made his way towards it when he realised it was a white woman. At first James hardly recognised Bella. Her face was dirty and her clothes torn and shabby.

'Bella! ...It's me! James!' he called out. She came out of the shadows and approached him. James took her in his arms. 'Thank God you're alright,' he said after a moment.

'They killed Richard,' Bella blurted out.

He stood back from her. 'Who?'

'It happened when the British were shelling the town. He's been dead for over six weeks.'

James took her in his arms again. 'Oh God Bella, I am so, so sorry.' Moment's later a black woman also came out of the outhouse and stood behind Bella. 'You remember Molly don't you James?'

'Yeah... how are you Molly?'

'I am fine, boss,' she replied timidly.

Bella told James that she had moved into Molly's quarters after the house was destroyed. The other servants had fled when the shelling of the town began. She also showed him Richard's grave. James asked her what she was going to do now. She said she wasn't sure but had enough money to live on for about six months. She thought that once the war was over she would try and get Richard's paper up-and-running again. Perhaps even try and have the house rebuilt, but that would require a lot of money. George joined them and after James had introduced him to Bella, he said they would have to get going. After saying an emotional goodbye James climbed into the saddle and the five men rode off. The visit to Bella's had left James in a solemn mood and feeling somewhat guilty at not being able to offer her any help.

After Heidelberg the 1st WAMI, now attached to General's Hunter's column, continued to steadily move southwards, crossing the Vaal River, into what was now called the Orange River colony, the Free State having been annexed by Britain. They encountered small pockets of the enemy on a number of occasions as they travelled between several towns, namely Frankfort, Bethlehem and Harrismith near the border of Natal colony.

On the 18th, July the 1st, W.A.M.I received orders to saddle-up with three days rations and join General Ridley's column that was in pursuit of De Wet and three other Boer Generals, accompanied by fifteen thousand commandos. The previous day, General Hunter and Pole-Carew's columns outside of Bethlehem had surrounded De Wet and the others, along with five thousand Boers. During the night however, De Wet and others had slipped through the imperial noose.

It was a hard, gruelling ride to a place called Palmietfontein north of Bethlehem, where the 1st WAMI caught-up with De Wet and the others on the afternoon of the 19th, July. The whole of the area was hilly with numerous small kopjes. The men were breathless having dismounted and then bolted along a ridge to a good position to launch their attack. The Boers were travelling through a valley and Major Moor gave the order to open fire at a distance of six hundred yards. The West Australians rifles kicked hard into their shoulders as the weapons discharged their lethal cargo towards the Boers. They had caught the moving enemy by surprise and several men were seen to drop to the ground.

The order was then given by Major Moor to proceed further along the ridge. The men ran most of the way and took up new positions. Once again they discharged a fusillade of lead upon the enemy, who, with very little resistance kept on the move. The West Australians were then ordered to remount their horses and gave chase after the Boers. James spurred his horse hard as he galloped through the tall brown grass with Major Moor leading the charge. After about half a mile of riding on the Boers right flank, the major wheeled sharply to the left and headed towards another ridge. As they got closer they came up against a wire fence which prevented them getting to the ridge. It took time negotiating the fence in order to get through it and by this time the Boers had occupied the ridge. The enemy opened up with a barrage of fire.

The major yelled, 'Dismount and take cover!'

James and the others quickly spread out and took whatever cover they could find, and then began shooting back. Moments later, James looked over at the man on his right and saw it was Private Collett. He was going to tell him to try and find himself better cover when he realised he was covered in blood. James crawled over to him with bullets kicking up sand, ricocheting off rocks and whizzing past his head. When he reached Collett he found there was nothing he could do, as he was already dead. Luckily, reinforcements soon arrived and the Boers finally withdrew from the engagement as the sun sank on the horizon. Once the shooting stopped the men got to their feet and then started checking for wounded.

'Where's the major?' Lieutenant Parker asked one of the men nearest to him. He then noticed someone approaching. The others with him turned around to see James was carrying the officer towards them. Lieutenant Parker rushed forwards. 'Place him down on the ground, Mitchell, so that I can take a look.'

James placed the major carefully onto the ground as the lieutenant crouched down next to him. James knew the answer, and as he walked away he heard the lieutenant cry out, 'Oh God no!'

Stretcher-bearers arrived and began collecting the wounded, which totalled seven men. The casualties would have been far higher if some of the men hadn't taken cover behind a kraal. The horses unfortunately had been left in an exposed area and nineteen out of twenty-six had been shot. Some horses were still alive and James flinched each time the gunshots echoed between the kopjes confirming they had been destroyed.

One of the horse-holders in charge of five horses miraculously survived without a scratch although all the horses were killed around him. The death of Major Moor understandably cast a gloomy atmosphere over the 1st WAMI. They had lost a highly respected officer who had led them through many battles and skirmishes, and most felt that the contingent would never be the same without him.

From Palmietfontein the 1st WAMI, still attached to Colonel De Lisle's Column, continued with the clearing of the Orange River Colony and also the Transvaal. The Boer Generals kept-up their relentless hit and run tactics much to the annoyance of the Empire. The farm burnings continued and the prison camps grew larger daily, as women, children and old folk were herded in through the gates.

In September 1900 James received a commission to the rank of lieutenant and by November 1900 the 1st WAMI were almost at the end of their twelve months stint. Most of the men were more than ready to return home to Western Australia among them George Gleniste. 'It will be darn good to see Billy again,' he said enthusiastically. 'And the farm... and your mother and sisters... and hear the sounds of kookaburras and didgeridoos again.'

James smiled. 'Christina said something similar to me when we were still in Bloemfontein. That seems like a lifetime ago now.'

'Have you heard from her recently?'

'No. ...The last letter from her was months ago. Mind you, I don't think the mail can keep up with us any longer, we just never seem to stop moving.'

'What are going to do about Christina?'

'How do you mean?'

'Well, obviously you are both in love.'

...'Yeah.'

'Is she going to divorce her husband?'

'I don't know,' James replied softly.

'Haven't you asked her?'

...'No.'

George scratched under his chin. 'And what about Veronica?'

...'What about her?'

'James, when we were leaving Perth you told all of us on the train that you were madly in love with her. You said that you had asked her to wait for you to return home.'

...'Yeah, I know.'

'So?'

'Things have become a little complicated since then, George.'

'I'll say.'

'Listen, I'm no longer sure how I feel about her... or anything else for that matter. Ever since Timothy told me that he wasn't Samuel's father, something inside me changed.'

'Did you ever write and ask her if it was the truth or not?'

James shook his head.

'How come?'

'I don't know George... I haven't had the time... and perhaps because I had also met Christina again... I don't know.'

'Well mate, you have got a little over five weeks left before we return home, so you had better start thinking about what you are going to do.'

James gave a sigh. 'I'm not returning to Australia. Well, not just yet anyway. There are a few things I have to take care of here first in order to live with my conscious.'

'Like what?'

'For one thing, I need to go to my aunt's farm and explain to her how Piet died... tell her that it was me who had killed him. Take her and my uncle and show them where his grave is. That's the least I can do for them.'

George couldn't believe what he was hearing. 'James, this country is still at war! What if the Boers capture you? ...If they discover that you were with the Australian army they'll kill you.'

James nodded. 'That's a chance I'll have to risk.'

'Jesus!' George threw his hands in the air. 'What about your mother and sisters? They will be expecting you to come home, you know?'

James gave another sigh. 'I, know... I'll write and try to explain to them. I'm sure they will understand.'

'I'm sorry, but I just can't believe any of this.'

'Well you should do, you know me well enough. I have things I have to do here before... I can leave. Besides, not everyone's going back at the end of our term, you know?'

'Oh yeah... like who for instance?'

'This is confidential just between you and me. I've heard that Lieutenants Darling and Parker are both getting promotions to Captain shortly. Lieutenant Darling is going to be the OC (Officer Commanding) of the 5th, Contingent. Lieutenant Campbell's becoming Captain of the 6th,

Contingent. Corporal Messer's going to the 5th, Contingent as a lieutenant, and so is Private Sherard.'

'Well good luck to them all... anyway, how come you haven't been offered a promotion with another contingent?'

...'I was George... I turned it down.'

'Why?'

'I suppose because I can longer support the crown with the burning of farms and the herding of women and children into prison camps. I didn't volunteer to come over here and do that. I find it distasteful and have no stomach for it. I came here to fight a war, which to be quite honest with you, I no longer believe in any longer. What the British are doing here isn't right and I no longer wish to be a part of it... Once I have done what I have to do, I'm returning home.' James and George embraced one another on the crowded platform of Pretoria Station. 'Have a good trip George, and give my love to everyone back home. Tell them I'll be home within two or three months... I'll miss you.'

'I'll miss you to, mate. You take care, you hear?'

They shook hands.

George turned and then climbed into the carriage. He stood on the balcony at the end of the carriage and waved. James waved back. The whistle blew and moments later the steam train puffed and hissed its way along the platform and then out of the station. A sudden feeling of loneliness washed over James. The last of the carriages grew smaller and then were gone. He turned and then walked along the platform and then out of the station.

* * *

FOR THE CONCLUSION TO THIS EXCITING, WONDERFULLY POWERFUL STORY, SEE 'THE PLOUGH, THE GUN AND THE GLORY - 2

ABBRIVIATIONS

N.S.W.A.M.C.	New South Wales Army Medical Corps
N.S.W.M.R.	New South Wales Mounted Rifles
N.S.W. L.	New South Wales Lancers
C.B.	Citizens Bushmen
A.B.	Australian Bushmen
N.S.W.I.B.	New South Wales Imperial Bushmen
S.A.I.	South Australian Infantry
S.A.M.R.	South Australian Mounted Regiment
S.A.B.C.	South Australian Bushmen Contingent
T.B.C.	Tasmanian Bushman Contingent
T.I.B.	Tasmanian Imperial Bushmen
Q.M.I.	Queensland Mounted Infantry
Q.I.B.	Queensland Imperial Bushmen
V.M.R.	Victorian Mounted Rifles
W.A.M.I.	West Australian Mounted Infantry

ANGUS HYSLOP

W.A.M.I.B.C.   West Australian Mounted Infantry
Bushmen Contingent

A.C.H.   Australian Commonwealth Horse

THE AUTHOR

Angus was born in Southern Rhodesia (now Zimbabwe). He
has worked and lived in a number of countries including
Northern Rhodesia (Zambia) the UK and South Africa. Over
the years he has also travelled to France, Canada and the
USA. Angus also holds formal qualifications in a number of
various fields.

Since 1991 he and his family have resided in Australia and are
Australian citizens. Angus wrote his first book in Perth
Western Australia in 1997, tilted 'Jaws Of The Lion'
Rhodesia before Zimbabwe. Since then he has written several
other novels and at present is writing another book.

* * *

Comments to author at flamelilybooks2005@dodo.com.au

OTHER EXCITING BOOKS BY ANGUS HYSLOP

'THE PLOUGH, THE GUN AND THE GLORY: 2' THE SEQUEL' In search of relatives... Return to Rambling Meadows... Uncertain future... Epilogue.

'SUMMER WIND' The story, which takes place in several exotic locations, is great contemporary adult fiction, and like the authors three previous books Summer Wind has everything to satisfy the most fastidious of romantic action thriller readers and would certainly make an excellent movie.

'JAWS OF THE LION' lust, romance, double standards and terrorist warfare in the dying days of Britain's last African colony, then called Rhodesia and now Zimbabwe. This exciting novel takes place between 1972 and 1980 and was the author's first book, which was inspired by actual events and his own personal experiences while living in Rhodesia and serving with the army reserve.

'AN AFRICAN ODYSSEY' a great book about a young couple who travel across Africa on motorcycles to England. Set in the sixties and seventies the story takes the reader into a world of corruption, poaching, tribal warfare, anarchy, slavery and poverty. If you enjoy the unexpected combined with action, adventure and romance then don't miss reading this amazing novel.

'AN AFRICAN ODYSSEY: 2' THE SEQUEL' Beyond Africa... Return to Africa... Farming in Rhodesia... Attacks by terrorists...

NEW EXCITING STORIES COMING SOON

'DILUTED INNOCENCE' a contemporary story of a seventeen year-old schoolgirl, Jade Langley, who finds her twenty-six year old art teacher, Tyron Williams, irresistibly attractive. She sets a daring plan in motion to seduce him, but what she doesn't realize though is that these things often go horribly wrong. An intriguing story of seduction, deceit, lies and murder that will keep you glued to the very last page.

'CONVICT 1830' in London, some years earlier, a young orphan girl 'Emily Davies' becomes an unwilling prostitute in her aunt's tavern establishment. Later, she is falsely accused of stealing a wealthy customers wallet and also of murdering him. She is imprisoned on the Thames River prison barges, but is later transported to Australia to serve out a seven-year sentence. During the eight-month voyage to New South Wales, she befriends a young man, Hudson Slater. The captain of the ship also takes a fancy to her and she is made to clean his cabin and entertain him at night. Later, Hudson and a few other convicts steal a rowing boat and escape from the ship taking Emily with them. The captain sets a bounty on their heads, dead or alive, and they live a life on the run... This story is compelling reading for those who enjoy an intriguing action adventure love story.

GUARANTEED EXCELLENT READING

ANGUS HYSLOP